The telephone shrilled, startling Beatrice into instant wakefulness, just as in her days in San Francisco.

It didn't happen often then, only when one of her patients experienced an emergency. Now that she had no practice and no patients, it shouldn't happen at all.

Beatrice and Mitch had each had their own telephone line, arranged to have specific rings. Mitch had hospital call, so his phone line rang many times more than hers. She got very good at sleeping through it, only waking to her own. He used to tease her, saying shrink hours were like banker's hours, half of everyone else's.

Now there was only one telephone, and the unfamiliar jangle of it startled Beatrice. She sat up in bed, blinking at the reflective hands of the clock on the dresser. It was three in the morning.

Adrenaline jolted through her heart, and a hundred possibilities sprang to her mind as she reached for the extension.

Praise for
Louisa Morgan

"Superbly written....At once surprising, suspenseful, and thought-provoking, this may be Morgan's most compelling book yet."
— *Booklist* (starred review) on
The Ghosts of Beatrice Bird

"With suspense, sympathy, and pathos, Morgan illuminates the pain of abuse and the path toward healing."
— *Publishers Weekly* on
The Ghosts of Beatrice Bird

"Morgan's magic is at full strength....Realistic historical detail, wisdom from Ursule's predecessors, proud feminism, devoted families and friends, and subtle, believable magic all combine to create a full and gracious reading experience."
— *Booklist* on *The Great Witch of Brittany*

"Captivating....Glides dreamily from start to finish; readers will be transfixed."
— *Publishers Weekly* on
The Great Witch of Brittany

"[A] robust tale of matriarchal magic in a lushly depicted Gilded Age New York....Readers will root for these powerful women as they struggle to overcome the social limitations of their time, whether through magic or force of personality."
— *Publishers Weekly* on *The Age of Witches*

By Louisa Morgan

The
GHOSTS
of
BEATRICE
BIRD

LOUISA MORGAN

Cover design by Lisa Marie Pompilio
Cover photographs by Trevillion and Shutterstock
Cover copyright © 2023 by Hachette Book Group, Inc.
Author photograph by Deja View Photography

Redhook Books/Orbit
Hachette Book Group
1290 Avenue of the Americas
New York, NY 10104
hachettebookgroup.com

First Paperback Edition: May 2024
Originally published in hardcover and ebook in Great Britain by Orbit and in the U.S. by Redhook in November 2023

Redhook is an imprint of Orbit, a division of Hachette Book Group.
The Redhook name and logo are registered trademarks of Hachette Book Group, Inc.

The Hachette Speakers Bureau provides a wide range of authors for speaking events. To find out more, go to hachettespeakersbureau.com or email HachetteSpeakers@hbgusa.com.

Redhook books may be purchased in bulk for business, educational, or promotional use. For information, please contact your local bookseller or the Hachette Book Group Special Markets Department at special.markets@hbgusa.com.

Library of Congress Cataloging-in-Publication Data
Names: Morgan, Louisa, 1952– author.
Title: The ghosts of Beatrice Bird / Louisa Morgan.
Description: First edition. | New York : Redhook, 2023.
Identifiers: LCCN 2023002989 | ISBN 9780316628808 (hardcover) | ISBN 9780316628792 (ebook)
Subjects: LCGFT: Psychological fiction. | Paranormal fiction. | Novels.
Classification: LCC PS3563.A6732 G56 2023 | DDC 813/.54—dc23/eng/20230203
LC record available at https://lccn.loc.gov/2023002989

ISBNs: 9780316628785 (trade paperback), 9780316628792 (ebook)

Printed in the United States of America

LSC-C

Printing 1, 2024

For Zack

One need not be a chamber to be haunted,
One need not be a house;
The brain has corridors surpassing
Material place.

—Emily Dickinson

1

Beatrice, The Island, 1977

THE SEASCAPE BEYOND the cottage window was beautiful in a monochromatic way. Tarnished silver clouds drifted in a somber sky, and pewter water shivered under restless whitecaps. Sparse evergreens framed the pale scene with their dark, slender trunks.

It was a charming vista, but a painful reminder of how dramatically Beatrice's life had changed. San Francisco was all color, pastel houses marching along the steep hills, scarlet trolleys rattling along their rails, wisps of fog slipping through the vivid orange girders of the Golden Gate Bridge. The island was nothing like San Francisco, and it didn't feel like home. She had to remind herself that she had been here only six weeks. It would take time.

She liked the cottage well enough. She had bought it sight unseen, but it lived up to the real estate agent's description as a "charming woodsy getaway." The door from the wraparound porch opened into a well-appointed kitchen, separated from a dining area by a short bar. A forties-style archway led to a small living room, where wide windows afforded a view of the water. The outside walls were a muted blue-gray, in keeping with the coastal setting. Thick juniper bushes curled along the foundation. The interior walls were cream and rose and butter yellow, warm colors for a cool climate. A short strand of beach, featured prominently in the real estate photographs, ran below the porch, linked to the cottage by a steep stony path.

The photographs and the descriptions had somehow failed to mention one significant detail. Steps from the cottage, a small cow barn nestled among the pines and firs, an unpainted lean-to jutting from one side. Beatrice couldn't decide at first if the omission was an oversight or a deliberate effort by the sellers not to introduce a detraction. She doubted many buyers would see the barn as a bonus, nor would they be happy to learn about its occupants.

In any case, the purchase hadn't disappointed her, even though her ownership felt temporary. It felt pretend, like setting up a dollhouse, or like playing hide-and-seek, which was a better metaphor. The cottage—indeed, the island itself—was Beatrice's hiding place. She was an animal gone to ground, a wounded creature seeking respite, pulling folds of solitude around herself for comfort.

Beatrice was unused to isolation. She had chosen this loneliness, and it brought relief of a sort, but it was the kind of relief that comes from the cessation of pain. She was learning that the absence of pain left space for other discomforts, like the weight of unrelenting silence and the yearning for places and people she loved.

The worst was missing Mitch. At night, in her sleep, she often turned to reach for him. When her groping hand found nothing but a cold pillow, an unused blanket, she woke, and lay aching with loss.

She doubted that Mitch, safe in their blue and yellow house above the bay, felt anything like she did. He had neither written nor telephoned. She could only assume he was still angry.

In fact, the heavy black telephone on the bar had rung only once since she moved in, and that was to remind her that the store at the ferry dock would sell any milk she couldn't use.

Milk, for pity's sake. Who would have thought?

Beatrice moved close to the window to watch a single intrepid boat, bristling with fishing gear, plow its way through the frigid waters of the strait. It was too far away for her to see the people on board, so it didn't trouble her to watch its progress. It trailed an icy wake as it circled the distant silhouette of the big island and disappeared.

Thinking how cold those fishermen must be made Beatrice shiver and turn to the woodstove that dominated her living room. It hummed and crackled, filling the cottage with the spicy fragrance of burning pine. The fire was comforting, but the stove consumed an astonishing amount of wood. The cord stacked against the side of the cottage was shrinking with alarming speed in the face of the cold snap. She really shouldn't put off calling Mr. Thurman to ask him to deliver more, but she dreaded doing it.

Mr. Thurman was a pleasant man. When she called him with her first order, he had rattled and jounced up the dirt road, the bed of his ancient Ford pickup piled high with logs. He had greeted her cheerfully and made quick work of the chore, accepting her payment with a tip of his flat wool cap.

But he hadn't come alone. He would never come alone. Seeing him—them—had ruined what was left of that day. Remembering it, Beatrice pressed a hand to the base of her throat, where the borrowed misery lurked.

Regardless, she would have to order more wood. The radio said tonight would be even colder than the night before, which had glazed the boulders on her bit of beach with ice. She crouched beside the stove to stir up the embers and lift in fresh chunks of pine. She had just closed the glass-fronted door when Alice's commanding call rang out.

Smiling for the first time that day, Beatrice straightened and leaned to one side to look through the archway. Through the window half of the kitchen door, she saw Alice and Dorothy standing below the porch, the two of them gazing expectantly up at the cottage.

Dorothy was tall and rangy, white with splotches of black on her sides and her crooked nose. Alice was tawny and petite, with big dark eyes and long eyelashes. She was considerably smaller than Dorothy, but there was no doubt that she was in charge. At this moment she clearly considered it her duty to inform the new dairy farmer that milking time had arrived.

Beatrice adjusted the stove damper, then crossed into the kitchen to pull on the rubber milking boots left by the previous owners, as well as the secondhand red-and-black Pendleton jacket, her last purchase in San Francisco. She had not expected cows, but she didn't mind them. A woman alone could do worse for company than two easygoing cows.

The elderly couple who sold her the cottage were fortunate in their buyer. Beatrice had grown up in South Dakota. Her father had been a country GP who often helped out the local ranchers when the vet wasn't available. Beatrice had gone with him on house calls from an early age, and sometimes their patients had not been people, but horses, cows, or the occasional pig that had cut itself on barbed wire. She was used to livestock.

She said, "Good evening, ladies," as she stepped down from the porch and crunched across the graveled yard to the little barn. Her voice creaked, reminding her she hadn't spoken aloud all day. As she set Dorothy and Alice to munching hay in their stanchions, she chatted to them, just to hear herself.

She started with Alice, who would stamp and low if she didn't. "You must have been reading Betty Friedan," she said, as she slid the milk bucket beneath the cow's udder and sat down on the three-legged stool. "You're a bossy little bossy, but that's okay. I like that in a cow." Alice gave a small, bovine grunt, and Beatrice took it for agreement.

For all the times she had helped her father treat animals, she had never actually milked a cow, though she had seen it being done. Now she found herself in possession of two of them. No one knew what might have become of the cows if she had refused to keep them, but she hadn't done that. She had figured out how to accomplish the task of milking through trial and error, aided especially by the patient Dorothy. Now the chore went smoothly for the most part. If it didn't, Alice never failed to apprise her of her errors, swishing her tail so it stung Beatrice's cheek, or overturning the bucket with one impatient hind leg.

Beatrice appreciated Dorothy's compliant ways, but she and Alice had more in common.

· · · ★ ★ ★ ★ ★ ★ · ·

After the next morning's milking, Beatrice eyed the supply of milk and cream that had accumulated in the refrigerator and made a face. There was no excuse for not taking it down to the store. She had already managed that twice, after feeling guilty for letting a gallon of good milk go sour.

The experience hadn't been too bad. The nun who managed the store and the tiny ferry terminal called herself Mother Maggie. She had accepted the milk and filled Beatrice's grocery list with a minimum of questions, evidently unbothered by Beatrice's reticence. She was far from young, perhaps too old to be operating a ferry dock, but she had a kind face beneath her short black veil. Even better for Beatrice, Mother Maggie's ghosts were mercifully pale with age. As long as she was the only person in the store, Beatrice wouldn't mind the chore.

She showered and changed. It felt good to put on something besides the wool pants that had gotten too big and the cable-knit sweater she had borrowed from Mitch and neglected to return. She wondered if he knew she had it. If he did, he would understand why she had kept it. It might even make him smile. She missed his smile. She missed his unlikely dimples.

She put on a fresh pair of slacks and a clean sweater, and took up her scissors to hack off a few strands of hair still straggling into her face. She had cut off most of her hair soon after she arrived on the island. The long dark strands lying on the floor around her—to say nothing of the ragged look of what was left—had put a period to what remained of her life. Her hair looked pretty rough, but there was no one to notice. Most of the time she covered it under her knit hat.

One of her patients had made the hat for her from leftover bits of yellow and purple yarn. It was a curious-looking creation, but the knit was smooth and regular, and the hat was warm enough for the damp cold of the island. Every time she wore it she thought of the young people she had worked with in the Haight: homesick kids, stoned kids, frightened kids. She cherished the hat, odd though it was, because it reminded her of them. They were sweet, but so hurt and confused, flower children struggling to accept that the Summer of Love wasn't what they had imagined it would be.

Beatrice pulled on the hat and her secondhand Pendleton, wrinkling her nose at the clash of red plaid wool with yellow and purple knit, deciding it didn't matter. She packed the bottles of milk into a straw-lined basket and set out in the crisp winter air for the hike down the hill.

Mother Maggie was the leader of a handful of nuns who made up a tiny island monastery. She took grocery orders and sometimes delivered them in the nuns' dusty yellow station wagon. The other sisters taught in the little school and took occasional shifts with the ferry ramp. Their brown habits were familiar to everyone on the island, but tourists smiled and pointed at the unusual sight of nuns as ferry operators. They took snapshots with their cameras, as they might with wildlife or historical buildings.

When Beatrice emerged from the quiet of the woods into the clearing around the terminal, she wished for the thousandth time that she had succeeded, in the face of her disability, in developing a strategy for dealing with people. It was what she expected her patients to do, build tools to handle their challenges, but she had failed to do it for herself. She remained raw and vulnerable, and though it hurt her pride, she had fled her problem instead of solving it.

She was glad to see that it was Mother Maggie operating the ferry ramp, which meant she was also working in the store. She wouldn't have to meet someone new. The ferry was churning its way back out into the bay as the nun trudged up from the dock, an orange safety vest zipped over her billowing habit. She caught sight of Beatrice and waved a welcome as she went into the store, leaving the door ajar behind her. By the time Beatrice reached it, Mother Maggie had shed the vest and exchanged her rain boots for Birkenstocks with thick gray socks.

"Good morning, Mother Maggie." Beatrice set the basket on the counter beside the cash register. "Six quarts here."

"Good morning to you, Beatrice," Mother Maggie said with a smile. "We'll be glad to have the milk. Are you settling in all right?"

"Fine, yes."

"The groceries you ordered are in. I'll bag them for you."

"Thank you."

The nun turned to put the milk in the big refrigerator behind her, saying over her shoulder, "Won't you stay for a cup of coffee? I was just about to make some."

Beatrice found, to her surprise, that she liked the idea of sitting down for coffee with Mother Maggie. She hadn't been in company for weeks, and the shades that trailed behind the nun were so faint as to be nearly invisible, their energy almost spent. She could surely ignore them for a little while.

She said, "I'd love some coffee."

"Good. Go grab a chair. I'll just be a few moments."

There were three wooden tables in the back of the room, arranged around a potbellied stove that hummed with warmth. Beatrice pulled a chair close to the stove.

She sat down and started to shrug out of her coat just as the door to the store clicked open with a jangle of its welcome bell. A tall, slender young woman stepped through.

Beatrice froze, one arm still in the sleeve of her jacket.

The woman wore an expensive-looking camel's-hair coat, a creamy cashmere scarf around her throat, and a pair of elegant leather boots. She had fair hair tied back in a low ponytail and a shining leather handbag on a shoulder strap. She was exceptionally beautiful, with long legs and smooth skin, but her slender shoulders hunched as if she were carrying a burden.

As in fact she was. Two burdens. Beatrice saw them distinctly.

One, hovering above her like a storm cloud, was a threatening charcoal gray so dark it seemed lightning might flash through it.

The other clung to her legs, tiny and tragic, the lavender and indigo of confusion and grief. It was accompanied by the faint sound of a child weeping. Beatrice's throat throbbed suddenly, painfully, choking her with anxiety.

Hastily, she thrust her other arm back into her jacket and blundered her way through the tables toward the door. Mother Maggie was saying to the newcomer, "Oh, hello. You just got off the ferry, didn't you?"

Beatrice didn't hear the woman's answer. She was already out the door, abandoning her basket, forgetting her groceries, having not so much as nodded to the woman who had come in, nor said goodbye to Mother Maggie. Her mouth dry and her throat aching, she stumbled toward the forest path that led to her house. She fled.

She was ashamed of it, embarrassed by it, but she was helpless to do anything about it.

Most people saw their ghosts in the dark of night. Beatrice saw them in broad daylight, and it was intolerable.

2

Anne, The Island, 1977

A SMALL WOMAN, wearing a man's plaid wool jacket and with short dark hair bristling beneath a multicolored knit cap, brushed past Anne without so much as a glance as she hurried out through the door. It gave Anne an unfamiliar sensation. She had often wished people wouldn't stare at her, but now, she found being ignored unnerving. She wasn't used to it.

Even at this point in her life, when she felt so diminished, people looked at her. They had always done so, openly or covertly, since she was a girl of thirteen. It was her height, the straight sweep of her pale hair, the fortunate arrangement of nose and lips and dark blue eyes, the blessing of unblemished skin. The combination inevitably attracted attention, and the people staring at her—men, but women, too—couldn't know how intrusive that was.

Anne understood she was physically beautiful. She had been told often enough. She had been complimented for her beauty, and not infrequently envied for it, but she had learned not to place her trust in it. It had not protected her. It had made her vulnerable instead. It was all too easy to equate admiration or desire with love.

The thought ?ak ned her knees, even as a nun, plain and

gray-haired, greeted her. Anne blinked and hugged herself, trying to recover her fragile composure.

"Come in." The nun peered at her through black-framed glasses as she tied a printed apron over her habit. "Are you all right, young lady? You look a bit shaky."

Anne's voice sounded an octave higher than the nun's, squeezing past the constriction in her throat. "I—I was startled."

It wasn't a credible reason. She should be accustomed to these bouts of anxiety. They weren't the small woman's fault. When Anne's anxiety rose, it seemed to bloom from nowhere, like steam from a suddenly boiling kettle. It rendered her light-headed and unsteady. More than once, tormented by an attack of nerves, she had expected her heart to simply give out and let her fall dead in her tracks.

James would have told her to take one of her pills, but she was done with them. The respite they offered wasn't real.

The nun said, "Perhaps you're just cold from your ferry ride. It's nippy on the water. Come over by the stove and warm yourself."

Anne stumbled after her on feet she could barely feel and accepted the chair the nun indicated, resting close to the potbellied stove. The burning wood filled the room with a resiny smell and a generous wave of warmth.

Anne loosened her scarf and extended her gloved hands toward the stove. When she spoke again, her voice had eased almost to its normal pitch. "Thank you, Sister."

"It's Mother, actually. Mother Margaret Theresa, but I go by Mother Maggie."

"Ah. Mother. Of course." Anne stripped off her gloves and held out her hand. It shook visibly, embarrassing her. "Anne Iredale." At the touch of the nun's hand, strong and dry and warm, she felt the burn of tears and lowered her eyelids to hide them.

"Ah, Miss Iredale! Yes, I've been expecting you. The nun pulled a chair up beside her and sat. She fell silent, her eyes down, her hand on her wooden pectoral cross. Anne wore one, too, tucked beneath her sweater. Hers was small and gold, suspended on a gold chain.

Anne let her eyes close as she felt the nun's prayers wrap around her, soothing her spirit the way the warmth from the stove soothed her chilled flesh. She released a long, sighing breath and opened her eyes to find Mother Maggie watching her.

"I'm sorry," Anne said softly.

"Nothing to apologize for. I hope you're feeling better. Maybe you need some food."

"Probably."

Anne couldn't remember when she ate last. In Seattle, perhaps, when she got off the train at King Street Station. That had been noon the day before. A bowl of clam chowder, she recalled, though she hadn't been able to finish it. It had been weeks since she ate a full meal, and the way her slacks hung on her reminded her of that every time she buttoned them. She blinked at the small cardboard menu Mother Maggie put into her hand.

"We have some homemade soup," the nun said. "It's off-season, so we don't keep a pot going as we usually do, but it's easy to warm up. Or I could give you scrambled eggs. Or my favorite, a cheese and pickle sandwich." When Anne hesitated, Mother Maggie added, "If you don't have the money just now, I can—"

"Oh, no," Anne said. "I have money." She had problems, but money wasn't one of them. Not yet.

She considered for a moment. Scrambled eggs sounded good, but risky. If she found she couldn't eat them, she would be wasting this kind woman's effort. Soup seemed safer. "I would love a cup of soup, if it's easy."

"Easiest thing in the world. The next ferry's not due for half an hour, so I have time."

Mother Maggie rose and patted Anne's shoulder before bustling off to the little kitchen behind the counter. At the comforting touch, tears rose again in Anne's eyes. She found a handkerchief in the pocket of her coat and dabbed at them, marveling that she had any tears left to shed.

Soon she was seated at one of the café tables with a pottery bowl of steaming chicken soup and a plate with crackers and squares of cheese. Mother Maggie excused herself to attend to her ferry duties, urging Anne to enjoy her lunch while she was gone.

The soup was thick and savory, and Anne was glad of her choice. Her empty stomach accepted it without complaint. As she ate some of the crackers and all of the cheese, she gazed through the back window of the store, watching the ferry maneuver itself up to the dock. There were no foot passengers that she could see, but two cars drove off and disappeared up the road to the west.

Anne wondered who was in those cars. Families, perhaps, heading to their quiet island homes. Mothers, fathers. Children. Did they laugh together? Argue? Would they sit down to a family dinner, perhaps play a board game afterward?

A dog appeared from somewhere, breaking into her reverie. A border collie, Anne thought. It followed at Mother Maggie's heels as she worked, then tagged after her, its flag of a tail waving, as she climbed the slope back to the store.

The dog followed the nun inside, and as Mother Maggie traded the orange vest for her apron, she called, "I hope you don't mind dogs."

"I love them. What is this one called?"

Mother Maggie grinned from behind the counter. "This is St. Peter. Petey for short."

"So sweet. I would have loved to have a dog."

"Why didn't you?"

"My husband doesn't like them."

In fact, James was terrified of dogs. He pretended he just didn't like them as a species, but she had seen him shrink from the neighbor's gentle old Lab and had watched him cross the street to avoid a dog being walked. She hadn't understood his fear until after they were married, when she saw the ugly scar on his calf from a dog bite. It upset her then and filled her with sympathy. It upset her even more now that she knew the truth. The well of her sympathy had run dry.

She held out her hand, and the dog trotted to her, sniffed her fingers with his graying muzzle, then retreated to curl up on a dilapidated cushion at the end of the counter. Anne rose with her bowl and plate and carried them to Mother Maggie. "The soup was delicious, thank you."

"Glad to hear it," Mother Maggie said, with a satisfied nod. "How about some coffee, or perhaps a cup of tea?"

Anne felt steadier for the food, and for being in the presence of Mother Maggie. According to the ferry schedule, there was one more boat she could catch, so she said, "A cup of tea would be lovely." She had given up coffee. Her nervous state was already more than she could bear.

She endured her nerves every day until five o'clock. Cocktail hour, the time she could have a drink without troubling her conscience. In her current state, she could have drunk scotch for breakfast, but she would not give James the satisfaction of turning his lie about her into truth. Even though he couldn't possibly know what she was doing. Even though he had no idea where she was.

Today, she wasn't sure where she was going to find her cocktail, and that in itself made her anxious. It wasn't until she had drunk a glass or two of wine, or even better, of scotch or vodka, that she felt relief from the flutter of anxiety that made her heart beat an uneven, panicked rhythm and sometimes made her feel she couldn't catch a breath.

The nun brought her a cup of tea and a saucer with four homemade butter cookies on it. She smiled as she set it down. "You look as if some calories wouldn't hurt you, Mrs. Iredale."

"Anne, please."

"Anne it is. May I join you?" Mother Maggie indicated the second chair at the table.

"Please do." It was funny how the ingrained habit of good manners persevered even under stress. She wondered if that would ever fade. Perhaps she would become a crotchety old woman who snapped at people and shouted at children.

No. She would never shout at children.

Mother Maggie settled herself into the chair with a little groan of fatigue. She had brought a cup of tea for herself, but when Anne edged the cookie saucer closer to her, she shook her head. "Lent," she said, wrinkling her nose with regret. "Cookies, among other things."

Anne's hand went to her heart, where she felt the edges of the cross under her sweater. "Lent," she breathed. "Oh, dear. I missed Ash Wednesday."

"Just last week," Mother Maggie said. "Not too late to start your observance."

Anne hid her dismay by lifting her teacup and taking a sip.

She had always appreciated Lent. It was a welcome season for her, a time to make sacrifices, to give from the bounty that was—that had been—hers and James's. She loved the rituals, the ash mark on her forehead, the meatless Fridays, the cathartic emotions of Holy Week.

And she had adored dyeing Easter eggs with Benjamin. Ben, James insisted on calling him, because he thought it was more manly. Anne supposed one day her son's friends might call him that, but she thought the name was beautiful in its original form. It was one of a thousand points of disagreement, things James resented out of all proportion.

But now it was Lent. Her usual Lenten sacrifice was her nightly cocktail when James came home from court, but she couldn't tolerate that this year. She would think of something else. She would find something else to give up—even though she had already lost everything.

"So, Anne. The sisters at the motherhouse told me you were coming. They didn't explain, and of course your reason is completely confidential, but I'm curious as to why you would choose the island. We're such a small community. There are bigger monasteries, ones much easier to get to."

Anne turned the cup in its saucer, watching the tea spin widdershins against the plain china rim. "I know, but I thought, perhaps— I've thought of trying to discern my vocation."

"You're thinking of becoming a postulant?"

Anne looked up from the teacup. "Y-yes. I think so."

"You sound as if you come from the East Coast. Boston, maybe?"

"Very near there."

"This was a long way to travel if you're not sure about your vocation."

Anne looked away, out to the dull gray water and the mist-shrouded island on the other side of the strait. A stiff breeze raised lively whitecaps, and ridges of waves cut the water in lacy curves. She had always loved the sea, but now she saw it as a threat. A temptation.

She took another deliberate breath. At least she was no longer shaking. "Mother Maggie, I'm a lifelong Catholic. Cradle Catholic, as we say."

"So am I. And grateful for it."

"I'm grateful, too. It's been a comfort."

"I've often felt that way." The nun paused. "That's not a vocation, though, is it?"

Anne dropped her hands into her lap and twisted the fingers together. "I wish it were."

"And why would that be, Anne? Why do you wish for a vocation to religious life?"

"Because I don't know what else to do."

3

Beatrice, San Francisco, 1967

"THE *CHRONICLE* KEEPS calling it the Summer of Love," Mitch said, as he hung his white coat on its hook. "I wish they wouldn't." He unwound the stethoscope from his neck and hung it over the coat. "Christ, Bea, they're making it worse. Kids are pouring in from all over, and they have no idea what they're going to do when they get here."

"Sex, drugs, and love-ins," she said.

"It wouldn't be so concerning if it were just the love-ins." Mitch put on his overcoat and stood by the door, waiting for her to change.

They had worked late in the community clinic, and Beatrice felt the familiar weight of weariness blended with satisfaction at having completed a long day. She said, with a rueful smile, "You understand why they come, though. Summer of love sounds romantic."

"There is nothing romantic about venereal diseases and drug overdoses."

"Not for you, obviously. Or me."

Beatrice wore a tweed jacket for work, striving for a professional look. She and Mitch were the same age, but even at thirty-eight, his hair was enchantingly dusted with silver while hers remained stubbornly dark. She imagined his blunt features had made him look like an adult since he was a kid himself, despite the dimples. His round eyeglasses added a nice touch of gravitas. She, on the other hand, with small features and long straight hair, looked all too much like her patients.

"Maybe," she mused, as she slid her arms out of the jacket, "I should cut my hair."

"Why?" Mitch said. "Your hair is your signature. You look like a petite Joan Baez. Much prettier, though," he added with a grin.

She twinkled her thanks for the compliment. "I look too much like the kids I treat."

"I thought women liked to look young."

"I'd like even better to be taken seriously."

She hung up her jacket, exchanging it for a wool cardigan. It was July, but the fog had persisted all day. The evening air would be chilly.

He said, "They take you seriously, Dr. B. They keep coming back, don't they?"

"Some of them."

"Most of them."

He held the door for her, then carefully locked the handle and the deadbolt. They only kept antibiotics and antiemetics in the clinic, along with basics like aspirin and cough medicine, but some street kids hung about the place in hopes of scoring more—narcotics, amphetamines, barbiturates. Marijuana and LSD and a half-dozen other psychotropic substances were freely available on every street corner, but for some, they weren't enough.

The single most effective medicine they kept on hand was Enovid. The Pill. Mitch prescribed it liberally, because he thought the flower children gathered in the Haight-Ashbury district had enough problems without adding pregnancy to the list. Beatrice agreed. The last thing she wanted was to see a generation of drug-addicted infants come into the world.

As they walked, she cast him an affectionate glance. "You're a good doctor, Mitch."

He bumped her shoulder with his. "So are you, Dr. B."

"Sometimes I don't feel much like a doctor. It's an uphill climb."

"That's just San Francisco." He took her hand and squeezed it. "Everything's uphill."

They left Haight Street, caught the bus on Page, and climbed off on Steiner to walk the rest of the way.

They had managed, between their two incomes, to buy a crumbling fin de siècle Victorian house, its narrow profile slicing into the middle of a row of other such houses, gabled and scrolled and ornamented with curlicues and even tiny gargoyles at the roof corners. The house's paint, where it hadn't peeled off, was a cheery bright blue, and the gingerbread was painted yellow and white and green. There was a cutaway bay window in front and an overgrown scrap of garden at the back, overlooked by a miniature second-floor balcony with an ironwork balustrade. In clement weather they spent a lot of time there, planning the painting and repairs and rewiring they would one day do. Mitch called the house La Signora.

Mitch worked half the week in St. Mary's Hospital, where he made a decent salary. The other half he worked for nearly nothing at the free clinic. Beatrice divided her time between the clinic and the modest private practice she conducted on the bottom floor of La Signora. Her office was two steps down from the sidewalk, a snug, peaceful place she loved.

By the time they reached home, the dinner hour had come and gone, as it often did. "How about a glass of wine and a bowl of pasta?" Mitch said.

"Perfect."

As Mitch ran water in the pasta pot, she brought a glass of wine and set it at his elbow. He nodded his thanks, took a sip, then began salting the water as she set pasta bowls and forks at their kitchen table. The table was painted the same blue as the house. With the flowered pasta bowls and printed napkins, even a simple dinner took on a festive air.

Mitch had been raised by an uncle who was a good cook and had seen to it that Mitch could prepare his own meals when he needed to. In medical school, he said, being able to cook on a hot plate saved him and made him popular in the dormitory. Tonight, even short on time, he managed spaghetti aglio e olio. He set a glass bristling with breadsticks beside the wide pasta bowl and a small dish of black olives on the other side.

"You're amazing," Beatrice said. She scooped up a generous amount of grated Parmigiano and sprinkled it over the pasta. "You'd make someone a terrific wife."

"So I've been told." He flashed his dimples. "How about you?" he prompted, poking her ribs with one finger. "Would you care to apply?"

She smiled, but her mouth was too full of pasta to answer.

It was an old jest. They had met at the clinic three years before and had hardly been apart since, but neither of them was much interested in marriage. Careers instead of children, they decided. And as it happened, both their careers were very much about caring for children.

The two of them, Beatrice had observed more than once, were much alike in most ways, aside from their cooking skills. They loved their work and each other equally.

Mitch had made his way through his medical training a bit faster than she had gotten through her doctoral program. He liked the balance of his contrasting professional lives, the busy hum of the hospital and the color and energy of the community clinic. Beatrice thought one day she would like to focus strictly on private practice, but at the moment the clinic needed her. The work could be frustrating, but knowing how important it was to her patients—knowing it all too well, often painfully—it was still gratifying.

"I don't think Linda Sullivan is going to make it out of here without a crisis," she said, when she had finished her pasta.

"Is she the redhead? The one who follows that guitarist around?"

"Yes, and taking whatever drug he hands her, as if it came out of a box of chocolates."

"You can't fix them if they don't want to be fixed, Bea."

"I know, but..." She pressed a hand to the base of her throat, where she always felt things. Her father had called her out every time she did it.

Busy Bea, there you go again. Borrowing other people's troubles.

She had always dropped her hand under her father's scrutiny, but that didn't make the ache go away. She told Mitch now, "Linda had a nasty childhood, and this guy—this boy—"

"Bea." Mitch put out a hand and took hers away from her throat. "Stop."

She slumped back in her chair. "I do try."

"Empathy is a fine quality, but not when it affects your private life."

Her little gift was more than empathy, of course. A lot more. But she didn't want to elaborate on that. "You're right, of course."

"And your father said the same thing I just did, as I recall?"

She gave him a lopsided smile. "Yes, smarty-pants. You recall perfectly."

Her father, in fact, had never known how intense her gift was. After the uproar when it first surfaced, when she was eight, he hadn't understood. He had gained some clarity about her gift as the incidents mounted up, but she had never tried to tell him the true extent of what she felt. Even Mitch, who was so close to her, who shared so much of her life, didn't understand.

She pushed away from the table and picked up his plate and then her own. "I'm thinking of refusing to see Linda again, in any case. She was clearly stoned today, and that's a waste of my time." She started for the sink, saying over her shoulder, "And hers. Wasted her high. Should have been making tie-dye shirts or something."

"I'm pretty sure half the patients I saw today were either stoned or about to get stoned."

"That does not surprise me. It's like a pot cloud when you step out the door into the street. They probably get high just walking through it." She ran water into the sink and squirted in some detergent.

"No doubt. I hate to add prescription medications on top of all that."

Beatrice chuckled as she turned off the faucet. "You can't fix them if they don't want to be fixed."

He wrinkled his nose in acknowledgment. "You know they're terrified, Bea."

"I do." She resisted the urge to touch her throat again.

"Jack Persons got his draft notice. He's going to run, I think. Canada, or Mexico."

"I can't blame him."

"No, of course not." He blew out a breath and reached for the wine bottle. "Come on, let's not think about them any more tonight. Leave those dishes, and let's forget work for a while. Bring your glass. I think the fog has cleared, and there should be a moon."

Side by side, they climbed the stairs to the second floor and went out onto the little balcony. There they settled into the two mac-ramé sling chairs that hung from the beams and watched a crescent moon glimmer above the East Bay. The last of the fog nestled here and there, hiding the cars and the lower neighborhoods, muffling the traffic noises. A guitar sounded from Alamo Square, with two plaintive voices attempting a Peter, Paul and Mary song.

Beatrice sipped the last of the wine in her glass and set it at her feet. She leaned back, taking care not to dislodge the openwork of the macramé. "I love it here," she said, for the hundredth time.

"I do, too," Mitch answered.

"My father wrote again. He still thinks I could practice in our little town. He'll refer patients to me, he says."

"That should keep you busy," Mitch said. She wasn't looking at him, but she heard the smile in his voice.

"Hardly."

"It's sweet that he wants you near him, though." He meant that, as Bea knew. His own parents had passed away when he was still small, and though his uncle had tried, it hadn't been the same. He added, "I would guess he's lonely."

"I worry about that." She lifted her face into the moonlight, thinking of her father and his cramped, old-fashioned office with its single exam room and tiny waiting room. "But there wouldn't be enough for me to do. Truly, Dad treats as many horses as he does people. He always jokes he'd be doing the exact same work if he'd become a vet."

"I don't think I'd want a vet treating my pneumonia."

"You sure?" She grinned at him. "Most ailments aren't all that different between humans and horses. Or cows. Or pigs, or cats, or…"

Mitch laughed. Moonlight glistened on his round eyeglasses and glittered on the silver in his hair. She watched him without turning her head, appreciating the line of his jaw and strong profile of his nose.

He was Italian, but the dark tones of his skin and the coarseness of his straight black hair reminded Beatrice of the Pine Ridge Indians who came to her father's office. Her father had a special affinity for them, and they rewarded him with glimpses into their rich culture. He treasured the gifts they brought him, and so did the young Beatrice. Their living room mantel boasted a beautiful pair of beaded moccasins on a stand. A cured bearskin hung on one wall, and an intricately carved bison figure had the place of honor on her father's office desk. As a girl, she was fascinated by those things, and by the artisans who made them.

There were a few from the Pine Ridge Reservation, though, who struggled with alcohol, or its substitute, codeine cough syrup, and that experience had prepared her for clinic work in the Haight. For the young people she and Mitch served, it wasn't alcohol or codeine, but heroin. Mitch treated the overdoses while Beatrice tried to persuade the kids to extricate themselves from their drug-saturated culture. That meant leaving the city. Going home. It was a hard decision for them to make.

It was a frustrating way to practice, and it made her grateful for her little list of private patients. She specialized in adolescents, which she had always wanted to do.

She didn't realize she had put her hand to her throat again until Mitch pushed at her with his foot. "What?" she said, startled.

"Stop thinking about work."

Beatrice smoothed the crease between her brows with a forefinger, blowing out a breath to release her tension. "Sorry. Train of thought led me back to Linda Sullivan."

"Come on, Bea. Climb into my macramé and we'll snuggle."

"The ropes will break!"

"Maybe. Then we'll go bump. Let's try it."

Giggling, she struggled out of her own hammock and wriggled her bottom into his. It wasn't big enough for the two of them, so she ended up more on Mitch's lap than in the seat. He snuggled her against him, murmuring, "There you are," in a throaty voice that stirred her blood.

As she had predicted, in the middle of a sweet, suggestive kiss, one of the ropes broke.

They slid to the floor, giggling like children, and behind an inadequate curtain of hanging macramé, they skinnied out of most of their clothes and made love on the deck, hidden from their neighbors by the balustrade. Moonlight shone on their bare flesh, but the foghorn sounded from the bay. The mist was coming back to envelop their colorful city in its cool silver folds.

Beatrice sighed with contentment. She pressed her face into Mitch's warm shoulder and wished she could save this perfect moment, cork it up in the empty wine bottle, keep it forever.

4

Beatrice, The Island, 1977

THE TELEPHONE SHRILLED, startling Beatrice into instant wakefulness, just as in her days in San Francisco. It didn't happen often then, only when one of her patients experienced an emergency. Now that she had no practice and no patients, it shouldn't happen at all.

Beatrice and Mitch had each had their own telephone line, arranged to have specific rings. Mitch had hospital call, so his phone line rang many times more than hers. She got very good at sleeping through it, only waking to her own. He used to tease her, saying shrink hours were like banker's hours, half of everyone else's.

Now there was only one telephone, and the unfamiliar jangle of it startled Beatrice. She sat up in bed, blinking at the reflective hands of the clock on the dresser. It was three in the morning.

Adrenaline jolted through her heart, and a hundred possibilities sprang to her mind as she reached for the extension. Mitch was ill. A friend had died. Someone was in trouble.

Out of habit, she said, "Dr. Bird speaking."

Oh, damn. She hadn't meant to say that at all.

"Dr. Bird, I'm sorry to bother you…"

How many emergency calls started just like that? Pretty much all of them.

"I'm sorry to bother you, but the medicine isn't working. I feel like I'm having a heart attack..."

"I'm sorry to bother you, but Bobby told me he wishes he would just die, and I'm so worried..."

"I'm sorry to bother you, but Anna's gone off her rocker again, calling her managers at two a.m., she's going to lose her job..."

"I'm sorry to bother you. You don't know me, but Abby, you know, the postmistress? She said you're a doctor. The nurse isn't on the island tonight, and—"

The caller, a woman, sounded young, her voice high and tight. Beatrice felt the shift in herself, the change from woman woken from a deep sleep to professional with a job to do.

It was like changing gears on a car, or a channel on the radio. One moment she was plain Beatrice Bird, middle-aged, weary, preoccupied. The next she was the person who had taken an oath to help people, to put their needs above her own.

She swung her legs out from under her blankets, and her throat began to ache with the need to do something to help. She said, "I didn't catch your name?"

"Oh! Sorry." There was a rising, panicked tone in the young woman's voice. "I'm Terry Bachelor, and it's my little boy. He's all over rash, and he's so hot, I—I don't know what to do!"

Beatrice said, with the firmness of long practice, "Well, Terry, first I want you take a deep breath. You'll want to be calm. Is there anyone else with you?"

"No!" Terry wailed. "I'm all alone, and I just—" The expected sobs tore through the telephone wires, and Beatrice drew a deep breath of her own.

"Terry. Terry, breathe. I can hear how tense you are, and that doesn't help, now does it?"

"Sorry, sorry," the young woman repeated.

"No need to be sorry. The thing is, Terry, I'm a psychologist, not a medical doctor."

"Oh, God!" Terry's voice rose again. "What am I going to do?"

Beatrice was sitting on the edge of her bed now, facing the uncurtained window. The woods beyond were invisible in the dark, but her own pale face, with its uneven thatch of short hair, was mirrored there. She remembered once wishing she could look older. That wish had come true, and sooner than she had expected.

Mitch would hate her cropped hair, but that hardly mattered now. This young woman—Terry—was falling apart on the other end of the telephone line. She would help her if she could. She would do what she knew how to do.

Beatrice spoke a little louder to cut through the girl's sobs. "Terry. Can you hear me?"

"Y-yes. Yes. S-sorry."

Beatrice didn't waste time telling her again not to apologize. She simply said, "Good, Terry, that's good." Always use their names, she had been taught. Speak their names, acknowledge their need. "We're going to talk this through together, you and I, and figure out what you need to do. First, you'll feel better if you don't panic, and I can help you with that. I want you to take in a breath, counting to four, then exhale to a count of six. Can you do that?"

Terry sniffled, then began the breathing exercise. Beatrice could hear her damp inhalation, and then her noisy exhalation.

"One more time, okay, Terry? Breathe in, and feel your shoulders relax. As you breathe out, feel your feet on the floor. Then tell me if you feel a bit calmer."

Terry did as she asked. "I—I think I feel calmer. It's just scary."

"Of course it is. How old is your boy?"

"He's two. Just turned two."

"And you're alone there with him?"

"I am now."

The telling response. Flowing beneath Terry's fear, Beatrice sensed the current of anger and resentment.

"Are you married?"

"Yes, but my husband's away."

"I see. A work trip?"

"No." There was a little pause as Terry sniffled, then blew her nose. "No," she said in a shaky voice. "He went fishing with his buddies."

Details. Details that had nothing to do with a sick child and everything to do with an angry spouse.

"No neighbors nearby?"

"No. Our place is way out on the Point."

Beatrice turned away from her reflection in the night-dark glass and tried to imagine the young woman on the other end of the line. This would be easier if she could see her face, but since she couldn't, she would rely on the childish sound of her voice, the inadvertent revelations in her choice of words, and the actual fact of a sick child in an isolated house. And that unique feeling behind her forehead, the one she had been familiar with since she was small.

"Tell me, Terry," Beatrice said, "what is your boy's temperature? And what's his name?"

"It's Joshua," Terry said. "I haven't taken his temperature. I've never done that, and I'm afraid I'll do it wrong."

Two years old, and she'd never taken the child's temp? That was revelatory, too.

"Do you have a thermometer?"

"I think so. Somewhere. He's just so hot, and this rash is all over his chest—and he's breathing really fast."

"Where is he?"

"In his crib."

"Asleep?"

"Y-yes," Terry answered, her voice dropping. "Do you think that's okay?"

"Well, Terry," Beatrice said cautiously, "I'm inclined to think that's a very good sign, but I'm not a pediatrician. You sound as if you're feeling a bit calmer now. You've done very well. Do you think you could take Joshua's temperature, and then call the emergency hospital on San Juan? They'll want to know how high it is, and maybe have some suggestions for you. Then you can call me back and tell me what they said."

"Okay. I guess so," Terry said doubtfully. "You have to put it in his—in his bottom, don't you?"

"Yes. Just put a little Vaseline on it, and it slides right in. He probably won't wake up."

"Okay." She didn't sound confident, but at least she wasn't hysterical anymore.

"Do you know how to read it?"

"Not really."

"Okay. Well, I'll talk you through it. Go look for the thermometer, and I'll hang on."

There was a clunk as Terry put the phone down. Beatrice sat where she was, bemused by the strangeness of this event. In the silence, she thought about how swiftly she had returned to therapist mode, how natural it was to ask questions and make suggestions and coax a patient—okay, Terry wasn't her patient, but at least a person in trouble—to think rationally and take productive action.

She waited. She had to pee, but she didn't want Terry coming back to the telephone and finding her gone. She crossed her legs and pulled her quilt across her lap against the chill. It occurred to her she didn't know the number of the hospital on San Juan Island, so she pushed off the quilt in order to rummage in the bedside stand for the phone book for Island County, then tucked herself under the quilt again.

Terry came back at last, and when she picked up the phone, she sounded better. "I found it, Dr. Bird," she said.

"If you have some alcohol to dip it in, that would be a good idea."

Terry went to do that, and Beatrice looked back at her image in the window. It was too bad about her hair, but she hadn't had much choice. She couldn't face a beauty salon, with its stylists and customers all lined up under bright lights, their ghosts trailing behind them—

"Okay!" Terry said breathlessly into the phone. "I did that. Now what?"

Terry didn't have an extension for her telephone, she discovered, so Beatrice described the process of taking a rectal temperature as clearly as she could. "Then bring the thermometer back to the phone and I'll tell you how to read it."

That was the hardest part, it turned out, but finally Terry understood how to read the bar of mercury, and to align it with the proper number. She said, at last, "101. That's high, isn't it? Is that bad?"

"No, that's not really very high," Beatrice said. "I still think you should call the hospital, just for your peace of mind. Do you know the number?"

"No."

Beatrice wondered again how old this young woman was. She had met such people in the Haight, girls and sometimes boys who barely possessed the skills to care for themselves, yet had left their homes and their families, drawn by the illusion of freedom, not just in their attitudes but in their behavior, in their sexual lives.

As she read out the number for the hospital, she thought of what she would do if this were actually her patient. There would be a list of things for Terry to do, homework that would include learning basic life skills and coping mechanisms for times like this.

But, again, this wasn't her patient. She didn't have patients anymore.

She said, "Call me back, Terry, after you've spoken to the hospital."

The call ended, and Beatrice hurried to the bathroom. She didn't bother turning on the light. The sky was beginning to lighten above the treetops. It would be milking time before long. She might as well make coffee, perhaps listen to the radio while she waited for Terry's call.

The percolator had not yet stopped its gurgling when the telephone rang again. Beatrice switched off the radio and picked it up. "Terry?"

"Yes, Dr. Bird, it's me. Terry."

"Did you reach the hospital?"

"Yes. They said it sounds like an allergic reaction. I'm supposed to give him Benadryl. And children's Tylenol."

"Do you have those things?"

"I don't know."

Beatrice suppressed a groan of irritation. "You haven't looked?"

"Well, I—the thing is, my husband should have—I mean, he's the one who does the shopping and everything."

The coffeepot stopped, and Beatrice poured herself a cup one-handed. "Terry, I'm sure they have both those things at the little store."

"But they're closed."

"They'll be open in a couple of hours."

"How will I get there?" the young woman said, her voice rising again as if she were on the point of tears.

It was notable, Beatrice thought, that the little one had slept through the whole exercise. By the time she got Terry settled on a plan to ask one of the sisters to bring her the medication in their station wagon, the sky beyond her windows was bright enough to see by. Alice, standing beside the barn, was gazing expectantly at the cottage.

"Now, Terry," Beatrice said. She tried to keep her voice neutral, neither authoritative nor pleading. "I don't know you, but I can guess you're not used to managing on your own."

"No, I'm not," Terry sniffled. "Gerald always does these things."

In a clinical situation, Beatrice would have asked questions, gently directed the conversation, but this wasn't a therapy session. It wasn't for her to guide this helpless girl into the 1970s and leave the 1950s-style feminine dependency behind. Terry was going to have to figure this out on her own.

Dorothy had joined Alice, and the two cows, one black and white, one golden brown, had begun to low, demanding her presence. Alice's voice was gently insistent. Dorothy's sounded like a tuba with a cat down its throat.

"The thing is, Gerald's not here at the moment, is he? And you're all your baby has."

"What do you mean?"

"Only that when things need doing—food prepared or medicine given—you're the only one there to do them."

"But I—Gerald should—"

This would have been a good time, in her office, to let the silence stretch, to let the girl work out the concept on her own. Instead, with the mooing of the cows becoming more demanding, she said, "I'm afraid I have to go milk my cows now, Terry."

"You have to *what*?"

"Yes, they won't wait. I know you can handle things. You know what to do."

"Wait, you milk cows? By yourself?"

"Of course. And I have to do it now, so if you'll excuse me, I'll say goodbye."

Beatrice gave Terry a moment to respond, but it was clear the girl didn't know what to say. She nodded to herself as she hung up the phone. She had done what she could, but that was a young woman who needed real therapy. It was classic, of course. She could guess at what Terry's parents had been like, and for that matter, what her husband must be like, but she wouldn't. She was just a neighbor. A voice in the night.

As she went to put on her milking boots, her throat burned with her frustration and regret over her own situation. What a waste. What a mess. And all her fault.

At least, she told herself, as she filled the manger with hay and closed the stanchion bars around the cows' heads, she was doing right by Dorothy and Alice. They munched cheerfully as she set her stool by Alice, pressed her forehead into the cow's warm flank, and began her chore.

As her bucket began to ring under the fragrant streams of milk, she felt better. Cows, as her father had often said, were the best of creatures. They knew what they wanted, and they knew what their job was. They were sweet, if a little selfish. They were perfectly satisfied by a feed of hay and a swiftly emptying udder.

Best of all, they had no ghosts.

Beatrice, South Dakota, 1937

She was eight years old the first time her gift caused her trouble, and it was pure, unsuspecting innocence.

She was in the third grade. She loved school and was reading books far above her grade level. She had lost her mother at an early age, but she adored her father, and they spent hours together when he was free. A Mrs. O'Reilly came in to cook and clean for them. She was a middle-aged widow with thinning hair and thick glasses who firmly believed children should be seen and not heard, but she was kind enough to young Beatrice, and she made wonderful brownies. She frequently lectured William Bird on his failings as a parent, but he mostly ignored her. The Bird home life was relatively peaceful. Beatrice was a happy kid.

Her classmate Erick Ericksen was not. Because the classroom was arranged alphabetically, his desk was right behind hers. He struggled with his schoolwork, and his clothes told the story of an impoverished home.

Being poor wasn't unusual in their small town. The Depression had hit as hard in South Dakota as anywhere, and no one had much money. The farm wives who came in to cook school lunches could see that Erick, with his homely haircut and too-thin face, wasn't getting much to eat at home, and he wasn't the only one. The cooks slipped extra cookies or an apple to any student who seemed in need. Beatrice didn't know until she was much older that her father helped cover the cost of such things.

Everything seemed as usual that cold January day. School had just resumed after the winter holiday. The theme the third grade had been assigned was due, and their plump, elderly teacher, Miss Snow, was coming through the room, collecting their handwritten papers.

Beatrice had just gotten her essay out of her desk and set it on the corner for Miss Snow when she began to feel strange. Her throat began to ache, just at the base, a pinching sort of hurt. She touched her neck, wondering what it meant, and then—suddenly—she *knew* there was something wrong with Erick.

There was no reason for her to know. She wasn't any closer to Erick than she was to her other classmates, but she was eight. She didn't question her knowledge. She just knew.

She twisted abruptly in her seat and stared at him. "What is it?" she hissed.

He stared back. "What?" There was no paper on his desk, no theme to hand in.

"What's wrong, Erick?" He gaped but didn't answer, and the ache in her throat grew sharper. She jumped to her feet and leaned over him, her fists on his desk. "Tell me!" she said. "Something's wrong! I need to know!"

She couldn't have explained why she needed to know, but the need drove all other thoughts out of her mind. She sensed Miss Snow's alarmed presence beside her, smelled the faint smell of mothballs on the teacher's cardigan, and felt her cold, rather shaky hand falling on her shoulder. It didn't distract her. She said, "Erick! You have to say! What is it?"

Color flooded Erick's freckled face, a rush of red that spread across his cheeks and down his throat, and then as quickly faded, leaving his cheeks ashen. His mouth opened, but he couldn't seem to speak. He gave a choking gasp, dropped his head to his desk, covered it with both hands, and sobbed, brokenly, steadily, a sound that would have shattered the hardest heart.

Beatrice jumped back, bumping into Miss Snow. The teacher hissed, "Beatrice Bird, what did you do? What did you say to Erick?"

In moments a different classmate was on the run to the principal's office. The rest of the class was up, out of their seats, gawping at the boy huddling over his desk, near hysterics now as he clutched the back of his head and wept. Miss Snow ordered Beatrice to move back, away from the outburst.

Beatrice did as she was told. With her palm pressed to her throbbing forehead, she stood beside Miss Snow's desk as the tumult overtook the classroom. Erick's cries intensified. Beatrice's sense of something wrong didn't abate, but Erick was beyond explanations. Beatrice had never seen anyone cry so hard. Answering tears of her own dripped down her cheeks, and for some reason she couldn't comprehend, she kept thinking of screams, though no one was screaming. It was like a nightmare, screams running through her mind while the compulsion to know what was wrong with Erick wouldn't release her.

The principal arrived, then the school nurse, and in short order Beatrice's father. He and the principal ushered the sobbing boy out and took him home, leaving Miss Snow to try to salvage what was left of the school day.

Everyone learned soon enough what it was all about. The uproar was not because Beatrice made Erick Ericksen cry. It was because of what the principal and Dr. Bird found when they took the boy home.

Erick's father had beaten his mother half to death. They found her in her bedroom, covered in blood, barely breathing. Her husband had left her there, told Erick and his younger sister their mother didn't feel well, and shoved them out the door to go to school with orders not to talk about it. Erick, nine years old, had listened to his mother scream for help the night before. He had even battered on the locked bedroom door, but his father wouldn't open it.

When the morning came he was torn between fear of his father, the need to help his mother, and the responsibility of getting his little sister to school. When Beatrice demanded to know what was wrong, all of his grief and confusion and fear burst forth in a solid fit of hysterics.

Once the furor had settled down, with Mrs. Ericksen safely in the hospital and Mr. Ericksen less safely ensconced in the county jail, Beatrice's father asked her to explain what had happened at school.

William Bird was, as Mrs. O'Reilly never ceased pointing out, not a strict parent. He told Mrs. O'Reilly often that with a child like Beatrice, he had no need to be strict. Mrs. O'Reilly was unimpressed.

"Got a mind of her own, that girl!" Mrs. O'Reilly would say dourly. "Leaps before she looks. Acts first, repents later. Takes any chance comes her way—"

William usually stopped her at that point. "I know, Mrs. O'Reilly" was his customary mild response. "Beatrice is impulsive. But she has a good heart, the best heart, and an outstanding mind. I think we can trust her to do what's right."

Mrs. O'Reilly would set down her plate of brownies with a thump and wander back to the kitchen, muttering all the way. Beatrice would cover her laugh with her hand, and her father would wink at her, and Beatrice would think no more about any of it.

It was different this time, but not because William felt he had to be strict. He was worried, and so, Beatrice would find out, was Mrs. O'Reilly.

William sat Beatrice down at the dining room table and took the seat across from her. "Tell me about it," he said, as he took off his cowboy hat. "Miss Snow says you wanted Erick to tell you what was wrong, and you wouldn't take no for an answer. Why was that?"

Beatrice sat chewing on her thumbnail, trying to find the words to explain. William waited, polishing his glasses, his round face creased with concern.

"I just—I had to know," Beatrice finally said.

"What does that mean, you had to know?"

"Something was wrong, and I had to know—I *needed* to know—what it was."

"But why, Bea? Why would you *need* to know?"

She thought for a long time, wrinkling her forehead. Finally she said, "Daddy, I think it was because Erick needed to know. He needed to know if his mother was okay, didn't he?"

"It seems that way, yes."

"So he needed to know, and that made me need to know."

William frowned. She couldn't help him, because she didn't understand herself. It wouldn't be the last time for such a conversation, and none of the following ones produced any real answer except that Beatrice was just made that way.

"Fey," Mrs. O'Reilly said, when people asked about the doctor's daughter after the incident. "Second sight."

William told Mrs. O'Reilly to stop saying things like that, but his orders to the housekeeper had no more effect than her admonishments about his talents as a father. It didn't matter much until Beatrice reached middle school, when anything different about any student was fodder for teasing and gossip. At that point—although she had other incidents like the one with Erick, if not so dramatic— Beatrice began keeping things to herself.

Mrs. O'Reilly nodded satisfaction at this development, proclaiming that Dr. Bird's daughter had "grown out of it." "Always said she would," she boasted. "Just needed a firm hand, that girl."

William smiled at that, but both he and Beatrice knew the truth.

Once, Beatrice knew Mrs. O'Reilly needed extra money. She had an image in her mind of a rocking chair, not Mrs. O'Reilly's. She didn't know whose it was, but she knew the money wasn't for Mrs. O'Reilly herself. She told her father, and William, used to her ways by then, gave the housekeeper a generous bonus for Christmas. Mrs. O'Reilly wept when she opened the envelope. She never explained why. Talkative though she was, she spoke very little about herself, and the Birds didn't ask. William said, "None of our business, Bea. If Mrs. O'Reilly wants us to know, she'll tell us." She never did.

Another time, when Beatrice accompanied her father on a call to one of the small ranches outside of town to help a mare in foal, she met the owner in the barn. Mrs. Clayman was a thin, dry little woman, widowed two years before, aging too fast as she tried to keep her place going with only one ranch hand to help her. When the foal was safely delivered, she offered William and Beatrice coffee in her kitchen, and as she served it, Beatrice knew, without a word being said, that Mrs. Clayman was pregnant, and terrified.

Beatrice was a doctor's daughter. She was only twelve, but she understood how pregnancies happened. She didn't know why Mrs. Clayman was afraid until she overheard two women gossiping in the mercantile about the widow woman pregnant by her hired hand. Bea asked Mrs. O'Reilly about it.

The housekeeper sniffed and tossed her head. "No better than she should be, that Margaret Clayman. No respect for her husband's memory, and him barely cold in his grave."

Beatrice turned to her father. "Why do people care about Mrs. Clayman having a baby? Everybody has babies."

William sighed. "Yes, everybody has babies, but someone decided a long time ago that only married women are supposed to have babies. Poor Mrs. Clayman isn't married anymore."

"Maybe they should be talking about her hired hand and not her."

Her father gave a snort that was half amusement, half irritation. "Exactly right. It takes two to make a baby happen."

"So they talk about the woman but not the man."

"Afraid so."

"That's not fair, Dad."

He reached out to touch her cheek, then to stroke her hair. "You're right, busy Bea. It's not fair. It's not fair at all."

There were other incidents, most less consequential than Mrs. Clayman's pregnancy. By the time Beatrice was fourteen, she had gotten used to knowing things without being told. Sometimes she understood them. Just as often she didn't. Sometimes they upset her. Sometimes they seemed so trivial she barely noticed them.

All she knew for sure about her talent was that she could neither predict it nor control it. It was part of the fabric of her life, knitted into the pattern of it just as Mrs. O'Reilly knitted designs into scarves and mittens and hats.

Beatrice never suspected it would one day control *her*.

5

Anne, The Island, 1977

ANNE WOKE TOO early, still on East Coast time. The sky was just beginning to brighten from black to a shade of gray that almost matched the silver of the sea shimmering beyond her window. She showered, ignoring her haggard reflection in the bathroom mirror, and dressed in the same clothes she had worn the day before. There weren't many choices in her hastily filled suitcase. There had been no time for thoughtful packing. As it was, she had only the cross she always wore, a few clothes, a small cosmetics bag, and a change of shoes.

Her purse had been full of cash, but the supply was shrinking steadily. Under the pressure of an uncharacteristic premonition, afraid things were going to go badly for her, she had withdrawn all of her housekeeping money. The curious look on the teller's face had made her hands shake, but she had persevered, left no balance in the account, and hurried out of the bank with several thousand dollars. It was, at the time, the most daring thing she had ever done. She had secreted the cash in her suitcase when she packed for the sanatorium, and since she never went inside, no one discovered it.

The money wouldn't last if she kept staying in hotels, though. She had to do something different. Today she would return to the island, speak again with Mother Maggie, beg for a place in the monastery. She didn't dare tell her the truth about why she was here. Keeping secrets wearied her, but she felt she had to do it. She hadn't confided her plans to her local priest, either, for fear he, like everyone else she had trusted, would tell James. James would track her down, put her where he wanted her. It would spell the end of her life in any real sense, the end of any hope she had for setting things right.

She finished repacking, locked her room, and made her way downstairs and out through the lobby. She pulled her camel's-hair coat tight against the clammy sea breeze as she walked down the slope to the beach, her strides stiff with tension.

It had been weeks since the devastating verdict that had thrust Anne into a waking nightmare. Only her grief pierced the sense of unreality that fogged her mind and weakened her muscles. None of it seemed real. It was all impossible. These things didn't happen to women like her: educated, well-brought-up women. Admired women. Women of means.

She had believed when she married James that she had settled into the perfect life: a beautiful home, a handsome older husband, a good car, a country club membership. The few friends she still had from college thought so. Certainly her parents believed it.

James was a judge. Men like him didn't mock their wives in public, then strike them in private. They didn't lock their small children in dark closets for the smallest infractions. Men like James didn't accuse their wives of being hysterics, or of being drunks. They didn't tell the court their wives were unfit mothers.

Anne reached the beach, a meandering, pebbly strand washed by winter waves. She turned south to let the slowly rising sun warm her face. Gulls circled in the cold sky, filling it with their hollow cries. The ocean was the color of old pewter, the sky full of shifting clouds. Deep green trees and banks of juniper lined the beach.

There was beauty in the scene, but Anne couldn't feel it. She smelled the salt in the air, and felt the revitalizing sting of it on her cheeks, but she was not energized. Everything felt colorless, without movement or sound or scent. She had never, in all of her thirty-one years, felt so alone. Worse than alone—bereft.

It had all unfolded like an awful dream, the kind where her legs didn't work, where no one listened to her cries for help, where she was blundering through dark alleyways, lost and confused. The nightmare still clung, though her bruises had faded. The gray waters called to her, offering relief from her agony, but it was a call she would not answer. It wasn't just that her faith forbade that irreversible step; she couldn't abandon Benjamin.

He must think she had, though. Anne wondered what James had told him. Did he say she was dead? Or that she was in the hospital, as he had intended her to be? He could even claim she was in jail, and that wouldn't be far wrong. She languished in a prison of loss and sadness and could see no way out.

She watched the waves slide up the beach, fingering her gold cross and praying silently for someone to protect Benjamin. For someone who would understand. For someone who would believe the truth.

If there was any answer to her prayer, she couldn't hear it.

Anne, Oak Hill, 1953–1964

St. Michael's was the only place Anne had felt completely welcome as a child. Her mother Phyllis attended Mass every week, bringing Anne with her. The priests and nuns knew them both by name, and always smiled down at Anne and asked about school.

It was also a place her father never came if he could avoid it.

Anne liked everything about St. Michael's. She was enchanted by the stained glass windows and the stories they told. She liked tracing the smoke of the censers swirling up into the vaulted ceiling. She loved the music of the choir, twisting around to watch the singers in their loft until her mother hissed at her to face the altar. She liked the miracles read out from scripture, the multiplying of the loaves and fishes, the changing of water into wine, the blind man receiving his sight. She savored the smell of incense and the thrill of the organ tones filling her head. Candles flickered everywhere, adding to the sense of mystery and magic. For Anne, St. Michael's was a place of wonders.

When she was small, her only disappointment with the church was that she couldn't be an altar server. She longed to ring the little bells, swing the smoking censer, carry the chalice. She wanted to wear the white robe with the pink vestment over the top and kneel close to the altar, where the magic happened, instead of yards away in the pews.

The nun who taught her catechism class had declared flatly, "Girls can't do that."

"But why?"

"The church forbids it," Sister Perpetua said.

Anne glanced up, caught by something in the sister's voice. Was that a slight tremor of resentment? She was still a child, and she didn't always understand unspoken feelings, but her mother often sounded like that when speaking to her father. Phyllis never argued with her husband, but her voice often held that odd note of suppressed tension.

"Women have other functions in the church," the nun added, but the tremor was still in her voice. "We have to be content with those."

It was the sort of thing Anne's mother said, if Anne asked why Daddy wouldn't let her take guitar lessons or have a kitten or play ball in the empty lot next door with the neighbor kids. She would repeat his objections. "Too expensive," or "Too messy," or a favorite, "No daughter of mine is going to act like a tomboy. I'm raising my daughter to be a lady."

Anne didn't argue with him, because it was pointless. If she complained, Phyllis would say, "Daddy knows what's best," or "Daddy wouldn't like it."

Phyllis was not delighted by the reforms of Vatican II. Anne was, though she kept her thoughts to herself. The nuns of St. Michael's, her teachers, had mixed reactions. The sisters liked their habits, and Anne could understand that, though she thought the wimples and veils must be restrictive. Some of them railed against giving up the Latin service, as did a number of parishioners.

Sister Perpetua was the unlikely leader who modeled the changes. She began wearing drab dresses that reached halfway down her calves. She abandoned the wimple, revealing a head of thinning gray hair to which she pinned a half veil. She embraced the new liturgy, and eventually others joined her. Girls were even allowed to be altar servers, but that change came too late for Anne.

Anne was thirteen when she became aware of people's eyes following her when she was in public. Some were admiring gazes, but others seemed hungry, as if she had something they wanted, as if there were something they would take from her if they could. She shrank away from these, her natural reserve intensifying into painful shyness. She had never been gregarious, but by high school she had withdrawn into a tiny circle of friends she thought she could trust.

Her only relief came from working in the church's food program, serving meals to people in need. She was years younger than the other volunteers, and they let her stay in the kitchen, wrapped in an overlarge apron with a scarf over her hair. No one could stare at her there. She found a community in the kitchen. She baked cookies, and made soup, and dreamed up creative ways to use donated vegetables. If she made a mistake, ruined a batch of biscuits or oversalted the soup, no one criticized. Sometimes they even laughed together as they found a way to fix the problem. Anne felt she fit in. She could be herself.

After a year of this, her father groused about the hours she spent there. "Waste of time," he said.

"It's not, Dad," Anne said. "I'm helping."

"Stay home and concentrate on your schoolwork. I want to see straight As."

Anne turned to her mother for support, but Phyllis didn't look up from the shirt she was ironing. She didn't say anything.

Anne said, weakly, "I got straight As last semester, Dad," but she recognized the small, sad vibration in her voice. It was the sound of surrender.

Her father said, "Did you? Well, good. Now do it again."

* * * * * ★ ★ ★ ★ * * * *

Anne, The Island, 1977

"You're back," Mother Maggie said. The dog, Petey, circled Anne's ankles, his plume of tail wagging.

"I am." Anne bent to stroke the dog, taking comfort in the cool, silky feel of his long fur.

She was steadier today. She had fortified herself with two fingers of scotch from a bottle hidden in the bottom of her suitcase. She wasn't proud of it, but it had helped her hands not to shake as she checked out of the hotel and steadied her steps as she boarded the ferry once again.

Anne watched the nun expertly work the levers that raised the ramp. Her hazard vest was a startling unmonastic orange against the dark brown of her habit. Her short black veil fluttered in the wind. When she finished, she dusted her palms together, then gestured to Anne to follow her up the slope to the store.

It was good to get out of the cold. Anne set her suitcase on the floor beside the counter, careful to keep a bit of distance in case her breath smelled of alcohol.

"If you have time, Mother Maggie, I would like to talk to you."

The nun smiled. "Of course, Anne, and good morning. Shall we have coffee, or would tea be better?"

Coffee, Anne thought, would hide the scent of her breakfast scotch. "Coffee would be lovely," she said. "Can I help with something?"

"Oh, no, thanks," Mother Maggie said. "It will only take a moment. Get yourself warm."

Anne moved to the stove, taking off her calf leather gloves and stuffing them in the pocket of her coat. She extended her hands to the warmth, noticing how white and bony they looked, an old woman's hands, with veins showing under the skin. She wondered how much weight she had lost. She hadn't had much to spare in the first place. James liked her to be as thin as she had been when they met, before Benjamin came along.

"Here we go," Mother Maggie said, and Anne turned to see the coffee service laid out on one of the little tables. There was a small sugar bowl and a white ceramic creamer in the shape of a cow.

Anne said politely, "What a charming creamer."

"Isn't it sweet? My niece sent me that. You'll want to try the cream," the nun said. "It's from Beatrice's cows, the woman who was here yesterday when you came. It's a treat, nothing short of miraculous. Come, sit."

Anne obeyed, pulling a chair close to the table. She drank some of the excellent coffee, made rich and sweet by the thick cream, and made herself nibble one of the gingersnaps arranged on a flowered saucer.

Her hostess laced her own coffee with cream before she took a sip. She eyed the gingersnaps but didn't take one.

Anne had worried about how to talk to Mother Maggie. She couldn't bring herself to outright lie. She had decided, as the ferry bobbed its way across the choppy strait, to tell the truth, but only some of it. The safe parts were bad enough.

When she had drunk as much of the coffee as her nervous belly could manage, she set the cup down and lifted her eyes to the nun's.

"I have nowhere to go," she blurted. "I got into some trouble."

Mother Maggie raised one gray eyebrow. "Are you expecting?"

Anne startled at that, losing her train of thought. "No!" she said weakly. "No, I'm not pregnant, I'm—that would be—no. It's worse than that. I got into some trouble with the police."

"Are the police looking for you?"

Anne shook her head. "No. Not the police." That was the wrong way to put it, she knew instantly. It implied someone else was looking for her.

"Do you want to tell me about it?"

Anne folded her hands tightly in her lap, trying to organize her thoughts. Her voice shook when she spoke. "There's not much to tell, truly, Mother Maggie. I had been taking tranquilizers, for a nervous—for my nerves. I drank some wine, which I shouldn't have done, and crashed my car. No one was hurt," she added hastily. "But my—my family—my husband—I had to leave."

"You were convicted, then."

"Oh, yes. I admitted it right away. There wasn't a trial or anything."

"I can see this is hard for you to talk about. I'm not quite sure why that situation sent you here, though. Couldn't your family forgive you? Help you to get past this, make reparations? People do it all the time."

As anxiety began to shiver through her body again, Anne said bitterly, "No. My—my family won't forgive me."

"Because of the car?"

It would have been easy to let the nun believe that was the reason, that the car mattered more than she did, but it wouldn't be true. It had nothing to do with the car.

Anne pressed her hand over her cross, feeling the smooth gold beneath her palm. "No, Mother Maggie." Her voice trembled. "It's more than that, I'm afraid. I hope you'll believe me, but I had to leave."

There was a pause. Behind her clunky eyeglasses, Mother Maggie's eyes were somber. "Anne, you must tell me. Are you a danger to yourself?"

"No," Anne said softly. "I will admit it has crossed my mind. But I'm a good Catholic, or I have always tried to be. I wouldn't do it. I have to find a way to live. A place to live. I can't—I don't know if I can ever—go back."

She fell silent. She had told the truth, up to a point. She was afraid to go further.

Mother Maggie's gaze made Anne feel as if the nun could see right through to her soul, and that was a comfort. Her past might not be clean. Her soul was.

Mother Maggie said, with an air of regret, "I can't take you in as a postulant, Anne. I'm sorry. We're not equipped here, with so few of us. There's no place to put you, for one thing. And I have to say, I'm not sure it's best for you. Becoming a sister is hard enough without a true vocation."

"I understand," Anne said, though her heart sank at the thought of moving on once again, searching for some place she could rest.

Where she could be safe. It would be like James to send private detectives to find her. She had hoped this little island could be her refuge. But now...

A surge of weariness washed over her, so intense she had to close her eyes. Her muscles felt as if they had turned to water, and she clutched the table's edge to keep herself upright.

"Here, here now." Mother Maggie jumped up and came to steady Anne with strong hands on her shoulders. "Here now, Anne, let's get you someplace where you can lie down. We'll talk when you're feeling stronger."

Anne obeyed meekly as the nun helped her to her feet, then supported her as they walked up a short flight of stairs. There were bedrooms above the store, and Mother Maggie led her to one of these, undoubtedly her own. She guided her onto a narrow single bed with a crucifix on the wall above it. Anne didn't notice anything else as she laid her head on the crisp white pillow and let her eyelids drift shut again. The scotch and the coffee seemed to meet and mingle in her bloodstream like two creeks joining in their run to the sea, loosening her limbs but making her shiver at the same time. She felt the warmth of a wool blanket drawn up to her shoulders, and the gentle, intimate maneuver of pulling off her shoes, the tucking of an extra blanket around her chilled feet.

She didn't really expect to sleep, but in moments she was shallowly drifting through a swiftly changing dreamscape full of faces and voices she didn't recognize. Soon, she slipped more deeply into a thick slumber unmarred by any dreams at all. She woke to the sounds of gulls squawking over the bay. Her sticky eyelids resisted, but she made herself open them, and she sat up, surprised to see how much the light had changed. It was the best sleep she had had in weeks. She wondered when she might have another.

6

Beatrice, The Island, 1977

THE TELEPHONE RANG in the early afternoon, startling Beatrice out of a nap she had not intended to take. She started up from the armchair, where she had fallen asleep reading, and fumbled her way to the telephone, thinking of Terry and her baby.

"Hel—" she began, then had to clear her throat. "Sorry. Hello?"

"Beatrice, it's Mother Maggie. Did I wake you?"

"It's okay," Beatrice said, still a little hoarsely. "I didn't get much sleep last night."

"I'm sorry. The thing is—I have a problem."

"Oh," Beatrice said, hoping she didn't sound too wary. She had a strong feeling she wasn't going to like this. "Is there something I can do to help?"

"Do you remember the young woman we saw yesterday? She came into the store just as you were leaving."

Beatrice's heart sank. "I remember her." Remembered her with painful clarity. The charcoal layers of the shade looming over her head. The tiny violet one clinging to her legs. The faint but unmistakable sound of a child crying. She braced herself.

Mother Maggie said, "Her name is Anne Iredale. She came back today. Now the tide is too low for the ferry to dock, and she's stuck.

I don't have a bed for her, and I thought—I haven't been in your cottage, but I understand there's an extra bedroom—"

There was a painful pause. Beatrice stared blindly at the uneasy gray water beyond her gravelly beach, seeking a way to get out of this. Searching, but not finding. Refusing would seem not only unsociable but cruel.

Beatrice had tried everything she could think of to endure her affliction, to no avail. Ultimately, it became intolerable. Her only respite was solitude, and in twentieth-century America, in any city or town or village, true solitude was hard to achieve. This island in the cold waters of the Pacific Northwest had been the closest she could come.

Mother Maggie said, "It's a lot to ask, I know, but she's a very nice young woman, and she seems terribly sad. I just don't know what to do with her."

"Did she tell you her reason for coming back?"

"She said she has nowhere else to go."

Beatrice's heart sank. Of course Anne Iredale's reasons would be different from her own, but she, too, had felt she had nowhere to go. It was horrible to have the sense that there was no safe place in the world. She said, "Mother Maggie, I—I'm not good with guests, really, but—"

"The ferry will be able to come tomorrow, according to the tide chart. Perhaps just one night? I do realize it's an imposition, but I really can't ask any of the sisters to give up their beds..." The nun's voice trailed off, but the image of Mother Maggie's tiny, satisfied smile sprang into Beatrice's mind. She gritted her teeth against the message her gift was sending. Mother Maggie had no doubt Beatrice would solve her problem.

Beatrice wished she hadn't picked up the phone.

The nun waited in dogged silence. Beatrice pictured her, the big black telephone receiver in one hand, the other pressed over her cross. Even as Beatrice gave the answer she wanted, her throat ached with anticipated misery. "Of course I'll help, Mother Maggie. If it's just one night, then—I'm sure it will be okay."

It wouldn't be okay. It would be ghastly, but she would have to bear it.

"Thank you so much, Beatrice." Mother Maggie didn't sound at all surprised. Nor did she sound as if Beatrice were doing her a great favor. Beatrice suspected she usually got what she wanted. The nun went on. "I'll bring her out in the station wagon in an hour or so, if that's okay. I'll bring your groceries with me, the ones you forgot yesterday."

Beatrice's cheeks warmed with embarrassment at the detail. Mother Maggie must have wondered what on earth was the matter with her, going off like that, leaving everything behind.

Mother Maggie said, "She's resting now. I don't completely understand what's going on with her, but the poor girl's exhausted."

After hanging up the telephone, Beatrice tried to remember what was in those groceries. She hoped there was something she could make for dinner. Dinner for two. She might be a reluctant hostess and an inadequate cook, but she would try not to be rude.

The cottage was clean enough, but she thought she had better tidy the kitchen, wash the scorched pan still soaking in the sink. She had burned her oatmeal that morning. As the smoke rose from the pan and the oatmeal crusted a discouraging shade of brown on the bottom, she could hear Mitch in her mind, saying, "Bea! Who burns oatmeal?" and herself responding, "Blame Mrs. O'Reilly."

She stared blindly out the window, thinking of how that exchange would have gone, and how they would have chuckled together. She whispered into the ether, "I should have listened to you, Dad."

My busy Bea, never one to be cautious.

I'm paying the price now.
Life is like that, sweetheart. Everything has a cost.
So I have learned.

Beatrice, South Dakota, 1944

Beatrice had just laid the table for dinner when the telephone rang. They were the only family in town with a dedicated telephone line, so when it rang it was always either for her or her father. It was almost always for the doctor. Mrs. O'Reilly picked it up in the kitchen and called, "Doc, it's for you."

William heaved a tired sigh and went to pick up the receiver. "Dr. Bird here."

Beatrice knew what the call meant. She could tell, hearing her father's responses to the voice on the telephone, that he would be going out to the reservation. Mrs. O'Reilly would have to hold his dinner.

William Bird was the only physician in an area of a hundred square miles, and he was on call all day, every day. When he hung up, he said, "Sorry, Bea. I'll have to go."

"The reservation?"

"Yes. There's a sick baby. Trouble breathing."

"I'll go with you," she offered.

Her father usually refused such offers on school nights, but this time he nodded. "I'd like that," he said.

Mrs. O'Reilly said, "Beatrice has homework."

"I can do it in the car," Beatrice said.

"I really don't think, on a school night..."

William said, "She can manage it, Mrs. O'Reilly. Nice for me to have company. It's a lonely drive in the dark."

Beatrice hurried to fetch their coats from the mudroom before Mrs. O'Reilly could change her father's mind.

"You can go home, Mrs. O'Reilly," she said as she shrugged into her coat. "I'll heat up the stew when we get back."

Mrs. O'Reilly harrumphed once or twice but gave in. "Mind you don't set the heat too high, or it will scorch."

"I'll be careful." They all knew cooking was not one of Beatrice's talents. She blamed it on Mrs. O'Reilly liking the kitchen to herself, while Mrs. O'Reilly often held forth on the need for a woman to cook when she married.

Beatrice had no intention of marrying. She wanted to be a therapist. A psychologist. She hadn't told her father yet, or anyone, but her mind was made up.

William settled his cowboy hat on his head, the one he always wore when he wasn't in the office, and lifted the car keys from their hook. "Grab a couple of clean towels, will you? And that big aluminum pot with the handles. They may not have a way to make steam."

Soon they were winding through the dark hills in their Victory Model DeSoto. The car was only two years old, one William had been allowed to buy because he was a physician, performing essential services. Beatrice was proud of its sleek lines, its up-to-date features. Better yet, every one of its amenities worked, including the radio. Her classmates always turned to look when she and her father drove by. It was one of the few times she felt popular.

Beatrice had her homework with her, an algebra text and a biology notebook, but she left them on the floor at her feet. She and William listened to a radio station out of Rapid City for a while, big band music and an occasional bit of war news. As they drove on through the darkness, the radio signal faded, blocked by rocky hills and stands of tamarack and fir, and then they talked.

Beatrice was aware, even at fifteen, of how unusual her relationship with her father was. She could tell him anything, and he always listened. He spoke to her of the war, of politics, of medical ethics, and of the challenges of trying to treat a diverse community of patients without the help of a nurse or another doctor.

"We're on our own out here," he was fond of saying. "Fortunately, we're up to it."

Everyone called William "The Doc," as if he were the only one in the world. His daughter was convinced he was the best doctor there had ever been. He was her hero, her friend, and her mentor.

She watched his profile beneath his felt cowboy hat, his blunt features illuminated only by the lights of the dashboard, and she listened as he ruminated on the poverty on the reservation, the lack of employment, the living conditions.

"Infant mortality is high there. We do what we can, but a lot of those folks don't even have running water."

"That's why we brought the pot, right, Dad?"

"Yes. I'm hoping this place is near enough to a creek that we can get some water, get it over a fire if there's no stove. It's not going to be easy," he said, with a warning glance. "This baby's really sick."

"I'm not afraid."

He reached across the gearshift to pat her knee. "I know you aren't. You're not very big, but you're the strongest girl I've ever known."

Gratified by this, Beatrice settled back in the seat of the DeSoto and contentedly watched the stars wheel above the Badlands until they reached Pine Ridge, and her father took out the note where he had written directions.

They found the house without difficulty, but Beatrice's heart sank when she saw it. It was a cold night in October. When she climbed out of the DeSoto, her breath misted before her face. The house—a cabin, really—was dark, only the glimmer of a candle showing from the small window that overlooked the slanting porch. A thin ribbon of smoke curled from the metal chimney, and chunks of firewood were stacked against an outer wall. As they closed the car doors, a man with the thick black hair of the Oglala emerged. He carried a rifle over his arm and stood bracing himself on the uneven boards of the porch, eyeing them. He wasn't a big man, but there was threat in his stance and in his stony-eyed silence.

"I think you should wait in the car," William said.

Beatrice touched the base of her throat as she gazed at the silent man on the crumbling porch. Her forehead tingled in that familiar way. "No, Dad. You're going to need me."

He looked down at her, his glasses glinting in the starlight. "Why do you think so, Bea?"

She stared up at the dark cabin as she said evenly, in a voice her father had learned not to argue with, "I have a feeling." It was the word they had settled on when speaking of her gift.

He gave a slight, resigned shake of his head. He adjusted his cowboy hat, hefted his medical bag, and opened his car door. Beatrice, the pot and towels in her arms, followed as he approached the cabin and the man with the rifle.

William put his free hand out. "I'm Dr. Bird. Are you Mr. Beaudry?"

The man nodded without speaking and without extending his hand. He pushed open a creaking door with his foot. William went up the two steps to the porch, but he waited for Beatrice to go ahead of him. Their eyes met as she passed him in the doorway, and his looked as grim as she had ever seen them. He said in her ear, "One sign of trouble and we're gone."

She nodded and went past him to the interior of the cabin,

watching her step in the dimness. The floor beneath her boots was uneven and felt splintery.

There were always tensions between the reservation and the town, but normally Dr. Bird was welcome everywhere. He was careful not to carry anything anyone would want to steal, since that merely complicated his work, but he counted on his reputation preceding him. He would probably not be paid for this house call, but that wouldn't deter him. It never did.

The inside of the cabin was nearly as dark as the outside. A small fire flickered in a cast-iron stove, and a single candle burned on a windowsill. It took a moment for Beatrice's eyes to adjust so she could see the three children lying on makeshift beds of blankets around the stove. There was one bed, a mattress and box spring set against an outer wall. A woman sat there, her head propped against the wall, a wheezing infant lying on her chest. If there were other rooms, Beatrice couldn't see them.

She had assisted her father before. As he went to crouch beside the bed, she stood at his shoulder, ready to do whatever was needed.

His voice was gentle. "Mrs. Beaudry, I'm Dr. Bird. Is this your baby? How old?"

The sound of the infant's labored breathing filled the cabin. The other children were unnaturally silent, and the woman's eyelids flickered as if she wasn't quite awake. She lifted them with obvious effort. In the candlelight, Beatrice could see that she was young, with smooth dark skin and long black hair. Her eyes were black, too, a deeper darkness, no light reflecting from them. She said in a hoarse voice, "Month or so."

Mr. Beaudry said, "Five weeks."

Beatrice watched her father reach for the baby to lay it on the bed so he could feel its temperature, listen to its little heartbeat with his stethoscope. It was too dark for the otoscope, so she brought the candle from the windowsill, and he grunted his thanks. He peered into the baby's ears, though she doubted he could see much.

He straightened and spoke in Mr. Beaudry's direction. "This baby has a virus that has settled in his chest. We're going to help him. First, some steam." He pointed to the pot Beatrice had set beside the bed. "Can you fill that with water? Do you have a pump?"

Mr. Beaudry grunted, "Creek across the yard."

"We need that pot full."

"I'll help. It will take two to carry it," Beatrice said.

"Bea, one of the children—"

"No, Dad." She shook her head, her eyes on Mr. Beaudry. She felt his need, his fear, in the nagging ache at the base of her throat. "They're too small, and it's heavy when it's full."

A muscle leaped in her father's jaw as he turned a hard gaze on Mr. Beaudry. Beaudry gazed back, his mouth tight. William said, "The rifle stays here."

Beaudry hesitated, eyeing the doctor and his daughter, but in the end, he laid the gun on the rickety table in what passed for a kitchen. He said to the oldest of the children, "No one touches that, Sam." The boy nodded. "Not you, either."

"Okay," the boy said.

"You can build up the fire."

"Okay."

Those two words were the only sounds from the children. Frightened, probably, with their mother in bed with a sick baby, and a strange doctor in their house. Were they frightened of their father? Beatrice didn't think so. She didn't yet understand what was happening in this house, but that familiar feeling, the compulsion of needing to do something, overrode her doubts.

She followed Beaudry out to the creek, and together, in silence, they filled the pot and carried it back between them, trying not to slosh most of it out as they walked. They found the fire nicely built up by the boy Sam, and Beaudry lifted the pot to the top of the stove. It began to blacken immediately. It would be ruined, but that didn't matter. They would be leaving it. They would order another at the mercantile.

William arranged a tent of towels, using the backs of two wooden chairs. He gently lifted the baby and moved to a stool beneath the tent. The steam began to billow out around the two of them. One of the other children started to get up, but Beaudry waved him back. "Boiling water," he said. "Sam, get the little ones some crackers. Keep 'em away from the fire."

The mother said weakly, "Is he better? Is he breathing?"

As if in answer, the infant gave a productive cough, and William lifted him to his shoulder to firmly pat his back. "It takes a while," he said. "But I don't think he has pneumonia. You'll have to keep up the steam until he's better." He looked at her above the baby's head as he lowered him from his shoulder. "I think you haven't slept in a while, Mrs. Beaudry."

Mr. Beaudry had picked up his rifle again when he came back in the cabin. He stood with his back to the door, the gun pointed to the floor. He said, "I'll take care of my baby."

"Good." Still William sat on, encouraging the infant to cough, patting his back, wiping the sputum from his lips. It was a long process, and Beatrice's legs got tired, standing beside the bed, but she had promised. She was silent, waiting for her father to decide they had done all they could for tonight.

William peered through the cloud of steam at Mrs. Beaudry, lying so still on the bed. "Mr. Beaudry, I assume your wife is nursing?"

"Yeah."

William said, "Okay. Bea, you come and hold the baby here, in the steam. I'm going to have a look at his mother."

Mr. Beaudry's stance changed instantly. The gun came up, although he didn't point it at anyone, and he planted his feet wide, as if he were expecting a fight. He said, "She's fine," in a manner obviously meant to prevent the doctor from examining his wife.

Beatrice was already reaching for the baby. Her father got up, very slowly, keeping his eyes on Beaudry. He let Beatrice take the infant, and she settled warily on the stool, tweaking the tent of towels to direct the steam. The baby was warm and soft in her arms, but her skin crawled with the tension in the room.

William said, "Mr. Beaudry, your wife is as sick as your baby. Maybe there's something I can do."

"Ain't nothing you need to do, Doc. She's fine."

"I'm not going to hurt her. I'd like to listen to her heart, her lungs. Take her temperature, make sure she's recovered from the birth."

"No."

"Did she have the baby here?"

"Yeah. All of 'em born here."

"Was there someone to help?"

"Yeah." Beaudry shifted the gun, just slightly, and squared his shoulders. "She's fine. Thanks for comin', Doc. Sam, take the baby."

"Mr. Beaudry, wait. Your wife looks very ill to me. I want to look her over."

"Nope."

"Have you done something to her? Hurt her in some way?" Beatrice heard the steel in her father's voice. She had heard it before, but she had never seen him face down a man with a gun.

"No!" Beaudry said, and his voice broke a little. "No, I ain't never hit a woman, and I ain't gonna start now. But she don't need no doctor."

"I've come a long way, Mr. Beaudry. I'd like to make that judgment for myself."

Beaudry shifted the gun again, though he still didn't point it at anyone. The boy named Sam had come to stand beside Beatrice, and he reached for the baby, but she shook her head. "No, Sam," she said softly. "Not just yet. You can help take care of your little brother later."

Sam turned his eyes to his father, torn between following his orders or doing what these strangers told him to do. William, with a nod to Beaudry as if to acknowledge the risk, picked up his medical bag and crossed to the bed. Now Beaudry lifted the rifle and pointed it at William, but Beatrice saw how the barrel shook, and he kept his finger well away from the trigger guard.

"Dad," Beatrice said, as he bent over the sick woman, stethoscope in hand. Her throat ached, and her forehead throbbed with knowing, the knowing of something she couldn't, shouldn't know. Her little gift, her second sight.

Her father turned his head to her without straightening, and Beatrice said quietly, "Mr. Beaudry's afraid you'll take her to the hospital."

Her father straightened then. "Did he tell you that?"

Beaudry made an odd sound, between a grunt and a groan. Beatrice said, "No."

Her father stared at her for several seconds, then shifted his gaze to Beaudry. "Is that your concern, Mr. Beaudry? That your wife may need to go to the hospital?"

"My sister went there," Beaudry responded. "Died. My kids need a mother."

"Of course they do," William said gently. "Let me see what's happening with your wife, and then we'll talk about what's best for everyone."

Throughout this exchange, Mrs. Beaudry had been ominously silent. Beatrice glanced at her, but her eyes were closed. Even in the dim light, she could see the beads of perspiration on her forehead. Her father bent over her again, checking her temperature, listening to her lungs, lifting her eyelids, which made her twitch and groan.

When he straightened, he said, "Beatrice. Give the baby to Sam now, and show him how to keep the steam directed. I'll chat with Mr. Beaudry."

Sam was waiting, and Beatrice coached the boy in caring for his little brother, even as she listened to her father speak to Mr. Beaudry. "Your wife," he was saying, "has the same virus as your baby, but she's exhausted, and she can't fight it off. If she gets any more ill, she won't be able to nurse, either."

Beatrice, rearranging the tent of towels and showing Sam how to do it, didn't look up, but she felt the presence of the gun looming through the darkness, as if it grew bigger and more lethal with the rising tension in the house. Mr. Beaudry was ominously silent as her father went on explaining why he believed Mrs. Beaudry would recover faster in the hospital, where the nurses could bathe her, help her with the baby, treat her fever, keep her comfortable. He said the agency would send a car for them both.

Beatrice put the baby in Sam's lap, gave the towels a final adjustment, and turned toward the kitchen where the two men were talking. Beaudry was ducking his head, running a hand over his eyes. The rifle hung in one hand, pointed again at the floor.

"She's a good wife. Don't want her to die," Beaudry said.

"Nor do I," William said. "Please believe me, she's more likely to die if she stays here."

"Don't trust those people."

William took a breath and held it for a moment. Beatrice knew it marked his effort to contain his impatience. "I promise you, Mr. Beaudry," he said finally. "I will go to the hospital with her. I'll make sure she's cared for. And once you have someone to watch your kids, you can go yourself."

"No car."

"I'll talk to the agency about that. If they can't send a car for you, I'll come myself."

Beatrice stepped into the ensuing silence. Beaudry lifted his head, and she looked directly into his midnight-dark eyes. "You can trust my dad," she said. "If he says it, it's true."

Mr. Beaudry gazed back at her. His face was intent, as if he was trying to see through her eyes to her mind, to gauge her understanding. Several seconds passed before he set the rifle on the table and nodded to William.

"Okay, Mr. Beaudry," William said, as if this had been any normal house call, any usual consultation. "It's arranged, then. The agency car will come for your wife and baby in the morning. I'll meet her at the hospital." It would disrupt his day, Beatrice knew, to make the drive up to Rapid City, but her father had made a promise. He would keep it.

Beaudry walked them to the door. William let Beatrice precede him, then followed her outside. As she climbed into the passenger seat, he set his medical bag in back, then got in beside her. Beaudry had already disappeared back into the lightless cabin. William sat for a moment, his right forefinger on the starter.

"I did need you, Bea."

"Yes."

Her father resettled his cowboy hat with his left hand and gazed at her from beneath the brim. "I object to superstition on principle, as I think you know, but Mrs. O'Reilly may be right about your second sight. Although I'd rather think of it as your intuition."

Intuition was not a strong enough word. Compulsion was a better one, but she didn't want to say so. "I just get these feelings, Dad."

He blew out a breath as he pressed the starter. "Sometimes it's best not to know things."

She didn't answer. For once in her life, she wasn't completely sure her father was right.

7

Beatrice, San Francisco, 1969

CHARLIE CROSSMAN WAS one of the most appealing young men Beatrice had ever met. He came to her in the community clinic, long-haired, long-eyelashed, with big, vulnerable blue eyes and the calloused fingers of a guitar player. He spent his days busking on city street corners and his nights, she discovered, suffering ghastly nightmares he couldn't remember, but which made him wake up screaming.

"My girlfriend sent me," he told Beatrice in an embarrassed undertone.

"You didn't want to come?"

He shrugged, not meeting her eyes. "She said, 'Why not try the shrink at the free clinic?'"

"Because...?"

There was a pause, and Charlie shifted in his chair, obviously searching for things to look at that were not Beatrice's face. When she didn't repeat her prompt, he finally said, "Because we're not getting any sleep. Either of us."

"You're living together," Beatrice said mildly.

Charlie colored, and his eyes flicked up to hers, briefly. "There are ten or so of us, sharing this house," he said. "Amy and I—well, we might get married someday. I don't know."

Beatrice made no comment. The kids often expected criticism, disapproval. Sometimes she thought they even hoped for it, because it was what they were used to, but she couldn't pretend she cared whether they were married or not. She cared that they used birth control, and she cared when they caught sexually transmitted diseases. Moral judgments didn't interest her.

Silence stretched in the little office as Beatrice smiled gently at Charlie Crossman, waiting. At last he said, "It's these nightmares."

"You have nightmares?"

"Yeah."

"What are they like?"

He shrugged again, and folded his arms across his middle. Defensive posture. "I can't remember them," he said. "But I wake up Amy, sometimes the whole house."

"How do you wake them up?"

He said, his flush deepening, "Yelling."

"Your nightmares make you yell, but you can't remember them?"

"Yeah, that's it."

Beatrice got very little out of Charlie that first day, but she persuaded him to try a couple of exercises, and to come to see her again. She thought his nightmares might be about being shipped to Vietnam, but it turned out he had asthma, and wasn't eligible. She worked with him for months, trying to get him to speak about his family, his mother, his father, his home. Her gift gave her a hint, but she couldn't think how to use it. The picture of a closet kept popping up in her mind, a closet with a closed door. She felt certain that the scary thing was behind that door, but she couldn't tell her patient that. She tried not to touch her throat as she felt his need to resolve what was troubling him.

Charlie was an exemplary patient. He was on time for their appointments. He was sober when he arrived, clean-shaven, long hair washed and brushed. He was invariably polite, if not voluble. It was frustrating to watch him struggle. Whenever he got close to a revelation, it was as if that door stopped him. He couldn't get past it, or open it, and she almost despaired of helping him.

The breakthrough came six months after he started working with her. The revelation swept Charlie up in a shattering earthquake of memory, and she was glad she was there to support him as he faced it.

That session was a long one, in which Charlie trembled and wept and then, exhausted, fell asleep with his knees awkwardly drawn up on her too-short couch. Beatrice went next door to Mitch's office, explained the situation, and acquired a mild sedative, something to ease him through the shock. When he woke, she gave it to him, with a second dose to take if his nightmares returned.

"But I'll see you again in the morning," she said. "We'll talk it all through when you've rested. It was a lot to take in."

"I can't believe it," Charlie said tiredly. "How could that have happened, and I forgot?"

"You didn't really forget, Charlie. It's not uncommon for victims of trauma to block their memories, and sexual trauma in particular tends to be repressed. Sometimes such experiences are hidden behind other memories, invented ones. Other times, as with your nightmares, they come out in unmanageable ways—but it's good when they do come out, so you can deal with them."

"He's dead now. Did I say that? My uncle is dead."

"You did."

"And now that I think of it, Dr. Bird—my nightmares started when we heard he died. My mom, though—I'm sure she had no idea what her brother did."

"That's possible," Beatrice said, which was true enough. She suspected Charlie's mother had aided her six-year-old son to bury memories that caused him pain. She wouldn't suggest it, though. She hadn't met the woman. She had to assume Charlie's mother had made the best choice she could think of.

"Charlie, why do you think you recovered this memory at last?"

He gave her a weak, watery smile. "I took LSD."

"You—what? You took what?"

"LSD. Amy bought some in the park. It's easy to get, and cheap. Everyone in the house took it, so it was safe. We took turns, in case anyone had a bad trip."

"You think it was the—the LSD—that helped you?" The idea intrigued Beatrice. Of the myriad of drugs circulating in the Haight, LSD was the one she knew the least about.

"I know it, Dr. Bird. It was there in my mind, as soon as I came down from the trip. It was—it was as if a door had been opened."

"A door."

"Weird, isn't it, Dr. Bird? The memory was right behind that door, locked away where I couldn't get to it. The trip opened that door."

Beatrice smiled at him. "That must have been an intense experience."

"The acid set my mind free. I could open that door, look behind it. I knew right where to go, what to do." He pushed himself up from the couch and shouldered the macramé bag he carried. "You should try it sometime," he said, smiling back at her. "It's amazing." He started for the door, pausing to say, "Thank you so much, Dr. Bird. I'll see you tomorrow."

She stayed in her armchair, watching him go, almost too tired to get up and gather her things. It had been a grueling afternoon. She was pleased with the outcome, for Charlie's sake, but she felt emotionally drained. Empty. His suggestion, "You should try it," barely registered.

* * * ★ ★ ★ ★ * * *

"A lot of people—doctors, especially psychiatrists—are experimenting with LSD," Mitch told her, when she brought up the subject.

"Still? Even though now it's illegal?"

The two of them were nestled in their living room, cocooned by the thick gray fog drifting against the windows. The yellow glow of streetlights glimmered through the mist, and the lights of the city blurred into amber and ivory spots, transforming the cityscape into an impressionist painting.

They stretched their legs out on opposite sides of the couch Mitch had inherited. It wasn't much to look at, that couch, but it was long enough for the occasional overnight guest to sleep on, and substantial enough to make love on if they felt like it. They each had a glass of wine, and Beatrice had set out a tray of cheese and salmon spread she had bought down at the wharf. A baguette rested on a bread board with a knife beside it. Mitch had upended a can of sardines on a saucer, and Beatrice wrinkled her nose at the smell. So far neither of them had eaten anything, but they were halfway through a bottle of Chianti.

Mitch said, "There's speculation that the drug has therapeutic possibilities."

"I assume the dosages are more or less random, since no one's regulating it."

"They have to be. People are just cooking it up in their kitchens, selling it on street corners." He shook his head and gave a small, disapproving snort. "Dangerous," he said.

"But Charlie's response was astounding. Struggled for months, and then the breakthrough." She took a sip of wine and savored it on the back of her tongue. "If the drug is helpful, how can that be bad?"

"I don't know that it's bad," Mitch said, in his precise professorial way. "I do know that it's not well understood. I read a journal piece about it the other day, written by a psychiatrist at Stanford. He tried LSD several times, and he thought it made him feel more able to relate to his friends, his wife—his patients, too. He wrote something about empathy. Sensing other people's emotions."

"Do you think it should be legal, then, the way it was?"

Mitch was adamant about that. "Absolutely not. I agree with the state on that issue. It may have its uses, but it needs to be tested under lab conditions."

"Have you tried it?" She poked him with her toe, grinning.

"I, Dr. Bird, am not the experimental sort. Uncle Matteo made me walk the straight and narrow." He pointed toward the sky, muttered, "Riposa in pace," then reached for the wine bottle. He poured more Chianti into his glass and then hers. "I still do. This is my drug of choice, thanks. This, and coffee."

"Oh, me, too," she said. She lifted her chin toward the cheese and the baguette. "Not much of a dinner, is it?"

"We'll eat a big breakfast," he promised, which made her laugh. They rarely had time for breakfast, and tomorrow was his hospital day.

"Ice cream?" she hinted. "After our fancy repast?"

He shook his head. "I'm too tired to go get it."

"Me, too." She sat up, drew the bread board closer, and began slicing the baguette. "This will have to do us for tonight."

"I'll take you out to dinner tomorrow."

She passed him a plate with several slices of bread and pushed the cheese and salmon closer. "Now that's a promise I'll hold you to."

He slid the sardines toward her. "You should try one."

She shook her head, laughing. Mitch knew she hated the things, but his suggestion reminded her of what Charlie had said. *You should try it.* She had forgotten about that until just this moment.

They went to bed early. Mitch fell asleep immediately, but Beatrice lay awake for a while, propped up on her pillows. She watched the fog curl and drift beyond the window as she wondered about Charlie, the release of his traumatic memory, and the agent that had made it possible.

8

Anne, The Island, 1977

THE MONASTERY'S OLD station wagon was too noisy on the rutted dirt road for conversation. Anne sat mute in the passenger seat, her arms folded around herself. She was always cold these days, despite her wool coat and leather gloves. She gazed into the stands of evergreen trees, recognizing pine and fir and cedar. The ground beneath them was thick with fallen needles, and their scent reached her even through the car's closed windows. Patches of winter-dry grass grew here and there, and wild rhododendrons tumbled along the sides of the road. Their leaves were a dull, dusty green, their buds already setting for spring. Occasionally she glimpsed the bay through a break in the woods, glistening faintly blue in the thin sunshine.

The road ran up the wooded hill to a bluff on the northeastern tip of the island. Where the road turned was a small barn with a lean-to tacked onto one side. Two cows grazed in its shadow, and they lifted their heads as the station wagon rattled by. Mother Maggie shouted over the car's racket, "Dorothy and Alice! Beatrice's cows."

Anne knew nothing of cows except for the milk that came to her house in glass bottles, but these were charming, set against the backdrop of forest and sea. The smaller one was a muted yellow, with long-lashed eyes like some sort of oversized puppy. The other was tall, black and white, with a comically crooked nose. How fortunate this woman was to live in such a spot, with two such gentle-looking creatures! It must be peaceful.

She could barely remember what it felt like to be at peace, and she sometimes wondered if she ever had been. The memory of the beckoning waves, and their temptation of eternal rest, hovered at the edges of her mind even as the station wagon bumped to a stop in front of a pretty cottage that looked as if it had grown organically from the surrounding forest.

Mother Maggie turned the engine off. As the cooling motor ticked, she gestured to the house. "Nice, isn't it? There was an architect, I think."

The cottage had obviously been designed to make the most of the ocean view, with a narrow porch and broad windows facing the water. The exterior was simple, even rustic, but its soft blue walls suited the landscape. The window and doorframes were a creamy off-white, like the clouds dotting the sky above. A metal chimney emitted a stream of clear gray smoke, and the lowering sun glittered on the windows. Three shallow steps led up to a small porch and a half-glass door.

The whole thing made Anne think of a fairy-tale cottage, Hansel and Gretel, or Goldilocks. She wished, with a spasm of longing, that she could show it to Benjamin.

They climbed out of the car, and Anne lifted her suitcase from the back before following Mother Maggie up the steps. The door opened before they reached it, and the woman she had seen so briefly the day before stood in a shaft of sunshine, crinkles appearing around her eyes as she squinted against the slanting light.

"Hi." She put out her hand. "I'm Beatrice, and you must be Anne. Sorry about the ferry. We're at the mercy of the tides, I'm afraid. Come in, both of you. I'll make a pot of tea."

Anne shook her hand. On the surface, it was a courteous welcome, but there was something amiss. Beatrice's handshake was cool and firm, her hand surprisingly strong. She was shorter than Anne, older, but with the compact figure of a younger woman. Her voice sounded assured, as if she was used to meeting people, but her eyes skittered away, not looking into Anne's face.

She turned aside just a moment too soon, fixing her gaze on Mother Maggie or past her shoulder at the waning blue of the sky— any place but at Anne herself.

Anne said, in her best houseguest way, "Thank you for letting me come, Dr. Bird. I'm so grateful." She had to speak to the back of Beatrice's oddly cut hair.

Without turning, her hostess said, "Please, call me Beatrice." She led the way through an archway into a lovely room of modest size, with a sofa and an easy chair set to face the beach. There was a low bookcase, every shelf filled, and an open rolltop desk piled with more books and stocked with stationery and envelopes and an assortment of fountain pens.

Fighting her sense of being unwelcome, Anne said, "What a charming room this is."

"Isn't it?" Mother Maggie said. She didn't seem to notice Beatrice's odd demeanor, or perhaps she was used to it. She crossed to the windows, the long skirt of her habit brushing against the furniture, and stood with her hands clasped, looking out. "I had no idea you could see the big island from here, Beatrice."

"Yes, when it's clear," Beatrice called. She had stepped into the kitchen, where Anne could see a big stove and an oversized refrigerator. The teakettle was beginning to steam. A blue-and-white china teapot and matching cups waited on a tray. "When the fog rolls in, it disappears. I think of it as Brigadoon, only existing from time to time."

"Brigadoon! Perfect," Mother Maggie said.

Anne, feeling as awkward as an adolescent, couldn't summon a comment, though she loved *Brigadoon*. She had seen it in New York on a trip with her mother. They had also seen *West Side Story* and, while she was in college, *Hair*. If it had been left to Anne, they would have seen more, but her mother said she was done after *Hair*. The nudity offended her.

Mother Maggie went to the kitchen to help Beatrice, and Anne found herself alone at the window, watching the lights of a boat bobbing through the dusk. The voices of her hostess and the nun faded away as she recalled her mother's voice on the telephone, the last time they had spoken. She had told her of her troubles with James, and her fear.

"That's the way it is for women," her mother had said. "It always has been."

"It's not the 1950s anymore," Anne protested. She had read Steinem and Friedan in college. She had watched two or three of her sorority sisters break the rules: ignoring curfew, sleeping with their boyfriends, refusing to wear the prescribed dresses to class. One rebelled against her parents by joining a peace march against the Vietnam War. That girl's family had withdrawn her tuition money, and she had to drop out of school.

Anne admired those girls and wished for their courage. She told herself that one day, when she was older, when she was independent, she would do what she wanted, just as they did.

That hadn't happened. James had happened instead. She had worked hard to be the wife he wanted, to fit into the role the way he saw it—the way her parents saw it. It was when Benjamin arrived that the desire to be stronger had stirred in her soul. She wanted— she needed—to protect her child, to defend him from harm. She thought if anything would make her march in the streets, it would be something that threatened Benjamin.

"Mom," she began. "Things are different now. Women can have careers."

Her mother had interrupted. "Women's liberation nonsense! Your father would be furious if he heard you talk like that. Do you think those working women are happy, with no family, no children? You have everything you could want: a beautiful home, money, a respected husband. If there are rough times, you have to deal with them."

Rough times. That was the way her mother saw it. Bruises, fear, a traumatized child, never knowing when a day would be ruined, or an evening, never knowing when a hand would slap, or lash out in a careless shove. Never knowing why. Never understanding what she had done wrong, never knowing how to protect herself. Rough times.

She was, in her own way, marching in the streets for her son. But she was all alone.

She recalled the angry click as her mother hung up on her, and then the angry slam of the front door as James arrived home in a temper. The final temper. The end of everything.

Anne blinked, jarred by someone speaking her name. Disoriented, she jerked away from the window, causing herself to stumble.

"Come and sit," Mother Maggie called cheerily.

Beatrice was pouring tea at a small polished maple dining table with four straight chairs ranged around it. A fat candle rested in its center, next to a saucer with a few sugar cookies, the kind from a package. There was a sugar and cream set that matched the teapot, and a little stack of paper napkins.

Beatrice said, "Yes, do sit down, Anne," without looking up. "Sorry about the store-bought cookies," she added, as they each took a chair. "I don't really cook."

"Sister Mary Frances will make you some cookies," Mother Maggie said. "She loves to bake."

"How nice," Beatrice said, in noncommittal fashion.

Anne accepted a cup of tea, struggling to control the tremor of her fingers. Her dose of scotch had worn off as she slept, and anxiety rose anew in her chest like the tide rising up the beach. She took one of the sugar cookies, which had colored sprinkles and a scalloped edge, but she couldn't put it in her mouth. She slid it onto the saucer next to her teacup.

She was aware that the other two women were conversing about little things: weather, groceries, the ferry schedule. She didn't say anything. She remembered knowing how to make small talk, but she seemed to have lost the knack. She made herself pick up her cup and take a sip of tea, and told herself she really must make some contribution.

"This is lovely tea," she said finally.

Mother Maggie and Beatrice both turned to her, staring, and she realized, with a rush of humiliation, that she had interrupted them.

Her cheeks burned with shame, and she covered her face with her hands. "I'm sorry," she mumbled, behind her palms. "Forgive me for being rude." Her voice rose and thinned, and she clenched her fingers against her forehead. "Oh, God," she muttered, as the wave of anxiety became a tsunami, making her light-headed. She felt for all the world as if her head were no longer attached to her body. She mumbled, hardly knowing she was speaking aloud, "I can't do this. I can't—oh, dear God, I'm so sorry, I—"

Anne had the distinct impression she was about to die, right here in the home of a stranger. It was awful. It was humiliating. She wished it would hurry up, set her free from this agony. Surely her heart was about to stop beating. She was breathing, breathing hard, but she was sure no oxygen reached her lungs. Her head swam, and her throat felt as if it were closing. She struggled to her feet and turned blindly toward the door. Fresh air, the wind on her cheeks—

Anne found Beatrice Bird in her path. The smaller woman gripped Anne's elbows with strong hands, turned her, and guided her firmly toward the easy chair in the living room. She pressed her into the seat, and with a hand on the back of her neck, said, "Put your head down, Anne. That's it, on your knees. You're having a panic attack. It will pass in a few moments. Breathe slowly, in and out, deep breaths."

Anne did as she was told, without making a decision about it, without her own volition. She found, as her breathing began to steady and the buzzing inside her head to ease, that Beatrice was holding her left hand while Mother Maggie held the right one in dry, calloused fingers. Anne didn't know how long she sat that way, slumped forward, her forehead on her knees, her hands gripping the hands of two women she barely knew. Who didn't know her.

In time, she drew one final, rasping breath, and pulled herself upright. She found Mother Maggie on her knees beside her, her eyes heavy-lidded with worry behind her heavy glasses. Beatrice seemed surprisingly calm, even efficient. She released Anne's hand, and stepped back. "Do you drink alcohol, Anne?"

"Y-yes," Anne admitted.

"A little whiskey, then, I think." Beatrice's voice was matter-of-fact. "I don't have any sedatives in the house, but whiskey might help."

Mother Maggie said, patting Anne's hand, "Beatrice is a doctor, Anne."

"Psychologist," Beatrice said, from the kitchen. She came back, carrying a small glass with two fingers of amber liquid. "Psychologist," she repeated. "PhD, not MD." She held out the glass to Anne. "But I can prescribe a bit of whiskey for nerves, as long as you don't have an alcohol problem."

Anne ignored the issue of an alcohol problem. She accepted the glass gratefully and drank the whiskey in three gulps. She leaned back in the easy chair, feeling the fire of the alcohol burn down her throat and into her mostly empty stomach. Its heat spread into her bloodstream, easing the pounding of her head and the stiff, helpless feeling in her chest. The relief was profound, but it was shameful, too, and she closed her eyes. "Thank you, Dr. Bird."

"Beatrice."

"I'm so sorry."

"It's all right," Mother Maggie said, though Anne thought she sounded doubtful.

Beatrice said, "Some things are not your fault, Anne, and a panic disorder is on the list."

Anne opened her eyes again. Mother Maggie still knelt beside her, but Beatrice had gone back to the kitchen with the empty whiskey glass. The chink of cups and saucers being moved signaled the end of their tea time.

Mother Maggie patted Anne's knee. "I thought you were going to faint."

"I thought I was going to die," Anne blurted.

From the kitchen, Beatrice said, "That's what they feel like, panic attacks. Like you're going to die. Something of a surprise when you don't."

Anne thought she might be speaking from experience. She said, "I'm so embarrassed. I'm sure you're wishing you weren't stuck with me for the night."

Mother Maggie tutted at that, as she clambered to her feet and straightened the full skirt of her habit. "Now, Anne. Have faith. Perhaps God put you right where you need to be."

Anne wished she could believe that. A faint snort from the kitchen implied Beatrice didn't believe it, either. Anne was about to apologize again when a low, groaning sound came from outside the cottage. She and Mother Maggie both started, and Anne came to her feet.

They turned toward the windows and saw the smaller of the two cows, the yellow one, standing beside the porch and gazing in through the window. She mooed again, and Beatrice chuckled. "Alice," she said. "She's the bossy one, letting me know it's milking time. If I don't get out there, Dorothy will join the chorus."

Mother Maggie said, automatically, "Can I help?"

"Not really. You go on home before it gets too dark. Anne can relax for a bit while I do my chores. Not sure what we'll do about dinner, but we'll figure something out."

"I brought your groceries. They're in the kitchen, on the counter."

"Thank you, Mother Maggie. I can't even remember what I ordered."

Anne stood where she was as Mother Maggie gathered up her keys, bid them both good night, and strode out to the porch and on to the station wagon, her habit swirling around her sturdy ankles. Beatrice followed, a milk bucket in her hand as she crossed the yard to the little barn. The two cows ambled after her. All three disappeared inside, and a light came on in the barn window.

Anne had no idea how long it took to milk two cows. Uncertainly, she moved into the kitchen, looking about for something she could do to be useful. She found the teapot and cups in the sink, so she rinsed them and stacked them in the drying rack. She picked up the untouched cookies and slid them back into the open package on the counter, then wiped down the bar, though it looked perfectly clean.

Out of things to do, she stood with her back to the sink, surveying the kitchen. The bar held a heavy old-fashioned black phone, a slim telephone directory, a notepad and pen, and a wooden basket with two onions and a head of garlic. There was a wine rack beside the refrigerator, full of bottles of various sizes and colors. The cupboard doors were glass, showing a modest assortment of china and stemware.

Under different circumstances, Anne would have felt enthusiasm over such a well-ordered kitchen, felt an urge to look for the pots and pans, discover what was in the big fridge, plan a meal, especially for a hostess who said she wasn't much of a cook. Anne was—or had been—an excellent cook, with a flair for creative combinations of ingredients.

The bag of groceries waited invitingly on the counter, but it seemed presumptuous to start going through it, and she didn't know where Beatrice would like things to go.

She wandered back into the living room and looked out into the darkness. The water gleamed here and there as the stars began to come to life. In the distance, the lights of the big island glowed, reminding her that she would have to go back in the morning, would have to find another destination. Another place to hide.

The thought wearied her, and she made herself turn away from the view of the tempting waves. She walked determinedly toward the kitchen to find something to do besides worry about tomorrow.

9

Beatrice, The Island, 1977

BEATRICE BURIED HER forehead in Alice's warm flank and closed her eyes as she milked, concentrating on the sounds of the bucket filling and the cows munching. The familiar smells of the barn and its inhabitants comforted her almost as much as the blessed absence of ghosts.

Anne Iredale's ghosts were as intense as any she had ever experienced. The base of her throat ached so badly she felt she might choke.

It had been easier, in a way, to deal with Anne's panic attack, because Anne was actually, physically, present. There were things Beatrice could do to help. Actions she could take. The little ghost was pure pain, and she had no power to alleviate it.

The bigger one was a different problem. It was a monster, menacing, angry, the kind constructed of nighttime shadows. Its cold silence pulsed with fury. With threats, and the very real possibility of danger. This was what poor Anne Iredale was carrying with her.

They were projections, of course. Beatrice understood that. Their origin was in the mind of the one who carried them: her sadness, her sorrow, her fear made tangible.

Alice's udder was empty. Beatrice stood up to shift the bucket and stool to Dorothy. Both cows were halfway through their feed of hay. By the time she finished, the manger would be empty and the bucket would brim with milk, and she would have the satisfaction of a productive chore completed. Tonight, she wished she could extend it, put off going inside the house, tackling the problem of dinner, making up a bed for her guest, but her conscience pricked her. What if Anne's panic returned? The young woman was clearly at the end of her strength.

Beatrice hurried with Dorothy. She opened the stanchions when she was finished, and then the barn door so the cows could go out. She hoisted the milk bucket, said good night to the girls, and walked back to the cottage in chilly darkness.

She was startled, as she stepped up on the porch, to smell onions and garlic sauteing in olive oil. It was a scent that had often greeted her in San Francisco, and it gave her such a jolt of nostalgia that she nearly dropped the milk bucket. She had to pause to collect herself before going inside. She tucked her chin, her little defensive gesture, and pushed open the door.

Anne Iredale spun when she heard her come in, a faint look of guilt on her face. She held a spatula in one hand and the handle of a frying pan in the other. "Oh, Beatrice!" she said. "I hope you don't mind. I just—I wanted to do something to help, and you said—"

Beatrice focused on getting the milk bucket to the counter without spilling. It helped her avoid looking at the indigo shadow clinging to Anne's slender legs, to distract herself from the misery of it. She began pouring the milk into the strainer. "I don't mind at all, Anne. As I said, I don't really cook. Did you find something you can work with?"

"There was pasta in the grocery bag, and an onion and a head of garlic in the basket. I found shrimp in the freezer, and I just—I kind of got started. It's the way I usually cook. Used to cook."

Beatrice forced herself to produce a vague smile in Anne's direction. It was one night, she reminded herself. When her unexpected guest departed on the ferry in the morning, she would put these ghosts out of her mind. It was not as if there was anything she could do about them. She could at least find it in herself to be courteous to an unhappy young woman.

"I appreciate it," she said. "Let me get this milk into the fridge, and I'll set the table."

As the sizzle of frying shrimp sounded from the kitchen, Beatrice turned down the lights in the dining room and lit the thick candle. The dimness would make Anne's ghosts easier to avoid. Even knowing they were in the house unsettled her, her throat throbbing in response.

Just the same, she rather looked forward to a meal she hadn't cooked. Anne had found a bunch of parsley in the vegetable drawer that Beatrice had forgotten about, and chopped it into the shrimp and onion mixture. She tossed everything with the package of linguine and added a hefty sprinkle of Parmesan cheese. Beatrice opened a bottle of her favorite Chianti, and the two of them sat down.

Beatrice focused on the wineglasses as she filled them. "This smells wonderful, Anne. Thank you for cooking."

Anne answered with an air of formality that Beatrice thought must be customary with her. "It's my pleasure. Your kitchen is lovely to work in."

"I'm glad you think so. It's more or less the way I found it, to be honest." Beatrice took a forkful of pasta. It tasted even better than it smelled, and the pain in her throat eased as she swallowed. "This is delicious." It was, in fact, equal to any of Mitch's creations. She tried not to notice that Anne barely dipped into the serving on her plate. She would not, she told herself, urge the girl to eat. She wasn't her mother. Or her doctor.

She also tried not to notice, or to judge, how quickly Anne's Chianti disappeared.

When her own glass was half-empty she refilled both glasses, taking care because the room was so dark. The candlelight barely illuminated the serving bowl and the food on their plates. Blessedly, it didn't reach to the uninvited guests at the table, enabling Beatrice to look more closely at Anne's face.

It was a truly beautiful face, clear-skinned, with large eyes of a distinct and unusual blue, a delicate nose, a fine-lipped mouth. It was the kind of face that turned heads and opened doors, eased the path through life. Her own face, Beatrice knew well, was unremarkable. This young woman was a classic beauty, despite being far too thin. She would have thought—

Anne interrupted her thoughts. "Did you move here from San Francisco?"

"I did. Less than two months ago."

"Such a beautiful city."

"It is indeed." Beatrice took another serving of pasta.

"You were working there?"

"Yes. In a community clinic, and I have—had—a small private practice."

Anne sat back with her wineglass in both hands, her pasta barely touched. "Island life is a big change from city life."

Beatrice speared a shrimp and gazed at it. "I needed the change. Quiet. Solitude. This island has plenty of both."

"I can see that." Anne took another sip of wine.

Beatrice sensed Anne's dismay as she realized her glass was almost empty again. Beatrice picked up the bottle and poured the last of the Chianti into Anne's glass. "And so," she said, "did you come in search of solitude, too?"

The darkest shade rippled behind Anne Iredale's shoulders, disturbing the gloom, jolting Beatrice so that her hand jerked, and she set the bottle down too hard on the table. It rocked, and nearly fell. She caught it in her hand to set it down more carefully.

Her guest said, "Not exactly. I hoped—I came to see Mother Maggie. I thought of becoming a postulant."

"Really? But that didn't—" Beatrice wasn't sure how to put it. Knowing it was a clumsy phrase, she said, "That didn't take?"

Anne drained the last of the Chianti in her glass, then shook her head. "No. It turns out they have no room for me, and Mother Maggie's view is that I have no vocation."

"Oh." Beatrice didn't know anything about vocations. She supposed Mother Maggie must have had one. Still did, no doubt. She could have asked Anne to explain, drawn her out about vocations and why she had thought she might have one, but she didn't want to extend the conversation. What she wanted was to escape to her bedroom, away from Anne's ghosts. Their aura of heartache and anger crept over her, and her appetite died. She laid her flatware across her plate and saw that Anne had given up on her own plate as well.

Anne jumped to her feet. "Please let me do the dishes, Beatrice."

"But you cooked," Beatrice said automatically. When Mitch cooked, she always did the dishes. Had done the dishes.

Anne deftly slid her plate from beneath her hands. "It's the only way I can thank you," she murmured, and disappeared into the kitchen.

Beatrice blew out the candle and turned up the lights. She heard the gentle clink of dishes and glassware as she put wood in the stove and closed the damper to bank the fire until morning. She was just starting toward the second bedroom to put out linens when Anne came back.

Without thinking, Beatrice glanced up. She saw Anne's slender silhouette against the bright lights of the kitchen. The ghosts were still there, the charcoal shadow hovering above her head, the sad little shade at her ankles. But there was something else…Something different. Something new. Something awful.

Beatrice hissed, "My God, what is that?"

Anne froze, her eyes wide and one hand halfway to her heart. "What?" she whispered, her voice barely audible. Slowly, shakily, she turned to look behind her.

Beatrice pressed one hand to her mouth as her heart raced. There was a third ghost. A third shade, rising ominously, swiftly. It was black and intense, so opaque that it blocked the light from the kitchen.

This ghost was not a mere shadow, an amorphous mass charged with meaning because of the emotions emanating from it: pain, fear, sadness, anxiety. The shades Beatrice saw grew out of the feelings that tormented her patients, her acquaintances, the strangers she passed on the street.

This wasn't one of those. This was the stuff of nightmares, of horror films, of campfire tales. It was separate. Its own entity. Its own phenomenon.

This, Beatrice thought, with an unaccustomed twinge in her chest, *this* was the worst yet.

There was nothing vague about it. There was nothing open to interpretation, or judgment, or instinct. Unlike the shades she was used to, it had form, a head, a shock of hair, hands that lifted before its face, as if to attack, or—or to hide itself? It carried with it a profoundly existential fear that stole Beatrice's breath. It exuded a pure horror that made her heart bump and skip.

And it stank!

Beatrice had seen hundreds of her ghosts: small, large, threatening, sad, frightened. Not once had there been a smell.

And this smell! It was putrid and dank, the stench of rotting flesh. Beatrice knew that smell. Sometimes she and her father found dead animals among the live ones, and they smelled like that.

This ghost made no sense. This was—an exaggeration. A monster. A creation of her own making—

It turned her stomach, and her gorge rose at the same moment that the vision, or whatever it was, faded to nothing and then, in an instant, vanished as if it had never been.

Perhaps it hadn't. The smell evaporated, too, but her stomach didn't settle.

Beatrice stared at the spot where it had been. She saw only her bright kitchen, where Anne had just been putting things away. Beatrice drew a desperate breath, struggling against panic.

She had hoped against hope this would not happen. She had fled here for the specific intent of getting better, being less sensitive, more rational.

This event erased all doubt. She was hallucinating. She was seeing things that were not there. That could not be there. Far from recovering, she was getting worse. The existential dread she felt was hers, and hers alone.

She tried to swallow, but her fear had gone straight to her belly. "Oh, damn," she grunted, one hand on her churning stomach.

"What is it?" Anne cried.

Beatrice tried to swallow away the nausea, but she couldn't get ahead of it. Words were coming from her mouth, but she barely knew what they were, what Anne would think of them. "I—oh! damn—I'm going to be sick."

She pressed both hands over her mouth, whirled to dash to the bathroom, and slammed the door behind her.

Anne, The Island, 1977

Anne nearly dropped her glass as she watched the color leach from Beatrice's face and the pupils of her eyes expand, nearly drowning the iris. Her nostrils flared and she folded her lips as if she smelled something awful. Was that because she suddenly felt sick?

Obviously, she did feel sick, was being sick—but before that, before her precipitous dash for the bathroom, she had looked past Anne at—at something. Something that shocked her. Frightened her. Beatrice didn't seem to be a person who would be easily frightened.

Her flesh crawling, Anne turned again, slowly, to look behind her. She saw nothing but the gleaming kitchen, the plates drying in the rack, the dark windows reflecting her own pale image, the lights like blurred stars in the panes.

From the bathroom she heard the unmistakable sounds of Beatrice being sick, then the flush of the toilet and water running in the sink. Anne turned back into the kitchen to put the last glass in the rack, then smoothed her slacks with her hands, wondering how she could ease the embarrassment her hostess would feel.

She decided on a glass of water. She found a lemon in the fridge, cut a slice of it, squeezed it into the water, and carried the glass into the living room.

Beatrice came out of the bathroom carrying a hand towel, her hair damp and straggling over her forehead. She accepted the glass of water, took a long drink, then sank onto the sofa with a groan. "Sorry," she said.

"I hope it wasn't the garlic," Anne said, knowing it was a lame thing to say. She was quite certain it was not her dinner that had made Beatrice sick. Something had happened. Something she didn't understand in the least.

Beatrice shook her head and sipped more water.

"If there's anything I can do for you…"

"You could turn the light down," Beatrice said. Her voice was guttural and hoarse, not the even, confident voice Anne had first heard.

"Of course." Anne found the switch on the lamp and clicked it until she found the lowest setting. Beatrice gave a long sigh and let her head fall back against the sofa. Anne thought perhaps the light hurt her eyes. She wondered if Beatrice had an illness she wasn't aware of. That Mother Maggie didn't know about.

Anne pulled the desk chair close to the sofa and sat down, leaning forward. "Beatrice. Do you need…Is there some medicine you could take? I could get it for you."

Beatrice's mouth twisted, and Anne sat back, fearful she had offended her. Beatrice said, in that same rough voice, "Thank you, no. The water's good. Just give me a moment."

"Of course," Anne whispered. The illusion of a polite evening was shattered. Already unsure of her welcome—rather, quite sure she wasn't welcome—she pressed a hand to her own stomach, which churned with discomfort. The room was getting cold, and the fire in the stove barely glowed. She thought of opening the damper, but perhaps Beatrice needed to save the wood for the morning. Instead, she pulled the sleeves of her sweater over her hands.

She had been trained, by her mother, by her sorority, by the example set by her mother's friends, to fill silences with talk, with witty comments and courtesies, but her mind was a blank. A tree's branches scraped and creaked against the side of the cottage, but there was no other sound except the distant susurration of the waves sliding up the beach. Obviously, she couldn't just get up and leave this stranger to her misery, though there seemed to be nothing she could do to ease it. She waited, shivering a little.

After perhaps five minutes, Beatrice opened her eyes and turned her head toward Anne without lifting it from the back of the sofa. When she spoke, her voice was stronger. "Sorry about this. So embarrassing. I can't remember the last time…"

Anne gazed into Beatrice's eyes. They were oddly fey, their fine gray irises like clear water over stones. She wore no makeup, but her lashes were thick and dark, making her eyes stand out even more. It was the first time she had seen them, because it was the first time her hostess had looked directly at her. She said with sincerity, "Please don't apologize, Beatrice. I've had many such moments myself."

Beatrice blinked, lifted her head, and pushed herself upright. Now she gazed at the darkened window, where the wind-whipped sea glistened with starlight. Anne watched her profile, the small, straight nose and short upper lip that made her look absurdly youthful. She didn't look like a doctor, a professional. If Anne had not seen her in action earlier, she might have wondered if it was true.

Beatrice said, "These 'moments' of yours—I doubt they're quite like my own."

Her tone strove to be matter-of-fact, but Anne's every nerve, scraped raw in the past weeks, responded to the tremor in her voice, the restless movements of her hands, the distress in her tense shoulders. Instinctively, Anne leaned forward again. "Do you want to talk?"

It was something she would have said to a friend. The words were out before she had thought them through. Did she want to absorb someone else's trouble? Did she have the strength? It wasn't as if she knew this woman at all, beyond a forced invitation to spend the night and a shallow dinner conversation in which neither of them had revealed anything about themselves.

Part of her recoiled at the idea of hearing some traumatic story, while another part of her—the maternal part, perhaps—couldn't ignore another person's pain.

Beatrice gave a halfhearted chuckle. "That's supposed to be my line."

Anne was glad the light was so low that Beatrice couldn't see the flush of embarrassment in her cheeks. "I do apologize. I didn't mean to intrude."

Beatrice held up a hand. "You were being kind. Nice of you, but believe me, you don't want to add my problems to your own."

Anne sat back in her chair, twisting her fingers together. "I think," she said quietly, "that it wouldn't make much difference. I could hardly feel worse."

Beatrice rose from the sofa. "What we need is another bottle of wine. We can drown our sorrows—or share them—whatever feels best."

Anne tried not to sound too eager. "Shall I get the glasses?"

"Just sit. I'll be right back."

Anne moved to the sofa so she could lean into its cushions, stretch out her long legs, and contemplate the turn the evening had taken. She wouldn't tell Beatrice her secret, of course. She didn't dare. She had learned that even people she trusted could betray her.

She could listen, though. It would be good to feel useful. It had been a long time since she had comforted anyone.

Except for Benjamin. She had comforted Benjamin many times. The idea of him, the memory of his warm small body close to hers, her arms around him, his head on her shoulder, made her heart ache so badly she had to press her palm to her chest.

Maybe, with an extra glass of wine, she could sleep. It would be such a relief, such a respite, to relax in this secret, safe place for a few hours. Perhaps for once she wouldn't be tortured by dreams of her baby, crying in vain for his mother.

10

Benjamin Iredale, Oak Hill, five years old

GRAMMA PHYLLIS SAID Mama had gone for a rest in a special place, but Benjamin knew she just said that so he wouldn't cry. He had seen Mama's face as she waved goodbye, and the brilliance of tears in her pretty eyes. Mama wasn't going for a rest. She was going away forever.

He tried really hard not to think about Mama when Papa came to pick him up from Gramma Phyllis's house. Papa didn't like him to cry. If Benjamin cried, Papa would say things like "Boys don't cry" or "Crying is for babies." Sometimes he said, "I'll give you something to cry about," and he meant that. It always hurt. Sometimes it left bruises. When Mama was here she could stop him sometimes, but now she wasn't here. There was no one to stop him.

Papa was the one who sent his mother away. Gramma Phyllis tried to pretend Benjamin didn't know that, but he did. He was a very smart boy.

He knew he was smart, and not just because his mother said so, or his teacher. He was the only one in kindergarten who could read. He had started to learn the letters on his blocks when he was only two, and by the time he was three, they had resolved themselves into words and sentences and stories. He loved collections, and he studied stamps and coins and read books the adults thought were too old for him, because they made him even smarter. He might not be good at soccer or T-ball—he was terrible at them, really—but he was good at puzzles and board games, anything that had to do with reading and remembering things.

Benjamin had known for a long time that Papa was mean to Mama. They both tried to hide it from him, especially Mama, but sometimes he heard Papa shout at her, just like he shouted at Benjamin. He heard the crashes when Papa shoved Mama, which was a lot like when Papa slapped him hard enough to make him fall down. Once Papa caught him watching and crying when he was twisting Mama's arm—bruises again—and Papa dragged him upstairs and locked him in his bedroom by himself.

At least he hadn't locked him in the closet with the light off. That was always the worst. Benjamin suspected that was why he started stuttering, but he wasn't sure, and no one ever said so. No one ever talked about it except to tell him to stop. He looked in all his books, and in some of Mama's, but he couldn't find anything about stuttering.

Stuttering was a hard thing to understand. He could remember talking smoothly, without any problems, but then the closet thing happened, and other things, and he started having trouble with certain words. He had lots of words in his head, but they wouldn't come out of his mouth. The teacher was nice about it, and always waited for him to finish what he had to say, but the other kids didn't. Some of them pretended to stutter, too, to make each other laugh. That made him stutter more, because he was always afraid they would make fun of him. Sometimes he stuttered more just because he was worried about it.

Benjamin thought his teacher probably knew his mother had gone away, and felt sorry for him. He had heard his Gramma Phyllis on the telephone, talking to her friends, and she was always saying that everyone knew. If she saw him listening, she tried to pretend she was talking about someone else, saying things like "Little pitchers have big ears." Benjamin pretended he didn't understand, but he did.

He understood Papa had done something to Mama the day of the crash. Her face was already bruised before they got in the car. It was the kind of bruise Benjamin sometimes had on his arm or his bottom, a big black bruise. He knew how much they hurt.

When he got too lonely, he tried to think about Mama sitting with him, letting him explain his stamp collection to her. He had stamps from Mexico and Canada as well as America. He also had several stamps from England, hidden on a back page. He tried to remember those times, nestled close to Mama on the sofa, but his mind tricked him. Instead of that good memory, he remembered watching her being driven away while he had to stay with Papa and Gramma Phyllis. He remembered how she got into the back seat of that strange car, her face frozen as if she had a mask on, and he knew it was so she wouldn't cry. He kept hoping she might come back for him, but she never did.

At first he kept count of the days since the car took his mother away, reciting them to himself at night, but that made him too sad. He counted his coin collection instead, and then he counted his stamps, even the ones from England. And when he had to cry, he did his best to wait until he was in bed, with the lights out and a pillow over his head so Papa wouldn't hear.

Often, when he was done crying and he took the pillow away, the lady was there in his room. She was sad, too. She smelled funny, and she made his room smell funny, but seeing her made him feel better. When she stood at the end of his bed, it was good. He could sleep then, because he wasn't alone in the dark.

11

Beatrice, San Francisco, 1969

CHARLIE CROSSMAN CAME to say goodbye to Beatrice on a sunny September morning, when the bay sparkled its clearest blue and the gulls' cries rang across the city like discordant bells.

He came into her office, though he didn't have an appointment, and she gestured him to the sofa. He sat on the edge of it, making it clear he didn't mean to stay. "I'm going home, Dr. Bird," he said. "I just wanted to tell you. The kids in my house are stoned all the time, and Amy and I aren't really—well, it's not working out. A lot of people are leaving, actually."

"So I gather."

"Mostly, I want to see my mother. I want to tell her it's okay. Tell her I understand now, I know how she must have felt—you know, the things you and I have talked about."

"I think you're making a very good choice." Beatrice leaned back in her chair and laid her notebook aside. "You've done wonderful work these past months. I'm proud of you."

"You made it possible," Charlie said. His cheeks reddened, but he held her gaze. "I'll never forget you."

She smiled, warmed by the sentiment, cheered by the idea that between them, real healing had taken place. "I'll remember you, too, Charlie."

He reached into the pocket of his denim jacket and brought out a tiny parcel. "I brought you something," he said, his eyes dropping now, embarrassed. "You don't have to use it if you don't want to, but—well, I wanted you to have some."

She put out her hand for the parcel and felt it with her fingers. "What's this?"

"It's acid."

"What? Did you say acid?"

"Yeah. LSD." He shrugged. "Just a little bit—for you to try if you want to."

"Really?" She held it on her palm, thinking how innocent the tiny package looked, and how much legal trouble it could cause.

"It really helped me, Dr. Bird. It just—it opened me up."

"It's not a pill? This doesn't feel like a pill."

"No, it's a liquid, dripped onto a piece of paper. It's really tiny. You just put it in your mouth and swallow it."

"Well. Thank you for thinking of me, Charlie." She put the little package in the pocket of her tweed jacket and followed Charlie to the door. He put out his hand, like a grown man, and she shook it. "You might send me a postcard," she said. "I'd like to know how it goes."

"I will. 'Bye!" He shouldered his backpack and jumped down the front steps, a boy again, speeding up the street to begin the next adventure of his young life. Beatrice smiled after him as she closed the door.

Mitch was in the corridor, writing something in a chart at the little shelf he used as a desk. He glanced up. "Was that Charlie Crossman?"

"Yes. He's going home," Beatrice said with satisfaction. "He's going to make things up with his mother."

Mitch grinned. "Well done, Dr. B."

She nodded, not trying to repress her own grin. "It feels good."

"Are you done for the morning? Have time for lunch?"

"No, sorry. I have another appointment in ten minutes."

"I'll bring you something. Seafood salad?"

"Perfect. Thank you." Beatrice went back into her office, absent-mindedly thrusting her hands into her pockets. Her right hand encountered Charlie's little offering, the packet of LSD-soaked paper he had described. She unfolded the stiff paper to find a tiny square printed with some sort of cartoon. It didn't smell of anything, or look like much, except that the colors of the cartoon had run, right in the middle. She held it on her palm and was startled to realize how much she wanted to try it.

Have a care, busy Bea. Look before you leap.

Oh, I don't know, Dad. Sometimes it's great to just jump in.

Beatrice had grown up helping her father in his medical practice. In his office, she had talked a patient with the DTs into lying down in the waiting room rather than ransacking the storeroom for codeine cough syrup. Once she had come close to delivering a baby right in the examining room. She had assisted in sewing up the haunch of a horse that had plunged through a fence, crouching in a muddy barn-yard to hold an umbrella and a flashlight. She had helped pull a calf who was turned the wrong way from the body of a struggling cow. None of it frightened her. Her father boasted that his daughter had the iron nerves of a surgeon.

Her mother had died when she was only two, and William had brought up his daughter to be as independent as a boy might have been. He despised what he called the postwar domesticity trap laid for women. He encouraged her to think for herself, to do what she wanted to do.

Beatrice responded with gleeful vigor. She was the first in her swim class to jump off the high diving board, the first to raise her hand in speech class, the first of her friends to smoke a bummed cigarette, the last to care about boys and dances and clothes. When she went off to college, she told her father she had decided to treat minds instead of bodies, and she was sorry if that disappointed him. He grinned, kissed her cheek, and said he was just relieved she hadn't taken it into her head to be a test pilot.

Mitch was not as tolerant of her risk-taking as her father had been. He would object to her trying Charlie's offering, but she wanted to do it anyway. She kept thinking of that little square of paper. She took it out to look at it, to wonder about it. She could think of reasons not to try it, but she was curious to know what it was like, what there was about it that made it popular, even now that it was illegal. And she loved the idea of opening closed doors. The square of paper might enhance her talent. Maybe instead of vague messages, she would actually *know* what her patients needed. Why turn down something that might make her a better therapist?

Thinking of her father's grin, she tucked the little packet back into her pocket to await the right moment.

* * * * * ★ ★ ★ * * * ·

Beatrice, San Francisco, 1969

Two evenings after Charlie's visit, Mitch had night duty at the hospital. His shift started at eight and didn't finish until six in the morning. Usually Beatrice felt restless and lonely on those nights, but this time, she planned to seize her moment. He kissed her and headed out around seven. She changed into a pair of cutoff jeans and a T-shirt and took the little square of paper with its faded cartoon colors out onto the balcony.

The lovely weather had held, bringing a warm evening air scented by the roses that grew topsy-turvy in the tangle of the garden. Beatrice loved San Francisco like this, the bay glowing azure in the twilight, the streetlamps sparkling along the streets like fairy lights. Jazz and folk music filtered through neighbors' windows, opened to the balmy air.

She settled into the surviving macramé sling and stretched her bare legs up into the warm breeze. She propped a pillow under her head and held the little square on her palm.

Of course Mitch was right. This drug should be regulated. She had no idea where Charlie had acquired it, or who had made it—or even how much LSD might be on this bit of garish paper. Charlie was a good kid, and he wouldn't mislead her intentionally, but still. It was a risk.

Just the same, she was safe at home, on her own balcony, and she wanted to do it. She wanted to know what the Stanford psychiatrist had experienced, what tectonic shift had freed Charlie Crossman from his demons.

I wish you wouldn't take chances, busy Bea.

Nothing to worry about, Dad. Just another adventure.

She smiled up into the evening sky, lifted her palm to her lips, and licked the paper into her mouth.

It was wonderful.

It started with the roses. She could still smell them, the lemony, sweet scents of the white ones, the heavier, spicier smell of the reds. But as the drug took her, she began to *hear* them. The whites were faraway violins, slender threads of sound winding up through the dusk. The reds were brass, trumpets and French horns, penetrating sounds that underlay the sounds of the city and turned all of it—car horns and stereos and ferries hooting in the bay—into one enormous symphony. It seemed the roses floated against the starfield, or their shadows did. The colors were vague, the shapes amorphous, but she had the distinct impression of flowers dancing before her eyes as they sang their strange songs.

She floated in the warm night air as if she were bathing. The rough texture of the macramé against her legs turned silky. The pillow cradled her head as if it were a hand cupping her skull. She was all sensation, and she surrendered to her heightened sensitivity without fear or anxiety, without intention or regret. The stars spun gently in a kaleidoscope of light that left shining contrails on her retinas as she listened to the symphony of roses.

Charlie had taken care with his little gift. As powerful as the experience was, it didn't last long. She settled back into her body as lightly as a ladybug descending onto a flower. She discovered her legs were cold, her neck stiff from the hard pillow, but neither could spoil the delights of her experience.

She wriggled free of the chair and went into the house. She showered, her skin shuddering with pleasure at the warmth of the water, the tingle of the spray on her breasts and arms and face. Her nightgown felt as if it had been woven of gossamer, and her hair falling down her back made her think of fairy wings.

She folded herself into bed with a smile on her face. She couldn't wait for the next day, to see her patients, to learn if there were changes in her perceptions.

And she wanted to do this again.

12

Beatrice, The Island, 1977

BEATRICE CHOSE A white wine from the fridge and opened it in the kitchen, where the light was bright enough to wield the corkscrew. She carried the bottle back into the dim living room with two fresh glasses and set everything on the coffee table in front of the sofa.

Anne said, "Shall I turn up the light?"

"Please don't," Beatrice said. She poured two glasses of wine.

Anne accepted hers, but she watched Beatrice over the rim before she took a sip. "Does it bother your eyes?" she asked. "The light, I mean?"

Beatrice shook her head. "It's not that." She sat down, then took a sip of wine, holding it in her mouth for a moment before she swallowed. Anne sat in the darkness, gazing at her, not saying anything as she drank her wine. Beatrice had the uncomfortable feeling that she had become the patient, when she had thought she might coax Anne to confide in her.

She had to look away from that gaze, though the darkness softened its intensity. Anne's eyes held a look Beatrice recognized, one that had been acquired through suffering. She couldn't have defined it, exactly, but it was something about the way the eyelids stretched, how the lashes trembled in the dim light. The look in Anne's eyes brought a decades-old memory to the surface, the haunted look of the widow Mrs. Clayman, pregnant, alone, desperate. Mrs. Clayman had also been worn thin with misery, and Beatrice had never forgotten the look of hopelessness in her face.

Heart aching with sympathy, Beatrice stared at the faint glow of the night ocean beyond the window. She supposed she should explain, now that the subject of the light had come up, but she found it difficult to speak the words. Somehow, she felt if she spoke them aloud, she would become vulnerable. Would be weakened. She wondered why she cared about that. How could it matter?

Finally, she said, "I'm afraid my behavior must seem—well, 'odd' is not really a strong enough word."

"Something frightened you."

"You could say that," Beatrice said. Her voice sounded bitter in her own ears. The truth was, though she couldn't bring herself to say it aloud, she was terrified. It didn't seem unreasonable to be afraid, in the face of her fear that her mind was breaking, collapsing, failing her.

Anne said, "I didn't see what it was."

"No. No one sees—" Beatrice broke off. "What's that?"

Beatrice gave a shake of her head and pressed the fingers of one hand to her lips. What was it about sitting here with this damaged young woman that tempted her to blurt out her truth? She hadn't meant to. Her intention had been to be kind to this girl, to focus on her. How had it happened that their conversation had turned the other way?

Anne Iredale sat silently, her arms folded around her, waiting. Beatrice felt the pressure of her attention, of her expectant posture. Her patients invariably felt this need to fill the silence, to answer the unspoken question, and just like them, she found herself squirming in her chair. How many times had her patients done just this, shifting their feet, pushing themselves back into their seat as if they could escape the need to speak, to dig deep into their feelings, their thoughts, their secrets?

Anne said, "Are you feeling all right? Your stomach?"

Beatrice flashed her a wry grin. "My stomach's okay," she said. She took a long sip of chardonnay and rolled its oaky flavor over her tongue. "I've just realized how close I am to telling you something I've never told anyone."

That wasn't quite true, though. She had told Mitch, and that had not gone well at all.

Anne regarded Beatrice with eyes full of sympathy. "I think," she said gravely, "that perhaps you *need* to tell me. Maybe that's why I'm here."

"Sorry? I don't think I follow."

"I mean, maybe God did put me here for a reason. Even though you didn't want me."

Beatrice drained her glass and reached for the wine bottle. "I'm afraid God and I are not well acquainted. I should say, not acquainted at all. But I'm sorry for making you feel unwelcome."

"I wasn't complaining!" Anne said hastily. "I'm sure you have a good reason for not wanting company."

"I do. And you're right. I'll try to explain, but I'm not sure you'll believe me." Mitch hadn't. He thought she was imagining things.

Anne released a long, trembling breath. "You might as well try me. Of late, to be honest, life has taught me to accept all sorts of things I would have sworn were impossible."

Beatrice poured more wine for both of them. "How old are you, Anne, if you don't mind me asking?"

The blue of Anne's eyes, when she turned to answer, had gone dark. China blue to cobalt. "I'm thirty-one. Going on a hundred."

Beatrice lifted her glass to her guest. "We have that in common, at least. I'm forty-eight, also going on a hundred."

Anne lifted her glass, too, and they drank together.

Beatrice didn't speak for a moment. They were such unlikely companions, the two of them. She had no idea whether Anne had gone to college, had a job, had siblings. Their lives had undoubtedly taken different paths, but both paths had led through loss and pain and struggle to bring them to this strange night. She knew no one could carry her burden for her, and that was true for Anne as well, and yet—somehow, with the empty night stretching ahead of them, in the darkened living room, there was a sort of weird relief in being in company, even the company of a stranger. Perhaps it was true that a burden shared was a burden eased. She wondered if she dared find out.

She pictured Charlie Crossman's sweet young face as she took another sip of wine, drew a breath, made a decision. She released the breath, and said, "It started with a gift from a patient."

13

Beatrice, San Francisco, 1969

BEATRICE LOVED HER home office on the bottom floor of La Signora. The room was just beneath the level of the sidewalk, and even on the rainiest of days, it had a sense of comfort and warmth. She had furnished it with three comfortable armchairs and a small desk, a gift from her father, where she could write notes after each session. She had added a large dream catcher, bought at one of the open-fronted shops at Fisherman's Wharf. She hung it in the small window to obscure the street-level view. It spun gently in the warmth from the radiator, its glass beads refracting the filtered sunlight. On a low table Beatrice kept a box of tissues, a sketch pad with several crayons, and a floppy stuffed kitten. Even teenaged boys loved the kitten, though they often pretended to laugh at it.

Patsy Ellmore started her therapy two days after Beatrice's brief LSD trip. Her mother brought her and objected when Beatrice explained that she would need to speak alone with Patsy for her first few sessions.

"She's only fifteen," Mrs. Ellmore said. She was a plump, polished-looking woman, slightly overdressed in the current midi-skirt fashion, high boots, thick false eyelashes. She eyed Beatrice's tweed jacket and jeans with an arched eyebrow.

Beatrice responded with the explanation she had given many times before. "I see many young people of Patsy's age and younger, Mrs. Ellmore. I find it best if we speak without anyone else present at first. It will help your daughter speak freely to me."

"Well," Mrs. Ellmore said uncertainly. "I don't know…"

Patsy faced the dream catcher in the window, her shoulders slumped and her fists buried in the pockets of her peacoat. She was a shorter, thinner version of her mother. She wore red cotton slacks and a checked turtleneck sweater under her coat. Her hair was long, tied into two thin braids with little red ribbons at the ends. She didn't look like a fifteen-year-old girl. She looked much younger, barely adolescent. Beatrice had the impression she had brought a doll with her, or a teddy bear, something small and dark she held in her arms, but when she turned around, there was nothing. She stared at the floor, her chin dropped, a classic aversion posture.

The image of a baby popped into Beatrice's mind, a baby lying still and cold, not moving. It made her forehead tingle, and she shivered.

Mrs. Ellmore clutched her handbag to her chest, and her brow furrowed with indecision.

"Patsy, you can sit in any chair you like." Beatrice moved purposefully to her own armchair as if everything was settled. She sat down and picked up her notebook, though she wouldn't write in it until the session was over. "Mrs. Ellmore, please come back in about fifty minutes. There's a nice café around the corner if you'd like to have coffee."

Mrs. Ellmore hesitated a moment longer, and then, with a glance over her shoulder at the back of her daughter's head, she sidled out through the door. Through its small window Beatrice saw her standing outside, though she had closed the door behind her. Clearly, Patsy knew she was there. The girl didn't move for at least three minutes, until her mother had walked away.

When she finally did move, Patsy took a few awkward steps, pulling on her childish braids with both hands. "I'm not fifteen," she said, in a near-whisper that made Beatrice lean forward to hear. "I'm thirteen."

Another shiver swept Beatrice's neck and shoulders, and the tingle behind her forehead became a throb. She laid her notebook on the small table beside her armchair and indicated one of the other chairs. "Tell me about that, Patsy. Why would your mother say you're fifteen?"

The girl shrugged her thin shoulders, her gaze skittering away, back to the dream catcher.

"Do you think she forgot your real age?" Beatrice took a sidelong look at her notebook, where she had written Patsy's date of birth when the appointment was made. It was true. The girl had just turned thirteen.

"My grandmother made the appointment, didn't she?" Patsy said, still in that breathy, childish voice.

"Yes. She was the one who called me, and I gather she's going to pay for your sessions. Is that all right with you?"

"I guess. Daddy won't like it, though."

"Does your father object to therapy?"

Another shrug, and a silence that stretched in the quiet room. Beatrice folded her hands in her lap and crossed her ankles. Patsy, after a few moments, moved to the chair and sat down, her thin legs stretched out before her.

Beatrice let the silence extend another minute before she asked, "Do you want to talk to me, Patsy?"

The shrug again. "I guess."

"What would you like to say?"

None of this exchange, or the lack of it, was unfamiliar to Beatrice. It wasn't unusual for young patients to need several sessions before they began to speak easily. She had techniques to ease them into the process, help them begin to trust her, to understand that they could say almost anything without having it reported to their parents. She waited for Patsy to decide to talk, letting her own unfocused gaze drift to the window. She wasn't thinking of anything other than being open, being patient, letting the peace and safety of the room wrap around the girl, when she heard very clearly in Patsy's childish whisper, although not aloud: *I'm not Melissa.*

Beatrice started, and checked her notebook again. Mrs. Ellmore was Mary. The grandmother who had made Patsy's appointment was Ethel. Then who—

She looked at Patsy and could have sworn the toy was there again, the doll or teddy bear, there and then gone in a heartbeat. The baby? Completely disconcerted, she blurted, "Who's Melissa?"

Patsy's face blanched all at once, so swiftly that Beatrice jumped up, fearful she was going to faint. The girl looked up at her with eyes gone wide, and her voice was suddenly shrill with panic. "Don't say that name! Daddy says never to say that name!"

Beatrice froze, shocked by the girl's abrupt vehemence. Patsy cried, "Who told you? Daddy will think it was me!" before bursting into tiny, doll-like sobs.

Automatically, Beatrice pushed the box of tissues forward, then sat back in her chair, drawing deep breaths to regain her composure. It was hardly the first time a patient had wept in her office, but this had come on so suddenly, and with what looked like real fear, that she wanted to tread carefully.

She waited, watching her young patient cry and shiver, truly distressed. When the squeaking sobs began to diminish into small, shuddery gasps, she leaned forward. "Patsy," she said quietly, "we don't need to say that name again if you prefer not to, but I wonder if you can tell me why it upsets you."

Patsy sniffled and pulled a tissue from the box to wipe her eyes and her nose. She averted her eyes again and wrapped her arms around herself. Beatrice waited a minute, then another, before she prompted, "Patsy, obviously something is frightening you. My patients often find that talking about what scares them is helpful. It can reduce the fear sometimes, take the energy away from whatever it is."

She stopped talking then, to let the girl think it through, decide for herself. As she waited, she wondered about the lighting in her office, if a shadow from outside had tricked her eyes into seeing something that wasn't there. Perhaps the dream catcher had blocked the sunshine and caused a shadow that made her think of a teddy bear. A toy. A doll. She squinted, trying to make it happen again, but it didn't. The throb in her forehead eased a little.

Patsy finally spoke, her eyes fixed on her shoes. "I'm not supposed to talk about it."

"Because your father told you not to?"

A nod, a final small shudder from the tears, and nothing more. Mrs. Ellmore returned a few minutes early, knocking and then coming into the office without waiting to be invited. Beatrice was certain she had been hovering nearby, waiting. Patsy had shut down, at least for the moment, so she gave up for the day. She made another appointment, wrote it down on one of her cards, and said goodbye to the two of them.

As she pulled the blind and locked the door, her discomfort lingered. Usually the process of settling her office at the end of the day was the signal to her mind to withdraw, or at least try to. She always intended to set aside her patients' troubles until their next session. Often she was successful in the effort, but Patsy Ellmore was a mystery. Beatrice couldn't help trying to guess at what the odd clues meant. Meanwhile, a thirteen-year-old girl was possibly in danger of abuse.

She thought of Charlie Crossman saying that his trip opened the closed door that had been tormenting him. It would certainly help her to help Patsy Ellmore—perhaps to protect her—if she knew what the girl was hiding.

* * * ★ ★ ★ ★ ★ * * *

Beatrice had no trouble acquiring more acid. Many were still making it at home, and she knew almost everyone in the Haight-Ashbury district. It was easy to buy some from the son of the Italian grocer around the corner from the clinic, who grinned and winked at her but made no comment on the strangeness of Dr. Bird buying LSD.

She waited until another of Mitch's night shifts. It was the perfect night, she thought. Mist shrouded the city in swirls, obscuring the tops of the houses, muting the baritone warnings of the ferry and the basso responses of the container ships in the bay.

She stayed indoors, stretching out on the sofa under an afghan one of her patients had crocheted in yarns of purple and green and orange. Mitch had declared the thing a shock to the eye, but it was soft and warm. Beatrice tucked it around herself, then opened up the little packet with its square of LSD-soaked paper and let it dissolve in her mouth.

This time the drug hit her hard and fast. She had the instant dizzy sensation of spinning up through the roof of the house and diving into the ripples of fog.

Her every sense was exaggerated. She perceived every gradation of color in the mist: silver, pewter, charcoal. Here and there tiny blooms of water drops gleamed like faraway stars. She smelled the scents the fog had absorbed, the spice of gasoline, the umber of woodsmoke, the tang of frying fish. She heard the folds of fog chime as they slid across each other, like bells ringing in a breeze.

And there, slipping between the misty layers, was a vague image of Patsy Ellmore's mother following her daughter through the mist, the two of them swimming like dream creatures through the fog. Beatrice's entire body prickled with gooseflesh, arms and legs and scalp, even her chest and across her cheeks. Patsy stayed just ahead of her mother, fleeing weakly, halfheartedly. Mary Ellmore reached for those long braids, almost, but not quite, catching them in her hand.

At first Beatrice was thrilled by what she saw, a clear dramatization of the troubled relationship. The daughter, struggling to be free. The mother, trying to hold her back, to hold on to her, to grasp the flying braids...

But there was something else with them, something tiny and dim, a darker gray than the fog, even more vague than the figures of Patsy and her mother. It was the same elusive shade Beatrice had seen in her office, when she thought Patsy was holding a doll. Even in her altered state, she sensed something wrong, something disturbing, something that took the pleasure out of her trip and added a churning stomach to her goose bumps.

Someone, she thought, was crying.

She touched her own cheeks to be certain it wasn't herself. Was it Patsy? But this voice, this weeping, was deeper, older. It was Mary Ellmore, surely, sobbing in misery as she tried to capture her fleeing daughter.

And then Beatrice heard Patsy again, that tiny voice whispering, *I'm not Melissa.*

Beatrice sat straight up on the sofa. This was too much, too weird. She was cold, despite the warmth of the afghan. She shook herself to escape the effects of the acid, to end the experience, but it was like trying to wake herself from a bad dream in the midst of a heavy sleep.

She didn't like it. She wanted out. She struggled to say it aloud, to demand it. She learned it wasn't as easy as that.

There was no escape from the twists and turns of her imagination. The layers of fog rang in her head, and the chimeras of Patsy and Mary Ellmore danced their strange ballet through the sky as Beatrice shivered beneath her psychedelic blanket, forced to wait for the acid to wear off.

She was still lying there when Mitch came home.

"I don't want you to do that again," Mitch said in a tight voice. "I could hardly get you off the sofa and into bed, and you weren't making any sense at all."

Beatrice held her hot coffee between her cupped palms, trying to blink herself into a normal morning state. She didn't want to admit it to Mitch, but she was still feeling the effects of the trip. Her brain felt swollen, crowding the inside of her head, as if she had grown extra neurons in the night. The lack of control of the experience unnerved her, but only a little. Mostly what she felt was excitement.

She said, "I think that Stanford psychiatrist was right. The drug could be helpful. Give me a fuller understanding of my patients."

"Do you not think you're already getting in too deep?" When Mitch was upset, he spoke as if he were a professor teaching a class, formal language, heightened enunciation.

"You mean my little gift. My second sight."

"Yes." He tipped up his chin to regard her somberly through his round glasses. "Yes, I mean precisely that. I'm hardly the first to warn you."

"Don't quote Dad at me. I remember everything he said."

"He was correct, Bea. You go too far, too fast, without thinking."

"I might have had a breakthrough last night. An intuitive leap, you could say."

"Come on, Bea! It's all of a piece with you, isn't it? You want to read minds. You want to know everything about your patients, even when they don't know it themselves. It will wear you out to work that way."

"I can handle it."

Mitch took off his glasses and polished them, peering at her with his dark eyes narrowed. "I very much insist you not do this again, Bea."

She couldn't stop herself. "Don't tell me what not to do, Mitch. Or what *to* do, for that matter."

His temper was as quick as her own, and the formality of his speech dissolved. "Jesus, Bea, this women's lib stuff again? Come on. You and I don't need that. We never did."

She glared at him. "It's women's lib because I want to make my own decisions?"

He put his glasses back on his nose and reached for his coffee cup, avoiding her angry gaze. "I just want you to be safe."

"I know." She took a slow, coffee-scented breath and set her cup down. "Sorry. I'm—mmm, still processing it."

"Fine. Let me put it this way," he said, pushing himself to his feet. "As someone who cares about you, I would feel a lot better if you didn't do this again." He started toward the bathroom, saying over his shoulder, "I'm going to shower. Early patient."

As he shut the door and started the shower running, an image of Mitch popped into her mind. He was standing in the shower, covering his face with his hands.

She had no need of acid to understand this moment. She had experienced that sort of revelatory image a hundred times. He had no early patient. He was escaping.

As Mitch had said, with surprising intuition of his own, it was all of a piece with her, and he wasn't wrong. She didn't know any other way to be.

But she heard Mitch groan, a sound of pure frustration, and that was new. Something about it sent her thoughts whirling back to the bizarre tableau she had seen during her trip. Patsy Ellmore. Mary Ellmore. Patsy, Mary, Patsy, Mary, a mystifying pas de deux in the fog.

I'm not Melissa. What did that mean?

14

Anne, The Island, 1977

THEY HAD MANAGED, as Beatrice told the first part of her story, to empty the bottle of chardonnay, and they both looked at it in dismay. Anne knew she had drunk enough wine for the evening, but she didn't feel in the least drunk, or even sleepy.

Beatrice said, with a wry twist of her lips, "Tea, I think."

Anne answered, "Agreed. Let me manage it, Beatrice."

"Good idea."

In the kitchen, Anne found the package of cookies no one had touched earlier and arranged several on a plate while the kettle heated. With the tea made, she arranged cups and cookies on a tray and carried it through the archway into the living room.

Beatrice accepted a cup and took a cookie onto her saucer. A small clock on the rolltop desk chimed the hour. "Good lord, it's midnight. I'm never up this late, not since college. This is a strange evening."

"I know."

"I've done all the talking."

Anne smiled at that. The action felt unfamiliar, as if the small muscles of her face had grown unused to the movement. She couldn't remember the last time she had done it. "Your story is fascinating. I hope there's a happy ending."

Beatrice shrugged. "An ending to Patsy Ellmore's chapter, in any case."

Anne took a cookie from the plate also, and when she bit into it, she found its richness surprisingly welcome. It made her mouth water, and she reached for another before she had finished the first. "Can you tell me the rest?"

"I'll tell you what there is of it. Let me build up the fire first."

Anne pulled the colorful afghan Beatrice had given her up to her chin and watched as Beatrice opened the damper and prodded the coals into flames. It was, indeed, an odd evening, an accident of timing she could never have predicted, an unexpected respite from her days of loneliness.

She had never met someone like Beatrice. It wasn't just that she was older. Anne had lost any sense of her own youth, so the age difference seemed insignificant. It was Beatrice's personality. She wasn't unfeminine, exactly, although Anne had no doubt her father would have thought so. There was a decisive streak in the way she spoke, the way she moved, certainly the way she lived, that excited Anne's admiration, even ignited a spark of envy.

She had hidden too long behind customs and attitudes that were better suited to her mother's era than her own. She had built an identity out of careful manners, meticulous grooming, a quiet voice, and perfect poise. It was a role she played, or a costume she wore. It occurred to her, watching Beatrice stoke up the fire, that Beatrice, despite her problems, knew exactly who she was. A doctor. A milker of cows. A woman with her own home, her own career, her own money.

She, Anne Iredale, had buried her true self under layers of propriety and convention, and she had no idea how to exhume it.

Beatrice returned to her chair. The shimmer of the flames reflected on her cheekbones, and she pulled her cardigan tighter around her small body. "I should have listened to Mitch," she said quietly. She cradled her teacup between her palms and blew across the surface of the hot tea. "I've always taken chances, and he knows—knew—that. His objections just—I don't know, got my back up. I was raised to be independent, to put it mildly, and I'm a bit fierce about it.

"I went on seeing Patsy Ellmore. We made no progress, though we worked together for months. It was the same, her mother reluctant to leave her with me, Patsy saying very little, getting thinner and thinner every week, crying during her sessions. I kept seeing the—whatever it was, doll, teddy bear—but I couldn't get her to tell me about it, or to tell me who Melissa was. She just kept saying she wasn't supposed to talk about it. Of course I was afraid she was being abused, but I had nothing to go on.

"The previous trip had scared me a little, but I decided the risk was worth it. I thought another dose might help me to help Patsy." Beatrice drew a long breath that whistled between her lips. "It did. But it's not hyperbole to say that it ruined my life."

* * * * * ★ ★ ★ * * * ·

Beatrice, San Francisco, 1970

Patsy Ellmore was getting worse, and Beatrice was worried. Patsy's grandmother sent the checks and made the appointments. Beatrice guessed she put pressure on her reluctant daughter-in-law to keep them. There was some dynamic there that was difficult to uncover, but at least it kept Patsy coming to see her.

Once, when the elder Mrs. Ellmore called to make an appointment, Beatrice asked if she would like to come along, but the grandmother demurred. "It's their problem," she said. "Nothing I can do."

"It's generous of you, though, Mrs. Ellmore, to pay for Patsy's treatment."

"I have to do something. Her father doesn't want her to have therapy, but you can see how unhappy she is. And so thin! I don't know if she eats anything at all."

"Do you know why?"

"No." The older woman's voice was sharp, dismissive. "If I knew, I wouldn't have to pay you. It's your job to figure it out."

Beatrice let that go, for Patsy's sake. Mrs. Ellmore was not the first family member to sidestep an issue. To expect a professional to manage it. To pay someone to make a problem go away. She tried, in her next session with Patsy, to bring up the subject of Melissa.

"I'm not supposed to talk about it," Patsy whispered, her head down.

"But you come here to talk to me, Patsy."

"Not about that."

"What will happen if you do talk about it?"

"Daddy will be mad. He gets—well, he gets really mad."

"Are you afraid of him being mad at you?"

"Not me," Patsy said. "Mom."

"Oh. So you don't want him to be mad at your mother?"

A shake of the head.

"Then what would you like to talk about, Patsy? How can I help?"

The little shrug, the averted gaze, the impression once again of a doll or a teddy bear in Patsy's arms.

What could it be? Beatrice wondered. She didn't want to tell Patsy what she saw. If it didn't make sense, didn't resonate with the girl, Patsy could slip away from her, and then who would help her? Not her mother. Not her grandmother. Evidently not her father.

There was a long pause, during which Beatrice could almost, but not quite, make out the shape of the shadow huddling in Patsy's lap. When she looked closely, she thought it was a faint blue-gray, shimmering with flashes of violet, but the shape was indeterminate.

The image made the base of her throat ache, that old, half-forgotten pinching pain.

She prompted, "Patsy? Why do you think your father gets angry with your mother?"

The girl's voice was a gossamer thread, nearly inaudible. "Because she gets confused."

"Do you know why she's confused?"

Patsy shook her head, but Beatrice had the sense they had made progress, a tiny bit, a tantalizing hint at what was going on in the Ellmore family. As Beatrice saw Patsy out with her mother, Patsy looked back over her shoulder, peeking up from beneath her childish bangs. *I'm not Melissa.* She didn't speak the words aloud, but Beatrice heard the words in her head as clearly as if she had.

It was that night Beatrice decided to try one more time, against Mitch's expressed wish. She stopped at the Italian grocer's and bought another dose. Mitch was at the hospital, and she hurried, intending her trip to be over before he returned. She skipped dinner, forgoing even her usual glass of wine after her last appointment. She went straight to the sofa, pulled the afghan over her, and put the little square of soaked paper in her mouth.

The dose was different from the last one she had bought. It took longer to affect her, and when it did, she felt as if she slid into a different plane of awareness, not spinning upward but plunging inward, diving into a welter of her own memories. She saw her mother on her deathbed and herself beside her, a tiny girl clutching her mother's hand as it grew cold. She saw her father with tears on his cheeks at her high school graduation. She saw her thesis advisor scowl as he pushed her completed dissertation across his desk.

And she *heard* them. She heard her mother thinking how terrible it was to die and leave her little daughter motherless. She heard her father wondering how he could bear to see his girl go off to college, grow away from him. Her thesis advisor was thinking how point-less a doctorate was for a girl who would never use it, would marry, have children, become a housewife.

There were other scenes. Her first meeting with Mitch, she heard his thought, *This girl is mine.* She saw a few of her patients, some successes, some failures. She saw her father's funeral, feeling again the breaking of her heart, the wave of guilt at not having been there when he died.

She heard his voice, disembodied but as warm as ever. *Don't cry, my busy Bea. Everything is fine.*

It was all surreal and yet utterly real, at one and the same time. She became aware that tears were drying on her face, that the room was growing cold, that the afghan had slipped to the floor and long strands of her hair had tangled around her neck. She was coming up from the depths, rising toward consciousness, when she saw a woman. She was dressed all in black, with a black pillbox hat. It had a short, heavy veil that hid her face, but Beatrice knew who it was. Patsy's mother.

And a baby. Not a ghost doll, or a teddy bear. A real baby. A still, pale baby, swathed in white satin blankets. It lay, unmoving, in a tiny white coffin.

This was not a memory of Beatrice's own. Whose was it? How had it crept into her trip?

Insight flashed through her, just as the Stanford psychiatrist said it did for him. The memory of her father's coffin had triggered this other one, this borrowed one. This was a memory transferred from her patient's mother to her patient, but Patsy had no way to process it. Her youthful mind turned her feelings inward, making her mis-erable. Her spirit turned it outward, projecting her confusion and resentment over the burden her unhappy mother had placed on her.

Mary Ellmore had lost a baby and had tried to replace her with a new one.

Melissa. The baby, the dead baby, was Melissa.

I'm not Melissa. No. But Mary Ellmore wanted her to be.

Poor Patsy, Beatrice thought, as she swam up from the ocean of memories. You're not Melissa, but your mother pretends you are. Imagines you are her lost child, fantasizes in order to ease her pain, makes you carry the sadness of her death with you. Your father is doing the only thing he can think of to stop it, to make your mother stop thinking about it. He wants to pretend everything is normal. He tells you not to talk about Melissa, and he orders your mother never to speak her name, as if that will negate her existence. As if it will erase the memory of a lost infant, make her cease trying to turn her second daughter into her first.

Patsy was not the one who needed therapy. It was her mother. It was Mary's psychosis that was tearing her daughter—her living daughter—to pieces.

15

Anne, The Island, 1977

ANNE STARED AT Beatrice, her mouth open in wonder. "She thought Patsy was—what, a reincarnation of her lost child?"

"Less logical than that. She was using Patsy to block the memory of losing her baby. She saw Patsy as Melissa, often called her Melissa, confused her birthdate, mixed up pictures of Patsy with baby Melissa's. Her husband couldn't cope. He had terrible fits of anger, and Patsy was terrified he was going to hurt her mother, and it would be her fault. Patsy's grandmother tried lecturing her daughter-in-law, and when that brought on fits of hysterics, she stopped seeing her altogether."

"But Patsy—"

"Patsy became the chess piece between them all."

"Such a weird story."

Beatrice nodded. "It is."

Anne bit her lip and hugged the afghan around her. Her own story was perhaps not so strange, but just as cruel in its way. She would have said it could never happen to her. Now she understood that nearly anything could, and the idea chilled her. She tried to distract herself with Beatrice's account. "You helped her in the end, didn't you? Patsy?"

"I did." Beatrice's lips curved into the first real smile Anne had seen on her face. It made her look younger, more girlish, with her cropped hair and ice-gray eyes. "It wasn't a cure, of course. That rarely happens. But Patsy discovered a reservoir of strength in herself and developed strategies for coping with her mother's delusions. Her father did, too. When Mary's inevitable breakdown came, he and Patsy found they were more alike than they realized. It was—" She broke off and gazed into the erratic dance of the flames. "It was life-changing for them," she finished. "And it might not have happened if I didn't figure out what was happening to that family."

"That's a success story, though, surely, Beatrice?"

Beatrice's lips curved again, but this smile wasn't warm and reminiscent. It was wry. Disappointed. Guilty. Anne knew a thing or two about those emotions.

"I count that as a success, yes. The problem was that my—well—" She spread her hands. "I don't have a good word. Our housekeeper, when I was a kid, called it second sight. I just called them feelings, and I had a lot of them. In any case, they intensified after my acid trips. Good for Patsy. Not so good for me."

"But surely, knowing what other people are experiencing when they can't speak of it—that has to be a wonderful attribute for a therapist."

Beatrice shrugged. "Maybe. But as they say, you can have too much of a good thing."

"So your—your second sight, whatever it is—it kept getting stronger?"

"It might have been okay," Beatrice mused, setting aside her teacup. "If it had stopped then. But it didn't."

The fire had begun to die down, and Beatrice got up to put in another chunk of wood. When she returned to her seat, she pulled up her feet to sit cross-legged in the chair. "I'm taking a long time to get to the point."

"You're a great storyteller," Anne said, with perfect sincerity.

Beatrice chuckled. "Well, thanks, but I'm sure you're past ready for the conclusion."

Anne put her own teacup aside and pulled the afghan tighter around her shoulders. She was reluctant to reach the end of Beatrice's story, because then she would no doubt be expected to share her own. She said, in what she hoped was an encouraging tone, "I'm assuming there were more patients you were able to help."

"There were," Beatrice mused. "Most patients know, at least superficially, what's troubling them, but there are always those who can't access a memory or a deep-seated anxiety. Who can spend years searching for answers. My little gift, whatever we want to call it, was particularly useful to those people, as it was to Patsy. It could be scary for them, too. I learned to go slowly. Not say too much at first. It was an exhilarating time for me in my practice, and I'm afraid I got a bit full of myself. 'Overconfident' is a nice way to say it. 'Arrogant' is a less precious description."

"But such important work," Anne murmured.

"Yes," Beatrice answered, just as softly. Her gaze was dreamy, fixed on the freshly fed flames, her small features glowing with their reflection. "Important to them. A girl who stopped eating because her dad, who she worshipped, pinched a little bit of baby fat. Another girl, brilliant kid headed for medical school, whose grades dropped overnight. She almost got kicked out of high school because she was being bullied but was too ashamed to tell anyone. A boy who couldn't understand why he kept thinking of suicide, something he had no wish to do, and no intention of doing. He figured out—with my help—that his parents had withheld the truth from him about an older brother who had taken his own life. They did it to protect him, but keeping the secret was destructive." She gave a nostalgic little nod. "That young man went off to study to be a teacher, and I'm sure he's going to be a wonderful one."

Anne shook her head, wordless at the suffering some people endured. And her own—did Beatrice's ability extend to her? Did Beatrice already know what her problem was, the trouble she was in?

"Beatrice," she ventured, after a moment. "Can you tell me—this gift of yours—what form does it take?"

Beatrice said softly, "Do you really want to know?"

"I—I think so."

Beatrice shifted in her chair and leaned a little forward, meeting Anne's eyes directly. The look of her was so intense, almost otherworldly, that goose bumps prickled on Anne's arms. Beatrice said, "You're wondering if I know what's bothering you."

Anne nodded, and a fresh wave of anxiety rose in her chest. The soporific effect of the wine she had drunk had worn off, and she was back where she started. Anxious. Bereft. Desperate.

"The thing is," Beatrice said, "it's not as if I always have answers. Sometimes I know things, which is okay. That can be put down to intuition. Other times, and this is what's gotten me into trouble, I see things. Sometimes they're useful, but mostly they're just upsetting."

Anne was almost afraid to ask. "Do you see something in me?"

"Not *in* you" was the answer, that fey light gleaming from Beatrice's gray eyes, like the gleam of reflected light in a crystal glass. She repeated, with a tiny sigh, "Not in you. Following you. Clinging to you. Hovering behind you. Worse, I not only see these things, I feel them. The emotions they represent—fear, sorrow, misery, worry—sink into me as if they were my own. I can't stop, sadly. I could at first, and at first it was only my patients, but then—" She sat back, pressing a palm to her forehead beneath the ragged fringe of her hair. "Now I see them everywhere. Following everyone."

"Everyone?"

"Everyone. Every person I see."

"Every single person? My God, Beatrice."

Beatrice dropped her hand to her lap. "Afraid so."

"But what you're seeing—I mean, trailing after people—"

Beatrice grimaced in acknowledgment. "I think of them as ghosts, which isn't accurate, really. They're not necessarily dead."

Anne drew a sudden breath of understanding. "That's why you wouldn't look at me."

"That's why."

"You're looking at me now, though."

"It's dark in here."

"Does that help?"

"Yes, a bit."

"But—when you saw me at the store—"

"Yes. Saw them. Felt them. That doesn't mean I know who they are, or why they're following you. More accurately, why you're carrying them with you." She tucked her chin, a defensive gesture. "None of this is logical. Nor scientific. There are psychologists doing ESP tests in laboratory settings, but I could never prove anything in a lab. It's real, just the same, undeniably real to me. Real enough to drive me from the city, from my home. I couldn't walk down the street without seeing a thousand ghosts, being battered by the emotions they represent. It became intolerable."

Anne hesitated, not wanting to cause further pain to her hostess.

Beatrice said, "I'll tell you if you want."

Anne started, and Beatrice's lips quirked. "You see? It's uncomfortable. I'm not reading your mind, but I *feel* what you're feeling." This time she touched her throat, just at the base, and gave a self-deprecating shrug.

"I'm sorry for that," Anne said. "I wouldn't wish these feelings on anyone." Except perhaps James, but she didn't say that aloud.

"Well, it wasn't your fault." Beatrice rubbed her eyes. "I'm going to have to sleep," she said. "Dorothy and Alice expect me up early."

"Of course." Anne came to her feet. "I've kept you up far too late."

"We've kept each other up," Beatrice said.

"You've been more than kind, Beatrice. I don't know what I would have done tonight. I literally had no place to go."

"It's okay." Beatrice pushed herself out of her chair and crouched to adjust the damper on the stove. As the fire died down to glowing coals, she said, without looking up, "Who is the child, Anne?"

Anne's breath caught. "The—the child?"

"A lot of pain associated with that child."

Anne's knees weakened, and she sank back onto the sofa. "You saw a child."

Beatrice looked back from her crouched position. "I still do."

Through a dry throat, Anne croaked, "My son. My Benjamin."

Gently, "Is Benjamin living, Anne?"

"Yes. You can see him?"

Beatrice straightened and faced Anne with her arms folded. "No. What I see is his—let's call it his imprint. It's like a shadow, feelings made manifest. As I said, I call them ghosts, but of course they're not that. I don't have a term for the phenomenon. I suspect there isn't one."

"I miss him so terribly."

"I know. I feel the pain it causes you."

"It's awful," Anne whispered. "Worse than dying. And there's nothing I can do about it."

Beatrice, The Island, 1977

As she milked Dorothy, Beatrice tried to think what had possessed her to reveal herself to poor Anne. It had not been her most professional moment. She had been tired, certainly, and had had a shock—was still reeling from that, in fact—but that was no excuse. She might be hallucinating, losing control of her mind, but spilling her troubles to someone she barely knew wasn't going to help. If she was on the verge of losing her mind, poor Anne Iredale wasn't going to be able to save her.

Despite all of those things, those truths, it had been a relief to tell her story. It gave her perspective, and Anne, despite her own troubles, was an excellent listener, giving of her own emotional reserves to a woman she had known only a few hours. It was impressive, and Beatrice was moved by it.

She had made up the guest bedroom and seen to it that Anne had everything she needed. She hadn't pressed her for her own story, but now, in the light of her own confession, she supposed she would have to hear it. The idea wearied her, and that shamed her, in the face of Anne's generosity.

Beatrice finished the milking and turned the cows out to graze. As she swept out the barn, the memory of that awful thing she had seen—or imagined she had seen—rose in her mind with the cloud of dust at the end of her broom. She had tried, as she lay waiting for sleep, to tell herself it was the same experience she had been having for months, a projection of Anne's, but she knew that couldn't be right. It simply wasn't the same. No amount of rationalization could change that.

Aside from not being attached to Anne, as her ghosts always were, it had looked profoundly different. That had not been an inchoate shadow, colors of mist, a cloud of feelings made visible. That thing had been distinct, and human.

And there was the smell. Did failing minds produce olfactory phenomena?

She shook herself and tried to put it out of her mind, focusing on her clean barn floor, the scents of sea and evergreens flooding through the open barn door, on the foaming warmth of the milk in its bucket and the wintry sunshine spilling in through the window.

She hadn't intended to get caught up in Anne's misery, and perhaps if she had not seen—the thing, whatever—she would not have done so. That experience had rendered her vulnerable, shaken her out of her isolated state. She was involved now, and turning her back on a young woman of obvious character and appealing grace was not in her nature. She had dedicated her life to helping people. It had been her motivation since she was nine, and she was learning that her need to live that life had not diminished under the battering of her own suffering.

She would strain the milk, and then she would ask Anne Iredale if she would like to stay. If so, she would call Mother Maggie to tell her. She would order more groceries, ask Mr. Thurman for wood, concentrate on this nice young woman, do all she could to distract herself from the shattering fear that her mind was disintegrating.

Asking for trouble, busy Bea. Again.

I know, Dad. But you'd do the same.

In her mind, she heard the echo of her father's old familiar chuckle and felt a stab of longing.

16

Beatrice, San Francisco, 1974

PATSY ELLMORE'S MYSTERIOUS little shadow had been the first inti-mation for Beatrice of what was to come. Subsequent shades were similar, amorphous fogs, more cloud than ghost, different colors depending on the feelings that generated them. They were faint at first, so subtle she could almost convince herself they weren't there, but they intensified as time went on. She found herself pressing her fingers to the base of her throat more and more often, unconsciously at first, then uncomfortably aware that there was a reason for it, that she was having an emotional response, distracting, unpleasant, unwanted.

How had her experimentation exaggerated a characteristic that was natural to her? She wondered if anyone else had similar experi-ences. She delved into the scientific literature, searching.

She found nothing. Like the Stanford psychiatrist, there were accounts of insights, of an expansion of thought, of fanciful trips that were by turns wonderful and terrifying. No one else saw ghosts.

Or if they did, they were wise enough not to publicize the fact.

Beatrice wasn't afraid at first. She was curious. She kept notes, with an eye to writing a scholarly paper. She imagined giving lec-tures, exploring the possibilities. The idea of being a pioneer in a unique environment intrigued her.

Then the day came when she realized it was not merely her patients whose ghosts she saw, more and more clearly every day. She began to see them attached to people to whom she had only a casual connection, and then to people with whom she had no connection at all. The grocer at the corner. The postman who delivered her mail. Bus drivers. Traffic cops. The fishmonger at the wharf. Passersby.

And she *felt* them, the first hint that she might be in real trouble. The grocer was attended by the ghost of his son, the same one who had sold Beatrice the little squares of colored paper. That ghost was in layers of brown and gray, shivering with a father's anxiety. The postman was trailed by several ghosts: an older woman who radiated sorrow, a younger woman full of anger and resentment, a youth exuding worry and fear.

Beatrice understood that what she saw were not actually ghosts. To begin with, she didn't believe in ghosts. These were weird manifestations lacking features, limbs, or bodies, things she thought were customarily ascribed to phantoms. They were made up of an unmeasurable and indescribable mix of colors, emotions, impressions, burdens. They were not her burdens, but they weighed on her as if they were.

It was too much to bear. She didn't want to do it anymore.

Busy Bea…

I know, Dad. I've stopped. I won't go any further.

But it was too late.

Beatrice, The Island, 1977

Beatrice found Anne already in the kitchen, wrapped in a borrowed bathrobe that was a bit too large and a lot too short. She had found a whisk, one Beatrice hadn't known she possessed, and was whipping eggs in a bowl with a practiced hand.

She looked up when Beatrice came in and said with an apologetic smile, "I thought I could at least make you breakfast before I leave. The ferry's not until ten, so I can—"

Beatrice put up her free hand. "Anne, wait. That is, breakfast sounds good, but first—I have a suggestion for you. If you're interested, that is."

Anne's hand stopped moving, letting the whisk rest in the foamy eggs. "A suggestion?"

"A thought. Something for you to consider."

Anne set the bowl down and wiped her hands on her bathrobe. "Of course," she said, but Beatrice saw the wariness in her eyes and took note of the tremor in her hands. Sympathy stirred in her heart, completely unrelated to the ghosts that trailed after Anne, staining the clarity of the morning sunshine.

Beatrice said, "My thought is—I know we don't really know each other well, but I think you should stay here with me. For the time being, at least."

Anne's eyes instantly began to sparkle with tears that shone sapphire blue against her pale eyelids. "But, Beatrice—you—the things you see upset you so—"

"It's true. I never have respite from them, and yours are no different. But nor do you have respite from them, Anne, and I think—I hope—perhaps I can be of some help to you."

Beatrice set the milk bucket on the counter. Anne's shades hovered on her peripheral vision, the large one dark and grim, a thundercloud, the little one a weak little shadow, hovering helplessly behind Anne's slender legs. Anne's child. Benjamin.

Beatrice set her teeth against the flood of emotion swirling around this poor woman. It was as if Anne were standing in a river of pain, the current buffeting her this way and that, threatening to drown her. The ripples of it made Beatrice's throat ache.

She used her task to steady herself, carefully tipping up the bucket, pouring the milk through the strainer. When it was done, she braced her hands on the edge of the sink and gazed through the kitchen window into the woods. The evergreens shivered in the wind, and the rhododendrons' leaves glittered with dew. Sunshine gilded the bare branches of the deciduous trees. In the little clearing around the barn, Dorothy and Alice grazed, peaceful and content. Ghostless.

Anne had not yet spoken a word, nor had she picked up the egg bowl again. Beatrice sighed and turned to rest her back against the counter. "I'm aware this is hardly the most gracious invitation, but I do want to be of some use. Counsel you, if you like, or just listen."

Two tears escaped Anne's brimming eyes, and she dashed them away with the back of her hand. When she spoke her voice was high and tight. "So kind, Beatrice. So—I really—the truth is, I have no place to go. I hate taking advantage when you barely know me, but…" Her voice broke on a sob, and she pressed her hand over her mouth.

Beatrice spoke in her most matter-of-fact voice. Her therapist voice. "I understand your reservations. I hope you'll accept my invitation anyway. I would say, my new friend, we have work to do."

Anne nodded, her hand still covering her mouth. As Beatrice handed her a tissue, she noticed that Anne's shades—both of them—had receded ever so slightly, the thundercloud shifting, lightening just a bit, the tiny ghost's cries subsiding.

Wondering at this change, she went to the telephone to call Mother Maggie. She heard the smile in the nun's voice, but no surprise, as she explained she had invited Anne to stay. She pictured the nun with her hand on her cross, confident in her belief that her prayers had made this happen.

As she hung up the phone, she saw that Anne had poured the eggs into a skillet, where they were bubbling nicely. The smell of toast filled the kitchen. She watched Anne set the table, butter the toast, neatly scoop the eggs onto two plates. She was as graceful as a dancer as she moved about these simple tasks, tall, elegant, a pleasure to watch. Beatrice wished there were no ghosts to detract from the sight.

She found her hand at her throat again, and she made herself drop it. She was committed now. She would make the best of it.

Busy Bea, are you sure about this?

No, Dad. Not sure at all. But I couldn't live with myself if I didn't try.

17

Anne, Oak Hill, 1974

ANNE MADE A tour of the dining room and the kitchen before going up to bed. Alicia, their housekeeper and sometime cook, had already left. Everything was in order, but Anne took up a flannel just the same, careful to polish the table and the countertops so they shone the way James liked them.

The dinner party had been a success. The babysitter had kept Benjamin quiet upstairs as the guests arrived, and he was asleep by the time the cocktails had been drunk. The lobster bisque, one of her specialties, had been perfect. Her pumpkin pie had garnered lots of compliments. The table, with its arrangement of fall foliage and mums, had been lovely, the crystal sparkling and the china and flatware perfectly arranged.

Anne alone, it seemed, had not enjoyed the evening. Between the main course and dessert, Benjamin had cried out for her. She rose from the table, but James had waved her back to her chair. With a smile full of charm and tolerance, he said, "Please, everyone, go ahead with your pie. It looks wonderful, Anne. I'll see to Ben."

Anne sank back into her seat, but as Alicia poured coffee and served the slices of pie, artfully topped with swirls of whipped cream, Anne's stomach clenched. The crying from upstairs had stopped abruptly. Too abruptly.

One of the lawyers' wives winked at Anne. "Lucky girl," she said. "A husband who's good with children."

Anne forced herself to smile, but though she pushed whipped cream and pumpkin custard around on her cut-glass dessert plate, she couldn't force a bite into her mouth.

She had to endure the after-dinner brandies, the cigars and cigarettes being smoked while her guests chatted, then the attenuated goodbyes that seemed so hard for people to execute. Now, assured the kitchen would meet James's approval in the morning, she hurried up the stairs to check on Benjamin.

He wasn't in his bed.

She peeled back the coverlet, hoping he had wriggled himself down to the foot, but there was no toddler curled up there. She bent to look underneath, in case he had fallen asleep on the floor, but no luck. She heard the shower running in the bathroom as James got ready for bed. She called softly, "Benjamin! Benjamin, where are you?" but there was no reply.

Her skin crawling with anxiety, she turned in a circle, sweeping the room, searching for a place he could be hiding, some odd place he might have curled up and gone to sleep. When her gaze reached the closet, she froze.

She always kept the closet door open, so the light inside could serve as Benjamin's night light. James had forbidden a night light. He said every boy had to learn to cope with darkness, and he might as well start early. Leaving the closet open with the soft overhead bulb turned on was Anne's little trick to keep everyone happy. The babysitter understood. She would have done the same.

But James had ~or ε up when Benjamin cried. James had done

something that stopped the boy's crying. James had closed the closet door and—

He had locked it. Anne could see the depressed button beside the doorknob. She should have disabled that odd lock long ago. She was across the room in a heartbeat, turning the knob to unlock it, reaching to switch on the light that James had to have switched off himself.

"Benjamin! Oh, honey!" she whispered.

Her little son was on the closet floor, curled into a tiny ball. He had no pillow, no blanket, no cuddly toy. His face was red and swollen from crying himself to sleep, and fronds of his hair curled stickily, soaked by his tears.

Gently, she pulled him up into her arms and carried him to the rocker in the corner. He stirred and clutched at her but didn't wake. How long had he cried before he fell asleep? How frightened must he have been, locked in a dark closet while his parents ate and drank and laughed downstairs?

What kind of father would do such a thing?

She answered her own thought. It was the same kind of father who had once abused a dog until it turned on him.

That night was the worst fight Anne had ever had with James until that point in their marriage. It didn't help that he was more than a little drunk and half-asleep by the time she came into the bedroom. Part of her knew it was no good to argue with him in that state. She had never done it before. Like her mother, she had always shrunk from confrontation.

But this was about Benjamin. She trembled with anxiety, but she also burned with fury. She couldn't wait for a better moment. She had to speak now.

She stood beside the bed with her arms tightly folded. "What possessed you to lock a little child in a dark closet?"

"He wouldn't stop crying," James mumbled, rolling over in bed so his back was to her. "We had guests. Important people."

"Important people! More important than your son?"

"Don't be melodramatic, Anne. It didn't hurt him."

"It was so cruel, James, unbelievably cruel! You know he's afraid of the dark!"

"He'll get over it. Needs to toughen up."

"Toughen up? He's not even three!" Her voice rose, and she pressed a hand to her lips. James hated raised voices. She had learned that before Benjamin came along. She had discovered too late that her handsome, urbane husband was all too much like her father, who wanted women's voices to be soft. Accommodating. Apologetic, even when there was nothing to apologize for.

James adjusted the pillow beneath his head without facing her. "I have court in the morning, Anne. Let me sleep."

She drew a trembling breath. Her control was not what it should have been. She had drunk two glasses of wine that evening, more than she usually did. She was tired, and shocked, and frustrated. She couldn't help herself.

She said, in a sharper tone than she had ever used in her life, "I could lock you in a closet, James! Would that help you sleep?"

James froze in the act of pulling the sheet up over his shoulders. Slowly, deliberately, he released the sheet and pushed himself up to a sitting position, then up and out of bed. His face was set and hard, the same face he used when he was sentencing some miscreant. Anne was shaking so hard she could barely stand as he picked up his pillow in both hands, and without changing his expression, he threw it across the bed as hard as he could.

Anne was too shocked even to duck. The pillow hit her squarely

in the face. It didn't hurt, not physically. It was the insult it represented, the careless fury, that took her breath away. It fell to her feet,
leaving her staring open-mouthed at the man she had married.

He gritted out, "Pick it up."

Stunned, confused, habituated to doing what he told her, she
picked up the pillow. With trembling hands, she lifted it and let it
fall on the bed just out of his reach. It was a tiny act of rebellion, and
she was stunned at her own daring.

He let that go. He stretched to pick up the pillow and settled it
back into its place. Coldly, he said, "Good night. Turn off the light,
will you?" He lay down again and pulled up the covers.

Anne stood where she was, feeling stupid and helpless, her anger
a pointless, exhausting emotion. It would change nothing, because
he didn't care. She had no power. None.

She was as trapped as poor little Benjamin had been in that
locked, dark closet. It was the first time she had admitted that to
herself, had allowed herself to truly understand the shape and form
of her marriage.

It horrified her so that she couldn't even cry.

The one thing she could not do, would not do, was to lie down in
bed next to James. She took off her clothes, put on a nightgown and
a bathrobe, and went to sleep on the floor in Benjamin's room. She
slept badly, the floor hard and cold under her bones. When she did
fall asleep, it was a light, uneasy slumber, and it was disturbed by
her son's faint whimpering now and again. He didn't wake, but she
did, and lay seething, staring at the graying sky beyond the window.

When James rose, he showered and dressed as if nothing had happened. If he was aware that Anne had not been in bed, or that she
was unusually quiet, he made no comment. If he noticed his son
flinch when he came near him at the breakfast table, he gave no sign.
He drank his coffee and ate his breakfast as usual. Before he left for

court he cast an assessing glance around the kitchen and took a peek into the spotless dining room. He gave a single, satisfied nod, picked up his briefcase, and was gone.

Anne's tears welled at last, and she let them drip down her cheeks in silence. Benjamin, seeing, said, "Mama c-cry?" and burst into tears himself. She snatched him up and held him close to her, taking comfort in the sweet smell of his scalp and the pliant warmth of his small body.

"Never mind, Benjamin," she murmured, over and over. "Never mind. Mama will take care of it."

It was an empty promise. It was, in fact, a lie. She had not taken care of it. She had destroyed everything.

· · * * ★ ★ ★ * * · ·

Anne, The Island, 1977

"I should have done something then," Anne said. "I wanted to do something, to stand up to him, but I couldn't think how to do that. I felt as if I had no options but to suffer through it, to watch my child suffer through it. I suppose I was a coward."

"I don't agree," Beatrice said calmly. "You were young, just out of college, with no experience and no means of your own. I suppose you could have packed up Benjamin and left, but with no money, and no help, where would you have gone?"

Anne put down her fork. The eggs had been good, and she had eaten her share of them without difficulty. The release she felt at sharing her burden had sharpened her appetite. "I don't know," she said. "But by staying, I made things infinitely worse."

"You couldn't have turned to your parents?"

"No. My mother thought I was lucky to marry someone with money, with position. She had grown up with nothing until she married my father, and staying with him was a matter of constant compromise. He was the sort of man who laid down the law and expected everyone around him to obey. I thought—naively—that James would be different. I thought—" She twisted her fingers together. "I was foolish. I was stupid, really. I thought he was in love with me. I thought I was in love with *him*, come to that."

"How did you meet him?"

"At our church, St. Michael's. Part of his image as a judge was to be an upstanding, churchgoing member of the community." She felt the old anxiety rising again, beginning in her middle and flowing upward to make her heart flutter. "Everyone thought I was so lucky, young wife, fine Catholic man, a beautiful child…" Her throat closed, and she couldn't go on.

After a moment, Beatrice asked, "Where is your son now, Anne?" Her voice betrayed nothing of what she must surely be thinking. How could a mother leave her five-year-old child?

This was the point, Anne thought, where things could get tricky. She pressed a hand over her breastbone, as if that would stem the rising tide of nerves, and cast Beatrice a panicked glance. She found only interest, perhaps a touch of sympathy, no judgment. And no impatience.

Anne drew a long breath and released it. "He's with his father. It's a complicated story."

Beatrice said nothing. Anne felt the pressure of her silence, the need to fill it, to tell it all.

"You're going to think I'm a terrible person. A bad mother."

"Do you think you are?"

Anne's throat tightened again. "Maybe," she said softly. "Maybe I am."

18

Benjamin, Oak Hill, 1977

EVERY DAY, WHEN Gramma Phyllis picked Benjamin up from school, she asked him questions. She would ask what he had for morning snack. He had the words in his mind for graham crackers and milk, but it took him too long to speak them. *Gs* and *Ms* were especially hard, and Gramma Phyllis would get impatient and go to another question. She asked if he had colored or fingerpainted, which was better, because he could show her the pages. If she asked what he liked best, or who he played with, he stammered and struggled to explain.

He didn't play with anyone. He didn't have a special friend at school, or any friend, really. He knew the words to describe that, but the effort to speak them stuck in his throat. No matter how he tried, the words wouldn't come out.

It was bad, because he knew Gramma Phyllis was upset when he couldn't talk to her. He thought she might even have hurt feelings, although he wasn't sure if grown-ups had hurt feelings the way a kid did. He might have asked her that, but those words were even harder to say than the regular ones.

The worst was when his father came to pick him up at the end of the day. Papa was cross to begin with, because he had a really hard job. He always reminded Mama of that when he came home at night, when he poured his drink and dropped his briefcase on the floor. But now, when Benjamin struggled to answer his questions, he got mad.

He didn't shout in front of Gramma Phyllis. He waited until they were in the car, and then he yelled at Benjamin in the back seat to knock it off, to stop pretending. Papa said Benjamin knew perfectly well how to talk. He was just being stubborn. Trying to embarrass him.

Benjamin hung his head so his father couldn't see the tears dripping down his cheeks. He missed his mother so much at those times that he thought he couldn't bear it. He wished she had taken him with her when she left. He wished she could have done something to stay with him. He wished he had run after her car, begged her to stop, to open the door.

He wished he could spend the night with Gramma Phyllis, because nights at home alone with his father were bad. His only respite was when he was in bed and the lady came to stand at the foot. She never spoke, or even smiled, but having her there was a comfort just the same. She made him feel he could sleep.

Sometimes, when he woke in the morning, he thought he could still detect a whiff of her smell, and it reminded him she would be there again when darkness fell.

19

Beatrice, The Island, 1977

BEATRICE CAST A sidelong glance at Anne, then beyond, to the ghosts drifting behind her shoulders. She didn't feel the way she had expected to. She had once again acted on impulse, invited this unhappy woman to stay even though she expected to be miserable.

Misery, to her surprise, was not what she felt. She felt relief, even pride, at having done something helpful. Something positive. There was no dearth of discomfort over Anne's pain, but the good outweighed the bad, and that lifted her spirits.

She should have known. She was the therapist. The psychologist. She should have applied her own hard-won knowledge to herself.

Beatrice sighed and laid her flatware across her plate. She had never expected her little gift to grow into a monster, to swell and expand and intensify until it dominated her. Once it had, she had failed to master it. It had controlled her instead, and she had done exactly what she tried to persuade her patients not to do. She had not confronted her trouble. She had run away from it.

But now, with Anne opening her heart to her, she felt something like the therapist she had once been. It reminded her of the governing force that had driven her since Erick Ericksen's crisis in the fourth grade. She welcomed back the compulsion to help. To heal. To counsel.

She wanted to listen as she once had, to sift through the various approaches she had developed the way a woodworker might sort through her tools. Her desire to ease Anne's pain was greater than the feeling of doom the angry ghost brought her, stronger than the pain in her throat caused by the small one. She did her best to push aside her distress. That meant a headache later, but she would accept the cost.

Anne was reaching for the plates to carry them to the sink, but Beatrice put up a hand. "Why not leave that for a little?" she said. "I'd like to know why you think you might be a bad mother." She recognized the note of acceptance in her own voice, the nonjudgmental tone she had found effective with her patients. It did not come as easily as it once had, but it was good to hear it once again, and it was a welcome distraction from her other, more personal fear.

Anne obeyed, leaving the dirty plates where they were, but she sat stiffly in her chair, her hands tightly wound in her lap. Beatrice sat still as well, her head tilted, listening. Waiting. Watching Anne struggle with whether to reveal her truth.

A full minute passed before Anne drew a ragged breath and blurted, "I should have fought for him."

"For your son?"

A nod, and a tremble of the lips that spoke to Anne's remorse.

"Was he taken from you?"

"Yes, he was. But even before that—when James—he was so cruel…" She loosened her hands to lift them in a helpless gesture. "I couldn't believe it. A little boy. I kept thinking I was doing something wrong, that it was my fault James was so angry, so impatient all the time. My mother said it was."

"Your mother said it was your fault?"

"Oh, yes." Anne lifted her face, full of sorrow. "Could I talk while I do the dishes? They bother me, sitting there."

"Sure. Come on, we'll do them together." Beatrice pushed herself up from the table, and as Anne gathered the plates, she picked up the butter dish, the jam bowl. "Tell me more about your mother. Were you close?"

"No. I don't know what that would feel like," Anne said, as she ran water in the sink and lowered the plates into it. "She was proud of me, though," she said. "Proud of the way I looked. The attention she received when we were together. I was a good student, but she didn't care about that so much. She liked me being a homecoming princess, which was odd, because I was too shy to date much."

"You said your father was strict."

Bleakly, Anne said, "He was the final—really, the only—word in our house. Mom was afraid of him, and I suppose I was, too. He never struck her, or me, either, to be fair. Mostly, he ignored me. Until I married a judge, that is. He loved that. He bragged about it to his friends. He boasted about our house, our neighborhood, the cars we drove."

Beatrice took a rinsed plate and began to wipe it with a dishcloth. "Is it possible you married James to please your parents?"

Anne paused, the dripping frypan in her hand. She stared into it as if she could see an answer in the scratched stainless steel. "Sometimes I wonder how different my life would be if I looked like other girls." She dipped the frypan back into the water. "My appearance was all anyone was interested in, aside from a few teachers. I hated people staring at me. Mom wanted me to take modeling lessons, but my father said no, and that time I was grateful." She lifted the pan again, absently scrubbing at it. "Once, Mom bought us clothes that were the same, to go to a mother-daughter luncheon. Everyone told her we looked like sisters. I remember how happy she was, flattered, while I was dying of embarrassment."

"Did you say so?"

Anne rinsed the frypan and set it in the rack. "No. We didn't talk about things like that. We never mentioned our feelings or argued. I never heard my mother raise her voice, and I didn't, either. Even my father never shouted. He just made pronouncements, and we did what he said."

She paused and gazed out the window into the woods, her dripping hands poised over the sink as she chose her words. "I didn't realize until I was in college that not every family was like that. I went home with a friend once for the weekend, and her whole family seemed to be always yelling, arguing over something. To me, it felt like everyone was out of control. I was terrified something awful was going to happen, but then they would all sit down to dinner, talking, laughing, all of it forgotten. I couldn't understand it. I never went there again."

"That's a bit sad."

"It is. She was a nice girl, and so was her family." She exhaled through tight lips. "I just didn't know how to handle it."

"Understandable."

"Now that I think about it," Anne mused, still staring out into the woods, "James never raised his voice in the early days, either. When I met him, I thought everything was working out the way it was supposed to. I had followed the rules. I met the right man and made a brilliant marriage. I was Cinderella marrying the prince. I never thought about what came after that day."

Beatrice took the pan from the rack and dried it. "So much fuss about weddings—the dress, the flowers, the gifts and invitations— what happens after doesn't get much attention."

"It's true. It's all about the big day." Anne pulled the plug in the sink, and as she watched the soapy water swirl away, she remembered.

* * * * * ★ ★ ★ * * * ·

Anne, St. Michael's Church, 1968

Choosing the wedding dress had been a long and laborious process. Anne always thought of it as The Dress. She couldn't think of it as hers, since it wasn't her choice, not a style she even liked. She had almost nothing to do with it, in fact, except wear it.

It was a confection of ivory silk, snug at the waist to show her slenderness, with lace and a swirl of white pearls at the bodice to hint at the bosom beneath. Her mother and she had set aside a selection of half a dozen wedding gowns, but after a long conference with the wedding planner about how the dress would look in the layout for the Sunday magazine, the two of them, alternately flattered by his attention and confused by his criteria, let him make the final decision. The Dress was not one of the gowns they had chosen.

The wedding planner had been hired by the groom, which was unusual. Phyllis thought it was exciting, and she told Anne she was the luckiest bride ever, being treated like royalty. She threw herself into the process, calling the wedding planner several times to ask what he thought of the veil, if there were enough pearls, should the skirt be more full so it could be spread across the altar steps for the photographs? No one asked Anne's opinion.

The whole wedding party had to gather four hours before the ceremony so the photographers could do their work. The six bridesmaids clustered to one side of the sanctuary, their matching cloud-pink tulle gowns swishing beneath the white statue of the Virgin in its niche. The groomsmen in their tuxes stood on the other side of the altar, laughing together, eyeing the bridesmaids, even though every one of them was a married man.

Anne, carefully buttoned into The Dress by her mother and the dressmaker, stood on the top step of the altar in a waterfall of creamy fabric. If Anne so much as moved her foot, one of the photographers barked at her to hold still. If the bouquet sagged a few inches, another of them would dash up the steps, careful not to step on The Dress, and rearrange her hands. They tweaked the veil, they tugged at her bodice, they adjusted the bouquet of white roses and baby's breath, they smoothed wrinkles out of the elbow-length white gloves she wore, pressing her arms this way and that for the angle they wanted. They said, "Beautiful, beautiful," over and over, until it no longer meant anything.

Anne felt like a Barbie doll, dressed, posed, arranged. The makeup artist had worked on her for an hour, and the hairdresser just as long. The flower arrangements that filled the church with the choking sweetness of gardenias were embarrassingly oversized, spreading their blooms so wide the altar nearly disappeared. She barely knew the pretty bridesmaids and was sure the wedding planner had chosen them for their figures. She supposed she was lucky she had been allowed to choose her own maid of honor, a girl from her sorority. There were ushers and valets and caterers and a smiling reporter in a smart skirt suit making notes as the whole show was assembled.

Anne was getting tired. She needed the bathroom, but without help with The Dress, that would be impossible. She looked around for her mother, but all she earned for that was another admonishment from a photographer.

James was nowhere to be seen, either. Wasn't he supposed to be in the pictures? In truth, she hadn't seen him in days, and she wouldn't have been surprised if he didn't show up at all. Part of her wouldn't have minded. The whole thing could have come to an end right there, and it wouldn't have been her fault. Once he had hired the wedding planner, he seemed to be done with the whole event, except for having his secretary send engraved invitations to all of his law colleagues and clients. Anne didn't realize until much later that there was an election coming. The judge's wedding was going to make great publicity.

James did, in the end, appear. The photographers posed him next to Anne and arranged the attendants on either side. James looked stunning in his tuxedo, elegant and refined, the faint touch of silver at his temples blending perfectly with the ivory of The Dress. James, too, said, "Beautiful," when he saw her, but that was all. There were no protestations of love, of happiness, of excitement. No asking if she was all right. If she needed anything.

Anne told herself James was too disciplined for that. He must love her, mustn't he? He had courted her. Proposed to her. Flattered her parents. Given her an enormous diamond, taken the wedding details out of her hands, dealt with all of it himself, or had his secretary do it. This was supposed to be her big day, the start of her beautiful life.

She stopped thinking about all of that. Her need to use the bathroom was becoming critical. Finally, with only a half hour to go before the ceremony, the photographers released them all. The wedding planner shouted, "Don't wrinkle anything!" as everyone filed out of the sanctuary. Phyllis appeared at last and held the skirts of The Dress while Anne made her careful way down the steps and off to the bride's room.

"Aren't you thrilled?" Phyllis said when they were alone, after Anne had finally been able to relieve herself.

"I'm exhausted," Anne said.

"But everything is so perfect!"

Anne, seeing her mother glowing with pride, nodded. "I know, Mom. It's all perfect. I just need to sit down for a moment."

The ceremony went by in a blur, but it seemed Anne had said what she was supposed to say, and James had smoothly placed the wedding ring on her finger. He had declined one for himself. He kissed her when he was told to and tucked her hand under his arm for the recessional, a satisfied smile on his face, which she told herself was happiness. She smiled, too, and kept smiling throughout the reception, the toasts, the dance, which was hindered significantly by The Dress, then the dinner, which she didn't taste.

She could hardly wait for it all to be over, for her to be alone with James at last, off to New York City for their honeymoon. Surely then, she thought, James would speak the words of love she longed to hear. They would sleep together, which they hadn't done—which she had never done, which her sorority sisters had teased her about— and she would feel really, truly married.

She woke early in their Manhattan hotel and lay thinking for a while. It was strange to share her bed with someone, but she thought she would like it, in time. She hoped she would like the other thing, too, although she had felt awkward and naive when it was happening. She had listened to her sorority sisters' bragging about their sexual encounters but had never been tempted to try it for herself. She had been glad about that when James asked her, because it seemed important to him that he was her first, her only. She was still glad, she told herself, and with time, she would get better at it.

She slipped out of bed, leaving James sound asleep, and went to shower and do her hair and makeup for the day ahead. James had made her unpack the night before so he could choose an ensemble for her. It was sweet, she thought. He wanted his new bride to look nice, and he was very good with clothes and shoes and hats. He had laid out a slim blue skirt with a matching jacket, and a white silk high-necked blouse. He had even chosen her earrings, and a pair of cream leather pumps with high heels. She thought he must not be planning much walking for the day. They would probably go everywhere in taxicabs, as they had last night from the airport. She had hoped to do some real sightseeing, but maybe that would come tomorrow.

She was startled, emerging from the bathroom wrapped in one of the thick robes provided by the hotel, to see that James was gone. A tray sat on the low table before a short sofa, laden with coffee, a sugar bowl and creamer, a little silver basket with fresh bagels and cream cheese. A copy of the *New York Times* rested nearby. Anne settled uneasily on the sofa, wondering where James might have gone, and why.

To her relief, he returned in moments, a sheaf of newspapers under his arm, a pleased smile on his face. "The hotel didn't have a Boston paper, so I went out to buy one. The spread is great. You looked like an angel." He bent, and though she lifted her lips to him, he kissed her cheek instead. "You were perfect."

20

Beatrice, The Island, 1977

BEATRICE OBSERVED THE faraway look on Anne's face as she pulled the towel from her shoulder, absently smoothing the creases before she hung it up.

"You're thinking of something," Beatrice prompted.

Anne gave her a wan smile. "Remembering. You've reminded me of my wedding day, and the days after. All the things I didn't understand at the beginning, that should have been warnings."

"You were young when you married, I think."

"Not that young. Twenty-two."

"Pretty young." Beatrice hung the pan she had been drying on its hook and pointed toward the living room. "Let's go sit in the living room, and you can tell me the rest."

And she could stare at the restless ocean instead of Anne's unhappy ghosts. They had retreated, but they were still there.

She built up the fire, then settled at one end of the sofa with Anne at the other end. The ocean was a cold green today, its surface rippling like cut emeralds under the cool early-spring sun. The evergreens danced in a light breeze, and three little sailboats sped past the mouth of the bay, racing each other, sails bellying in the wind.

Anne's gaze fixed on the water, but Beatrice doubted she was taking in the view. Her hands were squeezed together again, and her shoulders contracted as if she expected a blow. She said, "My wedding was a spectacle. Ostentatious. Everything controlled by James, even The Dress."

Beatrice heard the emphasis.

"My mother and I went shopping for a wedding gown, and it was one of the nicest days we had ever spent together. She was thrilled to be doing it, and we chose beautiful gowns." Her eyelids drooped under the weight of memory. "I loved those dresses."

"Didn't you wear one of those?"

"James wanted something more dramatic, because he had arranged for one of the Boston papers to cover the wedding." She breathed a long sigh. "My mother was delighted. I was overwhelmed. I just did what I was told."

Beatrice said, "How was the gown different?"

Anne gave a sour chuckle. "The Dress? I have to say, Beatrice, The Dress was a feat of engineering. Huge skirt, skintight bodice, about a thousand buttons. In the back, of course, so I couldn't get in or out of the thing without help."

"James managed everything?"

"Every detail. He even planned our honeymoon, and there were photographers when we went to dinner, or went up in the Empire State Building." Her face darkened. "He chose all my clothes. I had to walk all over Manhattan in three-inch heels."

"It's classic controlling behavior."

"Should I have known that? I didn't."

"You grew up with a controller, so it felt normal to you."

"I wanted to believe it was all because James loved me and wanted me to be happy, but that wasn't it. There was an election coming up. Everything he did was to enhance his image. I was just one part of it." She shook her head. "He cast me, as if I were filling a role in a play. I was to be the judge's wife." She made a wry mouth. "The judge's photogenic bride."

"And your son?"

"James never wanted children. I didn't do it on purpose. It just—it just happened, and I was so happy about it, but now…"

Beatrice took a swift glance at her, then turned back to the sea to avoid the ghosts. "You know, Anne, you're under no obligation to tell me anything. But I assure you it's all but impossible to shock me." At Anne's sudden indrawn breath, she added, "If that's your worry."

Anne unwound her hands and reached for the psychedelic afghan. "You might not be shocked, Beatrice. I am." She shuddered and pulled the afghan up to her shoulders. "Shocked to my very soul."

"Will it help to talk about it?"

"I don't think so, but I'll tell you. I hope you won't be disgusted with me."

"I promise you I will not."

"I am, though," Anne said in a low voice. "I'm horrified. I'm absolutely shocked by my own weakness, and it's cost me the only thing in the world that matters."

"Your child."

"Yes. Benjamin."

"How old is he?"

"Five. He turned five in November."

"What is he like?"

Anne's voice softened. "He's fair, like me, not dark like James. He's the sweetest little boy, sensitive and affectionate, precocious—" She stopped speaking, and her eyes sparkled with tears.

Beatrice waited while Anne swallowed and rubbed her eyes

with the heels of her hands. When she had collected herself, she said, "Benjamin likes to collect things. Coins, for their shapes and colors. Leaves in the autumn. Stamps, once he learned to read." A faint smile came into her voice. "He taught himself to read when he was three. James liked that, was always getting him to read when we had company. Showing him off. Until he started to stutter, that is."

"Benjamin stutters?"

"He didn't when he first learned to talk, which was really early, not even a year old. Then—well. I don't—well, I'm not sure why, but he stutters now."

Beatrice guessed that Anne knew why, but she couldn't accept it. She couldn't bring herself to add that to the weight of her guilt.

Beatrice spoke in a neutral tone. "What else did James like about his son?"

Anne spoke with instant bitterness. "Nothing."

"Really? Nothing?"

"He thought a boy should be athletic. Smart wasn't enough. He wanted his son to be bold. Rowdy, as I'm told James was when he was a child. Apparently his parents gave up trying to manage him when he was still young. He bragged about that, about throwing something at a teacher, refusing to conform to class rules, even beating up another kid who insulted him. He thought all of that was something to be proud of. And then there was the dog."

"The dog?"

"He didn't tell me the story himself. He just said a dog attacked him, but I heard his brother reminding him of it one night after they had both had a lot of wine at dinner, and whiskey after."

"You didn't mention James had a brother."

"Yes, Patrick. He was James's only family, but we rarely saw him. James always said they didn't get along, that his brother was jealous or something, but I don't think that's the reason. I think Patrick knows what James is, and—" She broke off.

Beatrice prompted, "There was something about a dog?"

"It was Patrick's dog, apparently. It seems James was mean to the dog, shutting it outside in the cold, hiding its water bowl, even kicking it if it was in his way. And then—" She wrapped her arms around herself, and the look on her face was a mixture of disgust and fear. "He went too far, I suppose. That night after dinner, Patrick and James had an argument, dredging up old fights, old resentments. It ended with Patrick accusing James of trying to kill his dog, making the dog fight back. He said it was James's fault their parents sent the dog to the pound. James shouted something about the dog being stupid, and mean, and Patrick slammed out of the house. He never came back."

"They were children when it happened?"

"I don't know exactly how old they were. But I have no doubt that even as a child, James was capable of abusing a dog. He's capable of abusing a sweet little boy. I'm afraid he's just cruel by nature. He has a reputation for it in court, known for being harsh. Some call it being tough, but I read about some of his cases, and his decisions seemed cruel to me."

"Did you tell him that?"

Anne gave a humorless little laugh. "Not exactly. I made the mistake of simply asking about one of them, early on in our marriage. I never made that mistake a second time. I found out how little James cared about my opinions, and I learned to keep my thoughts to myself, just as my mother did with my father."

Beatrice bit her lip over how profoundly her own history had differed, and how different her life had been because of it. Her father had always treated her as an equal. Mitch had, too. They respected her thoughts, whether they agreed with them or not. They never needed the label of feminist, despite Mitch's occasional gibes about women's lib. Their regard came naturally, without the persuasion of ideology.

As she listened to Anne's halting confession, her own sense of loss surfaced, and her heart grew heavy in her chest, as if one of the boulders on the beach below her cottage had lodged itself in her rib cage.

21

Beatrice, San Francisco, 1975

BEATRICE SAW GHOSTS everywhere, floating behind passersby on the street, hovering over women she saw in the shops, clouding around people she sat near in the movie theater. She saw them behind waiters in restaurants, and vendors on the wharf. The trolley was unbearable, crowded with shades and brimming with their misery, making Beatrice's throat ache with a ferocity she had not felt before. She kept hoping the strange experiences would ease. She spent a lot of energy trying to deny that the opposite was happening, but that was a wasted effort.

She began walking with her head down, wearing sunglasses even on foggy days, doing her best not to see. Then, on a night Mitch came in late from the hospital, there it was. The final moment, the worst of all. Her throat throbbed as she watched Mitch come through the door and hang his coat on the rack.

He was unaware of what followed him, but Beatrice gazed in horror at the fragile shade, pale gray shot through with indigo, swirling behind Mitch's shoulders. It clung to him in a cloud of worry and pain, trailing in the evening gloom like the afterimage of a flashbulb. No matter how she blinked, she couldn't make it disappear.

At the realization, tears sprang to her eyes.

Mitch crossed the floor with swift, concerned strides. "What on earth?" he said. "Has something happened, Bea? You're—you're *crying.*"

She rarely did. She had cried when her father died, and again at his funeral. Aside from that, she simply wasn't the sort of woman who wept. Mitch was aware of that. He knew her better than anyone living.

He folded her in his arms, and she dampened his wool jacket with her tears, dreading what she would have to say to him.

There was no way around it. One of her ghosts was in her own house, haunting her own partner. Her desire for the visions to fade, to let her be herself again, was in vain. She had hoped never to tell Mitch about any of it, but now...

She could prevaricate, make up some excuse for her tears, for the shock he had seen on her face, but she couldn't keep that up forever. Not when this ghost, with its attendant sadness, would be right there whenever she looked at Mitch. It would be with him when they sat down to dinner, when they worked in the clinic, when they went to bed. It would be there when they made love.

Beatrice counseled her patients to be direct when they could. She told them that hiding things, repressing feelings and fears, was poison to the psyche, and she had seen her patients' courage in the face of hard decisions like this one. She loathed hypocrisy. She had to be at least as strong as her patients had been. She had to face this without delay.

She pulled out of Mitch's arms and turned toward the kitchen, trying not to see the wavering shade behind him. It didn't help. The melancholy of this ghost was already imprinted on her spirit.

She tucked her chin, ready for conflict. "I'll get you a glass of wine, Mitch. Then I have to tell you something."

* * * * * ★ ★ ★ * * * *

Mitch's ghost was that of his grandmother. His nonna, left in her mountain village by her son, Mitch's father, when he and his brother emigrated to the United States. She had learned of his death through the mail, and had suffered a number of other losses since. She was entering her old age isolated and lonely.

"I knew you worried about her," Beatrice said. "But I didn't know how much."

"It's worse than worry. I feel guilty," Mitch said. "I've only been back to see her twice, once with my uncle, once right before I started my internship. All her other family, and so many of her friends, are dead now." He refilled his wineglass. "But I still don't understand how you knew that." His voice was tight with—what? Anger? Disappointment?

Or was it fear, like the fear that gripped her now? Beatrice felt her life slipping away, falling into ruins, and she couldn't think of a way to salvage it.

She and Mitch each sat at one end of the sofa, in the dark because neither of them had bothered turning on a light. It was a small sofa, but the distance between them felt huge to Beatrice, a chasm that opened and spread as she explained everything to Mitch in blunt language. With each detail she felt him withdraw further from her.

"Do you want me to explain it again?" she said. "You can imagine how hard it is to put such a—such an experience—into words."

It had been more difficult than she had expected. The phenomenon was as much emotional as visual, and there was no word to encompass it, to transmit the feeling and the experience to someone else. Ghost? Shade? Projection? None of those words were perfect fits, and she could find nothing better in the lexicon.

At least Mitch had not—at least, not yet—said she was crazy. He would never use that unmedical term, but he would have some way of saying it, of naming the fear that chilled her blood and weakened her bones. As her ghosts proliferated, so did her fear for her sanity. It was like waiting for a devastating medical diagnosis, trying to maintain an outward calm while inwardly trembling with anxiety.

From the darkness beyond the bow window, she heard the hollow hoot of the ferry from the bay, warning off other boats. The fog had drifted in to settle over the city in silvery billows that turned to gold around the streetlights. Beatrice yearned to go walking now, when the fog hid her ghosts so they couldn't torment her, but she didn't dare suggest it. She had to wait, let Mitch digest what she had told him, let him decide whether to be angry or sympathetic or disbelieving.

She watched the struggle play out on his face, lit only by the foggy glow of the corner streetlight. He said, in the professorial voice that always revealed how upset he was, "No, Bea, I would prefer you not explain again. You were perfectly clear—at least as clear as you could be in a situation that has no clarity at all."

"Mitch, you're a diagnostician. Don't you sometimes have insights, things you know without being able to explain why you know them?"

He turned his head toward her, but his body position remained stiff. "I fail to see how that relates to the current circumstance." Behind him, the shade of his nonna wavered in the shadows, as if to beg for his attention. Mitch saw Beatrice's eyes flick toward it, and his jaw tensed. "You're seeing it again."

"I am."

"Perhaps—" She watched him choose his words carefully. "Bea, I have to say this. Perhaps you just think you see something. This could be your imagination, your empathy, getting carried away."

"Do you really think I'm capable of making this up?"

"I didn't say you were making it up. I can see that you believe it, but I do wonder—maybe you should talk to someone?"

"A therapist?" She gave a bitter laugh, and her voice rose. "Give me a break, Mitch!" she cried. "If you won't believe that I'm seeing what I'm seeing—and feeling—then why would anyone else?"

He put up a hand. "Bea, please. You need to calm down."

"Calm down?" She found that her hands had fisted in her lap, and her legs shook with tension.

Mitch dropped his hand, then lifted it to pull off his glasses and rub the bridge of his nose with his fingers. "I apologize. That was the wrong thing to say. What I meant—what I'm trying to find words for—is that none of this is possible. It's just not logical."

"This isn't science," she said, lowering her voice to its normal pitch. "It's something else, something I can't name, something I might not have believed in one of my own patients. That doesn't mean it's not real."

"It's real to you," Mitch said. He replaced his glasses, pushing them up on his nose with one finger. They reflected the gleam of the streetlights, hiding his eyes from her. "You have to understand, Bea, that doesn't mean it's real to me. I've had patients—"

"I'm not your patient, Mitch."

"I didn't say you were." Mitch's jaw flexed. "But what happens now? Am I supposed to live like this? I don't know how we go forward, Bea. I have no idea what to do."

She cradled her half-full wineglass between her hands, watching the ripples in the ruby surface, searching for some kind of answer. "There is something you could do." She glanced up at him. "You could go see her. Assuage the guilt you're feeling."

"You're making this my problem, then."

"You asked what we could do, Mitch."

"Bea—" he began, then broke off. He picked up his glass and drained it. "I don't know what to think," he finally said.

"I know I shouldn't have taken the drug, Mitch. Believe me, I know, and I regret doing it. I'm sorry I ignored your advice. But that doesn't negate what you're feeling. You care about your grandmother. You worry about her."

"I'm not one of your patients, either, Bea, nor do I intend to become one," Mitch said.

"No, no, I wasn't—I mean, I was just speaking common sense, wasn't I? Tell me why you haven't gone to see her, since I can see how much you worry about her."

He let his head drop against the back of the sofa, a weary, helpless gesture. She wished she dared scoot over to him, put her arms around him, bring them back to where they had been before her revelation.

"There was always something in the way," he said. "Internship. Residency. Now the hospital and the clinic. When was the last time I took any time off?"

"I have the same complications," she said. "But I went to visit my father every year."

"It's hardly the same, Bea. I had no one to support me when I was in school, as you know. I worked all the way through, which still wasn't enough, and I have the bank loans to prove it. Even now, I'm under constant pressure, life-and-death decisions no one can make but me. How can I get free for a jaunt to the wilds of Trentino?"

It was true enough that William had supported her through her schooling. As to the rest of Mitch's argument, at another time Beatrice would have bridled at his implication that her work was less vital than his. Now she was too anxious even to mention it. Too frightened of what was happening. Of whether it was going to get worse.

The telephone interrupted them. Mitch's ring. He set down his glass and went to answer.

Beatrice put her own glass down and rose. If he had to go to the hospital, he would need something to eat. When she reached the kitchen, he was just setting the phone back in its cradle.

"I have to go," he said, and she had the sense it was a relief to him. An escape.

"I can make you a sandwich."

"No time. I'll get one in the cafeteria."

"Mitch—" But she couldn't finish. He put up a hand, seized his medical bag and his coat, and was gone. His sad, lonely ghost trailed after him.

* * * ★ ★ ★ ★ ★ * * *

Beatrice, The Island, 1977

The memories of that evening flashed through Beatrice's mind in the spaces between Anne's halting words. It had been the first of many tense discussions: formal, uncomfortable conversations, as if she and Mitch were strangers.

But this moment was about Anne Iredale. She refocused her attention as Anne spoke of her loneliness during Benjamin's infancy.

"Everyone—my friends, my mother—told me men aren't good about babies. They don't like the noise, the mess, the disruption. They said James was a typical father."

"Did you think so?"

"I assumed my own father had been the same." Anne hesitated, and shifted beneath the afghan. "I didn't doubt what they told me, but—the baby was so cute, so good! It was hard for me to understand. James never wanted to hold him or play with him or read to him. He wanted me to hire someone to come in every day to watch him, so I would have more time to make his dinner, iron his shirts, get my hair done. He wanted me to look good to go out with his clients, to be on his arm for special events." She added, "Especially if there were photographers present."

"Did you do it? Hire someone?"

Anne shook her head. "I wanted to take care of Benjamin myself. They're not babies very long, are they?"

"No, they're not."

"And I knew I wouldn't be allowed another one."

"You had natural maternal instincts."

"I suppose so, but James didn't like me to have my own ideas, any more than my father had. He expected me to obey his orders, and if I didn't—" Her sigh was small and sad. "He found ways to punish me."

"What ways?"

Anne slumped against the sofa arm, as if even talking about it wearied her. "It was little things at first, tiny things, really. Things I could dismiss, blame on James being tired, being under pressure, that sort of thing. Then—" Her voice dropped. "They escalated."

"In what way?"

"It wasn't too bad until Benjamin was born, although I learned early on not to say anything about James's work, or the news, or even about a book I might be reading. He considered my opinions ignorant. Silly. At first he laughed at me, as if I was a stupid child. Then, after Benjamin, he started snapping, telling me to be quiet, to—to shut up about things I didn't understand, especially in front of his friends. He said I—" An uncomfortable flush stained her pale cheeks. "He said I embarrassed him."

Anne went on, her words coming faster, as if her recitation had been bottled up inside her and was now pouring out in a rush. "Then he started asking for a full accounting of what I did every day. He asked me how long it took to do the laundry, to do the shopping, to make the beds. He checked the odometer on my car. He asked the housekeeper to corroborate, as if he thought I was lying to him." Another flush reddened her cheeks. "I had no one to talk to. Only my mother, and that was no help." She shivered. "He watched our joint checking account and asked me to explain every check I wrote, including the grocery store. I can remember him making me sit down and explain every withdrawal, tell him which shop I had been to, who had done my hair. Sometimes he made me go to my closet and take out a blouse I had bought, or a pair of shoes, and asked me what they cost." She stopped speaking, gazing out the window to the water shifting below the beach.

"You said it escalated," Beatrice prompted.

"Yes." Anne's voice went flat, as if to take the sting out of the ugliness of her words. "Once when I couldn't remember what I had spent some cash on, he lost his temper. I was holding the account book, and he slapped it out of my hand. I could see he wanted to slap *me*, but he restrained himself. Later—well, later on, he didn't. He pinched my arm when he didn't think the kitchen was clean enough. I could see his fingerprints on my arm for days. Once he shoved me out of the way when I was trying to put away his laundry, telling me I was doing it wrong. Pushed me into the closet door so I nearly broke my elbow. It hurt for weeks. He broke a picture frame he knew I liked, something my maid of honor had given me as a wedding present. I knew he did it on purpose, but I didn't dare say anything. I just got down on the floor and cleaned up the bits.

"It went on and on. I never knew when the next thing was coming. He said Benjamin's stuttering was my fault, that I was too permissive, too easy with him, that he needed more discipline. I tried to do what he wanted, to protect Benjamin, but it didn't help. He punished Benjamin anyway, and his stuttering got worse."

She gazed blindly out at the ocean. "I couldn't win, no matter what I did. I would have given up if it weren't for Benjamin. I would put up with anything for Benjamin's sake."

Beatrice started to say something more, something to encourage her to go on, but the smell stopped her.

It came from nowhere, that rank, nauseating odor of rot and decay. She whirled to look behind her, thinking the specter had reappeared, but there was nothing. Her mouth dry, her heartbeat thudding in her throat, she reached for her teacup and tried to pretend everything was normal.

22

Anne, Oak Hill, 1976

A BRAVER WOMAN would take her baby and leave. Anne wanted to be that woman. If only she could think of someone to turn to!

It was one of the worst drawbacks to being beautiful. Girls who might have been her friends didn't want to be seen in her shade. They would have denied it, but she knew they were jealous of the attention she received. Her maid of honor, the one girl she felt had been a real friend at school, avoided bringing her boyfriends anywhere Anne was going to be.

If they had been able to talk about it, if Anne had told her she recognized the problem, perhaps their friendship would have survived beyond Anne's wedding, but Anne had no idea how to broach the subject. In her family, they didn't speak of their feelings. They swallowed them. Anne thought her mother had been choking on her feelings all her life, and she had begun to think she would be forced to live the same way.

When the crisis came, she was at a loss. Her parents would never forgive her if she left the marriage they were so proud of. There was no doorstep she could show up on without an invitation. There was no place she could go with a baby in her arms and no money in her purse.

James had cornered her, as neatly and thoroughly as if he had shut her in a locked room.

It had taken too long for her to accept the truth of her situation. She had wasted time trying to persuade herself her mother was right. She had spent months trying to accept it as normal that when Benjamin was still nursing—another thing James had not wanted her to do—her husband often didn't come home for dinner. He didn't warn her, or call, he just didn't come.

Phyllis said she wasn't trying hard enough. She told her she should shower before her husband got home, do her hair and put on fresh makeup, put the baby down early so her husband could have her to himself. She cut out articles about how to keep romance in a marriage and gave them to Anne.

Anne knew they were old-fashioned ideas, but she tried them just the same. The first time she spent hours on a roast, with gravy and whipped potatoes, the things James liked. She took a bath, with Benjamin in his carrier beside the tub. She put on mascara and lipstick, and a fresh blouse over her slacks. It turned out to be one of the nights James was late, and by the time he showed up, smelling of whiskey and cigar smoke, her beautiful dinner had congealed into a disgusting gray mass.

James had given the ruined dinner one look, then marched past her to go up the stairs without saying a word. Anne was exhausted from a long day of baby demands, planning and cooking the ruined meal, hurrying to be ready when he arrived. She stood in the kitchen, still in her apron, weeping tears of frustration. The baby began to cry from upstairs, and she raced to deal with him so James wouldn't have something else to complain about.

She tried other times, different meals, different clothes, getting her hair done with the baby in her lap. None of it made any difference. After several ruined dinners, she began to plan dishes that could wait in the oven, so that if James came home—and she was never sure if he would—she could bring them out and serve them. It rarely worked. She began to think she would never get anything right.

A stain that wouldn't come out of a shirt meant the shirt was thrown at her with an order—not a request, but an order—to get it out before James got home that night. A mismatched pair of socks brought a flurry of curses and a completely turned-out sock drawer. When Benjamin was two and a half, he left a small metal airplane on the floor. James stepped on it and began shouting at his little son, threatening to take all his toys away. When Anne tried to intervene, he hurled the airplane at her, striking her in the chest.

The dinner party when James locked Benjamin in his closet came soon after, and not long after that, the shoving and slapping began. A dirty dish, an overcooked steak, a mislaid phone message, all enraged James, and angry words no longer sufficed for him to vent his temper.

Anne's and Benjamin's best evenings were when James stalked out of the house, leaving them to comfort each other in the rocker in Benjamin's bedroom. Sometimes it was Benjamin weeping, with a red mark on his back where his father had slapped him. Just as often it was Anne in tears, trying to pretend the new bruise on her hip or her leg didn't hurt.

She had tried at first to pretend that each incident was unique, that if she only did better, was more careful, tried harder, it wouldn't happen again. She consolidated her shopping trips, so the mileage on her car wouldn't add up enough for James to question her. She made careful notes about what she did with her cash, so that she could explain when he asked her. She spent hours doing housework that didn't really need doing, so she could account for her day, as if she were an hourly employee. She stopped speaking when James's friends were in the house, so that he would have nothing to criticize her for, but then he accused her of being rude, refusing to make polite conversation. She talked to Benjamin when James was out of the house, and he talked to her, but when James was present, they grew more and more silent, until their house felt like a war zone.

By the time Benjamin was four, Anne was in survival mode. All that held her together was the need to shield her son as best she could. Benjamin's stuttering got worse, which made James shout at Anne that his son was an embarrassment, and she should do something about it.

Anne's hands began to tremble involuntarily when James was around, which garnered no sympathy and earned a derisive remark about needing medication. She tried to speak to her doctor at her yearly checkup, but his advice was very like her mother's: Every marriage has rough patches. It takes two. Try to understand your husband's needs. Be grateful he's such a good provider. Remember how hard his job is.

In the end, her doctor prescribed Valium. Then he called James.

· * * ★ ★ ★ ★ ★ * * · ·

Beatrice, The Island, 1977

Beatrice startled at that, and the offending odor vanished with her sudden jolt of anger. "He did *what*?"

Anne spread her hands. "He told him everything. They're friends, which is why he was my doctor. James chose him."

"That's a terrible betrayal of your confidence, Anne. It's not illegal, but it's certainly unethical. Paternalism of the worst sort."

"He told James I might be a hysteric."

"How nineteenth-century of him!" Beatrice spat. "No one has used that term in decades."

"He's old-school, I guess."

"He's incompetent."

"Probably, but it wouldn't matter. He and James and the others, they're like a club. A boys' club. They do what they like, and no one dares criticize them." Anne's sigh was one of pure exhaustion.

"What happened after that?"

"James came home in the middle of the afternoon that day, after my doctor called him. He shouted at me that I had humiliated him, made him look bad. He said he needed a wife who was presentable, who was appropriate for his position, who was—who wasn't—" She shook her head and pressed her shaking hand over her mouth. When she continued, her voice was soft with strain. "He yelled at me for a long time, a long list of insults. Then—I had taken the Valium, and I suppose it made me less cautious. Or maybe I had finally had enough."

Beatrice said, "Yes. Maybe."

Anne said, "I would like to think that was it. In any case, I snapped at him, something I hardly remember, like 'Leave me alone.' He stopped shouting, and his eyes went so cold and hard, it was terrifying. When he pulled back his fist, I thought he might actually kill me. He didn't, obviously—I mean, he's cruel, but he's not a killer—but he did hit me really hard. With his fist. Right here." Her slender hand lifted to her left cheek.

Beatrice had to turn to her to see the gesture. Beyond the window the sky was a clear, chilly blue, the water gleaming with the winter sunshine. Indoors, the air was icy and oddly dim, the living room shadowed by misery. Darkened by the hideous shade of Anne's husband, which had now swelled to three times its size. It towered over Anne, swirling with nightmare colors, purple and black and gray. It hovered above her as if about to pounce, to suffocate her. Beatrice felt the ugliness of it in her chest as well as her throat.

"He leaned over me, where I was lying on the floor, and he told me if I ever told anyone, anyone at all, about any of it, he would see to it I was put away in an institution and I would never see my son again."

"Oh, Anne. How awful for you."

"I've never—I'm not used to speaking of these things, Beatrice, but—"

"Take your time."

"I made it worse."

"None of this is your fault, Anne. You must know that."

"The rest of it is. It is my fault, I'm afraid." Anne's voice was so bleak, her face so drained of color, that Beatrice had an urge to move closer, to put an arm around her thin shoulders.

She resisted the urge. That would have been the action of a friend, not a professional, and in this situation, she was very much the professional.

Instead, she got up and added wood to the fire. It blazed up, cherry flames licking at the little glass window of the stove, but even that couldn't banish the chill that had invaded her cottage.

She went back to her seat and spoke as calmly as she could. "There's nothing to be afraid of here, you know. You can tell me everything. Anything."

Anne began to speak rapidly, her voice thready and uncertain, hurrying as if to get it out now that she had started, to get it over with. "James left. I heard the door slam just as I was picking myself up off the floor. I looked into the mirror over the breakfront, and the bruise was already spreading. My cheek, my eye, my forehead, turning black and blue almost at once. I had to wonder if he had done the same to his first wife, and that was why she left. I remember thinking she was a wiser woman than I."

"You're his second wife?"

She nodded. "His first was named Glenda. He would never talk about her, though I did ask in the beginning. He said she left him without a word of warning, and he was furious over the rumors and gossip that caused, the questions he had to answer. She went back to England, to her family, but she never wrote or called or anything. He divorced her in absentia."

"That seems odd."

"I know. I saw a picture of her once, one he had apparently missed when he cleared out her things. She was blond and slender, like me. His type, I suppose."

"Naturally you would suspect if he struck you, he might have struck her."

"I tried not to believe it, but after that day—I did wonder."

"What happened after he left?"

"Benjamin woke up from his nap, and I tried to give him his usual snack, but my hands were shaking so badly I couldn't slice the apple. I gave him a cookie, then went straight to the bar James always kept stocked. I—"

Her face colored, and for a moment the rush of words stopped. When it resumed, every sentence dripped with shame. "I poured two fingers of scotch and drank it down in one gulp, anything to stop the shaking. I wasn't crying. I was too shocked for that. I couldn't believe he had hit me that way. A shove, a slap, those things seemed like nothing compared with that closed fist—it was so deliberate! I had trouble believing it was all real. Then I did a foolish thing.

"I thought if I drove to my parents' place, if they could see my face, see what he had done, they would have to believe me. They would have to understand how bad it had gotten. Surely, I thought, my mother—maybe even my father...

"But I had taken the Valium, and drunk the scotch, and I wasn't thinking clearly. I put Benjamin in the car. I didn't even take my purse. I made it about a half mile, and then I saw someone on a bicycle, maybe a child, I wasn't sure. I swerved and went right off the road."

"You weren't hurt? Benjamin wasn't hurt?"

Anne's voice hardened, and turned bitter. "Benjamin was fine, although of course he was crying. I was already hurt. When the police arrived, they thought my black eye was from the accident. James showed up right behind them, and he agreed, of course. He was so smooth, so convincing, and the way the police talked to him, deferred to him—I knew how much trouble I was in. He acted so caring, so concerned, cuddling Benjamin, helping me into his car. It was all pretense."

"What did the police do?"

"What everyone in Oak Hill did. They asked my husband what he wanted to do with me, as if I were a runaway child. He told them he would take care of me." Her voice grew weaker, as if the last of her energy had been spent. "He took care of me, all right. He took me home that night, but he had me in court the very next day. He accused me of being an alcoholic, of driving drunk with Benjamin in the car. The judge, another of his friends, granted James custody of Benjamin." She drew one last, exhausted breath. "James doesn't even *like* Benjamin."

Beatrice saw the engorged darkness of Anne's ghost ripple in a way that made her stomach turn. The little blue-gray cloud that was Anne's fear for Benjamin darkened, disappearing a moment later in the suffocating darkness that was his father.

"These are terrible things that have happened to you, Anne."

"Yes."

"And I repeat, not your fault. You've been abused no less than Benjamin."

"I suppose."

"I need you to believe that. To *know* that."

Anne's eyes sparkled with tears that were sapphire blue in the dimness. "Thank you," she whispered. "I was beginning to think James was right, and I'm an unfit mother."

The looming shadow behind Anne shrank, just a little, although it was still an angry, roiling charcoal. Beatrice looked away and drew a shuddery breath.

Anne said, "I'm tiring you, Beatrice. I know it's an awful story, but I—"

"We're both tired." Beatrice pushed herself up. "Let's stop for now, shall we? You could lie down. That might be best. I need to bring in some wood."

"I'll help you."

"Kind of you, but absolutely no need. Go and rest. I'll be back soon."

Beatrice needed a break. She thought if she didn't take a few moments in the fresh air, with no ghosts to trouble her, she wouldn't be much good as a therapist.

She needed to think, too. Not about Anne, but about the other thing. It hovered just beneath her conscious thoughts, a worry she couldn't completely banish, flirting with her sanity. The specter poised right at the edge of her mind and hovered there, awaiting the worst possible moment to manifest. She drew a breath through her nostrils, testing the air like a fearful animal. There was no scent, but she was still afraid.

23

Anne, The Island, 1977

ANNE LAY DOWN on the guest room bed, as Beatrice had said she should, though she didn't think she could sleep. She tried closing her eyes, but they wouldn't stay shut, and she found she was gripping one hand with the other so tightly that her nails had gone white. She forced herself to relax her hands, and then her legs, but still she lay awake. She wished she had a drink, but the little bottle of scotch in the bottom of her suitcase was empty.

The room was lightly furnished, a small pine dresser with an oval mirror, a straight chair in one corner. The bedstead, Anne guessed, had been left by the previous owner. It was also of pine, with a carved headboard. A puffy quilt spilled over the foot, the fabric in a patchwork of greens to answer the verdant depths of the pines visible through the small window. Anne pulled the quilt over her feet and turned on her side to gaze out into the woods.

The sense of unreality that had gripped her when James struck her had intensified in the past twenty-four hours. Being here, in this remote cottage, listening to Beatrice's odd tale of seeing ghosts, gave her the same weird sense that none of it could be actually real.

Anne believed in spirits. She had to. Her faith demanded it, and she had clung to faith throughout her ordeal. She had prayed for help, begged for guidance. Her faith helped to prevent her from walking into the cold seawater. She had turned to the spirits for protection for Benjamin, because she had nothing else she could do. She wasn't at all sure that spirits and ghosts were the same thing, but she had no confessor, no advisor, she could ask.

As her mind spun, Anne's muscles contracted again, making her hands and her legs ache. She wiggled her toes and fingers to relax them, made herself breathe, and held her little gold cross in one hand as she murmured an Our Father and a Hail Mary. It helped. She tried again to close her eyes, and this time, with her cross in her fingers, she finally drifted into a light sleep, lulled by the homely sounds of Beatrice stacking wood beside the stove, of the cows' gentle lowing, of the sigh of the wind through the evergreen trees around the cottage.

When the dream came, her own cry of fear woke her.

She lay still for a long moment, her heart thudding.

A gentle knock on the bedroom door made her sit up, clutching the quilt to her throat, although she was fully clothed.

"Anne? Are you all right?"

"Y-yes. I had a bad dream." Anne swung her long legs to the floor and tried to straighten her slacks. "Come in, Beatrice. I'm sorry I disturbed you."

Beatrice appeared in the doorway. She kept her gaze averted, as if she were checking that the curtains were straight or the dresser dusted.

"You didn't disturb me. But as long as you're awake, come and have some lunch. I heated some soup. Canned, I'm afraid." She stepped back, out of the room, and waited for Anne to follow her.

What Anne would have liked above all was a drink, but she couldn't bring herself to ask. Her heart was still fluttering from the dream. She said, "Soup would be nice. Thank you." She stood up, steadying herself with one hand on the wall, then followed Beatrice out to the kitchen.

· * * * ★ ★ ★ * * · ·

Beatrice, The Island, 1977

Beatrice recognized the effort Anne made to speak normally, to be courteous, to function. It wrung her heart with pity. As she sat across from Anne at the table, spooning up chicken noodle soup, she wished there were something concrete she could do to help.

Anne said, "I'm intrigued that you don't cook. You have such a nice kitchen."

"Nothing to do with me," Beatrice said with a chuckle. "I bought this place mostly furnished. I never learned to cook because our housekeeper didn't allow me in the kitchen."

"You had a housekeeper?" Anne raised her eyebrows as she reached for a saltine to crumble into her bowl.

"My mother died when I was small, and my dad was a busy doctor. Mrs. O'Reilly cooked and cleaned for us. She was a character, I must say, but her food was good."

"I had a part-time housekeeper and cook after I was married, but that was James's idea. I only used her when we were entertaining. I love to cook. Actually—" Anne's cheeks turned a faint pink. "Actually I wanted to be a chef when I was young, a real chef, Cordon Bleu training, the pleated hat, all of it. My mother used to watch Julia Child on television, so I thought—but my father said only men could be chefs."

"Not true, obviously, as Julia Child proved."

"I know." Anne laid her spoon down. "Many things my father told me weren't true. By the time I was a teenager, I understood that, but I was too afraid of him to say anything. I wanted to go to

Paris to school, and instead I went to the girls' college he wanted me to attend, studied what he thought would be best for me."

"And what was that?"

Anne's cheeks grew even rosier, and she fiddled with her spoon. "It's a cliché. Home economics."

Beatrice smiled. "It is, rather. But at least it let you take some cooking courses, I hope?"

"Yes. Some." Anne picked up her spoon again with an air of deliberately turning the conversation. "Beatrice, we've talked about me all morning, but I haven't forgotten you're facing your own problems."

"That's kind," Beatrice said. "But unlike you, I'm responsible for my own predicament."

"It's not as if you did it on purpose."

"In a way I did, though. I chose to take the drug, and I liked it, at least at first. I should have realized the changes it was making in me, but I liked those, too. At first," she repeated mournfully.

"We're opposites, aren't we?" Anne mused, dabbing at her soup with her spoon. "You're independent, accomplished, even—what's the right word? Assertive, I think. You're not pliant, the way I am. Submissive."

"My dad taught me to think for myself."

"My father taught me I wasn't capable of thinking for myself. That I should let him, or my husband, do it for me." She didn't sound resentful. She sounded resigned.

"An entire postwar generation of women were told the same. That women's place was in the home, and the husband's place was in the office. So many women who worked in factories during the war years were sent home so men could have their jobs."

"Things are changing, though, aren't they? Thanks to braver women than I."

"But you have been brave, Anne. You're here, aren't you? Not shut up in a sanatorium? That's bravery." Beatrice pushed her chair back and stood up. "Let's go sit by the fire, and you can tell me about your dream."

Anne gathered up the bowls and spoons, and before Beatrice could tell her to leave them in the sink, she was washing them, propping them in the rack, wiping down the counter. She dried her hands on the towel and hung it up neatly before following Beatrice into the living room.

The fire blazed up with a fresh log. Beatrice handed the psychedelic afghan to Anne and sat as before, at the end of the sofa. "Dreams can tell us a lot," she mused, gazing into the yellow flames. "But only you can uncover what your dream means. It may help to have guidance, but the real understanding is up to you."

"It was just a nightmare. I don't think it meant anything."

"You don't think nightmares are dreams?"

"I suppose they must be. But aren't they just my imagination out of control?"

"Maybe. Or maybe the dream is trying to release something your conscious mind tries not to see."

"I don't think so. It was scary, yes, but it seemed random. Just something triggered by our earlier conversation."

"What did we say?"

"Not you. Me. I told you about James's first wife, the one who went back to England. I haven't mentioned her in ages. He got angry if I did, furious. I learned to avoid the subject, but somehow telling you about Glenda brought on the nightmare. Sleeping in the daytime does that, don't you think?"

"Sometimes." Beatrice kicked off her shoes and tucked her feet underneath her, settling in to listen. "Tell me about it. About the nightmare."

"It was silly. I've never met her, after all, just saw one photograph."

Beatrice watched Anne's face, trying to focus on her eyes. She couldn't shut out the shadows wavering around her, but she set her jaw and told herself she would have to tolerate them.

Anne said, hesitantly, "Well. If you really want to hear it…"

"Of course I do."

Anne blew out a breath. "I dreamed I was in my house in Oak Hill, just Benjamin and me, so it must have been daytime. There was something at the back door. That door is glass, the kind that slides open, leading to a patio. There was a shadow beyond the glass, something weird and sort of shimmery. Very dark. The doors slid apart, and there it was." She shuddered. "I could tell it was a woman, but it looked like a bad photographic negative, dark instead of light, and blurry. I couldn't see her face, because her hands—her hands were up as if she thought someone was going to strike her—"

Anne paused suddenly, her gaze unfocused. "That's probably because of what I told you James did. He hit me before I could get my hands up to stop him."

"That would make sense."

"I was afraid to try to close the glass doors. I tried to grab Benjamin, but my arms wouldn't work, and I couldn't hold him. Then she sort of fell on him, or over him, and he disappeared. It was like watching him get swallowed up by a monster. I tried to scream, but nothing came out. That is, just enough came out to wake me up." She wrapped her arms around herself, shaking her head. "I told you it didn't make any sense. Just a nightmare."

Beatrice said, "Sometimes nightmares have their roots in the subconscious. It could be that you associate what happened to you when James struck you with your wish to protect Benjamin. Perhaps—" She stopped midsentence, her mouth still open. Her stomach turned over, and her gorge rose in her throat.

The phantasm of the night before appeared swiftly, unexpectedly, behind Anne, as if it had been called. It wavered in the waning afternoon light, contrasting with the shades Beatrice was accustomed to. The smell, that awful putrescence, filled the room. Worse, the sense of terror gripped her so that she could hardly draw a breath.

Anne, staring at her, whispered as before, "Beatrice? What is it?"

Beatrice raised a hand to her cheek and found that it had gone ice-cold. "It's back. It's like—it's like nothing I've seen before."

"It's still there?"

"It is. I'm afraid of what it means."

"What? What do you think it means?"

Beatrice blurted, "I think it means I'm losing my mind."

24

Beatrice, San Francisco, 1976

BEATRICE REACHED A point where she couldn't walk the San Francisco streets without tears streaming down her face at the sorrow and pain emanating from the people she passed. It was slightly better with her private patients. She could do something to help them, but every appointment left her drained. Twice she fled the clinic, her emotions out of control. She couldn't socialize with the few friends she had or with Mitch's friends from the hospital. Mitch withdrew further and further from her, making excuses to work late, taking extra shifts. Hiding. She understood. He was protecting himself.

It did no good to pretend she didn't see his ghost, his nonna. Others joined her, the shades of unhappy patients, frightened ones, angry ones, sad ones. She tried to pretend she didn't see them, struggled to shut them out, but it was no good. She couldn't do it, and Mitch knew she couldn't do it. He watched her expression change when she looked at him, and he grew more wary and frustrated by the day.

"I can't live like this," he finally told her. It was November, and their misery was mocked by the red and green holiday lights glimmering gaily through the foggy San Francisco night.

"Mitch—" Beatrice began, but then didn't know how to go on.

When he had come home that evening, a half-dozen ghosts of every color trailed him. Another, pale and shivery in the background, made her heart clutch with anxiety. It was her own, generated by his worry for her, his anger over what she had done, his grief at the destruction of the life they had built together. It was terrible. She pressed her hand to the base of her neck, trying to ease the ache that swelled there, that closed her throat so she could barely speak.

Mitch made a halfhearted attempt at dinner, but neither of them could eat more than a few bites. Beatrice lit a candle and turned off the lights over the table, but the relief that gave her was too little and came too late.

"Every time you look at me," Mitch said bitterly, "I see your pain. I dread walking in the door, because I know what I'll see on your face."

"I'm sorry," she said weakly, as she had said dozens of times.

"I want to fix it," he said, staring at his plate. "I want to cure you. I want to prescribe something, but I have no earthly idea what it would be. And to tell the truth, sometimes I'm not even sure—" He broke off and dropped his fork against the china.

"You're still not sure you believe me," she finished for him.

"Are you guessing about that?" He lifted his eyes to her, and her heart quivered at the familiar shine of the candlelight in his round glasses.

"No," she said, very quietly, dropping her gaze to her plate. "Not guessing."

"One of your feelings." It was not a question.

"I'd rather not talk about it, because you won't believe that, either."

"I'm trying, Bea."

"I know. I've tried as best I can to explain it to you. I wish there were a way to reverse it, to undo what I did, but I haven't found it." She added, lamely, "Yet." It wasn't enough.

He was silent for a time, taking off his glasses, rubbing them on his napkin. Finally he said, "What are we going to do?"

For a long moment, she couldn't answer him past the choking knot in her throat. She was afraid she would sob, and that wouldn't help. When she finally swallowed the knot away, she managed to say, "I think I have to leave the city."

She did her best not to see the relief on his face, and he did his best to hide it. He said, halfheartedly, "Can't you try—something? Anything?"

"I don't know what it would be."

"But surely you don't have to leave permanently. There's the clinic—"

"Which I can't bear to go into."

"You could talk to a doctor."

"I am talking to one."

"I mean a psychiatrist."

"It won't help. I might as well see a palm reader."

A tense, unhappy silence stretched through the dimness, until Mitch said in a hoarse voice, "Will you come back, Bea?"

She looked at him then, and she thought she could feel her heart break in her chest. "I don't know, Mitch," she whispered. "I just don't know."

When they said goodbye late in December, Christmas trees still sparkled behind lace curtains up and down the street, and carols drifted out of open shop doors and half-closed windows. As Beatrice packed the last of her things, Mitch spent the afternoon cleaning the already clean kitchen, then reorganizing the pantry cupboard, deliberately avoiding the sight of her filling boxes and closing her suitcase. He didn't look at her until the moving van came, was loaded by the driver, and left.

She closed the door behind the driver and turned with her back to it. Mitch emerged from the kitchen and stood with a kitchen towel in his hand, looking at her, his dark eyes hooded behind his round glasses. He said, "You don't have to go, Bea. We'll figure it out."

"How?" she said. She wanted to go to him, to hug him, but they were both on the knife edge of losing control, and he would hate that. *She* would hate that.

For these last days, their pain had been like a houseguest they couldn't get rid of, a presence that lurked in corners, ruined dinners, poisoned their evenings. She had barely been outside the house in a month. Walking among strangers was excruciating. It was as if she came face-to-face with all the sorrows of the world, the pain and loss, the tragedy, the fears. It seemed that feelings of joy and peace and contentment created no ghosts. Only the worst of emotions had that energy, and they left her shaken and sick.

She had resigned from the clinic and closed her home office, though it was heartbreaking having to call her clients and tell them. One teenaged girl cried, and Beatrice came perilously close to weeping herself. She referred all her patients to other therapists, telling both patients and counselors that a personal issue had come up. She sensed the curiosity in her colleagues, but no one pressed her to explain.

Mitch dropped his gaze, twisting the dish towel in his hands. "This feels so final. I know you're miserable—"

"I'm making *you* miserable," she said. Mitch's ghosts wavered behind him, shades of blue and black and charcoal, a multilayered shadow. Beatrice's throat ached unbearably, and she had to look away. In a voice that cracked with sorrow, she said, "I'm getting worse, Mitch. This is all I can think of to do."

It was Mitch who closed the distance between them. He wrapped his arms around her and pulled her close.

She pressed her face into his shoulder. "I'm sorry," she said, for the hundredth time. "I'm so sorry."

He said, "I love you, Bea." His voice broke, and he tried to hide it with a cough.

"I love you, Mitch." Beatrice shed two painful tears against his jacket. She tried to memorize the feel of him, the warmth of his body, his chin against her head. He took a long, unsteady breath, his chest expanding against hers, then retreating as he exhaled, leaving a chill in the air between them. He stepped back, and a chasm yawned between them as he clenched his jaw and gazed at her, helplessly shaking his head.

The taxi arrived moments later. As she climbed into it, Mitch's eyes glittered behind his glasses, and his ghosts intensified behind him, shuddering with emotion and pain. Beatrice watched him as the taxi carried her away. At the last moment she blew him a kiss. If he saw it, he gave no sign.

· · ★ ★ ★ ★ ★ ★ · ·

Beatrice, Seattle, 1977

She took the Coast Starlight from San Francisco to Seattle, riding the entire way inside her sleeping car in order to encounter as few people as possible. She overtipped her porter, whose name was Roderick, asking him to bring her meals from the dining car.

She thought that would bring her relief from the flood of emotions that swept from the crowd of people sharing the train with her. It didn't.

Roderick was almost the only person she saw during the journey, but a crowd of ghosts followed him, so many tragic figures she thought she might as well have braved the dining car. There were at least three women—a mother, perhaps? Grandmothers? Of course she didn't see details of them, only impressions, but their sadness was palpable. There seemed to be half a dozen workworn men emanating exhaustion and despair. There were children, three of them, tiny clouds of blue and indigo and violet, who came and went depending on the time of day, and made her feel anxious and afraid. All these people, she knew, Roderick carried with him, worrying about them, grieving for them.

Worse, she intuited Roderick's thoughts. She sensed his worry about one of the children, still waiting for a promised Christmas gift. She was certain, as she handed him her tips, that he was adding them up, trying to project the final amount. She had the impression it had something to do with one of his ghosts, an elderly man who appeared to be ill. Even when Roderick withdrew, sliding the sleeping car door shut behind him, the miasma of unhappiness remained.

She couldn't wait for the trip to end.

When she detrained at King Street Station in Seattle, she wore the darkest sunglasses she possessed, despite the gloominess of the weather, hoping to block out the ghosts. It was the first day of the brand-new year, and the train station was crowded with people returning home after the holidays, accompanied by their sorrows and worries and fears. Beatrice flagged a taxi to transport her to the first of the ferries that would ultimately deliver her to the island and collapsed into the back seat in exhausted silence.

By the time she walked down the ramp from the last ferry, she was too weary even to be startled at the sight of a nun, an orange safety vest over her sweeping brown habit, operating the ferry ramp. She dragged her suitcase up the slope, past a tiny store with a soda machine and newspaper stand outside the door. She checked the real estate agent's directions again, finding the landmarks he had mentioned, then turned to begin the hike to her cottage. She had bought the house without seeing it. In her haste and need, she had placed her trust in the pictures and the agent's promises.

Mitch had advised against the purchase, but Beatrice was desperate. She had spent the remains of her inheritance from her father on it. The agent had sent her romantic descriptions of the solitude and beauty of the island. Aside from the little store, there were virtually no amenities. There was not even a taxi service. There was a tiny schoolhouse, a small part-time library, and not much else. It had seemed perfect for Beatrice's purposes.

"You'd better not get hurt," Mitch had said. The agent's sentimental descriptions had failed to move him. "That island has no hospital. There's no clinic, no doctor of any description."

"I know," she had answered. "I'll be careful."

"I don't think this is the best choice you could have made, Bea."

"I know," she said again, too sad to argue.

A damp January wind whipped the ends of her hair as she climbed toward her new home. Around her, stands of evergreen trees dripped moisture, and small, drab birds she didn't recognize flitted through the wild rhododendrons that spilled along her path. The silence was underscored by the sound of the sea off to her left and the occasional rattle of tree branches overhead, disturbed by a gust of wind. Though her arm burned from the weight of her suitcase and her feet ached with cold, she felt more at peace than she had in months, soothed by solitude. Lonely, but she had expected that. She missed Mitch with a sharpness she hoped would pass in time. At least the ache of her heart was all her own, not the borrowed suffering of strangers.

She was considering stopping to rest despite the cold when the path abruptly led out of the trees and into a clearing where, about five hundred feet on, perched her new house.

It was smaller than she had thought it might be, but its setting was lovely, and she felt a jolt of anguish that she couldn't share it with Mitch. She lugged her suitcase up the three steps to the porch and tried the door. As promised, it was open. She dragged her suitcase over the sill and took three more steps, stopping to take in the well-appointed kitchen, the short bar and the dining room beyond, and an archway leading to the living room. It was freezing in the cottage, but a small woodstove in the living room beckoned. When she reached it, she found that the real estate agent had thoughtfully left it stocked with wood and kindling. A box of long matches rested on the iron hearth beneath.

The movers had come and gone, placing her furniture, for the most part, as she had directed. She would need to make up the bed, order groceries, and eventually restock the woodpile, but those chores would give her things to do, keep her busy, distract her from the sea change that had disrupted her life.

She was standing at the kitchen bar, reading the pile of papers the real estate agent had left for her, when she heard a low, insistent sound from outside. She knew that sound. She hadn't heard it in years, not since her girlhood.

She whirled and stared through the half window in the door leading out to the porch. Just at the bottom of the steps stood a petite, wide-eyed cow. A Guernsey, if she recalled correctly, golden brown and small. The cow lowed again and blinked her long eyelashes.

Behind her, another cow appeared, tall and rangy, white with black splotches. Her lowing was louder, deeper, more of a honk than a moo.

Beatrice looked down at the sheaf of papers in her hand and saw a note paper-clipped to a list of telephone numbers: *Hay in the barn for the cows. They need to be milked twice a day.*

"Cows?" Beatrice said aloud, glancing back at the creatures awaiting her. "No one said there would be cows."

Mitch would find this riotously funny. She wished she could call and tell him.

25

Anne, The Island, 1977

ANNE WATCHED BEATRICE'S eyes stretch wide and visible goose bumps rise on her neck. She twisted to look behind her. She couldn't see anything, but there was no doubt that Beatrice did.

She whispered, "What does it look like?"

"Like your nightmare." Beatrice spoke in a low, guttural voice. "Just as you described it."

"Does that mean—do you think you picked it up from me?"

"You're asking me if I think it's not real."

"I'm not sure what I'm asking. I mean, you see something I can't—I don't know—"

"It's gone now." Beatrice turned her face toward the view of the water. The slanting winter sun stole the color from her face. "And I can't answer you." She jumped up to begin a restless movement about the room. "If it's not real, then I'm getting worse." She stopped by the windows, one hand on a wall beside the glass, the other pulling her sweater closer around her. "There's something else," she said. "I don't suppose your dream was like this, but both times I've seen this—whatever this is—there's an awful smell."

"A smell?"

"It's terrible. The smell of rot, of decay—dead things."

"That wasn't in my dream."

"No. And I haven't experienced it before, with the other—phenomena." Her shoulders slumped, and her voice trembled a little. "I suppose I'm hallucinating. I don't know why there should be a smell associated with a hallucination, unless the drug..." She tucked her chin as she blew out a despairing sigh. "Obviously, I'm not better. I'm worse."

"I'm so sorry." Anne found she was shivering, not so much from the cold but from the eeriness pervading the cottage. "I wish I could..." She let the sentence trail off, uncompleted. What could she do, after all? She was a virtual stranger, and Beatrice's experiences were—well. *Weird* hardly covered it.

She pushed the afghan aside and went to kneel by the stove. Gingerly, taking up the oven mitt she had seen Beatrice use, she opened the glass door and pushed two fresh chunks of wood into the flames.

Beatrice didn't seem to notice. She spoke so softly it was as if she were speaking to herself. "The things I see, the ones I call ghosts, are real enough, at least to me." She lifted her arm to rub a spot off the window with the sleeve of her sweater. "They've proven to me that whatever their composition might be, the emotions are real. Relevant. If I could have dismissed them as figments of my imagination, believe me, I would have done that. Long ago."

Anne wanted to say something supportive. She didn't want to believe she was alone in a cottage with someone whose mind was deteriorating. She knew nothing of hallucinations or what caused them. She said, "I—I think I understand."

Beatrice leaned against the window frame. "It appears I'm beginning to see things that aren't connected to anyone, or anything."

"But this thing you thought you saw, or you *did* see—couldn't it be connected to me?"

"Maybe." Beatrice turned from the window. "More likely, it was never there at all."

"And the others? My ghosts?"

"They're still there. They'll always be there, unless we can do something to help you."

Anne got to her feet, careful not to brush against the glowing stove. "I don't know what it would be," she said.

"You could go back for your son. Get a lawyer, apply for joint custody."

Pain rose again in Anne's chest, and her hands trembled anew. "All I want in the world is to have my son with me, but if I go back, James will shut me away. That won't help Benjamin, and it would be the death of me."

Beatrice nodded, with visible effort. "I'm not giving up."

"I'm grateful for that, especially since you're clearly upset."

Beatrice's lips twisted. "We're a pair, aren't we?"

Anne wanted to smile at that, perhaps laugh a little, but she couldn't. With a catch in her voice she said, "We are indeed."

Beatrice's glance flicked toward the door. "Headlights coming up the road. Probably one of the sisters with the grocery order."

Anne saw the beam of headlights glance through the trees just as Alice lowed from outside the barn. A second later, Dorothy added her fractured baritone moo. "Your girls are calling you."

"Yes." Beatrice moved to the peg beside the door where her coat hung above her boots. "That's Mother Maggie's station wagon. Could you give her a hand while I do the milking?"

"Of course." Anne went to open the door. She saw Beatrice, before she went through, cast an uneasy glance over her shoulder. Anne couldn't help looking once more, too, sharing her apprehension. Again, there was nothing.

Mother Maggie, wearing a heavy coat over her habit, was lifting a box from the back of the station wagon. Anne went down the short stair to greet her and took the grocery box from her hands.

Once they reached the warmth and light of the kitchen and Anne had set the box on the counter beside the sink, Mother Maggie beamed at her. "You're staying on with Beatrice."

"I am for a time, yes. It's so very kind of her to ask me."

"It could be good for you both," Mother Maggie said.

Anne made herself produce an uncertain smile. She hoped it was true.

She began unloading the grocery box, lifting out a package of hamburger, a head of lettuce, a cucumber, a rather dispirited tomato, a package of cheese, and a box of crackers. There were two bottles of wine at the bottom, which gave her a craving so strong she had to brace her hands on the counter.

"Are you all right?" Mother Maggie said. She was standing on the other side of the bar, frowning through her heavy glasses.

"I'm fine," Anne said, trying to sound as if she meant it. She still had the hollow feeling that none of this was real. It was as if she were an actress playing a tragic part, speaking lines she had not written, walking through a set she had not designed. She thought if she knocked a wall down, she would find nothing but emptiness beyond, the remnants of her real life lost in the darkness.

Mother Maggie said, "The sisters of the motherhouse wrote to ask about you, Anne. I let them know you had arrived safely. They asked me to tell you you're in their prayers, and they hope you're at peace."

Anne wrapped her arms around herself. It didn't help. She trembled no matter how hard she hugged herself. She was sure her peace had been shattered forever by the awfulness of her final day in Oak Hill. A wave of pain swept through her, and she suppressed a groan.

· · · · · ★ ★ ★ ★ · · · ·

Anne, Oak Hill, 1976

She had been told she didn't need a lawyer. James said it, as did her father, and her mother didn't argue. There was no courtroom, no public argument, no chance to explain herself. James himself escorted her into the judge's chambers, leaving Benjamin with her parents on the hard wooden benches in the hallway outside. James's hand on Anne's waist no doubt looked solicitous, his somber expression full of concern for her. Anne wanted to scream at her parents, at the clerk, at the judge, that it was all an act, a pretense, but she didn't dare. She had no doubt that would only make things worse, and she still had hopes for a fair resolution. Surely if she was quiet, was submissive, everything would work out in her favor. Wasn't that what they had all said all along?

James's fingers were poised above the narrow belt on her wool dress. Those fingers were capable of a vicious pinch if she said or did something he didn't like. The grave line of his mouth and the lowering of his eyebrows didn't hide the triumph in his eyes. He was sure he had won.

She had begged him the night before not to do this. "What can I do, James? How can I show you—prove to you—"

And her husband, so solemn and sorrowful today, had laughed at her. He never laughed except over drinks with his friends, and this laugh was cold, devoid of humor. "It's already over," he said. "Tomorrow is just a formality. You've proved you're unfit."

"But I'm not!"

They had been in the dining room, but not seated. They had not dined together in weeks. They faced each other across the shining hardwood table with its centerpiece of scarlet Christmas candles and a white poinsettia in need of water. She had bought the poinsettia after Thanksgiving, trying to follow traditions, to do things the way James liked them. She had struggled to salvage what she could of their life together. It had been no use.

He said with relish, "You were drunk, Anne. You put Ben in the car and drove when you were drunk. You're lucky he wasn't killed, or you'd be in jail."

"I wasn't—that's not fair! The Valium—"

"Valium and alcohol."

"You *hit* me! You knocked me down, blacked my eye, you—you—"

He raised his eyebrows and tilted his head. She knew that gesture. She had sat in his courtroom once or twice, and had seen him use it on more than one witness, more than one defense lawyer. "Your own fault, Anne. You pushed me too far. You should have known better."

"I didn't push you! You're twisting things, and I—"

He threw up a hand. "Enough. There's no point. I've made up my mind."

"You've made up *your* mind! What about mine? What about Benjamin, who needs his mother? You can't be so cruel!"

His face went still, in that way she knew so well, and his voice dropped. "I can do whatever I want, Anne. Don't you know that by now?" He leaned toward her, ever so slightly. In an even deeper voice, he repeated, "Whatever. I. Want."

Her voice went high with panic. "James, why? Why are you doing this? You married me, you must have cared for me at one time! What changed?"

"Cared?" he said, as casually as if he were talking about what to have for dinner. "I wanted you, Anne. That's not quite the same as caring. I don't want you anymore, as it happens."

"James. Please. You can't take Benjamin away from me." She didn't want to cry, didn't mean to, but tears sprang to her eyes, dripped down her cheeks. She knew her mouth was crumpled, making her look ugly.

James started out of the dining room, saying over his shoulder, "I've told you a hundred times. My son's name is Ben." He left her standing in their elegant dining room, sobbing helplessly, while he went upstairs to bed.

The next morning, he escorted her into the judge's chambers, the judge he had selected himself, to hear her predetermined fate announced. She sat on the edge of a deep leather chair and listened to the judge deem her unfit to care for her own child. She didn't cry again. She didn't speak at all. She stared helplessly, hopelessly, at the man announcing the ruin of her life.

He didn't meet her eyes even once. He sat behind his enormous black desk, rows of law books framing his head, and read from the papers before him. Occasionally he looked up at James as if for approval, but otherwise he kept his head down, reading in a monotone, pronouncing his decision in a voice completely without affect.

It was over within minutes. There were no questions. There was no discussion. James opened the door, and Anne stood, walked through it, and went ahead of him down the cold granite stairs to the hallway where her parents waited with Benjamin.

James gave her five minutes to say goodbye, and it was clear her parents thought he was being magnanimous. Her mother had told her, in a frigid tone on the telephone, that she would care for Benjamin each day, and James would pick him up and take him home each night.

Anne had said nothing.

Phyllis had pressed her. "You do understand? We have no choice in this matter."

Anne didn't answer.

"Anne! We're making the best of an impossible situation. You've let yourself go, drinking and drugs, and this is what happens. It's generous of James to pay for the sanatorium. Maybe one day you'll feel better, and he'll take you back."

Anne finally broke her silence. Her voice was so cold, so distant, she hardly recognized it as her own. "Mother. James has no intention of taking me back. Can't you see that? He has no intention of ever allowing me out of the sanatorium."

"Now, that's not true, Anne! Why would you say such a thing? Your husband is a fine man, doing the best he can in a difficult—"

Anne had hung up the phone, gently, carefully, as if it might break. Or she might.

She spent her five minutes with Benjamin trying to explain, trying to say something that would comfort a five-year-old when he realized his mother wasn't coming home. She saw in his eyes, those vivid blue eyes so like her own, that he knew it was good-bye. He would never understand why. He was a smart boy, wise beyond his years, but he was only five. There were no words to comfort him.

In the end, she simply hugged him, holding his small, warm body as close as she could, burying her face in his hair, kissing his cheek, whispering her love.

When James pulled him away, she let him go without resisting. It would do no good for Benjamin to be subjected to a scene, and it wouldn't change the outcome. It nearly destroyed her to see how stiff he was in James's unfamiliar arms. James never hugged him. She had never seen James kiss his son. How could her parents not see how fearful Benjamin was of his father?

The car James had arranged to take her to the sanatorium was waiting. Her parents and James stood on the steps of the court-house, watching her get in, neither waving nor calling to her. She looked back once, but having seen the bereft expression on Benjamin's face, she couldn't look again.

She had packed the single suitcase she was allowed at the sanatorium with the greatest care. She had given up fighting James. She had made no argument in the judge's chambers. She had abandoned any attempt to get help from her parents.

Instead, she had laid her plan in the painful darkness of the night.

Beneath her expensive, quietly stylish dress, she wore her most comfortable boots. She carried her camel's-hair overcoat over her arm. When the driver left her at the door, setting her suitcase at her feet, she thanked him, tipped him, then watched until he drove away. No one came out to meet her. She was supposed to check herself in, to support the illusion that she was entering the sanatorium voluntarily.

Her mouth dried with anxiety as she glanced swiftly past the manicured lawns and shrubberies of the grounds, searching for the walking path she felt sure must be there. Her heart fluttered with anxiety until she spied it. When she found it at last, she picked up her suitcase, shouldered her handbag, and set out toward it. She didn't run, though she wanted to. She walked as quickly as she dared, hoping not to draw attention to herself.

James had chosen a sanatorium that happened to be less than a mile from the motherhouse of a small order of Catholic nuns, sisters devoted to service. Either it was the only bit of luck Anne had had in months, or her prayers had produced one small blessing. Once out of sight of the main building of the sanatorium, she left the path to sidle between a small boxwood and a dwarf forsythia that caught at her skirt and ran her stockings. She pushed through the shrubbery and found herself on a quiet residential street. The road she needed was only a block away. Half an hour later, she was knocking at the door of the motherhouse, a comfortable brick structure that looked more like her own house than a monastery.

A brown-robed, white-haired nun came to the door in answer to her knock. Anne put her suitcase down, pressed her palms together, and said, "Sister. I come begging sanctuary."

Anne, The Island, 1977

While she had been lost in the memory of that awful day, apparently Mother Maggie had still been speaking.

Anne said, "I'm so sorry. What did you say?"

"The motherhouse. The sisters there asked if they could do anything further for you."

"Oh. I—I assume they would never tell anyone where—"

"Where you are? Of course not. Sanctuary means sanctuary."

Anne nodded. "Thank you. And if you write back, please tell the sisters I'm grateful for their prayers."

Beatrice returned at that moment, having made faster work of the milking than usual. As she poured warm, foaming milk through the strainer, Mother Maggie told her, "Our sisters sent a casserole to thank you for your hospitality to Anne. Just tuna, because we don't eat meat, but it smells lovely. I'll go get it."

As she went back to the station wagon for the casserole, Anne said, "I've put the groceries away. It seems dinner has come to us, though."

"Perfect," Beatrice said. "I'll start the oven to warm the casserole. Why don't you open one of those bottles?"

Anne tried to disguise her eagerness as she applied a corkscrew to a bottle of pinot noir, not rushing, twisting it steadily, deliberately. Its label featured an evergreen grove above a rocky cliff and a white-capped surf below. Local, she thought. She told herself to take her time and actually taste it.

She drew the cork and laid it aside, leaving the bottle where it was on the counter. She made herself wait for Beatrice to suggest she pour the glasses, then did it with care, the proper five ounces, barely half a wineglass full.

When she finally allowed herself a sip, she imagined the alcohol slipping down her throat to ease the ache in her chest, to calm the firing of her nerves that made her hands tremble, to let her take a deep breath without feeling as if it would turn into a scream. She didn't really taste the wine, although she rolled it on her tongue and tried to savor it. She took two more sips in quick succession, eager for the relief they would bring. It was the best she had felt all day.

26

Benjamin, Oak Hill, 1977

IT HAD BEEN a bad evening. Papa was already cross when he picked Benjamin up at Gramma Phyllis's. He didn't ask questions on the ride home, and when they pulled into the garage, he just pointed at the door to tell Benjamin to go inside. Benjamin had to go back for his backpack, and he saw his father take a paper bag out of the trunk of the car. He hoped it might be dinner, because sometimes Papa bought hamburgers, and once a pizza, but that wasn't it.

He hurried to get through the door from the garage before his father could see him and scrambled up the stairs to leave his backpack on a chair. He carefully hung up his coat. His father hated to see clothes lying on the floor, or on the bed, or anyplace except the closet. There was a rule about it. Benjamin didn't like to look at the closet, even with the light on, so he closed his eyes as he put the coat on a hanger. He put it on the low rail, the one his mother had put in so he could reach on his own.

He knew the rules, so he washed his hands and face and combed his hair before he went downstairs for dinner.

Papa was taking bottles out of the bag and arranging them on the bar. He already had a drink poured, and he swallowed the last of it as Benjamin came in, then refilled the glass from one of the new bottles. He looked down at Benjamin as he loosened his tie. "Are you going to talk to me tonight?"

Benjamin looked at his shoes. He wished he could talk, because maybe Papa would stop being mad. He wanted to talk, to speak the words his father waited to hear, but they were trapped in his throat. He couldn't get them out. Tears pressed against the insides of his eyes, and he scrunched his eyelids to keep them from falling.

"There are places for kids like you," Papa said. His voice was rough, and he smelled like cigarettes. "Kids who have *behavior* problems." He said the word *behavior* sourly, as if it tasted bad. "That's what your teacher says at school. You have *behavior* problems, and we should get you some *help*."

That word sounded sour, too, but Benjamin didn't know why. He didn't know what getting some help would mean.

He didn't dare walk away while his father was speaking to him, even though now he really needed to go to the bathroom. He squeezed his legs together and waited for Papa to tell him what to do next.

"I'm not in the mood to make dinner for a kid who won't talk," his father said. "You're old enough to get something for yourself, Ben. Go on and do it."

The rush of relief made Benjamin worry he wouldn't make it to the powder room, but he did, barely. After he went to the bathroom he washed his hands again, carefully, even though he thought his father had gone into the living room. He could hear the television news on, but he never knew when Papa would try to catch him breaking one of the rules, especially when he was cross.

Benjamin took the loaf of bread from the breadbox and took two slices from the package. He found the peanut butter jar in the pantry and a knife in the drawer. He knew how to make a peanut butter sandwich, because Mama let him make his own, but he needed a plate. Mama always handed down a plate to him, because the shelf was too high, up over the counter beside the sink.

He thought for a moment of just making his sandwich right on the counter, but then there would be crumbs, and Papa might come in and yell at him. He could climb on one of the kitchen chairs, though. Mama didn't like him to do that, because she worried he might fall. But she wouldn't like him to get yelled at, either. She did lots of things to keep Papa from shouting.

He lifted the kitchen chair. It was almost too heavy for him, but he managed to carry it to the cupboard where the dishes were neatly arranged. He climbed up on the chair and opened the cupboard door as quietly as he could. He stood on tiptoe to stretch his hand up and was just lifting a plate from the stack when his father returned.

"Ben!" he thundered. "What do you think you're doing?"

Benjamin started, caught by surprise. His fingers slipped from the plate, and the plate fell from the cupboard to glance off the counter. It hit the peanut butter jar, which fell all the way to the floor and cracked into three jagged pieces. Peanut butter spilled out over the tiles, slowly spreading in a brown, sticky circle.

He would have cleaned it up if he had been given the chance. He often helped his mother by sweeping, and he was really good at finding little pieces of things, but Papa didn't give him a chance. Just as his feet touched the floor, his father's hard hand slapped his face, then gripped his arm and hauled him away from the chair, out of the kitchen, and toward the stairs.

Moments like these had taught Benjamin how bruises happened. Once he was alone in his room, he could already see the bruises on his arm from Papa's fingers, and another bruise developing on his leg. He had banged into the banister as his father dragged him upstairs, too fast for him to get his feet properly under him. There was a red mark on his cheek from the slap, too.

Papa had said, as he pulled him up the stairs, "B-b-be more c-c-careful next time, B-Ben." It was just like the kids at school. He laughed, too, but it wasn't a nice laugh. It was a mad laugh, the kind he had when he said he had a hard day.

At least he hadn't locked Benjamin in the closet.

Benjamin would have liked a peanut butter sandwich, but he had ruined the chance of it by dropping the plate. Gramma Phyllis had put a packet of raisins in his backpack as a snack for school, so he ate those. He put on his pajamas, brushed his teeth, and climbed into bed, though it was too early to go to sleep.

He turned his lamp on the lowest setting and read the last book his mother had given him, a Christmas present. He liked it because it had lots of pictures, but also lots of words, and he could read them all. None of the kids in his kindergarten class could read yet, and they sometimes asked him to read things for them. He always did, hoping they would be friends and not make fun of him, but it was hard, because even when he was reading, he stuttered.

When he finished the book, he turned his lamp off and lay in the darkness, listening to the drone of the television downstairs and the occasional ring of the telephone. He wished he could use the telephone to call Mama. He thought about that, wondering if she had a telephone where she was, and if she was allowed to use it. He sometimes thought she was in jail, and that was why she couldn't come to see him. He guessed Papa put her in jail because she wrecked the car. Papa put a lot of people in jail.

He pulled his covers up to his chin and closed his eyes, trying to picture Mama in his mind, her pretty eyes, her silky hair, her gentle hands. He could manage to see the individual things, but somehow, it was hard to put them all together.

He hadn't meant to cry again, but he found he was doing it anyway. His sobs were small and quiet, like the mewing of the neighbor's kitten. Papa couldn't have heard them over the sound of the television. The program was full of gunshots and loud cars.

He wasn't asleep when the lady came. He knew he wasn't, because he was still crying, wiping his nose on his sheet. He pushed at his eyes with the palms of his hands, trying to dry his tears in case Papa came in.

When he took his hands down, still sniffling, she was there.

Seeing her was restful, even though she smelled funny. She was always quiet, even more silent than he was. She had never spoken a word to him. She was sad, too. She wasn't as pretty as Mama, but she looked as if she might have been, once, if she hadn't gotten so sad, and if she weren't so pale. She was so pale he could see right through her to the Spider-Man poster on the far wall of his bedroom.

He knew she wasn't exactly real, not like he was. He was five, and he knew a lot of things. But it was nice having her there just the same, standing by the foot of his bed. He felt safer while she was there. He felt a little less lonely.

He fell asleep under her silent gaze, and didn't wake until morning.

27

Beatrice, The Island, 1977

MITCH WOULD HAVE prescribed something for Anne's nerves. Beatrice wished she could. She saw how Anne's hands shook as she drew the cork on the pinot noir, how carefully she waited to be asked before she poured the wine, how she struggled to take small sips, to hide how much she needed it. It was cruel to see her suffer so.

She's not your patient, busy Bea. Not really.

She's more than that, Dad. She's my friend.

That's worse.

I know.

She had persuaded Mother Maggie to stay and share their simple dinner, and to accept a tiny bit of wine in her glass. They sat around the dining table, which Anne had set with flatware and napkins, the hot casserole on a trivet in the center. Mother Maggie and Anne both bowed their heads for a brief grace, and Beatrice watched them in respectful silence. Though she didn't participate, she found the moment of stillness restful.

Something small and tender stirred in her heart, making her wonder. Was that vulnerability, or was it courage? She found her fingers on her breastbone, and snatched them down before she might have to explain. She couldn't, because she didn't understand it herself.

The tuna casserole was traditional, familiar to Beatrice from her days of hot-dish socials in her small rural town. It was rich with canned mushroom soup and topped with a layer of crushed potato chips. Beatrice could imagine Mitch's horror at this creation, but it was delicious and filling. Despite the upsets of the past two days, she was hungry.

Beatrice had turned down the lights and lit the thick candle. The comfort food lulled her, as did Mother Maggie's uncomplicated company. After weeks of solitude, it was a pleasure having friendly faces gathered at her table, and their ghosts were nearly invisible in the candlelight.

She drank a glass of wine and poured another to sip as she ate. She told herself to enjoy the moment and to stop thinking about what she had seen, or thought she had seen.

Anne appeared to relax a bit, too, the unsteadiness of her hands easing after she finished her first glass of wine. In her polished way, she began a pleasant conversation about the island, the ferry, and the nuns who ran it. She asked Mother Maggie about the history of the sisters and the little school they taught in. The whole scene was almost exaggeratedly normal.

When the wine bottle was empty, and the casserole dish nearly so, Mother Maggie said, "Well, this was very nice. I'm glad to have a chance to get to know you both."

"It's gotten dark," Beatrice said. "I can ride down with you, walk back."

"Oh, no need. I drive that road all the time. I do have ferry duty in the morning, though, so I should be on my way."

Anne said, "I'll wash the casserole dish and bring it back to you."

"Thank you. There's no rush for that." The nun brushed a crumb from the front of her habit, laid her refolded napkin beside her plate, and started to get up.

Halfway out of her chair, she froze.

Beatrice had already risen, but she stood stock-still, staring at the nun's face. Mother Maggie's eyes had gone wide behind her heavy glasses, and her mouth hung open as she gazed through the archway into the shadows of the empty living room. The only light there was the flicker of the fire from the woodstove.

Beatrice didn't need to turn, to see what had shocked Mother Maggie. She could smell it.

Only Anne, her fingers to her lips, had no idea.

Mother Maggie said, her voice low and reverent, "Oh, my, Beatrice. Did you know your cottage is haunted?"

Relief made Beatrice giddy. It weakened her knees so that she had to sit down again, her hand over her mouth to press back a sound that might have been a groan, or might have been a laugh. She wasn't sure, and it didn't matter, because—she was not the only one to see the specter! Her mind was no worse after all. She was not hallucinating. She was not descending into some drug-induced madness. If Mother Maggie was right, what she had been seeing was a real ghost. A true phantom, a revenant!

"Do you smell it?" she asked Mother Maggie, her voice shaking with emotion.

"Smell it? No. Do you?"

Aware that Anne was watching the two of them, mystified, Beatrice spread her hands in apology. "Anne has heard this already, because I—I've seen this before. And smelled it. The stench is awful."

"Stench?" Mother Maggie said, shaking her head. "No, I don't detect that at all. I just saw a spirit. A ghost, if you will. I have always preferred the word 'spirit.'"

"Is it still there?" Anne asked.

"No," Mother Maggie said. "I only saw it for a moment."

"And the smell is gone," Beatrice added. "As before."

Tentatively, as if she could make it reappear, Anne rose and moved into the archway to peer into the living room. Shaking her head, she returned to the table and sank back into her chair. "I don't see anything."

"Mother Maggie, what did you see?" Beatrice asked. "You're so calm. When I saw it, it was dark and threatening—it frightened me, to be honest. "

"I didn't see that," Mother Maggie said. "It was brief, of course, but clearly a woman. Dark, of course, there in the shadows, but not scary."

"You believe in ghosts, then."

Mother Maggie smiled. "I've been a religious since I was a girl. Of course I believe in ghosts, although 'believe' is not at all the right word. 'Experience' is a better one."

"Experience?" Anne said.

"Yes. I feel the same way about the question of whether I 'believe' in God. I have 'experienced' God, and to call it mere belief would be to deny the truth as I know it. As I feel it, and live it."

"Well, I don't," Beatrice said, with a touch of truculence in her voice.

"Believe in God?"

"Well, I meant ghosts, but... that, too. At least until recently."

"You saw this ghost before?"

"I did. I thought I was hallucinating."

Anne interjected, "Beatrice was worried about that."

"About hallucinating? I can imagine that would be worrisome," Mother Maggie said. "But now that I've seen it, too, you can put your mind to rest!" She beamed through her thick glasses. "Isn't that a blessing?"

Beatrice, despite her lifelong skepticism, was tempted to agree.

Anne said, "Mother Maggie, you seem so comfortable with the idea of ghosts. Or spirits, as you prefer."

"Of course," Mother Maggie said. "My family came over from Ireland during the potato famine and brought their tales of pixies and fairies and shape-changers with them. I grew up knowing spirits were everywhere: in the garden, in the woods, on the riverbank." She smiled at them both, no doubts dimming her bright gaze. "My spirits aren't frightening. They're quite ordinary. Just—the echoes of the living, sometimes more specific than others."

"Specific?" Beatrice said.

Mother Maggie gave a wistful, remembering smile. "The first time I saw a spirit was such a long time ago. I was twelve years old. There was a teacher in my school I was fond of, a Franciscan sister. She'd been there for years, since I was in the primary grades. One night, very late, I woke to find her standing in my bedroom doorway. She was dressed just as I was used to seeing her, in her coif and veil, sandals on her feet, wire-rimmed eyeglasses. I sat up and said something like, 'Sister Mary Anne, what are you doing here?' She didn't speak, but she gave me a little wave, and left. By 'left,' to be clear, I mean that she disappeared."

"Disappeared? As in, vanished?"

"It was dark in my room, but there was light from a night light in the hall. I didn't see her turn and walk out. She was just gone. One minute there, the next not."

Anne asked, "What did you do?"

"I went back to sleep."

"You weren't afraid?" Beatrice asked.

"Oh, no, not in the least. It was Sister Mary Anne. I had no reason to be afraid of her." Mother Maggie gazed absently into the darkened living room. The sea beyond the windows glimmered vaguely in the distance. "You can guess what happened. The next day we heard she had died in the night, peacefully, but unexpectedly."

"Gosh," Anne said.

"I suppose people accused you of imagining it," Beatrice said.

"They probably would have, if I had told anyone. I never talked about it until after I had several other similar experiences." She glanced at their expectant faces. "I don't think you need to hear them all."

"And you were never frightened," Beatrice said.

"No. I was surprised sometimes. I was often startled, as I was just now. But what is there to be afraid of?"

"I don't know," Beatrice answered slowly. "But this—whatever this is that you and I have now both seen—it seems frightening, for some reason. It seems to have some—" She spread her hands. "Some dark meaning. Some awful import." She dropped her hands and breathed a frustrated sigh. "I'm not explaining it well."

"I would like to hear why you think that, though." Mother Maggie leaned forward and spoke in the manner of a pedagogue teaching something important. "In my view, we each have a spirit, distinct from our physical bodies. There's a reason some of us see spirits, although we don't always know what the reason is. Why did I see my grandmother's spirit lift out of her body? I don't know, but I'm glad I did. I was holding her hand, and I watched her fly free after a long period of suffering. It was a moment of pure joy. 'Ecstasy' is not too strong a word for the sense of release I felt, the feeling of relief."

"That's amazing," Anne breathed.

"I saw spirits in churches, too. After I made my vows, stopped eating meat, spent hours in contemplation, I saw any number of them. Now I've seen another. It strikes me as a terribly unhappy one, but it doesn't frighten me."

"Do you think there's a reason for us to see a spirit?" Beatrice asked.

Mother Maggie leaned back again, taking her cross in her hand. Her eyes crinkled at the corners. "Beatrice, I believe there's a reason for everything."

Beatrice tilted her wineglass, watching the dregs swirl at the bottom. "I wish I shared your faith."

"I wish you did, too." It was not a remonstration. It was sympathetic.

"It seems so pointless, seeing a ghost, not knowing why."

Mother Maggie nodded. "No doubt it will seem pointless until the moment you learn what the point is." She sighed as she put her hands on the table and pushed herself up. "Now, I really must say good night. This has been a stimulating evening, but I'm far too late. We can chat again when you bring the milk."

· · · · ★ ★ ★ ★ ★ · · · ·

After Beatrice had seen Mother Maggie off in her car, she paused on the porch to savor the night. The clouds of early evening had cleared, and abundant stars twinkled in their contented, remote way. A waxing moon cast a stripe of silver across the dark water, and the evergreens were quiet in the still air. Beatrice wished Mitch were here to appreciate the beauty of it all.

Of course if Mitch were here, his ghosts would be, too. She was having enough trouble dealing with the ones attached to Anne.

But she wasn't losing her mind! Despite everything, despite having no idea why she was seeing a real ghost, she felt happier than she had in days. A real ghost! The fact couldn't help but change her perspective on—on everything.

When she went inside, she found the kitchen spotless and the casserole dish scoured clean and waiting on the bar to be returned to the sisters. Anne was by the windows in the living room, her profile illuminated by the moonlit ocean, her arms tight around herself. She turned at Beatrice's step.

"You didn't know I had gone to the sisters for sanctuary," she said.

"No. I'm so glad there was someone to help you." Beatrice settled on the end of the sofa and rested her head against the back, feeling suddenly weary.

Anne turned back to the window. She said in a low voice, "I was supposed to check into the sanatorium. Instead, I walked to the motherhouse."

"That was an amazing thing to do."

"It was the only time in my life I defied James. I was afraid of what he would do if he caught me, but I was more afraid that if I admitted myself to the sanatorium I might never come out. I still had hopes of getting Benjamin back."

"How did you manage to get here?"

"The sisters helped me. They got me a bus ticket, and I had some cash. Before all that happened, the fight with James, the car crash, I went to the bank and withdrew all my housekeeping money."

"That was clever."

Anne shrugged. "I don't know about clever, but I did have an intuition, I suppose, that I was going to need it. The money was certainly useful. I took buses, sometimes a train if there was one. The sisters had suggested I come to Mother Maggie because she's so far away from Oak Hill."

"She was expecting you."

"Yes. She didn't know why, though. The sisters are very careful about that sort of thing. They often help women in—well, in my position."

"Abused women, Anne. You were an abused woman."

Anne came to sit on the other end of the sofa, keeping her gaze on the silvery water in its frame of slender pines. "I still have difficulty thinking of myself that way."

"Why?"

Anne's small laugh was one of the saddest sounds Beatrice had ever heard. "Women like me aren't supposed to be battered women."

"It can happen to anyone. To men, too."

"Really?"

"It's very hard for men to admit."

"I can imagine." Anne touched her breastbone, where Beatrice knew by now her little gold cross hung beneath her sweater. "I doubt I'll ever stop being ashamed of it."

"Nothing to be ashamed of. You stood up for yourself, traveled all the way across the country on your own. I'm proud of you."

"You're very kind." Anne dropped her hand from her cross and twisted her hands together. "You know, Beatrice, I agree with Mother Maggie. We see spirits for a reason."

"But you didn't see it."

"I dreamed it, though. I think that counts."

"What do you think the reason is, then?"

Anne turned her pale face to Beatrice. "I think it's a warning. I just don't know what it's warning us about."

28

Anne, The Island, 1977

ANNE WAS GRATEFUL for the peace of the two days following Mother Maggie's visit. Her misery hardly abated, and her yearning for Benjamin would never diminish, but the dream didn't repeat, and she found ways to keep busy around the cottage.

She was aware that her presence still bothered Beatrice. Her hostess did her best not to show it, but when Mother Maggie called to invite them both to attend Mass at the little chapel perched on a wooded slope above the ferry terminal, Beatrice shook her head decisively. "I'm sorry, Anne. I couldn't bear it. Do go without me, though."

Anne did go to Mass when Sunday came. She refused Mother Maggie's offer to pick her up, choosing instead to walk. Beatrice loaned her a heavier coat and a knit cap, and in relative comfort she set out on a cool clear morning for the walk down the hill.

The chapel was rustic, simply adorned with a few primitive-looking icons and half a dozen pews with unpadded wooden kneelers. The nuns were already there when she arrived. Mother Maggie was watching for her from the doorway and waved her in. A handful of other islanders were present as well, and one small altar boy who looked as if he would run away in a heartbeat if he could. Anne felt a twinge of sympathy for him.

The visiting priest was young and rather shy. Anne had to cup her ear to hear his light voice. Still, she was glad to be in a church, especially during Lent. She was accustomed to the heavy stained glass windows, carpeted floors, and thick organ music of St. Michael's, but she didn't miss them. This nearly primitive building, with the rush of the sea and the cries of sea birds replacing the sonorous tones of an organ, seemed a better place to pray.

She gave herself up to listening to the beloved rite and speaking the responses. It was an interesting mix of Latin and English, a bridge between the Mass of her childhood and the revised one of Vatican II. She didn't plan to take Holy Communion, since she had not been to confession, but Mother Maggie gestured to her that it would be okay. When the wafer touched her lips, her tears welled at the familiarity of the gesture, and then again at the taste of the watered wine on her tongue.

On her knees after Communion, the tears fell. The ancient ceremony still touched her, despite the weakening of her faith. She surreptitiously dabbed at her wet cheeks as she got to her feet for the recessional. She shook hands with the priest on her way out of the chapel, and Mother Maggie introduced her to the other sisters before they hurried off to their chores.

Over a cup of coffee in the tiny café, with Petey underfoot, Mother Maggie chuckled over the macaronic service. "We're having it both ways," she said. "Latin, English. It's like our community, still wearing habits though they're no longer prescribed by the church. Too old to change, I think!"

It was true that the nuns were not young. Anne wondered at their lives, the labor of the ferry, the running of the store, teaching in the school. It was a lot of work, but they seemed to enjoy it.

Anne thought she would like to have a job. She would like being part of the working world, earning her own money, being useful.

She watched Mother Maggie bustling here and there in the little store, and decided she would find something to do.

"You should teach me how to do the milking." Beatrice's eyebrows shot up and she stared at Anne in consternation. "I'm serious, Beatrice. I'd like to learn. I'm not used to idleness."

They were seated across from each other at the dining table. The winter dark had already settled over the island, and the only light in the cottage was the candle on the table and the unsteady light from the woodstove. Mr. Thurman had come today to restock the woodpile, and when Anne sensed Beatrice's aversion to seeing him, she had gone out to speak to him in Beatrice's place. It felt good to take at least one thing off Beatrice's shoulders, and she intended to do more.

"It's not necessary," Beatrice said.

"I want to, though. Your cows are so sweet."

"You may not think so if one of them steps in the milk bucket, or slaps your face with a wet tail."

"Could you let me try? I want to help. It feels as if you're stuck with me for a while."

"That's not the way I see it, Anne. But let's see if you can fit into my milking boots."

The boots turned out to be a squeeze for Anne's long, narrow feet, but she didn't say so. She followed Beatrice out to the barn in the early morning, when the dew sparkled on the pine branches and dripped from the eaves of the little barn. The damp air was cold, but the barn itself was cozy, warmed by the bodies of Dorothy and Alice. She had no experience with cows, or really any animals beyond the occasional cat her family had kept, but these two gentle beasts, despite their size, weren't fearsome at all.

Beatrice said, "The tall one with the crooked nose is Dorothy. Alice is smaller, but she's in charge, and she'll let you know that if she gets the chance." She stuffed flakes of hay into the mangers, and the cows eagerly put their heads through the stanchions. "Best to start with Dorothy. She's more forgiving."

Anne was awkward at first, and her fingers began to ache with the unaccustomed movement, but there was something about the chore, the feel of Dorothy's sleek flank against her forehead, the sound of milk ringing in the bucket—when she could make it happen, and not squirt milk onto the floor or onto the cow's legs—that was soothing. She gave over to Beatrice to finish, so poor Dorothy wouldn't be only half empty, but she stood stroking the cow until it was done. Beatrice, seeing her rubbing her fingers, insisted on milking Alice. "Next time will be easier," she said. "Your hands will get stronger."

Anne nodded and pitched in with the cleaning of the barn afterward. She repeated the whole exercise in the evening, feeding, milking, sweeping. She didn't realize until they were back in the cottage, straining the milk and washing the bucket, that the cocktail hour had come and gone, and she hadn't missed it at all.

Beatrice, The Island, 1977

As the days went on and Anne found more and more things to do around the cottage and the barn, the shades that clung to her faded, a little bit at a time. Beatrice tried not to look at them as a rule, but as she watched Anne sweeping the barn, several days after her first milking lesson, she noticed the difference. They were still there. She feared they would always be there, but her unexpected guest was doing just what she would have advised any patient—try to stay active, find things to occupy yourself, exercise.

Anne was still far too thin, and her face held the same haunted expression as when she arrived, but she was making a heroic effort. Beatrice admired her struggle to be resilient, and it made her question herself. Had she tried as hard to manage her demons? She had fled San Francisco. She had left Mitch. Abandoned her patients, the clinic. The comparison with Anne was not a flattering one.

The first two weeks of March had blown in with rain-laden gusts and leaden skies alternating with cool, brilliant sunshine. They learned, as spring approached, that the previous owners of the cottage had planted bulbs, and by midmonth their tentative shoots wriggled up out of the tilled soil. Anne, delighted, named them: crocuses, the first to flower, then the slender stems of daffodils, even some thick-bladed tulips that had survived the winter.

"Those should have been dug up in the fall," Anne said. "But some of them are hardy." One of the tasks she had taken on was weeding the narrow flower beds, clearing space for the flowers to grow. "We'll have to watch out for the deer. They love a tulip salad."

Beatrice noticed the *we*, but she didn't comment. Thinking of the unkempt garden of La Signora, she wrinkled her nose. "I needed you in San Francisco," she said regretfully. "We had roses and a few other flowers, but they were all tangled together. It was a mess."

Anne nodded. "It's a lot of work to keep up a flower garden. It was one thing my mother and I did together that we both liked."

Beatrice couldn't answer. The memory of hearing her mother's dying thoughts flashed through her brain, and the pain of it stole her voice. Perhaps some things, she thought, should be left unremembered.

She was on the porch a week later, sweeping away clumps of pine cones and wet needles deposited by the wind, when the nuns' yellow station wagon rolled up in front of the barn. Dorothy and Alice gave it a brief, incurious look and went back to cropping grass. Mother

Maggie emerged, one hand on her short veil to keep it from whipping in the wind.

"Hi," Beatrice said. "I wasn't expecting you."

"I know." The nun's face was grave, the lines behind her thick glasses drawn more deeply than usual. Beatrice felt a pang of anxiety. "I had to come, though. Something's happened."

"Is everything all right?"

"Honestly, I don't know, Beatrice. Whether it is or not, my community has let Anne down, and I'm heartsick about it."

Beatrice propped her broom against the wall beside the window and straightened, steeling herself against fresh tension. "We need to go talk to her, I gather."

"I think we'd better."

Mother Maggie's steps were heavier than Beatrice had seen them before. She supported herself on the short banister as she came up on the porch. Her other hand clung to her cross. Beatrice said, "I can see you're really upset, Mother Maggie. I'm so sorry."

"I am," the nun agreed. "Very. I'm not sure what to do about this."

They went inside, and Anne met them in the kitchen. "Mother Maggie, how nice," she said, in her courteous way. "Would you like some tea?" She moved automatically to fill the kettle at the sink.

Beatrice said, "Anne, come and sit in the living room. We can have tea in a little bit. Mother Maggie needs to talk to you. Us, I mean."

Anne's voice thinned, a sure sign of tension. "What's happened?"

Mother Maggie's Birkenstocks dragged as she plodded toward the living room. "It's really best if we sit down."

Beatrice had never seen the nun upset. She had always seemed so dependably cheerful. This change of mood gave her an uneasy feeling.

Cool spring sunshine flooded the room, glimmering on the paperweight on Beatrice's desk, picking out the gold lettering on her older books. Beatrice turned her desk chair to face the sofa. Mother Maggie sat at one end, and Anne, her hands visibly beginning to shake, took the other. The afghan was behind her, and she pulled it over her lap so she could wrap her hands in its folds.

Mother Maggie said immediately, without preamble, "I didn't know what forced you to leave your home. When someone is granted sanctuary—well, you know this already."

Anne's voice trembled, too. "But now someone has told you."

"Someone has told me part of it. That doesn't matter. And it wouldn't matter if he had told just me. It's that he told your husband."

Anne's cheeks paled instantly. "Why?" she cried. "Why would someone do that?"

"How did you find this out?" Beatrice said.

"There was a lot of press at the time Anne went to the motherhouse. I know the sisters would never reveal anything, nor would the lay sisters, but there are oblates. An oblate is a lay member of the order, a person who participates in our rituals but doesn't take vows. One of the oblates, I'm sorry to say, was at our Mass here on the island, and he recognized Anne from the newspapers."

"And went straight to James," Anne whispered.

"So I am told. I'm deeply ashamed to say it, but I think he asked for money."

"He probably got it." Anne jumped to her feet, letting the afghan fall to the floor. "I have to leave. He'll find me, put me away, and I'll never see my son again!" The look in her eyes, the expanded pupils, the stretched eyelids, alarmed Beatrice.

"We don't think he knows where you are, Anne, but—well, we're not sure. Your husband is harassing the motherhouse, threatening a lawsuit. He says you're a fugitive."

"He'll sue the order, Mother Maggie. He's a judge. He has a lot of influence, a lot of power. He knows everyone, and people always end up doing what he wants. I need to get off the island before he figures out where I am!"

Beatrice jumped up and crossed to take Anne's trembling arm with her hand. "Don't be hasty, Anne. Let's talk this through."

"You don't know him!" Anne whispered. Her eyelids fluttered. She swayed on her feet, and Beatrice put an arm around her, fearful she was going to collapse. It felt strange to touch her this way, to feel the bony thinness of her torso, the chill of her skin. Her shades shivered behind her, dark blue and lavender and an angry, muddy gray. They made Beatrice's throat ache.

Anne said, "He'll put me in the sanatorium this time, he'll drive me there and lock me up himself, and there will be no one to help me!"

Beatrice coaxed her to sit down again. She retrieved the afghan from the floor and tucked it around her, then went to the cabinet to pour two fingers of brandy. Anne drank the liquor in one swallow. She let her head drop back against the sofa. She closed her eyes, and two thin, exhausted tears slid down her cheeks. Beatrice rescued the glass before it could fall from her nerveless fingers.

Mother Maggie huddled at her end of the couch, her head bowed, her lips moving in silent prayer.

It was the worst possible moment for Alice to begin to moo from the yard. A second later Dorothy's broken-tuba call joined in, a discordant sound that shattered the chilled silence. An unladylike curse sprang to Beatrice's lips, but out of respect for the company, she settled for clicking her tongue. "Mother Maggie, can you stay with Anne? I need to milk those two or they'll never stop."

The nun straightened with an obvious effort. "Of course. I'll stay right here. Where's that brandy, if she needs it?"

"I left the bottle on the table."

Anne didn't move or open her eyes. Her fair hair was spread over the back of the sofa, its gold strands glowing against the dark print. The only sign of her continued distress was the tremor in her hands. They lay palm up in her lap, a posture of surrender. Seeing it wrung Beatrice's heart and infuriated her at the same time.

She did curse then, curses as fervent and fluent as they were silent.

Beatrice started the milking with Dorothy. The placid cow munched her feed of hay and swished her tail now and then, but gently. She was her usual compliant self, barely moving as Beatrice worked as quickly as she dared.

Alice was another matter. She ignored the hay. She shifted her feet, threatening the half-full milk bucket, and her tail flicked back and forth with a vengeance, as if it were summer and she were plagued by flies. Beatrice tried to hurry with her, but the little cow wouldn't stand still, no matter how much Beatrice cooed and pleaded. It took twice as long as it should have to milk her, and it wasn't a thorough job.

Beatrice set the bucket on its shelf before she opened the stanchions, releasing the cows. Dorothy ambled out into the early darkness. Alice pulled her head from the stanchion and faced the door, but she hesitated. At Beatrice's urging, she took a few steps, but they were short, reluctant ones. She finally stopped entirely. She dropped her head and planted her hooves just short of the door.

"What is it? Come on, bossy. Out with you," Beatrice said with impatience. She felt the pressure of needing to be inside, to be with Anne, to make some sort of plan.

Alice refused to budge. Beatrice put a hand on her bony spine and was shocked to find that the cow was trembling. Alice twisted her head to give her a panicked look. Her eyes rolled, showing the whites, and her breathing whistled in her throat.

Beatrice looked around the barn, then peered through the doorway into the dark. She saw nothing that should have frightened the cow.

Animals have reasons, busy Bea. Even if we don't know what they are.

I know, Dad. I'm trying to figure—

The smell hit her then, as suddenly as if someone had blown fetid air into her face. She gritted her teeth against the stench and let her hand run along Alice's knobby spine as she inched forward to look out into the barnyard.

There was only a bit of moon and a few stars to lighten the darkness. The phantom floated against the backdrop of the glowing windows of the cottage. It was more distinct this time, more human. Its terrible eyes flashed in the dark, stark and furious. Its hands—those desperate, defensive hands—rose before its face, palms out. Beatrice could just see the shape of the head, the cloud of dirty, disheveled hair, though the rest of the body was little more than shadow.

Beatrice froze, one hand pressed over her nose, the other gripping the cow's withers. The specter was female. She remembered what Anne had said, that she thought of Glenda Iredale in her nightmare, and now Beatrice understood. She had never seen the photograph, had no idea what the woman looked like, but the impression of a feminine presence was unmistakable.

This specter was connected to Anne, to what was happening to her, to all of them who had become involved. It was responding to the emotions that rocked the cottage. It was answering the threat to Anne.

The phenomenon defied logic, but logic had fled Beatrice's life the first time she put an acid-soaked strip of paper on her tongue.

Alice shook so badly that Beatrice was afraid the cow might fall to her knees. She gripped the poor beast's neck with what she hoped was a steadying hand and forced herself to breathe past the sick feeling in her stomach. She spoke with as strong a voice as she could muster, even as her skin crawled with horror.

"What. Do. You. Want?"

The apparition instantly swelled to twice its size. Beatrice couldn't help stumbling backward, as if the substanceless vision might suffocate her. The mouth stretched wider, a scream without sound. The hands spread, grasping at air. The smell of rot and decay intensified, making Beatrice hold her breath against the choking fumes.

There was no sound at all, anywhere. Even the evening birdsong had fallen silent, as if the whole island were holding its breath.

Then Dorothy gave a long, questioning broken-tuba call. Her fractured baritone resounded against the trees and the stones, splitting the still air with a blast of bovine sound no one could have ignored.

The specter vanished. It took no time, not even the passing of seconds. One instant it was there, looming before the barn door. The next it was gone. The smell disappeared, too, as thoroughly as if it had never been. Beatrice dropped her hand to draw a desperate breath, and she found the air clean once again, fresh with the scents of hay, of cows, of pine and fir and sea. Even the birds began to twitter from the woods.

Alice slipped from beneath Beatrice's hand as she charged out of the barn with a clatter of hooves. She trotted to Dorothy, galloped past her, and disappeared into the cover of the trees. Dorothy executed a ponderous turn and trotted after, her empty udder swinging.

Beatrice leaned against the barn door, weak-kneed with shock and wonder. She drew more deep breaths of the night air, trying to quell the nausea that still quivered under her breastbone.

The door to the cottage opened, and Mother Maggie appeared.

"Are you all right? The cow sounded—I don't know, upset. Does she usually do that?"

Beatrice raised a hand. "I am all right, yes. The cows had a bad moment, and I just—wow. I guess I did, too." She straightened, and when she could trust her knees not to buckle, she started across the yard, then had to turn back for the milk bucket. Mother Maggie waited for her in the doorway, closing the door once Beatrice was up the steps and inside the kitchen.

Anne stood with her back braced against the counter, her arms folded tightly around herself. Her ghosts had intensified again, and she seemed to be surrounded by a dismal halo of murky shadow. She said, "What happened, Beatrice? You look as if you'd—" She stopped, blinking at the irony of the cliché she had been about to utter.

Beatrice carried the bucket to the counter. She reached into the cupboard for the strainer, but she left it on the counter and turned to the nun. "Mother Maggie. You said we see spirits for a reason."

Mother Maggie nodded. "I believe that, yes."

"I've just seen the ghost again. It frightened Alice, and it frightened me, but I think I understand why it's here." She blew out a long, tired breath. "I have a feeling."

29

Anne, The Island, 1977

ANNE PUT THE kettle on, then set about straining the milk, glad to have something to do. She brought tea and a plate of cookies into the dining room, where Beatrice sat at the table, as pale as the milk Anne had just put in the fridge.

"Beatrice," Anne said gently. "Here. Drink some tea and eat a cookie. You need to get your blood sugar up."

"That's good advice," Mother Maggie said. "Then you can tell us what happened."

"I'm embarrassed at how much it scared me." Beatrice picked up the cup Anne had filled and took a sip. Her eyebrows rose at the taste.

"I put brandy in it," Anne said.

"Perfect," Beatrice said, wrinkling her nose in acknowledgment. She took another sip, and her cheeks began to pink a little. "Good grief," she said, rubbing her hand over her eyes. "That was no fun. I thought Alice was going to fall down—and then I thought I was going to be the one to collapse, my knees were shaking so."

Mother Maggie said, "My goodness, whatever did you see?"

Beatrice drained her teacup, and Anne, seeing, half filled it, then retrieved the brandy bottle from the kitchen cupboard. She didn't put any more in, but she left it within Beatrice's reach. Beatrice gave her a weak smile. "Thanks, Anne. This helps." Anne moved the cookie plate closer to her, winning another smile. "I'll eat one. Promise."

"I'll hold you to that," Anne said. Beatrice obediently took a cookie from the plate.

Mother Maggie said, "I knew you two would be good for each other. Isn't it amazing how God puts us where we need to be?"

Anne remembered saying something similar to Beatrice when she first came. It might even be true. Gazing at Beatrice's pallid face, seeing her cheeks grow rosy from the brandy, she had to agree that she and Beatrice were doing well together. It had been a forced relationship at first, and they were very nearly opposites in personality, yet they had developed a friendship. It might have come out of their mutual need, but that didn't diminish it. It had been far too long since she had a friend, especially one she trusted and admired—and liked—as much as she did Beatrice Bird.

Beatrice poured a tot more brandy into her cup and took a sip. "I had finished the milking." Her voice cracked. "Sorry, I'm still—I don't know what I am. Shaken, I guess."

"Take your time," Mother Maggie said, but her eyes were bright with curiosity behind her thick glasses, and she was clearly in no hurry to leave.

"What happened—well, Dorothy went right out of the barn after I milked her, but Alice wouldn't move. She was trembling. I've never felt a cow quiver like that. I looked out to see what was frightening her, and—there it was. Worse than before, bigger, darker. And the smell—" She touched her fingers to her nose, and her lips twisted at the memory.

"The smell," Mother Maggie said, pursing her lips. "How strange that is."

"Are there rules about ghosts?" Beatrice asked.

"Absolutely not," Mother Maggie said. "Everyone's experience is different, I believe."

Beatrice drained her teacup and shook her head when Anne lifted the teapot to offer more. She slid the brandy bottle away from her. "That's not all, I'm afraid."

"There's more?" Anne said. Her hands had steadied as she worked, but now they began to tremble again. She had a hunch she would not like what was still to come.

"Yes," Beatrice said. "God, I can't believe—well, I guess we're already past that. The ghost—the spirit—was right in the doorway to the barn. I didn't know what to do, so I asked it what it wanted."

"You asked it? You mean, the ghost?"

"Demanded, to be blunt. I shouted at it. 'What do you want?'" Beatrice grimaced. "The damned thing blew up to twice its size, and I swear it was screaming at me. No sound, but screaming just the same. I couldn't breathe for the smell, and then Dorothy—well, you heard her." She spread her hands. "The thing disappeared then, and so did the smell."

She looked up at Anne, and then at Mother Maggie. "You believe me, I hope."

"Of course," Anne said.

Mother Maggie nodded. "I never doubted, Beatrice."

Anne said, "So if we see spirits for a reason, Mother Maggie, why is Beatrice seeing this thing? And why did I dream it?"

"Only you can answer that," Mother Maggie said. "It will come to you, if you let it."

Beatrice said, "I don't want to upset you, Anne, more than you already are. This phantom is terrifying, but I'm convinced it's not trying to hurt me. Or you."

"Then what—"

"Remember your nightmare?"

Anne gave a shudder. "I wish I could forget it."

"I have a feeling about why this thing keeps coming back."

"What's the reason?"

"It comes back so we can't forget it. So we won't ignore it."

A chill settled in Anne's stomach. She had the sense that Beatrice's feeling matched her own, as if their thoughts were connected. Horrified, she whispered, "Glenda."

Mother Maggie said, "Glenda? Who's Glenda?"

Beatrice fixed Anne with an intense gaze. "How much do you know about your husband's first wife?"

30

Anne, Oak Hill, 1971

ANNE BRACED HERSELF on the edge of the heavy chest of drawers, balancing the bulk of her pregnant belly. She had been on her knees too long, trying to get the last speck of dust out from beneath the bureau, and as she straightened, her back gave a nasty twinge. She stood for a moment, rubbing it, then wiping the perspiration from her neck and forehead.

It was an unseasonably hot October afternoon. The whole day had been too warm for the chore she had undertaken, but the baby was due in three weeks, and she hadn't finished organizing the nursery. The windows were wide open, but there was no breeze, and the air in the room was breathlessly still. The room smelled of the fresh paint she had applied to the walls, a delicate robin's-egg blue, because she was certain the baby was a boy. The crib lay in pieces against one wall, waiting to be assembled. A white changing table stood in a corner, and the bureau she was working on would hold baby clothes and diapers and receiving blankets. It had already been in the house when she married James, but it was a nice light-colored oak, perfect for a nursery. It was just the right size, and James evidently had no use for it. It had been sitting empty since she moved into the house.

Or so she believed.

She hurried, because it was almost time to start dinner, and James disliked having to wait. She tore open the package of pink-and-blue striped drawer liners and picked up her scissors to cut the sheets to fit. She did the top three, smoothing the vinyl into the corners and pressing it flat to the bottom. She cut the fourth sheet and crouched down to insert it into the last drawer.

She was reaching inside to press the piece of vinyl into the back corner when her fingers encountered something jammed into the back, as if the contents of the drawer had pushed it there. It felt like a piece of stiff paper, crumpled into a ball. She pulled it out and smoothed it against the carpet.

It was a snapshot, one that had been enlarged as if to be framed or to be kept in a photo album. The glossy photographic paper was broken and wrinkled, but not so much that she couldn't make out the picture of an unfamiliar woman's face. Anne lifted it into the slanting sunlight for a better look.

The woman was fair-haired and blue-eyed. She looked a bit older than Anne, but long-legged and slim in slacks and a neat blouse. In fact, she looked a good bit like Anne, or more properly, Anne supposed, she herself looked quite a lot like this woman. The woman was smiling at the photographer, whoever that was, while she smoothed her hair with one slender hand.

Anne set the photo to one side while she finished her chore and then, with a grunt of effort, got to her feet. She retrieved the picture and looked at it for a moment, wondering who this woman was, with her bright hair and pretty smile. It didn't seem right to simply throw the photograph away, and she was curious. Why was this picture abandoned in an empty drawer? Had it been crumpled up deliberately, or was it just forgotten, left behind when the drawer was emptied? She carried it downstairs with her and smoothed it out on the kitchen counter. She would ask James if he knew who this was.

She was stirring cream sauce for the potatoes when James came in from the garage. She put her spoon down to go to the powder room to check her hair and lipstick. She tightened her apron, listening to his movements as he set his briefcase down in the foyer. His heels clicked on the hall tiles as he walked to the living room bar, where he would pour his evening scotch into one of the cut-glass tumblers they had received as a wedding present. By the time he came into the kitchen, she was back at the stove, and she turned to smile at him. "Hi, James. Good day?"

"It was all right." He set his glass on the counter as he loosened his tie. "What's for dinner?"

"Scalloped potatoes, pork chops, green beans."

She expected a grunt of approval, since those were all things he liked. The grunt never came. The photograph she had found caught his eye before he could answer, and as he reached for it, picked it up, glowered over it, she realized she had made a mistake. He set it down with a deliberate movement, and tension rose in the kitchen like a cloud.

"What's this?" he said. His voice had gone hard, and his eyes narrowed.

"Just a picture," she said. "I found it in the bureau in the baby's room."

"That bureau was empty."

"It was, except for that, in the bottom drawer. I thought it must have been forgotten." Hoping the moment would pass, she slid the pan of potatoes into the oven and set the timer with fingers that shook slightly.

"Why did you keep it?"

She felt like one of the defendants in his courtroom, as if no matter what she said, it would be the wrong response. "I don't know," she said. She would have taken an involuntary step backward if she could, but she was too close to the stove. "It didn't seem right to just toss it in the garbage." And then, because surely he must know, she said, "Who is it?"

He crushed the already-creased picture between his hands. "I thought I got rid of everything. You should have thrown it away."

"Is that your wife? Your first wife, I mean?"

"What do you care? She's long gone."

"I know that, James, it's just so odd that I've never seen a picture. You've never told me anything about her except that she left."

"And I'm not going to tell you anything. She's history." He moved to the garbage can and dropped the ruined picture in among the coffee grounds and potato peels.

Tentatively, wishing this could be a moment of real communication, Anne said, "I would like to know, though. It's a part of your life."

"What do you want to know?"

"You were married for—what, eight years? Nine? No children, obviously, but you must have had things in common. What went wrong between you?"

James put his hands on his hips and gazed at her in a way that made clear there would be no sharing of confidences. "It's nothing you need to worry about," he said. "It ended. She left. That's all."

"But you—"

"I don't like to talk about it, Anne. I think I've made that clear. And why should you care? She has nothing to do with you."

"Isn't it natural that I care about it?"

"Hardly. It's obsessive."

"Obsessive?" Anne said, stung. "That's not fair. I came upon the picture by accident."

"What's wrong with you?" he snapped. "I've told you all you need to know. I was married before. My wife walked out, disappeared without a word. Embarrassed me in front of all my friends and colleagues. Even the press asked about her, and that was a nightmare."

"Gosh, I'm sorry, James. I didn't know—"

"Well, now you do. So forget it. Forget *her*, just as I have." He picked up his tumbler of liquor and turned his back. As he walked away, he tapped the trash can, where he had buried the picture, and growled, "I never want to see anything like that again in my house."

Anne, staring at his stiff back, mouthed, "*Our* house," but she was afraid to say it aloud.

She knew more about his first marriage than he realized. She knew his first wife's name because her mother had heard the story, had told her how Glenda Iredale had disappeared one day, just poof! She had, the gossip went, taken all her things and left.

"They say she went back to England," Phyllis had said, on the day Anne was trying on wedding gowns. "That's a good thing for you." She whispered, so as not to be overheard by the saleswoman hovering outside the dressing room. She was helping Anne do up a long row of pearl buttons. "You never have to run into her, or be snubbed by her friends who might be James's friends, too. It's as if he was never married at all! So lucky."

Anne had nodded and wiggled her finger to make her engagement ring flash under the dressing room lights. The sparkle of the big diamond seemed to assure her that she was enough, just as she was. She was going to be the judge's wife. He had chosen her. Loved her, she believed, and she liked her mother's idea. Glenda Iredale leaving without a word, disappearing completely and essentially overnight, made everything seem as if James had never been married before, as if Anne were the first, special, unique.

She forgot all about Glenda Iredale until after the wedding and the brief honeymoon in New York City. She didn't think about her until she moved into James's house. The house was large, elegant, situated in one of Oak Hill's best neighborhoods, where the paved driveways curved between manicured lawns. The generous fenced-in back garden met a carefully preserved greenbelt thick with elms and red maples. The house was a conveniently short drive to the courthouse, and a slightly longer one to the grocery stores and restaurants. It never occurred to Anne, following James's lead in everything, that they might have bought a new house, a different house. A house that would have been as much hers as his.

It was the furniture that reminded her that she was not, in fact, his first wife. The bedroom suite was a heavy, dark wood, and she assumed it had been his own choice. But the dining room furniture was oak, pale and lacy, with cream brocade upholstery on the chairs. The sideboard matched it, with glass doors and carved decorations. The furniture in the living room had similar touches of femininity, sofas in pastel patterns and coordinating upholstered chairs. She never asked to change it. She liked it. She thought Glenda must have had good taste. Once or twice, she wondered if her predecessor regretted leaving her pretty things behind.

The old china and silver had been the only thing removed before she married James. While they were in New York, the wedding planner had put all their wedding gifts in place, filling the kitchen with new utensils and copper-bottomed pots hanging from a cast-iron rack. Her own carefully chosen china lined the sideboard, with a new set of stemware on the top shelf. She loved all of it: the gleam of the metal spatulas, the glow of the pots, the shine of the crystal goblets that had been a wedding gift from James's office staff.

She believed James had arranged it all to please her, so she didn't question it. At least the kitchen felt like her own place.

The garden did, too, for the most part. It seemed James's first wife hadn't taken much interest, not the way Anne did. Anne loved gardening, arranging shrubs in attractive patterns, planting flower beds and containers to provide color through the different seasons. She had wanted to plant roses in the far back corner, where they would catch the summer sun. She offered to rake out the burn pile so she could spread compost and prepare the soil, but James had drawn the line there. He said it was too much work for a pregnant woman.

Feeling cared for, cherished, she had accepted his statement at face value. Still, sometimes she looked at the burn pile, which was hardly used anymore, and wished she could transform that corner as she had the rest of the garden.

The nursery was also hers, and he didn't interfere with her there. Later, she would realize it was because he had no interest, but at the time she believed he meant to indulge her, let her decorate the way she wanted, with her own colors, her own choices of baby furniture. She wished she had never found the photograph, and not only because it spoiled the feeling that the room was hers and the baby's. She had never wanted to put a face to the woman who had fled from Oak Hill and vanished. She had never expected to feel sorry for her. Now, having seen her pretty face, her bright eyes and happy smile, she did. She couldn't help it.

She wondered over the fact, the reality, of Glenda Iredale. Glenda, with her blue eyes and shining hair, had lived in this house. She had slept in the same bed where Anne now did, sat on the same furniture, cooked in the same kitchen. Did Glenda Iredale, pretty as she was, also have trouble making and keeping friends? Did she wish people would like her for herself and not her face or figure? Had she been as much in love with James as Anne was? How had that love died? Why had she walked away from her beautiful house, her carefully chosen possessions?

The next morning, after James went to the courthouse, she dug the crumpled photograph out of the kitchen garbage. She cleaned it off as best she could with a paper towel and gazed at the image for a long time, wishing it could answer her questions. She couldn't resist offering a brief prayer for the woman whose house she now occupied, who had left such nice things behind for Anne to enjoy. She hoped that whatever had gone wrong, whatever had caused her to flee, Glenda Iredale was happy.

Anne took care to stuff the picture back into the kitchen garbage, then to empty everything in the outside bin. Afterward, with a faintly guilty feeling, she proceeded to go through every drawer in the house, to see if anything else had survived the purge. She found nothing. She even went into James's study, which he had forbidden her to do, and cautiously looked through the file drawers in his big black desk.

He was an organized man. Organized to a fault, she thought, although she would never say that she found him a bit obsessive. Every file folder was labeled, every form and receipt in chronological order. She found a folder marked *Official Papers*. It held their marriage license, their marriage certificate, James's birth certificate, and all the official paperwork declaring him a lawyer, and then a judge. She found the deed to the house, the titles to their cars, even James's parents' death certificates.

There were no divorce papers, though. Nothing to show that James had been married before. Surely there should have been a community property statement, or some kind of settlement for his first wife—alimony, or a share of the house, or something. She found nothing.

With great care, Anne put everything back exactly as it had been. She pushed the chair in at the desk and straightened the area rug where it had wrinkled. She looked back at the room before she went out, making sure there was no sign she had been there.

He must have filed the divorce papers at his courthouse office. Or whatever lawyer had handled the divorce had kept them for him. The best thing she could do—what her mother would certainly advise—would be to focus on the baby coming, and to put Glenda Iredale out of her mind. To behave as if there had been no first wife at all.

31

Beatrice, San Francisco, 1968

HER PATIENT'S NAME was John Wayne Belkom, but he asked her to call him Johnnie. "My father named me for John Wayne," he said. "My parents call me J. W., and I hate it. I hate *him*."

It was a remarkably clear beginning to their first session, and Beatrice settled back in her chair, appreciating the boy's clarity. "You mean, John Wayne the actor?"

"Yeah, the actor. I hate the way the guy walks, the way he talks, the movies he makes. I just hate him."

"That sounds like a complicated reaction. I suspect a backstory," Beatrice said, smiling.

The boy laughed. He was a slight youngster with a light, pleasant voice. "Right on, Dr. Bird. I don't need you to tell me that I hate John Wayne because my parents absolutely *revere* him."

Beatrice chuckled, charmed by the use of the word *revere* by a fifteen-year-old boy. "Tell me more about that. Sometimes we like the same things our parents like, but apparently, you don't feel that way."

"It depends," he said. "My folks love Chinese food, and I do, too. My dad likes jazz, and I love it. My mom is into fashion magazines, and I dig those. But movies—John Wayne—no."

"Any particular reason?"

"Well." Johnnie's grin faded, and his thin, expressive features drooped. "Yes. My dad likes him because he's a *man's man*—that's what Dad always says. And Mom likes what Dad likes, so there we are."

"You don't like the 'man's man' idea?"

The boy looked down, zipping and unzipping his jacket. Beatrice waited. She already felt that this patient would be very good at formulating his thoughts, given time and patience. In fact, she had liked him from the moment he stepped into her office.

Objectivity, busy Bea.

I know, Dad. But this boy—

The way he walked, the delicacy of his gestures, the air of vulnerability on his young face, all touched her. She knew what troubled him, of course, without him revealing anything. She also understood that if he hadn't already figured it out for himself, he soon would. She wished he could just embrace it, accept what he was, but she knew all too well the prejudices, the judgments, the obstacles such a boy would face.

He said after a few moments, "The thing is, Dr. Bird, I'm not like that at all. I mean, not a man's man. And every time Dad says something about John Wayne, I feel like he's reminding me he wishes I were that kind of son. You know, tough. Strong." And in an undertone, "Mean."

"Mean? You think your father wishes you would be mean?"

Johnnie shifted his shoulders and wrinkled his nose. "I guess not really. I don't think he believes being mean is a good thing, but—I get teased for not being athletic, for being short, all of that, and Dad wishes I would fight back."

"How do you feel about that?"

"I guess it would be easier if I were that kind of guy. I'm not. I just wish they would leave me alone."

Beatrice leaned back in her chair and linked her fingers in her lap. "Why don't you tell me the things you like to do, Johnnie? Not sports, I gather."

"Not unless you count chess as a sport." Johnnie gave a wry chuckle. "My dad doesn't."

"What else do you like?"

The boy shrugged. "Reading. Listening to music. Playing my recorder."

"A recorder! That's interesting. Have you played long?"

"I started in junior high. I wanted to take lessons, but Dad—" He shrugged again and spread his hands. "He thought brass would be better, play in the marching band and so forth."

"And your mother? Does she have an opinion about the recorder, or about chess?"

"She likes hearing me play, but she won't argue with Dad. Mostly I play when he's at work." Johnnie started zipping and unzipping his jacket again. "Don't get me wrong, Dr. Bird. I love my mom, and my dad, too. They're good parents, but…"

Beatrice waited for him to go on, but when he seemed to have run out of steam, she prompted him. "You love your parents, but you have conflicting feelings?"

"I guess."

"Is that why you've come to see me?"

There was another long hesitation, but Beatrice could see on the boy's face that he was working to come up with a good answer.

Finally, he stopped fiddling with his jacket zipper and met her gaze directly. "I'm confused," he said, with an air of making a confession. "I think some pretty strange things."

"Can you tell me what they are?"

"No, I—I don't like to say them out loud."

"I think all of us have strange thoughts once in a while. Sometimes they don't mean much, but if they worry us, it can be helpful to explore where they come from. What they mean."

He gave a long sigh, and Beatrice had to quell her own sigh as the wave of sadness that emanated from him engulfed her. She suffered a sudden shiver of anxiety that made her look more closely at him. There was nothing about his expression or his appearance that should alarm her, but the feeling was undeniable.

On his second visit, they talked about his school life, in which he felt like an outsider except for the chess club. She asked about that, and he said, "My dad makes fun of our coach. He says he's 'light in the loafers.' Other things like that."

Beatrice barely suppressed a shudder at the dismissive insult. She said as evenly as she could, "You like your chess coach?"

Johnnie nodded. "Yeah. He's nice to everybody." He zipped and unzipped his jacket. "Even nerds like me."

"Do you think 'nerd' is a nice word to use about yourself?"

He shrugged. "It's what I am, though. Not an athlete. Not a tough guy. Just—"

"Well, Johnnie, I've been out of high school a long time, but I wouldn't have liked being called a nerd."

"You probably weren't one." A fleeting smile brightened his face, and his eyes twinkled with sudden humor. "Come on, Dr. Bird, admit it. You were popular. Homecoming queen or something."

That made Beatrice laugh. "If you only knew! No, I was all about books and study, and helping my father with his medical practice. I was the furthest thing from a homecoming queen you could imagine."

"You were allowed to help your dad?"

"I was. He was a country doctor, and there wasn't anyone else to assist him. It was exciting sometimes, and satisfying. Hard work, but I liked it."

"So now you're a doctor, too."

"A different kind, but yes."

"I'll bet your dad is really proud of you."

Beatrice looked closely at her mercurial patient and saw the sudden swell of tears in his eyes. "Are you thinking of your own dad now, Johnnie? Can you tell me about it?"

His lips trembled, and he shook his head.

She put up a calming hand. "It's okay. I know this is hard. You're doing very well. You're brave even to be here."

It was during Johnnie's third and last session that she suggested that if he didn't want to speak his disturbing thoughts aloud, perhaps he could write them out. "I'll give you a notebook," she said. "You can bring it next time, if you like, and maybe we can talk about it then."

When the session was over, she stood by the door watching his slender back as he walked down the street, the spiral notebook she had given him tucked against his chest. Her sense of anxiety sharpened as she locked the door and went about turning out lights and filing her notes.

There was no question about what troubled him. She didn't need her little gift to know that Johnnie Belkom was in a battle with himself and was terrified that his John Wayne–revering parents would never forgive him. He wasn't the first such patient she had counseled, and she knew she would need to give him more time, earn his trust, let him speak his truth to her and make his own decisions about what came next.

She wanted to let it go, to wait, to follow the appropriate process, but her concern intensified as she thought about him.

She reached for the telephone, then paused with her hand on the receiver. What could she say if she called? He hadn't told her much yet. He hadn't shown signs of a boy in serious peril. She had only her feeling, and that wouldn't carry much weight with Johnnie's parents.

She pulled her hand back, leaving the receiver where it was, even though her forehead throbbed uncomfortably.

Second sight again, busy Bea?

I don't know, Dad. I can't decide.

For once, the ghost of her father produced no advice. She checked her calendar to make certain Johnnie was scheduled to see her again the next week. She argued with herself for a while, torn between acting on a feeling she couldn't explain and respecting the privacy of her young patient.

In the end, she did nothing, and she never saw Johnnie Belkom again.

· * * * ★ ★ ★ ★ ★ * * · ·

Beatrice, The Island, 1977

It had been years, but Beatrice would never forget the sick horror that gripped her when she received the news that Johnnie Belkom had taken his own young life. His parents had come to see her, begging for insight into why they had lost their son, but there was nothing she could say. She had met with the boy only three times, and he had never been able to bring himself to speak his fears aloud.

She had no comfort to offer his grieving family.

The thing about death, as she already knew, was how final it was. How irreversible. In Johnnie Belkom's case, it was also unnecessary. Now, the same feeling of horror she had when Johnnie Belkom died shuddered through her solar plexus when she thought about Glenda Iredale.

She said to a puzzled Mother Maggie, "Glenda Iredale was Anne's husband's first wife. It's her ghost I've been seeing."

"Are you sure?" Mother Maggie asked.

"Yes. Because I think—no, to be honest, Mother Maggie, though it's hard to explain, I'm sure—that the phantom Anne dreamed of, the ghost I have seen three times, is Glenda."

"But that would mean—" Anne began, then pressed both hands to her mouth. "Oh, no. That would mean she's—oh, my God."

Beatrice winced at the shock that swept from Anne, and at the sudden darkening of the big shade that hovered behind her, swelling, shimmering, threatening. She watched Anne's pupils swell, her hands begin to tremble.

"Oh, Beatrice," Anne said faintly. She swallowed, trying to moisten her mouth. "Oh, no. You can't mean—does this mean—"

"I'm sorry. It does."

Color surged in Anne's cheeks, and as quickly subsided. In a barely audible voice, she said, "Glenda's dead."

"She must be."

"And she's warning us." Anne's hands came up to hug herself, digging her fingers into her arms. "But why? I mean, for what? Oh—oh, my God. Benjamin."

"We already know your husband is a violent man, but this—"

Anne jumped to her feet. "I have to go back. I have to do something!"

Beatrice stood, too, and reached to put a hand on Anne's arm, even as her throat throbbed with the agony of Anne's fear. "Wait, Anne. Be patient. We have to think."

It wasn't much help, of course. As with Johnnie's parents, Beatrice had no real comfort to offer. Glenda Iredale was trying to warn them, and she had no power to ease the impact of that.

Anne cried, "But do you think—did James—" She pressed her hands to her cheeks, as if she could contain her panic that way. "He said she left!"

"I know," Beatrice said.

"Is it possible he—Surely he couldn't have—" Anne buried her face in her hands, muttering behind her palms, "It's too awful to think about!"

Mother Maggie looked from one to the other of them, frowning in confusion. "I don't know what's happening."

"I'm sorry about that," Beatrice said. "But this is Anne's story to tell."

"It's yours, too," Anne said. Lines of strain showed around her trembling mouth. "Your ghosts. That's the beginning."

Beatrice coaxed Anne to sit down again. "You're right, Anne. Breathe deeply, okay? Slowly. I'll start, and you can tell Mother Maggie the rest." She sat as close to Anne as she could, saying, "Mother Maggie, you're going to be exhausted tomorrow morning."

"I'll ask one of the sisters to fill in for me." The nun's face glowed with excitement. "I can hardly leave now!"

"I suppose not. And if it's true that spirits have a reason for appearing, perhaps you can help us make sense of this one."

It was another long night in the cottage. The March wind whipped the tree branches so they scraped again and again against the roof. The faint light of half-obscured stars glimmered on the dark, restless ocean. The little woodstove battled with all its might against the encroaching chill as Beatrice told her story once again, going back this time to her girlhood, and the early signs of her little gift. Second sight. Feelings.

"I still don't have a name for it. I've always called the things I see and feel my ghosts, but now that I've experienced a real one, my vocabulary fails me."

"Fey, my mother would say," Mother Maggie said. "You're fey."

She tilted her head, regarding her. "Beatrice, do you see—your ghosts, whatever they are—do you see them around me?"

"I see them around everyone. That's why I fled the city to come here. I couldn't tolerate it anymore."

"And mine—?"

"Yours are bearable. They're old, and faded, and they don't project the misery Anne's do. I doubt they ever did."

It was a relief to watch Mother Maggie nod in acceptance, neither challenging nor doubting. It had been much harder explaining to Mitch, who questioned everything. Who believed Beatrice was imagining things.

Still, the nun's face grew grave as she took in Beatrice's history, and then, when Anne took up the narrative, of how Anne came to seek sanctuary. Anne's ghosts shivered behind her in the candlelight. Beatrice wanted to look away, but she didn't. She faced them, especially the menacing one that was James, and she swore to herself she would do all she could not to let him win.

She knew that James Iredale had murdered his first wife. Her knowing would never stand up in court, or even get her past a police interview, but her forehead throbbed with the knowledge. She didn't doubt it for a moment.

If she were Mother Maggie, she would be praying for evidence, for a stroke of fortune, anything to reveal the truth, but she didn't know how to pray. It would be hypocritical of her even to try. And now, with Anne beside herself with worry for her child, the ghost of her husband was as ugly a shade as Beatrice had ever seen.

32

Anne, The Island, 1977

ANNE TRIED TO sleep through what remained of the night, but she turned and turned in a tangle of sheets, anxiety setting her heart racing. She kept seeing Benjamin locked in a dark closet until he cried himself to sleep. Benjamin with a red handprint on his back where James had slapped him for spilling his juice. Benjamin cringing away from his father on a Christmas morning, when James tried to teach him to ride his new bicycle, and James, in a cold rage, stomping on the thing until the wheel was bent beyond use. Benjamin sobbing when she left him at kindergarten, white-faced and silent when she picked him up.

She had told James that Benjamin wasn't ready for kindergarten, and he had laughed at her, called her overprotective, indulgent. "You'll ruin him," he said.

"James, he's not five yet. He should wait a year."

"He'll be five in three months" had been his response. "I was four when I started school, and I did fine." He wouldn't hear any further argument, and she, already cowed, insecure, doubting her own judgment, gave up.

She had tried talking to her mother, but that hadn't done any good. "He'll get used to it," her mother had said, echoing James. "Boys need to toughen up."

Anne didn't want Benjamin to toughen up. She loved him the way he was: gentle, sensitive. He cried over a dead sparrow, worried over a bedraggled squirrel caught in the rain. He loved bedtime stories, and showing off his collections, and laughing at their own private, silly jokes. He never laughed in his father's presence, and over time, he stopped talking in front of him altogether. James refused to see that scolding his son for stuttering—or threatening to take his toys away, or his books, or worst of all, his stamp collection—only made things worse.

Anne wished with all her heart she had found the courage to take Benjamin and go before the crisis had come. She would have had nothing, and she didn't know where she might have gone, how she would have managed, but it could hardly have been worse than now. Now Benjamin was at the mercy of a man who had none.

She tried to comfort herself with the thought that she had found a surprising ally in Beatrice Bird, a bright spot in the bleak landscape her life had become. And Mother Maggie, almost as stalwart in her quiet way. They had both promised, before Beatrice went to her bed and the nun lay down in a nest of blankets on the couch, that they would take up the problem in the morning. And Mother Maggie, of course, had said she would pray for them all.

Anne did the same. She pressed her hand over her cross and prayed for Benjamin's safety. She prayed for someone to watch over him. She prayed for strength and hope for herself. She prayed that James wouldn't find her, and she prayed that Beatrice would find some way to expose him.

None of it seemed to help. She felt as if she were sending her prayers into nothingness, like writing a letter and tossing it into a fire. They brought her no peace.

* * * * * ★ ★ ★ * * * *

Somehow, still whispering prayers, Anne fell into a restless doze. She didn't know the hour when she woke, but beneath the spatter of rain on the cottage roof, she heard the coffeepot percolating.

Hastily, she rose, washed her face and brushed her teeth, then pulled on her now-dilapidated wool slacks and sweater. She left her bed unmade. She was too late to do the milking for Beatrice, but she could at least do something about breakfast.

She hurried out into the kitchen in her stocking feet, hoping not to disturb Mother Maggie sleeping on the sofa, but as she passed the living room, she saw that the sofa was empty, the blankets neatly folded and stacked at one end.

Beatrice was in the kitchen. The milking equipment was already washed and drying on the drainboard. She was pouring a cup of coffee. She had shockingly dark circles under her eyes, as if her face was bruised by fatigue. When Anne came in, she put a finger to her lips before she poured another cup, added cream, and handed it to her. Anne raised her eyebrows as she accepted the cup, and Beatrice pointed through the archway to the living room.

Mother Maggie knelt on a cushion taken from the sofa and placed by the windows. The folds of her brown habit pooled around her feet, and her veil was neatly bobby-pinned to her hair. Her head was bowed, her hands clasped before her. The windows were rain-streaked, glistening in the gray light, and the shimmer of raindrops reflected in her glasses like the flames of votive candles.

Anne resisted an urge to go and kneel beside her. She cradled her warm cup and leaned her hip against the bar, alternately staring into the creamy swirls of her coffee and watching Mother Maggie at her prayers.

By the time the nun crossed herself and maneuvered herself stiffly to her feet, Anne's cup was empty and Beatrice was halfway through her second. As Mother Maggie came toward them, Anne said, "Good morning."

Mother Maggie nodded to her. "Good morning, Anne. Did you sleep?"

"A little. Did you?"

"Oh, yes," the nun said easily. "I always do. It's one of the benefits of putting my trust in God. I never lie awake worrying."

Anne had to look down into her empty cup, not wanting to reveal how badly her own lifelong trust had eroded. "Shall I make some breakfast?"

"Not for me, thank you," Mother Maggie said. "I need to get down to the store as soon as possible. I've missed one shift already."

"I'd love a scrambled egg," Beatrice said. Anne had the impression she said it more out of a wish to give her something to do than real hunger.

She took a carton of eggs from the refrigerator. Mother Maggie bid them goodbye, and they heard the cranky rumble of the old station wagon as she started it up and backed out of the yard. The rain had eased, and Alice and Dorothy emerged from their lean-to and began to graze the waterlogged grass.

When they sat down to toast and eggs, Beatrice asked, "Are you all right, Anne? Yesterday was intense."

"It wouldn't be truthful to say I'm all right. I'm not, but then I haven't been for weeks. I'm trying to think if there's anything I can do." She took a piece of toast and spread marmalade on it but couldn't bring herself to bite into it.

"I am, too." Beatrice ate half of her scrambled egg before she laid down her fork. "I'm so sorry. This is terrible."

"Everything seems to get worse and worse," Anne said bluntly. She looked past Beatrice, through the archway to the front windows and the sea beyond, where the wind whipped spindrift across the gray water, and rain-heavy clouds hung in layers of slate and pearl. The big island was invisible, and neither boat nor bird penetrated the vista.

It was as if the cottage existed out of time, even out of the world, floating alone in an ashen landscape. The idea made Anne's skin prickle. The inside of her head felt numb as she struggled to follow the currents churning around her. She thought if she could only concentrate hard enough, she would know what to do, but her mind whirled with memories and fears.

She said, finally, "I'm terrified to think about where all this is going. And I'm furious with myself for letting it get this far."

"You couldn't have known."

"I should have," Anne said bitterly. "I knew he was violent. Not that he was a—I mean, assuming he did this, but even if he didn't—I should have taken my son, defied my husband and my parents—"

"And your doctor, and your friends, and the police?" Beatrice shook her head. "That's a tall order. James trapped you, as abusers do, and he did a damned thorough job of it."

Anne forced herself to take a bite of egg, and then one of toast. Her mind roiled with possibilities, everything from flying back to Oak Hill to face them all despite the risk, to fleeing the island so James could never find her. None of the possibilities were good ones, and they all ended the same: herself alone, her child in danger, no way out.

She pushed back her chair and stood up, leaving her plate where it was. "Beatrice, may I use your telephone? I'll pay the long-distance charges."

"Of course," Beatrice said quickly. She, too, stood up. "Do you need a telephone directory?"

"I don't need a directory," Anne said.

"Okay if I ask who you're going to call?"

"I'm going to call my mother."

* * * ★ ★ ★ ★ ★ * * *

Dialing her parents' telephone number made Anne's heart flutter, but her hands remained steady. The number hadn't changed since she was in high school, and as it rang, she pictured the white princess phone in her bedroom. She had spent hours on that telephone, until her mother would pick up her own phone—an ancient black rotary contraption from the fifties—and order her to hang up so she could make a call.

It must have seemed strange to Beatrice that she would want to talk to her mother now, after all that had happened. It felt odd to Anne, too, but she felt a compulsion that wouldn't be denied. She *needed* to make the call. As the phone rang in her ear, she fiddled with her cross, then made herself drop her hand. The habit seemed pointless now. She was, as she had been for too long, on her own.

Phyllis picked up after the second ring. "Hello?" She sounded breathless, as if she had run to the phone. As if she was afraid of missing a call.

Anne leaned against the wall beside the bar and swallowed to moisten her throat. "Hi, Mom," she said.

Phyllis gave a sudden, uncontrolled sob. "Anne? Annie, is that you, really? Oh, my God, Annie! Where are you?"

"Mom. It's good to hear your voice." Anne was surprised to find how true that was. She put her hand over her eyes, aware of Beatrice busying herself at the sink, trying not to listen.

"Anne, James was here! Just an hour ago—and he took Ben away!"

"Benjamin was with you?"

"I have him every day," Phyllis said. "I take him to school and pick him up after, and I have most of his things here. Had."

"What do you mean, you had his things?"

"Ben stays over when James is busy at night. James let me go to the house to get his clothes and books, his stamp collection, that quilt he likes."

"Mother, slow down. Tell me what's happening. Why did James come for Benjamin? Shouldn't he be working?"

"He wouldn't say," Phyllis said, and another sob choked her voice. "He just—he was angry, I could see that, but I don't know why. I haven't broken any of his rules. He has so many rules, Anne! I can hardly keep track."

The unfairness of this ignited a flame of temper in Anne, something so unlike her that for a moment she couldn't recognize it for what it was. Her mother had refused to listen to her for so long, had made so many excuses for James, and now...

But this was no time to argue. "Where did he take Benjamin?"

"I don't know. He wouldn't tell me anything, and I—honestly, I was afraid to press him. His face was so—so cold—I don't know. I've never seen him like that. He's usually so controlled, but now—"

Controlled, yes. And controlling, which she understood now, thanks to Beatrice.

"He let me put some things in Ben's backpack—some clothes, his stamp collection, because he spends hours on it, and I think—He didn't really say, but somehow I got the impression they're going on a plane."

"A plane? Why?" Anne had an image of Benjamin, his slight frame weighed down by his backpack, running to keep up with James in an airport, or down a jet bridge. It chilled her.

Phyllis was still talking. "I couldn't fit the quilt in, though, it's too big. I was worried Ben would be cold. I wanted to get his sweater, but James wouldn't wait. He said he was in a hurry."

Anne dropped her hand. "Never mind that! Didn't James say anything, give any reason?"

"He just said—well, you won't like it—"

"Mother. Out with it." Anne had never in her life spoken to either of her parents that way, but her patience was at an end.

It was a relief not to be debilitatingly anxious, despite her worries for Benjamin, but to be truly, righteously, justifiably angry, at James, at her parents, at everyone who had enabled the entire mess. The fire of her temper warmed her, quenched her nervousness, put steel in her voice. "Tell me what he said, Mom."

"He said, 'I'm going to get her.'"

Anne's heart literally skipped a beat, and she pressed her hand to her chest. "'Get her'?" she said, her voice cracking. "He meant me?"

"He was furious when you didn't go into the sanatorium like you were supposed to. There were pictures in the newspaper, Anne, because you ran away. There was a picture of you in your wedding dress, one of the wedding photos, that beautiful one with just you on the altar, the skirt spread out—"

"Mother!"

"I'm sorry, Anne, I'm trying to tell you—so you'll know—it's all such a mess! James told your father you had embarrassed him, running off like that. He said you were a danger to yourself. You're not a danger to yourself, are you, Annie? I would hate to think that—"

Anne turned to the window again, seeking calm in the vista of choppy water and shifting clouds. Here and there, shafts of cold sunlight broke through the cloud cover to glisten on the waves. "I am not a danger to myself, Mom. It's James who is the danger. To me. To Benjamin."

"But, Anne, how can that be? I mean, I can see how you would be afraid of him, how he can be kind of scary, but—he's a *judge!*"

Anne's jaw had tightened, and she blew out a breath to release it. "I have to go, Mom. I'll call you again."

"Wait! Anne, wait. At least—give me your number!"

"It's not my number, so no. I can't do that."

"But I want—"

"Goodbye, Mom." Anne settled the receiver back into its cradle, but not gently this time. She let it fall with a resounding, decisive click. She did it deliberately, with intention. Her mother might as well know, from this moment forward, that she could not give Anne orders, or even advice.

She sat still for a moment, her hand still on the cool black plastic of the telephone, her heart thudding in her ears. *I'm going to get her.* That meant he knew where she was.

She wanted to flee, pack her things, catch the next ferry, disappear. But James had Benjamin. She couldn't abandon Benjamin to the rage James would be in if he found she had escaped again.

It was clever of James to use Benjamin as persuasion. It was yet another trap for her, and it was perfectly set. It was the cruelest ploy, the meanest thing he could have done.

It didn't surprise her in the least.

33

Beatrice, The Island, 1977

BEATRICE HAD NEVER seen such a rapid transformation in a patient. Watching Anne process what was happening, seeing her dig down for the courage she needed, was impressive. She had wanted to give Anne privacy as she made her call, but it was a small house. She heard everything, not only what Anne said but a good bit of what her mother had said, her voice carrying through the wires, shrill with tension. Anne's own voice had been steely, definite, nothing like her usual self-deprecating manner.

By the time Anne set the telephone receiver back in its cradle, her ghosts had changed. The little one was silent, its color the pale blue-gray of worry. The other one still clouded behind her head and shoulders in layers of gray and black, the colors of fear, but both were diminished, as if her anger and determination overpowered them.

Their effect on Beatrice changed, too. Weeks before, seeing these ghosts had caused Beatrice real misery. Now their effect was dimmed, distanced by the changes in Anne herself.

"I heard a lot of that," Beatrice said. "Not trying to eavesdrop, it's just…"

"That's fine," Anne said tightly. "It saves time. James is coming, and he's bringing Benjamin."

"You understand why he's doing that?"

"I do. He knows if he has Benjamin with him, I won't leave. And my mother—she just handed him over, as if he were a toy, or a missing wallet. Just—"

"Not completely her fault, Anne. Your mother has no real rights. Grandparents don't, and it can be hard on them. Even if she had the courage to stand up to James, to refuse to let Benjamin go with him, the law is all on the father's side."

"And in that city, James *is* the law. No one opposes him. But my parents still don't understand what he is."

"It can be a difficult thing to accept."

"I knew she wouldn't believe it. I just had this—compulsion, I suppose—to call, right at that moment. I suppose I was right to do it, although I don't see what good it does." Anne sank into a chair at the table and put her head in her hands. "He'll make me go back. He knows I won't make a scene in front of Benjamin, scare him more than he already is. He'll drag me away, shut me up in the sanatorium, as he planned all along. He knows exactly what he's doing."

"I wonder what he hopes to gain," Beatrice said.

"It's all about him," Anne said dully. "He has to control everything, and everyone. I broke the rules, and he's making me pay."

Hard white lines framed her mouth and her eyes, and Beatrice felt a stab of sympathy. Anne had been manipulated into a corner. Her devotion to her son would keep her right here, forced to wait for what was to come.

Beatrice wished she could pray, like Mother Maggie did. She would pray for an idea, for a strategy, for some way to deal with the trouble that was coming for her friend.

Have faith, busy Bea.

What? You, talking about faith, Dad?

Well, sweetheart. I've learned a thing or two.

The idea made Beatrice chuckle to herself, despite everything.

They knew, she and Anne, that James couldn't reach them for at least a full day, possibly even two. Anne made a simple but delicious meatloaf, which they ate with green beans from the freezer. They shared a bottle of wine, and Beatrice took note of how little of it Anne drank.

Her ghosts continued to withdraw, little by little, as they finished their dinner and did the dishes. It was such a curious phenomenon that Beatrice finally asked. "What are you thinking, Anne? I know you're anxious, and so am I, but you seem to be coping. You seem almost calm."

Anne turned from hanging up the dish towel and leaned back against the sink. She folded her arms, but it wasn't the same torso-gripping gesture Beatrice had seen her make so often. "I don't feel exactly calm, but I feel—I guess 'relieved' is the best word. This is coming to a head. These past weeks have been ghastly, but at least I'll get to see my son again, and I'll have the chance to confront James. I can't imagine that will go well for me, but at least this purgatory will come to an end."

She unfolded her arms and reached for a paper towel to dry the counter around the sink. "Mostly I'm angry. Angry at James, of course, and at my parents for not understanding, not supporting me. I'm angry with myself, too, but I'm not going to be that helpless woman anymore. That Barbie doll, to be dressed and posed and used. I'm done being a victim."

As Beatrice listened, she saw Anne's ghosts shimmer and fade until they were almost as pale as Mother Maggie's. "I'm so proud of you," she said, her voice throbbing with emotion. "You're facing your demons with far more courage than I've shown with my own."

Anne gave her a narrow smile. "I'm no therapist, dear Beatrice, but I've been spending a lot of time with one. I think *she* would say you're being too hard on yourself."

Beatrice smiled back, and though the night was cold and full of dread, she felt a flicker of contentment beneath her breastbone, a tiny candle flame burning in the darkness. She didn't suppose she could save Anne from James's fury, although she would try. But Anne had found herself, her true self, and Beatrice knew she had something to do with that. She was still a therapist.

She managed to sleep almost all of that night, which she realized with surprise when she woke in the chill of a gray morning. The exhaustion of too many nights of little sleep and too many days of worry had at least given her one night of uninterrupted rest. She rose, washed her face, brushed her teeth and her hair, and was already dressed when Alice began to call her out to the barn, and Dorothy's broken baritone joined in.

When the milking was finished, Beatrice looked into her bucket and saw that the cows' output had diminished. They were starting to dry up. No one had told her when they calved last, or really, anything else about them. She would have to decide what to do about that, if anything. She wouldn't mind keeping them as pets, but the sisters liked having the milk to sell, and the cream for themselves. Beatrice was in favor of granting them that small indulgence.

She put the problem off as something to deal with another day. She let the cows out and turned to cleaning the barn. A weak sun had risen to shine palely on the new green sprouting in the woods. Today might be warmer than yesterday, easier on the fishermen and the ferry riders. She had finished her chores and was just starting up onto the porc   ket in hand, when she heard an engine. She paused, watching the .urve of the road to see who was coming. It wasn't the sisters' noisy station wagon, nor was it the thumping motor of Mr. Thurman's truck. It was too soon, surely, for it to be James Iredale, though the thought of him sped her heartbeat.

It was an unfamiliar car, black, jouncing against the muddy ruts as it emerged from the trees. There was something tentative about the way it nosed into the yard, as if the driver wasn't quite sure where he was headed. Wary, still without any great plan to deal with James when he did arrive, Beatrice stood still. The kitchen door opened behind her, and Anne came out to stand beside her, two reluctant paladins bracing for an assault.

When the car door opened and the driver climbed out, Beatrice nearly dropped the milk bucket. "Mitch!" she breathed, her voice startled into a barely audible whisper.

Anne said, "Is that Mitch? *Your* Mitch? But you didn't know—"

"No, I didn't," Beatrice said, recovering her voice. It rose with excitement, with relief, with hope. "But here he is! Mitch!"

He lifted his hand and started toward her. Anne took the bucket from Beatrice's hand, and Beatrice, dignity abandoned, flew down the steps and across the yard to throw her arms around him.

At first, she gave herself up to the warmth of his embrace, the familiar soapy smell of him, the lovely feel of his chest through his coat, pressed to hers, warm and solid and familiar. He murmured in her ear, "There you are," and she didn't know whether to laugh or cry.

When she could, she leaned back, not releasing him, but far enough so she could see the dark twinkle of his eyes through his round glasses, and the flash of his dimples as he grinned at her. She lifted her face to kiss him. "Mitch, I can hardly believe—oh, my God, you're here! You're really here!"

"Such powers of observation, Dr. B."

She hugged him again, and spoke into his collar. "I've missed you."

"Missed you, too," he said. "And now I miss your hair."

Self-consciously, she put a hand to her ragged locks. "I know it's awful. I just couldn't deal with it the way it was."

"It will grow back."

"It will if I let it!" she said with a hint of her old spirit.

It was his turn to laugh. "Same old Bea." He kept his arm around her as he looked around the place. Dorothy and Alice peered out of the lean-to at the visitor. "Cows?" Mitch said. "A barn? I don't remember those being in the real estate agent's descriptions."

"I wrote to you about them. You didn't answer." She realized at that moment that there was something different about him, and she exclaimed, "Your nonna! She's gone."

"She's right where she's supposed to be," he said. "I've just come from visiting her. Took a detour from Milan through Seattle."

"I'm so glad. What a wonderful thing for you to do!" She pressed her cheek against his shoulder. "Oh, Mitch, your timing..."

"Good or bad?"

"Spectacular."

He took her hand. "I wanted to see you. It's good to know you were right about my nonna, and now her ghost is gone, if that's what it is. You're looking right at me, and—Oh, Bea. I couldn't bear it when you wouldn't look at me. That hurt."

"I know," she said. "I'm so sorry."

He squeezed her fingers, and she took it as an acceptance of her apology. "So," he said, glancing up at the house. "I thought you were alone here, but it looks like you have company."

"In a manner of speaking, yes. I have a lot to tell you!" She looked up at the cottage and saw that Anne had disappeared inside, giving them their moment. "Come inside. You must be exhausted. You rented the car, I guess?"

"Yes, at the airport. Getting here is no simple matter, Dr. B."

"True." She took his hand to lead him to the porch. "How long were you in Italy?"

"Three weeks. I took some time off from the hospital, which was tricky, but it worked out. I'm due back soon."

"And your nonna?"

"She's getting old, of course, but she's well. I was there long enough to make sure she has what she needs, to check with her doctor. One of my cousins has promised to drive up and visit her. I swore I'd be back, and she was very clear she meant to hold me to that." He gave a rueful grin. "She made me go to Mass every day, and she scolded me for not getting married. I had forgotten what a character she is."

He pulled her close and kissed her again. She gave herself into it, her heart brimming with love for this man who had come so far, had accepted so much that he didn't understand.

"Does this mean you've forgiven me, Mitch?"

He squeezed her closer and murmured in her ear. "After you left, I had time to think about everything. I realized that—even if you were imagining things—it was miserable for you, and if there was even one thing I could do to make it better, I should do it. And apparently—if you're not seeing my grandmother anymore—I was right."

Her heart lifted. The very sun seemed to shine brighter because of Mitch's arrival. The ocean breeze smelled sweeter, and even her island cottage glowed with renewed charm.

In a very short time she would have to tell Mitch more things he couldn't understand, but for now, she savored the touch of his lips, the pressure of his hand, the warmth of his body, the sweetness of his soul. She wished she could freeze time and just live in this perfect moment of reunion forever.

34

Anne, The Island, 1977

ANNE CARRIED THE milk bucket into the kitchen and began the straining process. She meant to give Beatrice and her Mitch their privacy, but she couldn't resist glancing through the window over the sink. Mitch was neither tall nor particularly handsome, but he radiated good nature and intelligence, which she thought was better than being handsome. She was sure she would like him. She couldn't make herself stop watching the two of them.

Beatrice looked softer and more vulnerable than she had ever seen her. She looked younger, her face shining with happy surprise. The attraction between the two of them, Mitch and Beatrice, was so strong it was almost visible, a magnetism that drew them close to each other, eager to touch and be touched, to look into each other's faces, to lock eyes in the intimate way unique to lovers.

Anne had never experienced such an attraction. She had never dared look up into James's face like that. She had never seen her mother and father gaze into each other's eyes as if they were looking into a mirror. Mitch was a head taller than Beatrice, but Beatrice's eyes met his as those of an equal.

Anne's chest gave an unaccustomed squeeze. She turned back to straining the milk, hoping it wasn't the shameful feeling of envy that constricted her heart. She wanted to believe it was just happiness for her friend, recognition of a loving and mutually respectful relationship.

Her hands slowed at her task as she thought about it. It would be easy to be jealous. The kindness in Mitch's face, the gentleness in the way his compact body moved, even the boyish dimples in his cheeks, stirred her wounded spirit. James was completely different, tall and striking, with his long, narrow nose and hard gray eyes that matched his silvering hair. She remembered, as if from a very long time ago, how her maid of honor had exclaimed over his looks and giggled over his handsome tuxedoed figure at their wedding. She was afraid she had, too.

But she had never looked at James the way Beatrice looked at Mitch. Not ever. Not once. She wished she never had to look at him again, but the knowledge that he was coming, that she would have to face him soon, jolted her heart in a completely different way.

Her hands didn't shake, though. She already knew it was going to be bad. She was ready. She was resigned.

By the time she had strained the milk and scrubbed the bucket, the kitchen door opened, and the two of them came through. Beatrice said, "Anne, this is Mitch Minotti. Mitch, Anne Iredale."

Anne put out her hand to shake his. "I've just made coffee, Dr. Minotti."

"Mitch, please," he said with a smile. "And I'll call you Anne, if that's okay."

"Of course." She moved to the cupboard for cups and the sugar and creamer. "You must have left Seattle terribly early this morning."

"In the dark, yes. My plane landed at a god-awful hour, but honestly, I hardly know what time it is now."

"Jet lag," Beatrice said.

"I guess. I slept a bit on the flight, though."

"That's good," Beatrice said. "Because we have a lot to tell you. I'm so glad you're here, Mitch, but you must know—we're expecting trouble."

He raised his eyebrows. Anne said, "I'll make some breakfast first. Give you strength."

"Wow," he said. "This must be bad."

Anne and Beatrice looked at each other, and Beatrice gave a slight nod. "It's bad enough."

They sat in the living room for a long time, finishing their coffee, as the sunlight moved from the woods behind the cottage to the waves washing the beach. Beatrice spoke at length, and Anne watched in wonderment as Mitch simply listened, his chin on one fist. He didn't criticize or roll his eyes, or breathe sighs of exasperation, as James would have done. He asked a question once or twice, but mostly he sat with one elbow on the arm of the sofa, the other hand holding his coffee cup. He nodded once or twice, gazing meditatively at the sun-bright water and the occasional sailboat dancing before the wind.

Beatrice asked Anne once if she wanted to tell her own story, but Anne shook her head. "You'll do it better, Beatrice, and you know it as well as I do now."

Beatrice didn't demur but went on with her recitation. Anne was sure Beatrice felt the pressure of time passing in the same way she did. James's arrival threatened, closer and closer, like a thundercloud blowing in their direction.

Anne fully expected a bad outcome, but she would hold Benjamin, absorb the sweet little-boy scent of him. She would reassure him that she had not left him on purpose, and she would remind him she would always love him, no matter what came.

If James got in her way—well, she didn't know what she would do, but she would do something. She was done with being passive. She was no longer the compliant girl he had manipulated. She had found her strength, and she would use it. She would fight for herself to the very end.

She caught her breath at the idea, causing Mitch to cast her a quick glance of concern. She gave a quick shake of her head and looked down at her folded hands, not wanting to interrupt Beatrice.

Beatrice was bringing her recitation to its close. "I know I've given you a lot of unscientific details, Mitch. I don't expect you to take everything on faith—although our friend Mother Maggie advises it—"

"Mother Maggie?" Mitch said. "Sounds like a nun."

"Oh, she definitely is," Beatrice said, with a wry little laugh. "A lovely one, actually. I hope you'll meet her. In any case, there's one more bit of information that brings us to where we are today, this afternoon, maybe this evening.

"Anne had a premonition, or a compulsion, whatever you might call it. It made her call her mother at her home back in Oak Hill. She learned that James had picked up Benjamin in the middle of the day, and James said he was coming to get Anne. We assume he's going to fly, and do what you did. Rent a car. Drive up the coast, take the ferries. He could arrive at any time."

"With the child."

"He knows I won't run if he has Benjamin," Anne said. "He'll use Benjamin to force my compliance, and he's not wrong. I want to see my son more than…" She pressed her lips together, unable to complete that sentence. After a moment, she said instead, "He'll take me back to the sanatorium, of course. And this time he won't trust me to walk in on my own." She spread her hands, gratified that they were steady. "Once I'm in, there will be no coming out."

"Who is this judge who ruled you unfit? What doctors testified?"

"The judge just did what James wanted him to. Everyone does that in our town. There was no testimony by anyone, not even me."

"Hardly ethical," Beatrice put in.

"Certainly not," Mitch agreed.

He took off his round glasses to polish them, and Anne saw how dark his eyes were, with laugh lines fanning from the corners. If only, she thought, she could have had a doctor like this one, who listened. Who accepted what he was being told, despite the discomfort of her complaints, the embarrassing details of her story.

"No lawyer of your own, then?" Mitch asked.

"My father said I didn't need one, that there was no point in bothering with it. I understood too late how foolish it was to accept that without question. I took no action to protect myself. It was all over before I understood what was happening."

"Well," Mitch said, putting his glasses back on. "Obviously, there has to be an appeal. With an actual lawyer, and not before some judge who's one of your husband's friends."

"James won't let it happen."

"It's not up to him."

"It shouldn't be. But in that town, it is."

Mitch pressed his lips together, shaking his head.

Beatrice leaned over to glance at Mitch's watch. "It's not too late. I think I'll run down to the store and get some things for dinner. Can I take your car?"

"Wouldn't you like me to drive you?"

"There's no need for that. You should rest. We have no idea what this evening is going to bring. Go and lie down."

Anne said, "That's a good idea. If anything happens—I mean, if anything changes, Mitch, I'll wake you."

Beatrice said, "I won't be half an hour. Let me show you the bedroom."

"Probably a good idea," he said. "Although I can't imagine sleeping with all of this to think about!"

"I know," she said, rising from the couch. "It's a lot of drama."

"Well," he said easily, smiling up at her. "I'm used to drama."

He got to his feet, and Beatrice led him off while Anne gathered up the coffee things and carried them through to the kitchen. Beatrice returned, the car keys in her hand, just as Anne was drying the cups and putting them in the cupboard.

"I think he'll sleep a bit," Beatrice said. "Doctors get good at that."

"Do you remember how to drive a car?" Anne said.

"Oh, my goodness, yes. I've been driving since I was twelve."

Anne nodded. "Impressive."

"Not really. Just country life. All the kids learned to drive early." She jingled the keys in her hand. "I'm off. Back in no time."

Anne followed her to the door and watched as she deftly backed and turned in the yard, then bumped away down the ruts. Anne stayed where she was for a long time, watching the empty road.

Beatrice, The Island, 1977

Beatrice parked the car just outside the store and went in. She had hoped to see Mother Maggie, but it was one of the other sisters behind the counter. The ferry was just navigating into the bay, so she hurried her purchases, knowing the sister would need to go out to operate the ramp. She bought bread and cheese, a jar of tomato sauce, a package of pasta, hamburger, and on an impulse, a roll of salami and some olives.

She hurried out with her grocery bag, hoping to get ahead of the trickle of disembarking ferry passengers. There were an unusual number of them, no doubt because of the sunshine sparkling on the water and the inviting sheen of spring growth on the trees and bushes that lined the island's steep banks and the road leading inland.

Beatrice was encouraged by the sense that she was doing better with her reaction to the ghosts she couldn't avoid. She still saw shades clinging to everyone, stranger and friend alike, but she felt she had made important progress. Just the same, she did her best to avert her eyes as she unlocked the car door and climbed in. She allowed herself to be distantly aware of the people: a young family with three excited children in tow, an older couple who leaned on each other as they climbed the slope from the dock, a pair of teenagers in bell-bottom jeans and floppy wide-brimmed hats. The teenagers could have come straight from the Haight, and they sparked a twinge of homesickness in Beatrice. The shades trailing behind them were light, insubstantial, almost invisible in the sunshine.

She had just turned the key in the ignition when she saw someone who surprised her. A man, tall, trim, wearing a loose black trench coat that looked out of place in the bright afternoon. He was getting out of a black car, very like Mitch's rental. He locked the door and turned to go into the store.

Beatrice had put the car in reverse, but she paused with her foot on the brake, staring at the man. She barely registered his face as she searched behind him, above him, for the ghosts she was used to seeing.

There was nothing. No ghosts. No looming fog of pain or sorrow. No pale, aging shades, like the ones belonging to Mother Maggie. No shadows of the hurts or disappointments of young people. This man had no ghosts at all.

Beatrice made herself back the car and turn into the road, biting her lip as she pondered. Something had changed, but she didn't know what. Was it her? Was her curse beginning to fade?

Or was that man truly without any ghosts of his own?

She drove as quickly as she dared up the hill. She should have been glad, she supposed, to see someone not trailed by the shades of misery that so troubled her, but somehow, she didn't feel glad at all. She felt mystified and, in some way she couldn't define, uneasy. She pushed it all out of her mind, eager only to return to Mitch. She pressed on the accelerator, suddenly needing to be home, in her cottage, comforted by Mitch's miraculous presence, making certain Anne was all right.

The telephone rang just as she walked in with her shopping.

Anne stood staring at the phone, her hands to her mouth. Beatrice set her bag on the counter and crossed to the bar to pick up the phone. "Hello?"

"Beatrice, it's Mother Maggie."

"Yes," Beatrice said in a colorless tone.

"Sister Mary Frances is working at the store this afternoon, and she said a man stopped to ask directions to your place. She felt uncomfortable telling him, but she didn't want to lie."

"It's all right, Mother Maggie. We've been expecting this."

"Are you going to be all right?"

"We have to be."

Beatrice hung up the telephone. That was the man she had seen. The man with no ghosts. She should have known who it was immediately, but she was distracted by Mitch's arrival, by the crowd coming off the ferry. She should have known that man had no ghosts because he had no conscience.

She said, "He's here, Anne. He's on his way up the hill."

"Benjamin?"

"Sister Mary Frances didn't mention a child to Mother Maggie. I saw James, though. Saw his car."

"How did you know it was James?"

"I didn't, but I should have. And I didn't look in the back seat. I barely noticed the car, because I was staring at him." She lifted her gaze to Anne's. "No ghosts, Anne. Not one. Not the slightest shade or mist or cloud."

"Oh," Anne breathed.

Mitch appeared from the bedroom, just putting on his glasses, his hair rumpled from the pillow. He and Beatrice spoke to Anne at the same time. "Are you okay?"

Anne drew herself up, and her eyes were as brave a blue as the spring sky. "I am. I just want to see my son."

35

Benjamin, Boeing 727, 1977

GOING ON AN airplane with Papa wasn't nice like it had been with Mama. Benjamin and Mama had flown to New York City once when Papa was doing an important job there. They went to visit him and stayed in a hotel. Mama brought books to read on the plane, and a puzzle they could do together, and a coloring book with a brand-new box of Crayolas. He was allowed to drink a root beer, which made bubbles go up his nose. When he had to go to the bathroom after he drank it, Mama walked down the aisle with him and waited outside the restroom so she could walk him back to his seat. When there were bumps, she held his hand and explained about wind currents and air pockets and things, and he wasn't scared at all.

The flight to go get Mama was a lot longer. Papa hadn't brought anything for Benjamin except his backpack. They didn't have books for kids on the airplane, or puzzles except in the back of a magazine, and those were too hard. Papa had a lot of drinks, and after they ate the dinner that came on little trays, Papa fell asleep.

The dinner was nice, with mashed potatoes and chicken and gravy, but Benjamin drank all the milk that came with it, and that meant he needed to go to the bathroom. He carefully undid his seat belt and climbed out of the seat. He knew where the restroom was, because he could read the small green sign. He worried a little about going by himself, because Mama wouldn't have liked that, but it turned out to be okay. The lady in the dark-blue uniform who had brought the dinner saw him coming up the aisle and opened the restroom door for him. When he came out, she was waiting to walk him back to his seat and refasten his seat belt. He was worried Papa would be mad because he went to the bathroom by himself, but Papa was still asleep.

The lady in the uniform asked if Benjamin needed anything, and he shook his head, afraid if he tried to speak he would stutter, and Papa might wake up and hear him. She didn't seem to mind, though. She smiled at him and smoothed his hair with her fingers the way Mama used to do. She was almost as pretty as Mama.

Benjamin fell asleep for a little while, but then he woke up, and there was nothing to do. He couldn't look at clouds or the scenery going by under the plane because it was really dark outside. He thought it must be the middle of the night. Most of the people on the plane were reading or sleeping, like Papa. He heard snoring, and some soft conversation, but that was all.

Benjamin was careful to be very quiet. He undid his seat belt so he could wriggle down to pull his backpack out of its place beneath the seat in front of him. He unzipped it and slid out his stamp collection. He settled it on his lap, but he refastened his seat belt before he opened it. He knew that was a rule with airplanes, because the lady in the uniform had told them all before the airplane left the ground. Benjamin was good with rules.

After a few moments he was able to lose himself looking at his stamps, taking in the colors and designs, remembering where they had come from, whether he had found them himself, like the ones in the back, or they had been presents, from Mama or from Gramma Phyllis, or once in a while even from Papa, when an unusual one came into his office.

He flipped through the pages, careful not to jostle any of the stamps. He glanced up once to make sure Papa was still asleep, and then he turned to the back of the book, where the English stamps were.

And the envelopes. He had fished them out of the burn pile because it was obvious Papa wasn't going to read them. He must not have wanted them. They weren't even opened.

Benjamin hadn't opened them, either. He had just used his safety scissors, very carefully, to snip off the stamps and put them in his book. He was afraid to try to put them back in the burn pile, because they were supposed to be already burned up. He didn't put the envelopes in the wastepaper bin, either, because Papa might notice he had cut off the stamps, and be mad at him. There was a deep pocket in the very back of his stamp book. He didn't know what it was for, but it was a good place for him to hide the envelopes with their corners cut off. He would have liked to put them in the outside garbage, but he wasn't allowed to go out to the street by himself. It was one of the rules.

The English stamps were interesting. They had a lady's face on them, with a crown on her head, and they were all different colors. He wondered who the lady was, but there was no one he could ask. Some just had the lady with the crown, but others had pictures he thought must come from books, people in funny clothes and sometimes houses, like in little towns. When he was bigger, he would find out what those pictures meant.

When Papa stirred and began to wake, Benjamin closed the stamp book and worked it back into his backpack. He put his arms around it and hugged it to himself as the trip went on. He wondered if Mama knew they were coming to get her. He wondered if that would make her happy or sad.

When the airplane landed, Papa brought his suitcase down from the overhead storage and helped Benjamin put his backpack on. "Come on," he said, even though it wasn't their turn to step into the aisle. "Come on, we still have a long way to go."

He made Benjamin go ahead of him. When they got near the door, the lady in the uniform who had brought their dinners and who helped Benjamin go to the bathroom was waiting. She crouched down and held out a pretty pin to Benjamin. It was in the shape of an airplane, like the one they had just flown on. "It's a pin to show you flew with us," the lady said, with a friendly smile. "It's just like the ones the pilots wear. Here, I'll pin it on you, shall I?"

"Just take it, Benjamin," Papa said, in that cranky tone. "You can put it on later."

Benjamin took it in his hand, but as the lady stood up, he saw the look she gave Papa. It wasn't a nice look. Not friendly, the way she had looked all through the flight. Benjamin could see she was cross. Her eyes narrowed, and her lips pressed together. It was the kind of look he usually saw only on Papa's face. He had never seen anyone look at Papa that way. He wondered if Papa was going to shout at her.

He didn't, though. Before Benjamin could put the pin in his pocket, Papa grabbed his hand and dragged him out the door.

They stopped at a big bathroom, where Papa told Benjamin to go to the bathroom and wash his hands, while he did the same. Benjamin was just going into the stall when Papa added, "And throw that stupid pin away. It's just junk."

But Benjamin remembered the smile the lady gave him, and the touch of her fingers on his hair. He didn't throw the pin away. He wanted to remember how nice she was, and how she could give Papa an angry look and not get yelled at.

It was going to be another secret. He put the pin way down in his pocket so it wouldn't fall out. He could look at it later and think about how it was just like the ones the pilots wore.

36

Anne, The Island, 1977

ANNE FELT WEIRDLY calm as the three of them waited for James to arrive. She thought it was the sense of acceptance that stilled her hands and eased the thudding of her heart. She had done all she could, everything and anything she could think of. She hadn't shied away from anything. Whatever happened now was not up to her.

For the first time in days, she put her palm on her cross and offered a prayer for protection for herself, for Benjamin, for Beatrice and her sweet Mitch. She crossed herself, aware of Beatrice's raised eyebrows at the gesture, and gave her a tiny smile.

Mitch went to the kitchen door to look out into the diminishing evening light. He came back through the archway to the living room and stood by the front windows, his brow creased with worry. "Pretty cottage, Bea," he muttered.

"I know," Beatrice said. "I don't know what we can do, Mitch."

"Not much."

Anne went to stand in the archway, one hand on the wall as she watched for the headlights that would both bring her enemy, James, but also bring her Benjamin. The cottage felt unnaturally quiet, with neither wind nor waves disturbing the twilight. It occurred to her that it was almost milking time, and she almost laughed to picture

James Iredale confronted with two milk cows. James loathed horses, and he was deathly afraid of dogs. He wouldn't even touch the calico kitten the neighbors had gotten, which they brought to the house for Benjamin to pet. What would he think of Alice? Of Dorothy?

She pressed a hand to her lips to stifle a wild giggle. Apparently, she wasn't as calm as she had thought. She drew a long breath through her nose and exhaled slowly. This was no time for hysterics. She needed to be steady, to be calm for Benjamin, to let him see his mother as he knew her. She hated to think of how lost he must feel, how confused. And now, after a long flight, and heaven knew how long a drive, he would be here.

Her arms tingled with the longing to hold him.

"Oh, gosh," she said suddenly, turning to Beatrice. "Benjamin will be hungry!"

* * * ★ ★ ★ ★ ★ * * *

Beatrice, The Island, 1977

It seemed just as well to let Anne go into the kitchen, busy herself finding bread and cheese for a sandwich for her son. Unless James hadn't followed directions, which seemed out of character, she wouldn't have time to finish making it. Still, it might help to ease the incipient hysteria, which Beatrice could sense in her own chest. The tension was maddening.

This must be, she thought irrelevantly, what it felt like to be under siege, as in a war. To be more or less trapped, waiting for an assault to come.

She went to stand by Mitch, taking his arm, finding balance in his sturdy presence. A wave of gratitude made her press her cheek to his shoulder. They stood facing the archway, their backs to the picture windows, all their attention on the road.

Mitch said in a wry tone, "I'm hoping there won't be any violence from this guy, Bea. I'm not much good at that. Better at putting people back together than taking them apart."

Beatrice straightened. "James Iredale is a violent man, but it seems to be reserved for people weaker than himself. A child. A woman. More than one woman, I fear."

"If you had any proof, we might be able to take some action."

"Anne and I both understand that all too well. My 'feelings' won't count for anything. And there are no police on the island in any case. There's a nurse." She gave a small, hollow chuckle. "Lots of nuns. Not much help."

"Well. Maybe Iredale will listen to reason."

"I doubt it."

"Yes, I'm afraid I do, too. But we'll do what we can." He pressed her hand tight under his arm, and they remained where they were, side by side, gazing out into the gathering dusk. The cows hadn't begun their nightly calls, which was unusual. Beatrice supposed it was possible, if they were beginning to dry up, that they might not even ask to be milked.

The clatter of a dropped knife in the kitchen brought both Mitch and Beatrice to full attention. Headlights carved through the sparse woods, and a moment later, a car spun into the yard. It could have come from the same rental company as the one Mitch had used: a black, four-door sedan, fairly new. It slammed to a gravel-spitting stop behind Mitch's car, which was still parked below the porch. The driver's door flew open the moment the engine was off.

Beatrice and Mitch moved into the archway, and Anne came to join them, the three of them forming a tense triangle, watching in silence as James Iredale climbed out of his car.

He was tall and lean in a well-cut black trench coat, unbuttoned, the belt hanging loose. He was, just as Beatrice had guessed, the same man she had seen going into the store, and just as then, he had no ghosts. It was odd for her to see him that way, as if he were undressed somehow. Exposed.

He slammed the car door behind him, turned the key in the lock, and strode past Mitch's car.

Anne moaned, "Where's Benjamin?"

No one had an answer. They watched James Iredale come toward the cottage, and Beatrice could see how a young woman's fancy might be sparked by such a man. He walked with confidence, and though his face was rigid, his features were classically handsome: a straight nose, a strong jaw. His hair, silver at the temples, was thick and well-cut.

Beatrice recognized his type. The fathers of her most troubled young patients were often like this, polished façades hiding a unique kind of meanness, a particular sort of self-regard that was nearly impossible to pierce. Her heart sank as he stepped up on the porch. He made a formidable opponent. There would be no easy way out of this conflict.

Mitch said quietly, "Anne? Go into your bedroom and close the door. Let Beatrice and me start this conversation."

"But Benjamin—"

"We'll know where Benjamin is soon."

Beatrice said, "Mitch is right, Anne. Hurry now, before he—"

James Iredale's fist struck the kitchen door, three times, hard.

Mitch gripped Beatrice's hand to hold her back while Anne hurried to her bedroom. Not until they heard the click of the door did Mitch let go. "I'm going to answer this," he said grimly. "We'll see if he tries to bully me."

He passed through the archway into the kitchen, walked at a deliberate pace to the door, and opened it.

"Who are you?" James demanded, without other greeting.

Mitch was shorter than James, but his demeanor was very much that of a man in charge. A man used to wielding authority. Beatrice could imagine him in the hospital ER, addressing a recalcitrant patient. She rather wished he had his white coat to wear, with the signature stethoscope slung around his neck.

Despite his lack of costume, his tone was steely and his manner assured. "I'm Dr. Minotti. I believe I know who you are. Would you like to come in?"

Mitch rarely introduced himself by his title outside of a medical situation, but Beatrice approved. Let this man know who Mitch was. For that matter, who she was as well.

She went to Mitch's side and looked up into James Iredale's face. His eyes were cold, his mouth thin-lipped and hard. Under close scrutiny, his good looks disappeared and he looked like what he was: an arrogant, cruel man.

And no ghosts. No projections of sorrow, or guilt, or worry. Nothing to show that he had any feelings about anyone except himself.

She narrowed her eyes to peer at him more closely, in case she had missed something.

There was nothing. Not even the faintest shadow clung to his shoulders or drifted behind his head. Not even the palest echo of an ancient, nearly forgotten worry, or hurt, or memory.

Beatrice had always thought that if she were to meet someone with a similar affliction to her own, they would look at her and see her mother's ghost, her father's, and of course Mitch's, all imbued with the grief of separation. She supposed they would see the shades of patients she still worried about, patients she had failed, patients she had lost. This man was unencumbered by any of that.

A sociopath, of course. She knew how common they were. She had always assumed she must have met a few without knowing for certain. In this case she had no doubt, and the conviction chilled her to her bones. Somehow, some way, they had to extricate Anne and her son from this man's control.

If she had been a believer, she would have thanked God for Mitch coming when he did.

She would have been praying with all her heart for a way out of this mess. Since she couldn't do that, since it would be shamefully hypocritical, she nursed a desperate hope that Mother Maggie and the sisters were doing it for her. She hoped they were giving it all they had.

James Iredale didn't answer Mitch's introduction with one of his own. He stepped through the door, his trench coat swirling around him. "What's a doctor doing here?" His tone implied he expected an answer. Was used to getting answers when he demanded them.

Mitch was in no mood to oblige. "The question is, Iredale, what are *you* doing here?"

It was gratifying to see James stiffen and an instant of doubt flash across his face. It vanished quickly.

His sculpted chin jutted. "None of your business," he said icily. "Who are you people? Where's my wife?"

"We'll get to all that," Mitch said, and Beatrice cast him a glance of admiration. He seemed completely unperturbed, although she knew that couldn't be true. He glanced out through the door that James had left standing open to the deepening gloom. "Where's the boy, Iredale? Where's Benjamin?"

"If you mean my son Ben," James said, biting off the child's name, "he's in the back seat of the car. He's asleep."

"It's too cold to leave him out there," Beatrice said. "Give me the keys, and I'll get him."

James ignored that. "I haven't heard your name."

Mitch nodded in Beatrice's direction. "This," he said, "is Dr. Bird."

"Another doctor? What's going on?"

"She's a doctor of psychology. And if I know her, you're not going to learn anything until you fetch Benjamin out of the car and into the warmth."

"Ben," James repeated. "I'll get him when I'm damn good and ready."

"We're at an impasse, then," Mitch said.

"How dare you? I don't even know who you people are, or why my wife is here with you! You do realize she ran away from a sanatorium? You're harboring a fugitive! I'm tempted to call the police right now."

Beatrice smiled, and she liked the way it felt on her face. Cool. Cynical. Unruffled. It didn't matter that it was pretense, that her stomach roiled with nerves, because he couldn't know that. One feature of being without empathy was a lack of awareness, and that was useful in this moment.

She said, "There are no police to call, Mr. Iredale. It would take two hours for any to get here from the big island—if you could convince them they're needed."

"I don't believe it."

"No?" Beatrice stepped back, and pointed to the kitchen bar, where the telephone. "Telephone. Be my guest."

He didn't move. He put his hands on his hips and stared down at her, clearly doing his best to be intimidating. He had, she could guess, a lot of practice with that look. He said, "What kind of god-forsaken backwater doesn't have police?"

"I don't think 'godforsaken' is the best adjective here. The island has no police, but it's quite well-stocked with Catholic nuns."

"You're breaking the law!" he spat.

"I don't think so," Mitch put in. "As I understand it, Iredale, your wife's commitment to the sanatorium was voluntary. The law doesn't apply."

James looked down his nose at Mitch, and his lip curled in a patronizing way that made Beatrice want to slap him. "I'm a judge, Doctor. I'm quite sure I know the law better than you do. Take my word for it. I have legal custody of my son, and it's illegal for you to interfere."

"Why did you bring him all this way?" Beatrice asked.

He didn't move his head, but his eyes flicked toward her. "That's a remarkably stupid question. I don't suppose your PhD is worth much in this situation."

"Watch it, Iredale," Mitch growled.

James gave a bark of humorless laughter. "You people are interfering in my family business. Look, I'm taking my wife back where she belongs, whether you like it or not. Now where is she?"

Neither Beatrice nor Mitch answered. James marched past them, and though Beatrice stepped forward with the intention of blocking his passage, Mitch shook his head. There was no point, maddening though it was. Beatrice gritted her teeth and followed Iredale as he moved through the archway, past the living room, his gaze raking every corner. Mitch was close behind as Iredale went into the short hallway. He looked into Beatrice's bedroom, which made her skin crawl with indignation, then turned to the only closed door.

It was the bedroom Anne was using. Iredale didn't bother to knock. He crashed the door open with a careless shove and went inside. Mitch and Beatrice stood helplessly in the doorway.

Anne wasn't there.

It was hard to believe she had managed to squeeze through the little bedroom window, but it stood open to the cool air of the evening, filling the room with the scents of the junipers growing against the outer wall. The bedroom was empty, and there was no other way out.

James shoved past Beatrice and Mitch once again, stamping across the little hall to look again into Beatrice's bedroom, then, without apology, into her bathroom. He thundered back through the archway into the kitchen, opening the pantry closet, scowling into the coat closet beside the door.

Mitch was close on his heels. "Listen here, Iredale. You can't behave like this in Dr. Bird's home."

James whirled to glare at him. "Who's going to stop me? A man like you? And no police you can call?"

Mitch rarely lost his temper, but Beatrice knew he was about to. She sensed it rising, like a pot coming to a boil. She put a hand on his arm, and his muscles trembled with tension beneath her fingers. She said hastily, "We should talk, Mr. Iredale. Why don't you sit down, and I'll bring you some water. Let's—"

His answer was another shout of mirthless laughter. He marched back to the door, banging it against the wall as he went outside. The handle left a dent in the plaster.

"Out of his mind," Mitch muttered.

"Let's be cautious. This sort of man can be dangerous if he feels he's been pushed—"

"I know, Bea. I've seen it all, remember. Let's go."

Anne, The Island, 1977

If she had been five pounds heavier, she might not have fit through. Pushing up the sash of the window had bruised her hands, and she had scraped her thighs on the windowsill, snagging her wool slacks, but she made it out. She nearly tumbled into a juniper bush but managed to steady herself on the wall, only losing one of her shoes. She untangled herself, retrieved the shoe, and ran toward the rental car James was driving, her heart near to bursting with need.

She leaned down to look through the back passenger window, and there he was. Benjamin, her precious boy. He stared up at her, wide-eyed, visibly shivering. She pulled on the door handle, but the door was locked.

"Benjamin!" she cried, still jiggling the handle. "Benjamin, honey! It's Mama! Are you all right? Can you open the door?"

He tried, pulling on the button, but it wouldn't move. Clearly the child lock was engaged. He pressed both of his hands against the window, sobbing, "Mama! Mama!" She ran around to the driver's-side door, but it was locked, too. They were all locked. She couldn't get to him.

She cast about her for some way to break a window, but she knew how hard a car window was to break. She had crashed a car, and though the windows sprouted spiderweb cracks across their surfaces, none of them broke.

Benjamin was crying now, open-mouthed, helpless. She wanted to pound on the window in her frustration, in her need to get to him, but it would only have frightened him more. "Benjamin, try the lock again! Can you lift the lock?" she cried, but they were out of time.

She heard James's raised voice from inside the house, then the crash of the front door opening. She paused just long enough to say to Benjamin through the closed window, "Don't worry, sweetheart! It will be okay!" and then she ran.

37

Benjamin, The Island, 1977

BENJAMIN HEARD WHAT his mother said, but he knew she didn't mean it. It wasn't going to be okay. He heard Papa shouting the way he did when he was really mad. No one could stop Papa when he was mad. Everyone was afraid of him, even Gramma Phyllis. He didn't shout at Gramma Phyllis, but Gramma Phyllis was really careful not to make him angry.

Papa had said they were coming to get Mama, and here she was. Somehow Papa knew how to find her. After the long airplane ride they rode in a strange car and took three different ferries. They stopped at a McDonald's before the first one, but that had been a long time ago, and the hamburger Papa bought Benjamin was small and dry and barely warm. He couldn't eat it, and now he was hungry and cold, and he had to go to the bathroom, too.

He was glad to see Mama, but he didn't think Papa was glad. He didn't come to get her because he missed her, not the way Benjamin did. Papa wanted to send her to that rest place again, whether she wanted to go or not. He hadn't said so, but Benjamin knew it was true.

And now he couldn't get the door unlocked so he could get out of the car. He wanted to hug her so much it hurt.

Everyone thought he was too young to understand all the things that had happened, but one of the good things about not talking very much was you could listen a lot. He had listened to Gramma Phyllis on the telephone. He had listened to his mother and father arguing. He was listening when Papa hit Mama and she fell. And he was listening the morning they went to see the judge, and Mama begged Papa not to keep her away from Benjamin.

Begging Papa never worked. Benjamin had begged Papa not to lock him in the closet, but he did it anyway. The worst thing now would be if Papa hurt Mama worse than he had before. Papa was really mad.

Benjamin wished he were big enough to protect his mother. He wished he were older. He wished he could get out of the car so he could run after her. So he could run away from Papa. He twisted to look out the back window, but Mama had already disappeared in the darkness.

He was glad she ran away, but it wouldn't do any good. Papa would know where she was hiding. He always knew everything.

Well, almost everything. He didn't know about the English stamps.

Benjamin hugged his backpack to him, shivering with fatigue and cold and anxiety and a pressing need for the bathroom. It was almost as bad as being locked in the closet.

38

Beatrice, The Island, 1977

BEATRICE AND MITCH hurried out to the porch after Iredale. There was no sign of Anne, but Beatrice could see the little boy's fair head in the back seat of the car. She pointed him out to Mitch, who dashed down the steps toward him.

Iredale paced along the porch, shouting for Anne. His voice echoed from the trees, sending a little flock of night birds fluttering up from the shrubbery. Iredale's presence was shocking, a breaking of the island's peace, a bombshell of anger and resentment.

Beatrice didn't see the cows, though it was past their usual time. She worried Iredale's yelling had frightened them into the woods. The night wind from the water had picked up, and the last of the day's fragile warmth seeped away before it. She drew a deep lungful of the briny air, trying to control her temper, struggling to think clearly. Strategically. The little boy crying in the locked car made her furious.

She said, with as much control as she could muster, "Please, Mr. Iredale. Bring your son inside. It's cold out here."

"That's Judge Iredale to you, lady," he snapped.

The arrogance of that made her even angrier, and the shell of her control cracked. "This isn't your courtroom. I have no intention of calling you Judge. This is my place, my home, and I'm telling you that child should not be locked in a dark, cold car."

Mitch was trying the door handles of the car, one by one, without luck. Beatrice saw him bend to speak to the child through the closed window.

She tried again, reining in her fury so she could speak in a level tone. "Listen. I know you're angry, but be reasonable. Unlock the car, and bring Benjamin inside so we can—"

"Ben!"

"What?"

"His name is Ben!"

Beatrice blew out a breath at that, and the cool smile, the one she had been proud of earlier, returned to her lips. "That bothers you, doesn't it, Mr. Iredale? It irritates you that you can't force me to call him the name you like. Does it break one of your rules? I've heard all about those, but you have no power here. I don't have to follow your rules."

Even through the gloom, she saw his face suffuse. His lips pressed together until they almost disappeared. He took a step toward her, one clenched fist rising, an eyelid twitching as his self-control disintegrated.

From his place beside the car, Mitch called, "Get hold of yourself, man! You're not judge and jury here."

Iredale spun toward Mitch and lunged down from the porch. At that moment, Beatrice looked past him to the barn. The sliding door was partway open, just far enough for a slender woman to sidle through. There was no light inside, but it was a logical hiding place. It was the only hiding place.

Iredale spotted it at the same time. With an exclamation of triumph, he strode past Mitch and on across the yard, his trench coat flapping like the wings of some enormous crow. He shoved the barn door open further, enough for him to slip through. As Mitch spun to run after him, he slid the door closed again, shutting himself inside. Beatrice heard the ominous clank of the iron bar falling into its rests. She had never, in her months here, locked that door. There had been no need.

If Anne was in the barn, as she certainly must be, James had locked her in with him.

Mitch said, "Is there another way in?"

"Not a door. There's a window, but no sash. We'd have to break it."

"There's really no one we can call?"

"No one. A lot of nuns."

"Jesus. I hope they're praying."

* * * * ★ ★ ★ * * * *

Anne, The Island, 1977

Anne knew how her husband's face would look. She had seen it too many times: eyes narrowed, lips pressed thin, face dark with anger. She was glad Benjamin was safely locked in the car, though she knew the dark scared him. He would at least be spared the inevitable ugly scene.

She supposed she could have run into the woods or down to the beach, but it wouldn't have made a difference. She couldn't go far. James had Benjamin, and that meant he had her, too.

This was her last chance to fight back. To take a stand. It was going to be nasty, and probably painful, but she had to do it. She couldn't surrender without some effort to regain her self-respect. Not anymore. Never again.

The cows hadn't come in yet, so the barn was empty. With no real plan except to postpone the confrontation with James as long as she could, she slid the door open just far enough so she could fit through. It didn't occur to her to lock it behind her. There was a steel bar hanging at an angle above the door, waiting to be dropped into the curved rest set into the wall, but she had never seen it done. She didn't know how the thing worked.

Nostalgia added to her heartbreak as she stepped into the little barn for what would be, she had no doubt, the last time. The fresh straw smelled tangy and sweet, like citrus. The bales of hay in the back room seemed to have stored up sunshine from the growing season, giving it back in the dark winter months with a pungent grassy scent. The whole barn felt warm and welcoming and, deceptively now, safe.

It wasn't safe, though. Even as she ducked behind the stanchions into the back room where the straw bales were stacked, she heard the door slide open on its rails and then, with a menacing clang that made her stomach clench, the locking bar fall into its rests. She shrank in upon herself, arms folded around her middle, her chin tucked low.

The only person who would have locked that door was James. He had stopped shouting, and that was a bad sign. It was always worst when his anger went cold. She thought he preferred this stage of a fight, when he was no longer burning with fury but rigid with contempt. It was the stage that most terrified her, when the last vestiges of his self-discipline had dissipated.

She heard his footsteps in the milking room, softened by the straw on the floor, then the tap of his heels as he came around behind the stanchions. She was cornered.

There was another sound, too, one she couldn't identify at first.

James rounded the end of the manger, his coat hanging loose around his tall figure like the robes of some mad monk. He had picked up the shovel they used to clean the barn, and she realized that was the other sound she heard. It was the clank of the shovel against the concrete floor. The shovel gleamed through the darkness, reminding her that it was metal, heavy, and hard.

James looked much as he always did, lean, patrician, the silver in his hair catching what little light there was. His hard eyes glittered with the look that struck fear into prosecutors and defendants and cowed rebellious jurors. Anne gritted her teeth, forcing herself to straighten her spine, to drop her arms, pull back her shoulders. She would hold her ground. There was no point in attempting a retreat behind the stack of bales. There was nothing to be gained by it.

In that low, cold, familiar voice, her husband said, "Stop being stupid, Anne. You thought you could get away from me, running off like that?"

Anne palmed her cross. "If I went into the sanatorium you would never have let me out."

"It was the safest place for you," he said. "You should have taken the chance when you had it, but you've ruined it now. I was being generous at the time, but no more. I've had enough." He was moving steadily toward her, rapping the shovel against the floor with every step. "Now a more permanent solution is required."

"Permanent?" Despite her resolve to be brave, to face what was coming, Anne's voice trembled. She suddenly felt as if she were floating above herself, no longer connected to her body. It was as if she herself had become a ghost, without substance, with only the most tenuous hold on life. It was exactly the feeling she had with a panic attack, the feeling that she was about to die, that her heart was going to give out, her breath stop.

No, she told herself, no. Not now. This was not the time. She would not give him the satisfaction. Make him do it himself.

She clenched her hands so that her nails bit into her palms, and strangely, that helped. She took one slow breath, and as her ribs expanded with it, she felt better. She wrestled her body back together, willed it to function as it was meant to.

She felt—was this pride? At the very least, there was a fragile sense of satisfaction that she was standing up to her abuser.

"It will be so sad," James said, his lip curling. "Young mother trips over a shovel in a dark barn. Falls to the concrete floor. Hits her head, and tragically—" He made a gesture with the shovel. "Tragically, there is no ambulance on this idiotic island, no hospital, not even a clinic." As he was talking, he took three more deliberate, ominous steps.

He was close enough now for Anne to smell him. She caught a trace of his usual aftershave, but perspiration had broken through his deodorant, and his breath was sour, even from a distance. A long plane flight, she thought, and a drive. No time to shower. Brush his teeth. Had he stopped at all? Had Benjamin had a chance to eat, to go to the bathroom? Was he cold, out there in a locked car, in the dark?

Those thoughts flashed through her mind in an instant and unleashed a flood of pure, powerful fury. She stood her ground, braced for what was to come, and spoke just loudly enough for him to hear. "So, James, you mean to kill me. As you did Glenda."

He stopped abruptly, and the shovel wavered in his hand. She felt the atmosphere shift in an instant, a crack appearing in the smooth surface of his arrogance. Even his voice changed, the tone higher, with a tiny tremor of doubt. "What—what did you say?"

Anne's voice was steady. "You heard me. I know you killed Glenda."

"You're insane! No one would believe that! I told you—"

"You told me many things." Anne interrupted him, lifting her chin, challenging him with her eyes in a way she had never done. It was dangerous, she knew, but gripped as she was by a righteous anger, she didn't care. "Including lies about your first wife. It's going to come out, you know, no matter what you do to me."

"Ridiculous!" he hissed. "Who do you think you are, Anne? You have no proof of any such thing! No one's going to believe a drunk, an unfit mother, a runaway wife!" There were only three feet between them then, and he covered half of the distance in one step. He lifted the shovel with both hands.

The threat was so close, so real, that Anne could feel the blow before it came. She knew the sickening contact of that metal blade with her skull, the loss of balance, the end of consciousness. She sensed the forward edge of her death, the violent rending of the veil. She felt the resulting ecstasy of oblivion, and the temptation was almost irresistible.

It was like standing at the edge of a precipice, knowing she was going over, unable, possibly even unwilling, to stop herself. Time slowed to a crawl, a deadly pace that allowed her to hear the shovel's progress through the air, register the slight grunt James gave as he lifted it above his head, even note the cessation of her own breath as she waited for it. She had ample time to recognize that this would be the end.

She didn't mind so much for herself. She was so very weary of the struggle. But Benjamin would be left motherless, with no one to protect him from being slapped and insulted and locked up in the dark, because no one would ever believe the truth.

She closed her eyes and whispered a one-word prayer. "Help." It was not a prayer for herself. It was a prayer for Benjamin.

And even as the prayer left her lips, the smell hit her.

It was the first time she had smelled it, and it was exactly as Beatrice had described. Intense, suffocating, foul, as if she had plunged her face into a putrid sea of mud. Just like Beatrice, she felt her gorge rising, threatening to make her sick.

Her eyes flew open.

It was much like her nightmare, but the shape was darker, thicker, larger. Its back was to Anne. It faced James instead, towering over him, a flickering, wavering, half-transparent phantom that was both vague and yet unmistakably the form of a woman, with arms and legs and a mass of disordered hair.

"Christ!" James's voice was as high and shrill as a boy's. He fell back, staring up at the apparition, eyes stretching wide with disbelief as he took in the shivering, billowing shape of it.

The arms of the specter reached out to envelop him in their suffocating embrace at the precise moment Dorothy gave her broken-tuba bellow. It was a shockingly discordant blare of sound, as if an orchestra's brass section had all gone mad at the same time. It was louder than Anne had ever heard it.

James dropped the shovel, throwing a wild-eyed look over his shoulder, then an even wilder one back to the phantom. His mouth worked, but no sound came from it. The ghost's shadow intensified, and with it the ghastly scent of decay. Of rotting flesh. The unmistakable, undeniable smell of death.

Choking, as if he were strangling, James spun away from the specter. He stumbled and fell hard to his knees on the concrete, then scrambled up to lurch toward the door.

Anne perceived all of it in that slow-motion way, seconds passing as slowly as minutes. Not until James began to struggle with the iron bar locking the door did time resume its normal flow. She watched the surging shadow of the phantom swell around him, blinding him as he fumbled with the bar. He gagged and cursed by turns.

Anne followed him. She did in fact trip over the shovel, but she caught herself without falling. The size and shape of the ghost stunned her. It was no wonder Beatrice had been shocked when she saw it, and it was no surprise she had misunderstood its meaning.

James managed to lift the bar at last and nearly fell again in his haste to be out of the barn and into the cold evening air. Mitch and Beatrice were beside his car, trying in vain to get Benjamin out. They both turned, mouths agape, to stare.

The awful smell filled the yard. Alice threw up her head, then whirled and galloped off into the woods without making a sound. Dorothy remained behind, the shattering sound of her mooing mingling with Benjamin's frantic calls from inside the car. "M-M-Mama! M-Mama! D-don't let them hurt the lady!"

Mitch swore, "Jesus, Mary, and Joseph!"

James, his keys in his hand, shouted right in Mitch's face. "I don't know how you pulled that off, you bastard, but it won't work!"

39

Beatrice, The Island, 1977

James shoved Mitch aside with such force that Mitch lost his balance, staggering to one side as James stabbed at the lock in his car door. He tried three times before he got the key in, undoubtedly scratching the paint. He threw himself inside, banged the door shut, and slammed his palm down on the locking button before Beatrice could open the back door.

He ground the engine as he turned the key in the ignition, and that sound, more than anything, told Beatrice how shocked he was, how disturbed by what he had experienced, whether he accepted it or not. He gunned the motor, and the car jerked backward with a spurt of gravel and dirt. He had to do it twice to get his car headed downhill. Beatrice and Mitch had to leap out of the way. He banged away down the road, jouncing in the ruts, swerving violently, so that it seemed he might run off the road into the trees.

Anne screamed, "Benjamin!" and tried, uselessly, to run after the car. Beatrice heard the child screaming from the back seat. Mitch's horrified expression told her he heard it, too.

Then the car was gone.

And so was the phantom. It dissolved into the darkness, taking its scent of death and decay with it. The return of the fragrances of pine and salt air startled Beatrice with its suddenness, as if she had put her head out of an open window. She drew a long breath, letting the spicy freshness cleanse her senses of the specter's ghastly smell.

Mitch, standing in the middle of the yard, spoke in a voice that shook. Beatrice had never seen him like that, this man who saw terrible things all the time in the emergency room, coped with every kind of trauma and illness. She sympathized. She knew how stupefying the first sighting of this phenomenon could be.

He said, even as he dug his own keys out of his pocket, "Bea, is that one of the ghosts you see? That awful thing? No wonder you can't stand it!"

* * * * * ★ ★ ★ * * * *

In moments all three of them were in the car, driving down the road to the ferry terminal.

"Is there anyplace else he can go?" Mitch asked.

"No," Beatrice said. She was in the front passenger seat, ready to give directions. "There are other roads, but they all circle back to the terminal. The ferry is the only way off the island."

"You know we can't detain him. We can't prove anything."

"We have to get the child away from him somehow."

"I know. Somehow."

Anne sat white-faced and silent in the back seat. The echo of the little boy's screaming was still making Beatrice's heart race, and she could only imagine how Anne felt.

"Should have called Mother Maggie," Beatrice muttered.

"There's no time for that, Bea. We can't be far behind him. When's the next ferry?"

"There's only one at night. Seven, I think? I'm not sure."

Mitch glanced at his watch. "It's nearly that now. They're probably boarding."

Anne stifled a tiny gasp, and Beatrice cast a glance back at her. "Hang on, Anne. We'll be there soon."

40

Benjamin, The Island, 1977

BENJAMIN'S SCREAMS WERE high and hard, ricocheting against the car windows, louder even than the roar of the engine. Papa would be really mad when he stopped driving, but Benjamin couldn't help himself. It was all so awful, Mama running into the dark and the lady coming out of the barn, then Papa shoving that man so he fell over...

Benjamin had seen the lady follow Papa, chase him to the car. He could even catch the faint scent of her through the closed windows. But how did she get here? He thought she lived in his bedroom, or maybe in one of the other rooms of his house. How could she be here on this island? Did she know how to take airplanes and ferries and things?

And there was Mama, right behind her. Thinking about Mama made him want to scream again, but now the ride was so rough he couldn't.

It was noisy, with terrible bumps and jouncing, as if the car was going to tip over. Papa hadn't let him out, and he had thought for sure, since they came to get her, that he would get to see Mama. Even if she had to go back to that rest place, he would get to see her first!

Papa wasn't making any noise at all. He drove crooked, jerking this way and that, like bumper cars at a carnival. The headlights flashed across tall trees and rolling bushes, making crazy patterns as the car swerved. Benjamin lost hold of his backpack when it slid to the floor, but he was too busy holding on to his seat to pick it up. Papa didn't slow down until they reached the ferry place, where the little store was, and then he slammed on the brakes without any warning.

Benjamin shot forward, striking his forehead against the back of the front seat. He cried out in pain.

The ferry was at the dock, and cars were already driving up the little ramp, their headlights gleaming on the ferry's white sides. There were only three of them. Papa's car was number four. He got in the line, glancing over his shoulder several times. He wasn't glancing at Benjamin, though. He was looking back at the road. Benjamin thought he was looking for Mama and those other people, but maybe he was looking for the lady.

Benjamin rubbed his forehead, and he looked back, too. He hoped he might see Mama running after him. He didn't know how she could get in the car, though, with the doors locked, and he couldn't get out. He didn't understand why they were leaving without her.

He had to ask, though it was hard to squeeze the words out of his throat. "P-Papa? Wh-wh-what about M-Mama?"

Papa didn't answer. He hunched over the steering wheel, closely following the other cars driving onto the ferry ramp.

Benjamin said again, "N-n-no, Papa! C-c-an't we w-wait for M-M-Mama?"

"Be quiet," Papa said, but not very loud.

Benjamin looked over the top of the front seat to see that the car ahead of them had driven onto the ferry. It was their turn. Papa put the car in gear and it started to roll forward. They were almost on the ramp when Papa said, "Goddammit!" and stopped the car.

A woman in a funny brown robe and an orange vest stood in front of the car, waving her hands and shaking her head. She had a little black scarf pinned to her hair, and she wore thick black-rimmed glasses like the woman at the library. The headlights made them shine so Benjamin couldn't see her eyes, but he could see that her hair was gray.

The woman set three orange cones on the ramp in front of the car, then came around to the driver's-side door. Papa rolled down the window.

"I'm sorry, sir," she said. "The ramp malfunctioned. It will take a few minutes to fix."

"Hurry up!" Papa said. "This is the last ferry, isn't it? I need to get off the island."

"That's right." The woman didn't seem to care if Papa was upset. "It's the last ferry. We'll do our best. Just sit tight." She straightened, but she added, "If your little boy needs the bathroom, you have time."

"He's fine," Papa snapped, without asking Benjamin. "Just get to it."

The woman nodded, but she took a moment to peer in at Benjamin before she walked away. She had a black-and-white dog trotting at her heels, and she wore some kind of work gloves, like the ones Mama wore to work in the garden.

Benjamin said, "I d-d-do h-have to g-go to the b-bathroom."

"You can wait until we're on the ferry," Papa said. He rolled up the window, double-checked the lock on the door, and sat glaring out through the windshield. He didn't turn the engine off. He didn't look back at Benjamin, but he didn't shout at him for stuttering, either. He tapped on the dash with his fingers, an angry beat-beat-beat, and he swore under his breath at the lady in the brown robe as she moved back and forth, setting more orange cones.

Benjamin crossed his legs tight, hoping he wouldn't have an accident. He wished Mama would come. He wished Papa would let him out to go to the bathroom. He wished—

"What the hell—" Papa's voice had gone high again. He threw himself back against the seat. "Not again! Christ!"

The car hadn't moved. Benjamin leaned forward to see what had happened.

It was the lady. His lady. The lady from his bedroom, and then from the barn, and now…

She sort of floated to the window and leaned down to look in, not at Benjamin, but at Papa. Papa made a strange noise and pulled as far away as he could get in his seat, even though the window was closed, and she couldn't get in.

It had grown really dark outside, but there was a light from the store, and headlights coming up behind them. Benjamin could see the lady better than he ever had in his bedroom. She was still transparent, as if she were drawn on one of the tracing papers he used at school sometimes, and her shape was uncertain, wavy, like a fog when the breeze blows. Her face didn't look sad, though, not the way he was used to. It looked angry. It reminded him of the way the stewardess on the airplane had looked at Papa.

The lady put one hand on the car, right above the window, and leaned down so that her face came very close to the glass.

Papa drew a noisy breath and shouted, "Get away from me!" It wasn't his usual shouty voice, though. It was high and tight. Papa sounded scared.

Benjamin didn't understand what happened next. He thought the lady was pointing at something inside the car. Was it him? Was the lady pointing at him? A terrible smell filled the car, like the garbage can when Papa forgot to put it out on the street.

The lady had never smelled that strong in his bedroom.

She pressed her face against Papa's window, closer and closer, pushing it against the glass so hard that it flattened and spread, her features disappearing into a cloud of something dark. It spread all across the windshield until it wasn't a face anymore. It was smoke, or fog, or shadow, and it completely covered the glass. Benjamin couldn't see out, couldn't see the ferry, couldn't see anything.

Neither could Papa.

Papa made an even weirder noise, sounding as if he was choking. "Dammit, dammit, dammit!" he grunted. He crawled over the gearshift, away from the driver's seat. He fell against the passenger-side door, scrabbling at the lock until it opened.

Benjamin froze, staring in confusion at the black cloud blocking the windshield. The lady had never done anything like that in his bedroom. What did she want?

41

Anne, The Island, 1977

ADRENALINE SPURTED INTO Anne's bloodstream. Her head pounded with it. She gripped the sides of her seat as Mitch's car racketed down the dirt lane, its teeth-rattling bounces shaking her like a bone being shaken by a dog. Still she wished it would go faster, silently urged Mitch to press harder on the accelerator. She had only one chance to catch up with James before he reached the ferry.

There was no time to think about the ghost, fantastic and shocking as it was. She had seen the thing surge after James, a tsunami of energy and fury, but it was all so confusing, so confounding, that her mind couldn't track the sequence of events. It had come into terrifying focus at the moment that James got his car into gear and backed up, again and again, trying to reach the road, then careened down the hill with her baby inside.

If Mitch had not caught up with her, urged her to get into the car, Anne thought she might have run all the way down to the ferry dock in the dark, in her soft boots, with neither coat nor flashlight. If he hadn't had a car—if there had been only Beatrice and herself—but she couldn't think about that. She set her jaw, pressed her hand over her cross, and prayed for something, someone, anything that could prevent James from driving onto the ferry with her terrified child in the back seat.

So stricken was she that she could hardly believe it when she saw that he had, indeed, been stopped. Mother Maggie bustled back and forth across the dock, setting orange cones, waving dismissively at James. Anne could see through the car windows that James was pounding the steering wheel with impatience. Exhaust poured from the tailpipe, meaning he hadn't even turned off his engine.

The ghost reappeared just as Mitch's car reached the landing. Even Mother Maggie saw it, turning to stare as the shadowy shape rose, spread, swarmed over the driver's side of the car to completely block the windshield.

Mitch had barely applied his own brakes before Anne was out of the car and racing down the slope. She reached James's car at the very moment he was scrambling away from the blinded driver's seat, struggling to climb over the gearshift to the passenger side. He clawed at the lock on the door, popped it open, and fell headfirst out onto the ground.

Anne heard the other locks pop open at the same moment, the sound of reprieve. The answer to her prayers. She ran to the rear passenger door and yanked it open. She pulled Benjamin out, gathered him up in her arms, and backed up the slope, hardly looking where she was going, moving as fast she was able away from the car, putting as much distance as she could between her and James.

She was focused so tightly on Benjamin that she hardly understood what followed. Benjamin clung to her, crying, "Mama, Mama," over and over. She was peripherally aware of a jumble of movement, a slamming of doors, the stentorian blast of the ferry horn, and the gunning of a car engine. She ignored it all, letting it swirl around her, not touching her, not interfering with her relief at having her son in her arms. Benjamin clung to her neck so tightly she could barely breathe. He was heavy for her, but she carried him anyway, her arms burning with effort. She stumbled straight up the short slope to the store. Panting, she pushed the door open with her foot, carried Benjamin inside, and set him on the floor beside the potbellied stove.

She knelt beside him, looking into his eyes, smoothing his mussed hair, soothing a growing bruise on his forehead with her fingers. "Benjamin! Sweetheart! Are you all right? Did he hurt you?"

He choked back a sob. "M-Mama, I h-h-have to go to the b-bathroom!" Crying a little herself, she stood, took him by the hand, and led him to the restroom off the little café.

When they came back, Mother Maggie was just coming inside. She hung up her safety vest and worked off her boots. Petey spotted Benjamin and trotted toward him. Benjamin had no experience with dogs, since his father was so afraid of them, but Petey seemed to understand. He sat a little distance away, head on one side, his tail beating against the floor.

Anne said, "This is Petey, Benjamin. He's a really friendly dog." She gave the dog a tearful smile. "Petey, this is Benjamin. I think he'll like you."

Petey, tongue lolling, jumped up and came to nuzzle Benjamin. Benjamin said, "P-P-Petey!" as he stroked the sleek head. Petey nuzzled him again, nearly toppling him, but there was a smile on Benjamin's tear-streaked face as he clutched the dog's fur.

Mother Maggie came to join them. "This dog is the best thing for the child right now, Anne. Petey's wonderful with kids, and yours has been through a lot."

Anne dried her eyes with her fingers. "You stopped James from going on the ferry!"

Mother Maggie's glasses flashed, and her lips twitched. "Me? We had a ramp problem, just for a few minutes there." She shrugged. "Just a glitch, all fixed. He's on the ferry now, on his way back to the big island."

Anne glanced around the store, but the other sister had disappeared somewhere, and there were no customers this late. "You saw it, didn't you, Mother Maggie."

"The spirit? Oh, yes. I recognized her from before, so—" She shrugged. "A little problem with the ramp suddenly developed. Funny how that happened."

Benjamin looked up from where he was stroking Petey and being licked on his face at the same time. "D-do you m-mean the l-lady, Mama?"

"Lady?"

"The lady! I th-thought she l-lived in our house, but she f-f-followed us here. I d-d-don't know how she d-did that."

Anne crouched beside him, and Petey decided she needed a lick, too. His tongue was rough and dry, his breath warm on her face. "Benjamin, what lady are you talking about?"

"The l-lady from my b-b-bedroom."

Anne felt Mother Maggie's rapt attention as she said carefully, "She was in your bedroom? Did she scare you?"

He shook his head. "N-no, it was g-g-good. You w-weren't there." He kept his eyes on Petey as he spoke. Anne suspected that it was easier for him to look at the dog as he asked in a tiny voice, "Are you c-coming home now?"

"I don't know," she said, in a voice not much stronger than his. "But you and I get to be together for now. For a while."

"I w-want to stay with you."

"I want that, too," she said, though a lump grew in her throat as she reflected that it wasn't likely.

James would be back. He would never let her win. He would never let anyone get the better of him.

She swallowed, and kissed Benjamin's tousled hair. "For now, sweetheart, we'll go home with my friends. You must be hungry."

Mother Maggie said, "I have some fresh bread to send with you. Some cookies, too."

"Does that sound good, Benjamin?"

He nodded, and took her hand. "I w-w-went on an airplane, M-Mama."

"I know you did, honey."

"I d-didn't g-get to b-brush my teeth."

"You can do that soon." She looked up at Mother Maggie. "Do you know where they are? Beatrice and Mitch?"

"Mitch?" Mother Maggie said. A heartbeat later the door opened and the two of them appeared.

Beatrice strode across the store to Anne and threw her arms around her, an action so unlike Beatrice that for a moment Anne couldn't think how to respond. She recovered in time to return the embrace, and when they pulled apart, smiling, Anne took Benjamin's hand. "Benjamin, these are my very good friends, Dr. Bird and Dr. Minotti."

"Beatrice, please," Beatrice said. "Or maybe you'd rather call me Bea, Benjamin. And this is Mitch. We're your friends, too, even though we've only just met. We've heard so much about you."

Benjamin, suddenly shy, hid his face against Anne's hip. She patted his back. "It's okay, honey. Take your time. A lot happened today."

Beatrice turned to Mother Maggie and introduced Mitch, then said, "I'm sure everyone's famished. That was the last ferry for tonight, right, Mother Maggie?"

"Right."

"Good."

"Why good?" Mitch asked.

"Because he can't come back. At least not tonight."

"Oh." Mitch nodded. "Then yes. Good."

Beatrice exhaled a huge sigh. "Peace, at least for the moment. Come on, Anne, and Benjamin, you, too. Let's go home."

The odd thing was, Anne thought, as all of them started toward Mitch's rental car, that the cottage did feel like home. The island felt like home. She wished James would give up and go away, and she and Benjamin could just stay, but that was the most unlikely outcome she could imagine. James would never give up.

* * * * * ★ ★ ★ ★ * * * ·

Beatrice, The Island, 1977

Beatrice had her hand on the passenger-side door of the rental when Mother Maggie called her name. "Beatrice, wait! I have something for Benjamin."

Beatrice turned back. Anne was already in the back seat, still holding tight to her son's hand as if afraid he would disappear. They were murmuring together, Anne nodding indulgently, Benjamin whispering some confidence.

Mother Maggie bustled across the parking lot, something bulky in her hands.

When she reached Beatrice, she held it out. "This fell out of the back seat of his father's car. It feels full. I think it's his backpack, and I expect he'll want it."

Beatrice took it from her, surprised at its weight. "Thank you."

Mother Maggie patted her arm. "I like your Dr. Mitch," she said. "What a godsend that he showed up when he did."

"Yes," Beatrice said. She grinned at the "godsend." Mother Maggie was at it again.

"It seems the sisters' prayers were effective," Mother Maggie said with a twinkle.

"So far," Beatrice said warmly. "I hope you'll keep them up."

"Why, Beatrice Bird," Mother Maggie said. "Listen to you, asking for prayers."

"I'll take anything that can help. We're not yet done with James Iredale."

"No, I see that. He's not a person who lets go easily, even after what he saw today."

Beatrice felt the pressure of Mitch and Anne and the little boy waiting in the car, but she had to ask. "You saw her again, didn't you, Mother Maggie?"

"I did. She didn't seem frightening to me, but she certainly frightened James Iredale." Mother Maggie's twinkle faded, and she gave a solemn nod. "Such a powerful spirit," she murmured. "So sad, but so determined. I'm grateful she shared her energy with me. She made me understand I had to stop him from driving onto the ferry." Her gaze drifted toward the ramp, stowed now, the ferry berth empty.

On an impulse, Beatrice leaned forward and gave the nun a brief hug. "Thank you so much for helping," she said. "We're lucky you were here."

"Well now," Mother Maggie said lightly, her twinkle returning. She put her hand on her cross as she stepped back from the car and gave Anne a little wave. "I don't think luck had much to do with it."

* * * * * ★ ★ ★ * * * ·

While Anne put together a quick pasta dish with a jar of tomato sauce and the hamburger Beatrice had bought, Mitch worked on the broken latch of Anne's bedroom door, but it was beyond repair. "Have to replace it," he said.

They had all had a shocking evening, and the hour was late, but their appetites were good, especially Benjamin's. Except for clutching his backpack in his lap as he sat at the table, he seemed content, although he wouldn't let his mother out of his sight. When Anne went to the bathroom, Beatrice had to go sit next to him and reassure him his mother would be right back.

Having Benjamin in the house was surprisingly easy for Beatrice. Only two ghosts trailed behind him.

One was his father, dark and gloomy, but somehow two-dimensional, like a cartoon. Beatrice supposed the little boy thought his father had been defeated, which kept his ghost at a distance, as if it couldn't reach him.

The other shade was sad, rather sweet, gentle. It was his lady, Beatrice felt sure. For little Benjamin, his lady was not at all the furious phantom that had terrified James Iredale or the billowing specter that had alarmed Beatrice. For Benjamin, his lady was a comfort. The anger and hatred she projected was not directed at a lonely five-year-old.

Interesting, too, that Mother Maggie also saw a sad, gentle soul, the way Benjamin did. What was the difference? Perhaps the two innocents in the drama were the only ones who perceived the real Glenda Iredale.

Beatrice wasn't comfortable with that explanation. It seemed naive. Simplistic. The ghost was the very embodiment of contradiction, and it made Beatrice ponder the power and the problems of blind faith.

Come on, busy Bea. Maybe there is no explanation. Maybe a ghost is just a ghost.

Yeah, Dad. That could be.

Beatrice grinned, and when Mitch raised his eyebrows to ask what had amused her, she shook her head. Her father was right. There was no explaining it.

By the time the pasta bowl was empty, Benjamin was nodding sleepily. Mitch offered to carry him into Anne's bedroom and help her put him to bed. Beatrice cleared the table and put the few dishes they had used into the sink to soak. She was yawning when Mitch came back.

"I feel the same," he said. "I'm so tired my head aches."

"Oh, Mitch, I can imagine. You haven't had a good night's sleep in days, I should think."

"Not really, no. I don't sleep that well on airplanes. I think the seats are deliberately designed to keep you awake."

"Come on, then. Let's get you into a real bed. Towels and soap in the bathroom."

"I should get my suitcase out of the car. Clothes and so forth."

"Never mind that. I have extra toothbrushes. I'll bring your suitcase in tomorrow. I have to be up early to do the milking, anyway."

"Did your other cow come back?"

"I saw both of them out in the lean-to. They're drying up, but they did miss their milking tonight. They'll want it in the morning."

"That big one did a great job with Iredale. A cow hollering at you from one side while a ghost chases you from the other—no wonder he lost it."

"That's some voice, isn't it? Like a bass-baritone with laryngitis." Beatrice yawned again. "I wish that could be the end of it. Too much to hope for that James was frightened enough to go back to Oak Hill and leave Anne alone."

"I don't think that will happen," Mitch said. "That would mean he had given up control."

Not until they were in bed, curled drowsily together, did Beatrice say, "You haven't said much about the ghost. About actually seeing it, I mean."

He mumbled, half-asleep already, "Part of me thinks it was just my imagination. A subconscious suggestion brought on by a stressful situation. You're the shrink. Don't you think that might be it?"

"No, I do not," she whispered, poking him with one finger. "I think, Mitch Minotti, that you saw a ghost, and now you're doing your best to explain it away."

"I don't believe in ghosts," he said, without opening his eyes. "They're not real."

"Fine," she chuckled, her own eyelids drifting closed. "You stick with that."

He might have answered, but she didn't hear it. She was sound asleep the next instant. She slept better than she had in months. The warmth of his body snuggled next to hers was familiar and soothing. The sound of his breathing, even the occasional snore, eased her loneliness. When Alice began her morning summons, she resisted for a time, reluctant to open her eyes, loath to abandon Mitch's warm side for the chill of the early morning. At least it was light outside, the turning of the season bringing earlier sunshine.

Mitch murmured, "Sounds like you're on call."

She laughed sleepily. "I guess I am." With a yawn, she slid her legs out from under the quilt and set her bare feet on the floor. It was icy beneath her toes, the warmth of spring not yet penetrating the walls of the cottage. She muttered, "Brrrr," and Mitch sat up.

He blinked at her, looking boyish and vulnerable without his glasses. "Can I help?"

"You cannot, but thank you." She bent to kiss his tousled head. "Lie down, go back to sleep. I'm so glad you're here."

When she was dressed, she turned to look down at him, his hair rumpled against the pillow, his face relaxed. It was such a good feeling to have him in her house, in her bed, that she felt softened by it. Tenderized. It gave her a cotton-candy feeling in her middle, and it made her question everything she had done.

As she made her way out to the barn, she wrestled with that. In a way, her heart had betrayed her, because now—after all this time without him, when she was just beginning to deal with her loss—he would go home to La Signora, and she would be left here on her own once again. She would have to start all over getting used to being alone. She had no doubt it would be harder the second time.

· · * * ★ ★ ★ * * · ·

"I expect," Anne said quietly, as she stirred oatmeal at the stove, "that James will be back today, or perhaps tomorrow." She had washed the dishes from the night before while Beatrice did the milking, dried them, and put them away. The glass-fronted cupboards sparkled in the spring light, and Anne had laid out cereal bowls, spoons, and prettily folded napkins.

Beatrice admired all this as she strained the milk. Benjamin and Mitch were both still sleeping.

Anne said, "He'll think we tricked him. Or he'll decide he imagined the whole thing. Sleep deprivation, or something."

"Mitch is tempted by that same thought. It's a bizarre experience to process, and he is—as he will insist—an objectivist." Beatrice moved the big jar of milk to the fridge.

"I'm having trouble myself." Anne turned down the heat under the oatmeal and laid her spoon on the counter. "A nightmare is one thing, but yesterday..." She gave an involuntary shiver. "It wouldn't be that hard to talk myself out of it. It's not as if the ghost really looked like her." She wiped her hands on her apron. "James will never accept anything supernatural. He doesn't believe in anything."

"But you met at church?"

"Another deception. I think he went to church to enhance his image."

"Or to find a pretty wife."

"Yes. A wife to replace the one he got rid of." The words were bitter ones, but her voice was even. Composed.

She rubbed her eyes, and Beatrice noticed how weary she looked.

The shade of James hovered behind her like a hazy, giant crow. At least, for now, there was no small, sad little shade clinging to her legs. "Did you sleep at all?"

"Some." She managed a tired smile. "I thought I would feel better if I could see Benjamin for just a little while, if I could reassure him, but now—I can't bear the thought of being apart from him again." She looked away as her eyes began to redden. "I thought I would get stronger, but I feel the opposite. Another separation—even thinking about it is agony."

"I know the feeling," Beatrice said, but stopped herself from saying anything further. Her situation wasn't the same at all. She and Mitch were adults. They could make their own choices. She said only, "We're trying to think of something we can do. You could leave right now. Get on the first ferry with Benjamin, and—"

"I wish I could, but I think I missed my opportunity to flee with my son. James could be waiting for me to do just that, and I'd be in even more trouble than I am. It would be like him to be waiting with law enforcement, trying to catch me at taking Benjamin away.

"He's right, of course. I lost legal custody of my son, fairly or not. James was shocked yesterday, but by this morning he will have recovered. It's not in his nature to accept losing. He always, always wins."

There was nothing Beatrice could say to that, but she wished with all her heart it weren't so.

42

Anne, The Island, 1977

IT WAS GOOD to see Benjamin tucking into a bowl of oatmeal like a normal five-year-old. Anne indulged in a fragile sense of contentment, determined not to focus on how temporary it was. Mitch sat next to Benjamin at the table, conversing easily. By the time they finished breakfast, they had arranged to walk down to the beach together, and Benjamin had promised to show Mitch his stamp collection. It was a charming scene. A deceptively normal scene. A little boy at breakfast, fair hair shining in spring sunshine, chattering to someone he trusted.

"I c-couldn't b-bring my c-coins," he told Mitch. "Th-they w-w-were too heavy."

"But you have the stamps," Mitch said, his eyes crinkling pleasantly behind his glasses. "I love stamps."

"I h-have s-some from England," Benjamin said proudly. "I'll sh-show you those last."

"Okay."

Anne and Beatrice cleared the breakfast things while Mitch and Benjamin disappeared into the living room, Benjamin lugging his backpack. None of the adults betrayed the tension they felt, but Anne felt it in every breath, every casual word, every ordinary gesture.

Beatrice said, "Benjamin seems pretty calm, considering the drama of yesterday."

Anne's brief moment of peace faded. "He doesn't understand," Anne said. "He thinks it's all over."

"I suppose it's possible."

"No." Anne pointed with her dish towel to the phone on the bar. "That will ring at any moment, Mother Maggie telling us he's back, and with reinforcements."

"Reinforcements?"

"James is an expert at throwing his weight around, and his reach is surprisingly long. It's weird that I used to be impressed by that. I didn't realize how much he could hurt people." She hung up the dish towel. "He'll have a lawyer, or a sheriff, or something." She glanced toward the living room, where they could hear Benjamin's piping voice describing various stamps, and her eyes stung. "I really shouldn't have mentioned Glenda. I was so angry, I wasn't thinking. He won't have forgotten that."

Beatrice paused in the archway, tilting her head to one side. "You know, it has faded a good deal," she said.

"What has?"

"The ghost of James. The one that has hovered over you all this time."

"Maybe it's because I'm not afraid of him anymore. Because I'm so certain it's over."

"Anne. Don't give up."

Anne untied her apron and hung it on its hook. "Don't worry, Beatrice. I'll keep trying to get Benjamin back. I'll do my best to get free of whatever punishment James wants to inflict on me, and I'll try to be smarter about it. But for now I'm just accepting."

"Well. It's obviously a healthy development, judging by the ghost diminishing. And of course Mitch and I will stand by you."

"Thank you. I'll never forget your kindness."

"It can't be over, Anne. It just can't."

"I would love that to be true, but I won't torture myself with false hope."

Beatrice looked as if she were about to say something else, but Mitch interrupted, calling from the living room in a low voice that throbbed with excitement. "Bea? Come in here. Anne, you, too. Quick!"

* * * * ★ ★ ★ ★ * * * *

Benjamin, The Island, 1977

Benjamin liked Dr. Mitch's sparkly brown eyes. He wore funny round glasses, and he had small, careful hands that turned the pages of the stamp collection gently. He was the nicest doctor Benjamin had ever met. He smelled like soap and oatmeal. He didn't interrupt when Benjamin explained the stamps to him, and he didn't seem impatient when Benjamin stuttered. Somehow that meant he stuttered less, and that was good.

They went all through the collection, the stamps with birds and flowers, stamps with special dates on them, a few really old ones and some that were brand new. Benjamin told Dr. Mitch all about them, and Dr. Mitch listened as if he was really interested, not fidgeting or interrupting or looking out the window.

Dr. Mitch said, as they reached the next-to-last page, "You read very well, Benjamin."

"I kn-know. I'm the only one in k-kindergarten who can read."

"I'm not surprised. Now, what's this one?"

Benjamin glanced up at him, hoping he wasn't pretending. Dr. Mitch was looking at the last page, pointing to the first stamp at the top.

"Th-that's from England," Benjamin said.

"Cool. How did you get it?"

Benjamin felt a flash of anxiety. Maybe he should have left those stamps out, just kept them for himself to look at. He said uneasily, "It's k-k-kind of a s-secret."

"Okay. Secrets are cool, too." Dr. Mitch pointed to the next one. "That one's also from England, isn't it?"

"This whole page. They're all from England."

"Very interesting. They're beautiful."

"I like the p-p-picture of the lady with the c-crown. She's the q-q-queen, I think."

"You're right. Her name is Elizabeth. Queen Elizabeth."

"Oh. I d-didn't know that."

"Pretty cool to find out, isn't it? Thank you for showing me your collection. It's great."

Benjamin said politely, the way Mama had taught him, "You're welcome." He picked up the book. He was beginning to slide it into his backpack when he sniffed. A smell drifted into the room. He knew that smell. It made his nose wrinkle, and he looked up, startled. The stamp collection slipped through his hands and fell to the floor.

She was back.

Benjamin had been sure, after she frightened Papa away, that the lady was gone for good. She had vanished. He assumed she went home, even though he still didn't know how she could get here without going on an airplane.

But now—now she was standing behind Dr. Mitch, kind of like she had in his bedroom, except now it was morning. The sunlight made her look as if she were made of glass, the kind of colored glass he saw in church. In his bedroom, at night, she was dark and misty, but here she was blue and white and her hair was kind of gold, like Mama's. She was still misty, though.

He stared at her for a long moment, and she gazed back. She looked awfully sad. She would have been pretty if she weren't so sad. He lifted a hand to wave at her, but she didn't wave back. A moment later she was gone.

Dr. Mitch hadn't turned around, hadn't noticed the smell. He had picked up the stamp collection book. "What's all this?"

Benjamin saw that Dr. Mitch had lifted the book upside down. All the letters—the ones he had hidden in the inside pocket, the ones from the burn pile that had borne the stamps from England—had fallen out, and lay scattered on the floor.

Dr. Mitch was staring at them as if they made him angry.

"I d-didn't open them," Benjamin said in a small voice. "I j-just c-c-cut off th-th-th—" He couldn't finish. He couldn't push the words through his rebellious throat.

"I can see that," Dr. Mitch said, but slowly, the way Papa did sometimes when he was about to yell.

"Th-they w-w-were in the b-b-burn p-pile!" Tears started up behind Benjamin's eyelids, and he squeezed his eyes shut to hold them in.

"Were they, Benjamin? In the burn pile? And you saw them and pulled them out."

Benjamin sniffled, and nodded. When he heard the little tear of paper that meant Dr. Mitch was opening one of the envelopes, his eyes flew open. Through the haze of tears he watched Dr. Mitch's face change as he read the letter inside. His mouth went hard. His eyes behind his glasses didn't sparkle anymore.

Then he called out for Dr. Bea and Mama to come in right away, and Benjamin knew he was in trouble. His tears burst forth, and he sobbed. He couldn't help it.

43

Beatrice, The Island, 1977

BEATRICE DROPPED THE wooden spoon she had been on the point of putting away and dashed through the archway into the living room, with Anne close on her heels. They saw Benjamin kneeling on the floor, his stamp book upside down and open beside him. Anne went straight to him. She crouched beside him, and he sobbed into her shoulder.

Beatrice saw that the lady's ghost that had clung faintly to Benjamin was gone. Not even a halfhearted outline remained. No shadow of her, no impression that she had been there. There was only the shade of his father, grown darker and larger, looming over him. It made her throat ache with misery.

Before Beatrice could think about this, she caught sight of the letters spilled out across the wood, more than a dozen of them lying this way and that between Benjamin and Mitch, who was also on his knees. They were all unopened, as far as Beatrice could see, except for the one Mitch held in his hand. Each envelope had a neat cutout on the upper right corner where the stamp should have been. Some of the envelopes had scorch marks, as if they had been burned. Others were smudged with ash.

"Mitch, what on earth!" Beatrice cried. "Why is Benjamin upset? Is it those letters?"

Mitch, his jaw rippling with tension, lifted the letter he held so Beatrice could take it. "Read that. And the envelope." He handed that up to her, too.

Slowly, the letter and envelope in her hands, she settled cross-legged on the floor beside him. She started with the envelope.

"Glenda Iredale. Oak Hill? But—"

"Read the letter." Mitch put out a hand to touch Benjamin's shoulder. "No need to cry, son. You're not in trouble. Not in trouble at all."

"B-b-but P-Papa," Benjamin sobbed. "If he s-s-sees I t-t-took the letters—"

"He won't, Benjamin. Trust me."

Anne, her mouth a little open, her eyes wide and very blue in the morning light, gazed at Beatrice as she began to read.

"The date is 1966." Beatrice raised her eyebrows at Mitch, who nodded and gestured for her to go on. " 'Dear Glenda,' it says. 'We were surprised not to hear from you at Christmas. Were you traveling? I hope it was someplace lovely, and that you had a very happy Christmas wherever you were. We are all well here. Your gran took a little tumble, so we've brought her to stay with us. I think that will be permanent. It's getting hard for her to live on her own, with stairs to climb and so forth. She has been asking about you, and your dad is wondering, too. It's been too long since we received a letter. Please do write soon, and tell us all about what's happening there.' " Beatrice had to stop and swallow. " 'As always, dearest daughter, your loving Mum and Dad.' " Her voice cracked as she read the signature line.

There was a long moment of stunned silence. Benjamin, his face tucked up against his mother's shoulder, had stopped sobbing as he listened to Beatrice read. Anne's eyes glistened with her own tears. Mitch had taken off his glasses and was polishing them with unnecessary vigor.

Beatrice lowered the letter to her lap and gave Mitch a meaningful look. He growled, "That bastard," and she nodded.

Anne said, in a tone that vibrated with wonder, "Read the others, Mitch. Are they all from Glenda's parents?"

Mitch picked up another, and then another, tearing the envelopes open with his thumb, scanning the contents. "They are," he said. "There could have been many more, of course. These are just the ones Benjamin saved from the burn pile."

For a fleeting moment, Beatrice saw the flicker of the ghost hover behind Benjamin and Anne, a sorrowing image, pale, nearly colorless, almost invisible. It dissipated swiftly.

She said, "What do you think, Mitch? Are these evidence?"

"Evidence enough, I would say. At least to prompt an investigation."

"I'm shocked no one thought to ask," Beatrice said. "Didn't she have friends in Oak Hill? Someone who expected to hear from her, or someone who wanted to go visit?"

"I doubt he allowed her to have friends," Mitch said.

"The garden," Anne said.

"What?" Beatrice and Mitch both turned to her.

Benjamin still knelt in the circle of her arm, his fair eyelashes sparkling with his recent tears. Anne was nodding, saying almost to herself, "That was it. That was why."

"What is it about the garden, Anne?" Mitch asked.

Anne lifted her head, and Beatrice thought again how beautiful she was, with her clear skin and sculpted mouth, her perfect profile. Anne said, "I always wanted to rake out the burn pile, clear that corner of the garden to plant something. Roses would have been nice, but James said no." She looked down at the pile of unopened envelopes, which Mitch had now organized by date. "Those poor parents," she murmured. "I wonder if they ever came to Oak Hill, looking for her?"

"The police will find that out." Mitch gathered up the envelopes. "They should have checked all this before."

Anne said, "That was the power James had, over the police, the courts, everything. Even if someone had suggested it, he would have prevented them. Those men protect each other."

"I understand," Mitch said. "I see it all the time. But in this case—" He tapped the handful of envelopes against his thigh. "Listen, I have a friend in law enforcement who advises the security people at the hospital. He might know who we can call."

Benjamin reached to pick up the stamp collection, adjusted the disarrayed pages, and set it carefully on his knees. He stared at it, blinking slowly as he thought things through. Mitch was getting to his feet, rubbing at his stiff knees. Beatrice uncrossed her legs and stood up, too, but she kept her gaze on the little boy.

At last Benjamin said, "Those l-letters—they were about the l-lady, weren't they?"

His mother said gently, her hand on his back, "Yes, Benjamin. They were."

"What happened to her?"

"We're not sure yet, sweetheart."

He thought for another moment, and Beatrice and Mitch exchanged a glance. "She's pretty sad," Benjamin said.

"Is she?"

"Yes. I can tell." He looked up at his mother. "I think someone hurt her."

44

Anne, The Island, 1977

ANNE DELIBERATELY KEPT herself busy all day. She spent most of her time in the kitchen, putting together sandwiches for lunch, then marinating a salmon fillet Mother Maggie had given them. Beatrice and Mitch had gone down to walk on the beach, taking Benjamin with them. She watched them through the front windows, Beatrice's short hair ruffling in the wind, Mitch's covered with a cap. Benjamin, wrapped in a borrowed sweatshirt that hung past his knees, crouched along the tide line, pulling things out of the sand and placing them carefully in an old milk bucket Beatrice had found in the barn.

Anne chose to avoid the barn, at least for the moment. She didn't need a reminder of the look of menace on James's face, the anticipation of the blow he had every intention of delivering. She would never forget the sights and smells of a furious phantom, though now it seemed more like a remembered nightmare than an actual experience. She felt the aftershocks of the experience in Beatrice, too, and in Mitch, for whom the phenomenon was shockingly new.

They would find peace in the ripple and rush of the waves against the beach. She hoped Benjamin did, too. She could see he had attached himself to Mitch, and she hated to think how little time he would have with his new hero. He had never had a man in his life he could look up to. One he could trust. One who didn't terrorize him. One who didn't abuse him, she reminded herself. *Call it what it is. If nothing else, you have learned that much.*

When the telephone rang, late in the afternoon, her nerves flared. She picked up the receiver, but only after drawing two deep, steadying breaths and clearing her throat so her voice would be steady when she answered. "Beatrice Bird residence."

"Oh, hi," came a man's voice she didn't recognize. "This isn't Bea, is it?"

The tension in her belly released, but it left her feeling breathless. She said, a little unsteadily, "No. I'm Anne. Did you want to speak to Beatrice?"

"Actually, it's Mitch I need. Dr. Minotti? He left me a message."

"Can you hold a moment? I'll get him."

"Tell him I'm calling from the hospital in San Francisco."

Anne laid the receiver down and went out through the kitchen door and around to the front porch so she could call down to the beach. The air was warmer than it had been, with the first promising scents of spring in the air. She saw newly forming buds on the rhododendrons below the porch railing, and she wished she could till the soil beneath them, add some compost, clear away the dead leaves from the year before. The hellebores growing at the side of the cottage were in full bloom, and the delicate spears of daffodils trembled in the ocean breeze. Anne thought she could be perfectly content if she could stay right here, in this quiet, lovely spot. She could nurture these flowers, milk the cows, and watch her son explore the beach in peace.

She braced herself on one of the newel posts of the porch so she could lean over the railing. "Telephone for Mitch," she called.

Beatrice lifted a hand in acknowledgment. Mitch came jogging up the path. Beatrice followed more slowly, Benjamin and his laden bucket in tow. Rather than eavesdrop on Mitch's call, Anne pulled her sweater tighter around her and went down to meet them.

She was crouching beside Benjamin, getting a tour of his beach treasures, when Mitch came back outside. Beatrice said, "Did you talk to him?"

"I did."

"Can he help?"

"He's going to try."

* * * * ★ ★ ★ * * * *

Beatrice, The Island, 1977

Anne's dinner was excellent, and the four of them lingered at the table as if they were a family, long after every bite of salmon and rice and freshly baked brownies had been demolished.

"I don't know how you did that," Beatrice said. "Brownies? I love them, but I never have anything like that in the house."

"Well, these aren't from scratch. Mother Maggie put a mix in our last delivery, and I thought it would be a shame to waste it."

Beatrice understood the implication, that soon Anne wouldn't be here to make brownies, with or without a mix. Or to make anything else, for that matter. She said only, "I'd love to have a taste of your scratch brownies. See if yours are a match for Mrs. O'Reilly's."

Anne said, with only a trace of sadness, "I would love to find that out, too. One day, perhaps."

Benjamin yawned, and Mitch smiled down at him. "Pretty tired, buddy?"

Benjamin tried to say no, but he yawned again. Anne started to get up, saying something about a bath and bed, but Mitch put up his hand. "I can do that, Anne. You've been cooking all day. Why don't you sit with Bea for a bit?"

Beatrice said, "It will be fine, Anne, I promise. Mitch has about a hundred nieces and nephews. Italian family."

It was clear Benjamin thought it was a wonderful idea. He and Mitch collected his backpack from the living room, complete with the stamp book, and disappeared into the bathroom. Anne said, "Mitch would be a wonderful father."

"He would have been," Beatrice agreed. "Afraid we waited too long. And of course—" She shrugged. "Never got around to getting married."

Anne gazed at her with what Beatrice was glad to believe was affection. The ghost of James was almost invisible in the muted light, no darker than a spring rain cloud. "Did you ever consider it? Getting married, I mean?"

Beatrice twirled her empty wineglass. "We did, once or twice, but it didn't seem important. Times have changed so much, it wasn't a priority."

"I guess I was behind the times."

"We all change at our own pace, if at all. My father wasn't very traditional, but still, my dad would have preferred us to get married. Those are the mores he grew up with."

"Mitch's parents?"

"He grew up with his Uncle Matteo, but yes—his uncle, all his relatives, thought he should marry me, rather than living in sin!" She chuckled. "I've always thought—" She paused, wary of giving offense.

Anne smiled in acknowledgment. "Tell me what you think, Beatrice."

"Well, it's just my opinion, but I think most of the objections to people living as Mitch and I do—did—are based on not being able to control women who aren't interested in marriage. Women who feel complete in themselves."

"I agree with you," Anne said. "It's tempting to wish I hadn't married James, that I had defied my parents about—well, about everything. Except then I wouldn't have Benjamin, and he's worth all of it."

"That he is," Beatrice said warmly. "He's a darling."

Anne drew a breath and gazed out to the water, where stars sparkled on the dark waves. "I'm so worried about him. My mother won't stand up to James. My father certainly won't interfere. That means there's no one. Who is there to protect Benjamin?"

"Try not to worry too much, Anne. The letters might persuade the police to do something."

Anne said with resignation, "They should dig up the burn pile. I doubt they will."

* * * * * ★ ★ ★ * * * *

Morning dawned bright and clear, the few clouds almost unnaturally white, glowing as if they had been painted on the vivid sky. Beatrice left Mitch brewing coffee while she did the milking. Anne and Benjamin slept late, not emerging until the smell of bacon enticed them out. Mitch, wrapped in one of Beatrice's aprons, stood at the stove and waved his spatula at Benjamin when he came in. The little boy trotted into the kitchen, his face glowing with anticipation.

Benjamin brimmed with plans for the new day. He wanted to see the cows. He intended to go back to the beach for more shells and stones and sea glass, to start a new collection. He promised to tell Dr. Mitch all about his coins. He barely stuttered as he announced all of these activities. It was a remarkable transformation, touching to see, but it made Beatrice's heart ache. Benjamin's respite would be brief, and she couldn't bear to think of his disappointment when his idyll reached its cruel end.

Anne was a different matter. The ghost of James still hovered behind her, its colors shifting from ashen gray to muddy brown as she listened to Benjamin's happy chatter. Beatrice saw the grief in her eyes and felt her anxiety in her own chest. There was nothing she could say to help her. All she could do, all any of them could do, was wait.

Mitch monitored the telephone while Beatrice and Anne took Benjamin to the beach. The three of them crouched on the sand to sift through the detritus left by the retreating tide. Benjamin was thrilled to find a sand dollar that was almost intact, and he added three pieces of sea glass to his newest collection. He discovered that if he stamped hard on the ropy bits of sea wrack, water squirted out, making him giggle. He did it over and over again, until his trouser legs were dripping seawater. They stayed on the beach until Benjamin started to get hungry.

"I can make you a peanut butter sandwich," Anne said when they reached the porch.

He shook his head. "I d-don't like p-peanut butter."

"You always like peanut butter!"

"I d-don't like it anymore."

Anne's gaze met Beatrice's above the little boy's head, and she gave a slight, mystified shrug. Beatrice said, "We have chicken noodle soup, in a can."

"I l-like that," Benjamin declared, and with that problem solved, they went in through the kitchen door.

Anne heated the soup and took a box of crackers out of the cupboard. "This is the last box," she said.

Mitch said, "Make a grocery list. I'll drive down to that little store."

"That would be good," Beatrice said. "There will be something in their freezer we can make for dinner. And get some wine while you're at it."

"Let me give you some money," Anne said, but Mitch waved her off.

"I'm good," he said. "I'll be back soon."

Beatrice went out to the porch to watch him back the car and bump away down the dirt road. She heard the hoot of the ferry horn, and she took a moment just to breathe, to absorb the welcome warmth of the afternoon. Even the birds chittering from the woods seem to be celebrating the return of the sun. These last days, she reflected, had been as full and wild as her early days on the island had been empty and silent.

She leaned on the railing to gaze out at the water. The afternoon sun made tiny, brilliant ghosts of light dance across the surface, and that made her think of Iredale again, and his utter lack of any shades.

He was, without a doubt, the most dangerous man she had ever encountered.

45

Anne, The Island, 1977

ANNE, SETTLING BENJAMIN for a nap, heard the basso honk of the ferry horn sounding in the bay. Benjamin was half-asleep already, the sand dollar clutched in his hand, but he stirred. "Wh-what's that, Mama?"

"That's the ferry," she said. "It's a really loud horn, so we hear it all the way up here."

"I l-like it." He snuggled deeper into the pillow.

"I do, too." She bent to pull the quilt up to his shoulders and to kiss his forehead. "I'll be right out there in the living room. Is that okay?"

"That's okay," he mumbled.

She waited until he was asleep before slipping out of the bedroom. She left the door open a few inches and went to the sofa. She picked up a book that lay on the coffee table but put it down again, too tense to read. She heard Beatrice step out onto the porch and start across the yard to the barn. She listened to her son's light breathing from the bedroom and heard the cries of the seagulls dipping this way and that above the coastline.

I could live here, she thought. *If only James would let it all go, I could live right here. Benjamin loves it, and I could get a job. Teach in the school or something. Help out at the store.*

Of course it was just a daydream, she knew that, but it was a sweet one, and she let herself linger on it until—

She felt him come in. She hadn't heard a car, or the opening of the door. She hadn't heard his heavy footsteps through the kitchen, but the thrill of alarm shooting through every one of her nerves told her he was there.

Slowly, she turned her head to look over her shoulder.

He loomed in the archway, too tall for this little house. He made a dark, ugly figure despite his superficial good looks. He radiated evil so strongly that she might have been Beatrice, with her feelings. Her second sight.

James was a terrible man who had done terrible things. Now she had to face him alone.

He spoke in that low, gravelly tone that meant trouble. "Where's Ben?"

"How did you get here, James?"

"Walked on the ferry, walked off." His features were frozen into a mask. Only his lips moved. "It was easy, Anne, and your meddling nun didn't even notice me. Weird seeing a nun work the ferry, but in any case—lucky you. Here I am."

"Why can't you leave us alone, James?" She spoke in a low voice, too, hoping not to wake her sleeping child. "You don't care about Benjamin. You never wanted a child except to make yourself look better, look like a family man. You can walk away, leave us here." She pushed herself to her feet and stood with her arms tightly folded around herself. "I won't ask for anything. I don't want alimony, nor community property. I don't care about any of that."

"Ridiculous," he grated. "Everyone cares about that. Money. Property. Position."

"I promise you I don't. I just want to raise my son in peace."

"Sure," he said. "Happy to arrange that. Just get me those damned letters, and I'll go."

"Letters?" Her face went cold, and her hands, as if all the blood rushed from her head. James's lips twisted in a sneer, turning his face into that of a cartoon villain, a caricature. It would have been ludicrous if she hadn't been so afraid of him.

"Don't be an idiot, Anne," he said, his voice dropping even lower. "Did you think the Oak Hill police wouldn't tell me? The chief called my hotel last night."

"James, I—"

"I told you. Give me the letters, and this will all be over."

But it wouldn't. She knew in her bones that he was lying. He meant to make her pay for defying him, for embarrassing him, for daring to disobey his orders. He would take the letters. They had been tied into a neat bundle, and they lay a mere two steps away, on Beatrice's desk. When he had them, he would hurt her. He might hurt Benjamin, too, and say she had done it. She was hysterical, was she not? Mentally damaged. An unfit mother.

She lifted her chin. "No."

"What do you mean, no?"

"I mean, James, that I will not give you the letters, nor will I voluntarily give up my child. It ends here."

He blinked once, and his mouth contorted with anger. "You have no idea what I can do to you, Anne."

"Oh, I think I do. I know you now. I know who you really are."

"Well," he said. "You're a fool, but you're right about one thing. It ends here."

She braced herself as he lunged through the arch, his hands out for her neck. She was trapped between the coffee table and the sofa. She took a side step to get free of the table, to have a path of escape.

It did no good. He was on her before she could move any farther.

He seized her arm with his brutal fingers, dragging her out from behind the coffee table, grabbing her neck with his other hand. She cried out, and at the same moment, Beatrice came in through the kitchen door.

James whirled, holding Anne in front of him, his arm coming around her middle, clutching her so tightly she could barely breathe.

Benjamin had heard her cry. He appeared at the end of the short hall, looking tiny and fearful in his borrowed sweatshirt. "M-M-Mama?"

Beatrice said, "Mr. Iredale, stop! You can't—"

"I think you'll find I can," he snapped, and jerked Anne backward, so hard her feet came off the floor. He kept his arm around her waist and his other hand tightened on her neck, just beneath her chin. He was breathing so hard she could feel the movement of his belly against her back. His body burned with temper.

Anne couldn't make a sound. She could think of nothing but the need to breathe. As black spots danced before her eyes she tried to squirm, to claw at James's hand, but her efforts were feeble ones. She had no strength.

The blackness won, and she went limp in James's grasp, just as her son shrieked, "P-P-Papa! D-d-don't!"

Benjamin ran full tilt into the living room, his bare feet skidding on the floor. He screamed again at James and launched his small body forward as if he would tear his mother from his father's grasp.

James, without hesitation, lashed out with his right foot. Anne felt the shift in his balance and the flex of his belly muscles as he kicked.

Benjamin stopped screaming. He didn't cry, or whimper, or even groan. He didn't make a sound.

· · · * * ★ ★ ★ * * · ·

Beatrice, The Island, 1977

Beatrice, coming through the arch, saw Iredale's kick, saw the screaming little boy fly across the room to strike the arm of the easy chair by the window. With a chill, she registered his ominous silence afterward.

Iredale's face was a mask of stone as he went about the task of killing his wife.

"Stop!" Beatrice shrieked. She ran toward him, too, but she knew, even as she rounded the sofa to try to intervene, that she was not strong enough. She needed help.

Where is she? Where is a ghost when you need her?

Hang on, Bea. She's right there.

And she was.

She appeared without warning, surging from the bedroom where Benjamin had been sleeping, charging toward Iredale. The foul odor preceded her in a wave. A black miasma surrounded her head, and her body pulsed so darkly that Beatrice half expected to see it shot through with lightning. The air in the cottage turned instantly icy, despite the fire crackling in the stove. Beatrice's breath misted before her, and a fog of it hung before James's face.

There was nothing from Anne, which terrified Beatrice even more.

She was two steps from James when the phantom flowed between them, looming like a thundercloud, swelling until its head touched the ceiling.

Iredale's eyes stretched wide. "Not again—" His grip on Anne eased enough for her to draw a desperate, noisy breath, and her exhale clouded in the frigid air as her feet scrabbled for purchase on the floor. Beatrice could see her struggles, but even in the face of the specter of Glenda Iredale, he held her fast.

Iredale shrilled, "You people!" His panicked voice was nearly unrecognizable. "How are you doing this?"

Beatrice was about to deny doing anything, but the ghost intervened. The shape of her blurred and shivered, growing more fearsome and less human with each passing second. A horrifying grimace flashed through the darkness as her arms lifted, her outstretched hands became claws, and she plunged them deep into Iredale's chest.

He gagged and groaned, his hold on Anne releasing as he struggled to push the phantom's hands away. He couldn't do it. His hands drove right through her cloudy form, useless, scrabbling. Hers gripped, and squeezed, and didn't let go. It was hard for Beatrice to see Iredale's face as his body curled in on itself, and he gave a moan of pure agony.

It wasn't possible, but it was happening. It couldn't be real, and yet it must be.

It was obviously real to Iredale. He gave up trying to get free of the ghost and pressed his hands to his chest, his breathing ragged, every bit as desperate as Anne's had been moments ago. "Stop it," he grunted. "Heart attack—stop it—"

But the ghost was not done. The stinking, dark, awful essence of her stuck fast to him, a limpet clinging to a stone. Her swollen body smothered him. Her strange, misty hands were invisible inside his chest, and she radiated a sense of fury that stunned all those watching.

Anne was on her knees, then on her feet, staggering toward her son, just as Mitch banged through the kitchen door and stopped in the archway with a muttered curse.

Iredale groaned, "You're killing me—stop—" He fell back a step, two, three, until his back was to the windows, his figure silhouetted by the sparkling water beyond.

The specter gave a last, swirling burst of energy. It flowed around Iredale, then suddenly blew apart, in a way that made Beatrice think of extinguishing a candle. It was there, and then, in a burst of sparkling darkness, it wasn't. The air in the cottage warmed instantly, and the putrid smell evaporated.

Iredale, bent at the waist, gasped for breath through slack lips. Both of his hands pressed to his chest, and his eyes, the pupils swelled with shock, were glassy and unfocused. His hands, so hard and vicious only moments before, shook as if with palsy. For long seconds he didn't straighten. The bizarre tableau of the five of them seemed suspended in time, as if captured in the flash of a camera.

The scene broke as Mitch strode across the room to kneel by Benjamin, who lay limp in Anne's arms. Mitch lifted his eyelids, felt his wrist, patted his cheek. He murmured to the little boy, words Beatrice couldn't catch.

James stuttered out his complaints, his voice weak and thready. "Sh-sh-she can't—what have you done to me? My heart—I might have died!"

What had Mother Maggie said? Something about there being a reason to see a spirit. James Iredale had come face-to-face with the spirit of his crime. His ghost. His guilt. His sin.

Beatrice sensed his horror as he realized they knew. She and Mitch and Anne knew what he had done. Others must know, too, or they would very soon. He was exposed.

Little by little, Iredale straightened, tugging at the lapels of his trench coat, wiping the spittle from his lips, smoothing back his disordered hair.

And behind him, though he didn't see it, floated the shade of the woman he had killed. It clung to his shoulders, a shroud of silver and gray and purple, the colors of guilt and fear.

No one else would see this particular ghost. This was Beatrice's phenomenon. It was not the angry phantom who had intervened when he kicked his son, or the specter who interfered when he choked his wife, but the sort of shade that would haunt him forever. He had no empathy, nor did he possess a conscience. This shade, his very first, sprang from his existential dread.

Beatrice saw it, but she didn't care. It didn't make her throat ache. It neither grieved her nor pleased her. She felt nothing, not even triumph.

That would come later, maybe, when the shock had passed and she had processed the events of the past moments. For now she said, in a gritty voice she barely recognized, "Iredale. Get the hell out of my house."

"You can't do this," he said, but there was no threat in it. It was a whine. The whimper of someone who was beaten. Who had lost.

"It's done, Iredale," Mitch said. Beatrice turned to look at him and saw with relief that Benjamin was stirring, blinking, breathing. Mitch's eyes glinted darkly behind his glasses. "I called my friend from the store. It seems the Oak Hill police went to your house. Dug in your garden."

James Iredale stared at him as if he couldn't understand the words he was hearing.

Mitch said, with satisfaction, "They found her this morning, Iredale. They found the remains of your first wife."

46

Benjamin, The Island, 1977

BENJAMIN KNEW A lot of words, but he didn't know what *remains* meant. He wanted to know, but he couldn't ask just yet. He would have to wait until he got his breath back.

He wasn't sure exactly what had happened. He remembered his father kicking him, because it hurt, right in his stomach, and it meant he couldn't breathe for a while. He kind of had to close his eyes for a bit, but then Mama was there, and Dr. Mitch, too, rubbing his back, patting his cheek, looking under his eyelids. He knew it was Dr. Mitch because he still smelled like soap and oatmeal.

It felt good, having them both there. When his stomach let go so he could breathe again, he opened his eyes, hoping Papa would be gone.

He wasn't gone. He was still there, but he didn't look mad anymore. He looked afraid. He didn't look sorry that he had choked Mama or kicked Benjamin. He just looked scared.

Benjamin thought *remains* must be something that scared him.

Dr. Mitch patted his shoulder and said, "You take it easy, buddy. Take some nice breaths and stay here with your mom." Benjamin thought that was a good idea. Mama's arm around him made him feel safe, even though his stomach hurt a little.

Dr. Mitch got up, and he and Dr. Bea went to Papa, one on either side. They walked him back toward the archway as if he couldn't find the way on his own. Papa looked back once, blinking at Benjamin and Mama as if he had forgotten who they were.

That was strange. But it wasn't the only strange thing.

The lady had been in his bedroom again. He had seen her there when he woke up. She looked like her usual self, sad and sweet. Then he heard Papa shouting, and Mama's cry, and he ran out. He thought maybe the lady had followed him out to the living room, but then Papa kicked him and he didn't know what happened after that.

He snuggled closer to his mother and whispered, "Did he hurt you?" Mama squeezed him. "Yes, honey. It doesn't hurt now, though."

"My stomach doesn't hurt, either," Benjamin said. It wasn't completely true, but he didn't want Mama to worry.

Benjamin heard car doors open and close, and a moment later Dr. Bea came in by herself. "Mitch is driving James down to the ferry. He'll make sure he gets on."

Mama released Benjamin, and the two of them stood up. He looked up at her and saw that she had bruises on her neck. He wondered if he had bruises on his stomach.

"I hope that's safe for Mitch," Mama said.

Dr. Bea said, "It is. James won't try anything now." She gave a lopsided smile and touched her temple. "I know it."

"Good."

Dr. Bea leaned down to speak to Benjamin. He liked looking into her eyes. They were a pretty gray color, shiny, like ice cubes. She said, "You okay, honey? What happened was bad, I know, but it's not going to happen again."

"I'm okay," he said. "But how do you know it's not going to happen again? Is it because of remains?"

Mama drew a sharp breath, but Dr. Bea nodded as if it was the best question he could have asked. "Yes, Benjamin," she said. "It is because of remains. That's an unusual word, isn't it? We'll explain it to you. There's a lot to explain, actually. Do you mind waiting a little bit?"

Benjamin thought about it for a moment. He wanted to know why the bad things weren't going to happen again, but he also liked being with Mama and Dr. Bea and Dr. Mitch, and he didn't want to worry about what came next. He said, finally, "I don't mind. B-but—" He paused, trying to think how big a question he could ask.

"Yes, Benjamin." Dr. Bea waited for him while he thought. He liked that. She didn't make him feel like he had to hurry, which always made his stutter worse.

"D-Dr. Bea, am I going to stay with Mama n-now?"

"Yes, you are. That's good news, isn't it?"

"Yes." He felt a smile start on his face, and a lightening in his chest, like when he had a balloon and it started to float in the air. It felt good, and the ache in his stomach didn't matter so much.

"So for now, let's go get some water, and I think I have some cookies. Dr. Mitch wants to examine you when he gets back, because you were hurt, but that's nothing to worry about."

Benjamin nodded. He didn't think he had to worry about Dr. Mitch. "Okay." The three of them started toward the kitchen, and Benjamin said as they walked, "I worried about you, Mama. I worried a lot."

Mama said, taking his hand, "I worried about you, too, sweetheart. I'm glad we're together now. We won't worry so much when we see each other every day."

47

Anne, The Island, 1977

MITCH RETURNED TO report that he had seen James onto the ferry without incident. "All the fight has gone out of him. He's a judge. He knows how much trouble he's in."

"Can he just disappear?" Beatrice asked. "Run away from prosecution?"

Anne said, "He'll never do that. He was frightened, but once he calms down, he'll talk himself out of it. He'll think he can control all of this. He'll have great lawyers, and he has a lot of influence with the police."

"Pretty sure they're going to charge him," Mitch said. "According to my friend, the police chief tried to prevent the detectives from going to investigate, but he couldn't pull it off. Iredale doesn't have the absolute influence he thinks he has."

"No guarantee of a conviction," Beatrice said.

"No. But destroying the letters that came for his wife is telling evidence, and since Benjamin saved so many of them, that's going to be hard to deny."

Anne was wary of the urge to feel celebratory. She resisted her own desire to believe it was all really and truly over. She watched Mitch examine Benjamin, palpating his tummy, asking him questions, and decided that at least she could be happy that Mitch felt no permanent harm had been done. She would focus on that.

She was startled when Mitch asked how she was feeling. "I'm fine," she said. "It was just—such a weird experience."

He put a gentle hand on her chin and turned her head left and then right. "Throat hurt?"

Actually, it did. She had been too preoccupied with Benjamin to notice. She said, "A little," sounding a bit like her son.

"Those are nasty bruises, but they'll fade. You can swallow all right?"

"Yes. I'm all right."

And she was, she realized. She—they—had been through a traumatic experience. A profoundly shocking experience. But they were, indeed, all right. Or they were going to be.

Except for poor Glenda.

Benjamin seemed to follow her train of thought. "What about the lady?"

"What about her, Benjamin?"

"When I woke up I saw her in my bedroom, and then I heard you. Where is she now?"

"None of us knows where the lady went, Benjamin."

"Did you see her before she went?"

"We did."

"She's good," Benjamin said with confidence.

"Yes," Anne said softly. "Yes, Benjamin, the lady is very good." She felt a swell of relief that lifted her heart and eased the tension in her body. "Very good," she repeated, stroking her son's hair.

"Will she come back?"

"I'm sorry, sweetheart, but we don't know that, either."

* * * * ★ ★ ★ * * * *

Beatrice, The Island, 1977

Mother Maggie appeared at the cottage several days later, driving the station wagon. A young woman was with her, toting a toddler on her hip. Mother Maggie brought in a fragrant pan of lasagne, and the young woman produced a brown paper bag filled with home-made cookies.

Mother Maggie introduced her companion. "This is Terry Bachelor. She's been helping the sisters and me in the store. She made the cookies."

Beatrice shook the young woman's hand and eyed her curiously. The name was familiar to her, but she couldn't place it until she noticed the shade floating behind her shoulders. A young man. Her husband, she thought. Terry's feelings about him were confused, and the shade reflected that in its shifting gray and blue and brown layers.

"Terry!" Beatrice said finally. "I remember."

The girl smiled shyly. "That's me, Dr. Bird." She set her child down. "This is Joshua."

"Ah, I see Joshua is well."

"It turned out not to be serious. But as you said—I mean, I figured out—I needed to be able to do things for myself. So I took the job at the sisters' store."

"How does your husband feel about that?"

Mitch made an impatient noise, and Beatrice grinned at him.

Not the time, busy Bea.

I know, Dad. I know.

"He doesn't really like it," Terry said. "But he likes the money. And the discount." As she spoke, the shade of her husband rippled behind her, fading ever so slightly.

Beatrice said, "Well, that's good to hear. My goodness, that lasagne smells amazing! Will you stay and help us eat it?"

"Thank you, no," Mother Maggie said, twinkling down at Benjamin, who was already devouring his second cookie. "Really I just wanted to invite you to Mass on Easter Sunday."

Anne said, clearly startled, "Easter?"

"It's Holy Week."

"Oh, gosh. I completely lost track."

"That should be no surprise. What drama you've experienced!" Mother Maggie included them all in a gesture. "We would be happy to have all of you join us."

Beatrice said, "I wouldn't know how to behave at a Catholic Mass."

Mitch laughed. "Just do what everyone else does, Bea. And yes, Mother Maggie, that sounds great. We'll be there."

"Are you staying on, then, Dr. Minotti?"

"Not much longer. I'm due back at the hospital in a couple of days. And the community clinic has been closed for weeks now. I need to get back to work."

Beatrice was grateful Mother Maggie didn't pursue the subject, though she could see the sparkle of curiosity in her eyes. She and Mitch hadn't talked about it yet, and she wasn't sure she was ready to. She had a lot of thinking to do.

They all stood on the porch to wave goodbye and lingered there for a few moments after the station wagon had rattled away, with Joshua waving goodbye from the back seat. The weather had grown balmy, and the evening air was sweet in her lungs. A thick stand of daffodils had bloomed beside the porch steps, surprising Beatrice and delighting Anne.

"Daffodils propagate really well," Anne said. "That bed might have started with half a dozen bulbs, and now look at it."

"They're so beautiful. Yellow, white, pink—I had no idea they came in so many colors."

"I love the flowers here," Anne said. "Hellebore, rhododendrons, daffodils—and I think I saw a dahlia poking its head up."

Benjamin, showing no interest in the flower discussion, disappeared through the kitchen door, and Mitch, grinning, followed him. "Man things," he said, as he closed the door.

Beatrice chuckled, then smiled at Anne. "You're looking so much better already."

Anne's answering smile was the widest Beatrice had ever seen from her. Her eyes were bright with it, as blue as the spring sky. She was still too thin, but Beatrice thought a few weeks of peace, with her son beside her, would help with that.

Anne said, "I can never, ever thank you enough, Beatrice. And Mitch, too. I know Benjamin will need to talk about what happened, and I have no idea where we're going to go or what we're going to do, but we'll be together. It means everything. It's all that matters."

Beatrice said, "I'm here to talk to Benjamin when you think he's ready."

"Thank you. I don't know how to explain the ghost of a dead woman to a five-year-old."

"I doubt anyone knows that," Beatrice said.

"And then," Anne added, "there's going to be the issue of his father being responsible. He'll have a thousand questions, and I don't know how to answer them."

Beatrice touched her arm. "Don't worry. He's an unusually bright boy, and his trust in you is obvious. I think the best thing is to say things plainly, in language he understands. I don't usually work with patients so young, but I believe they understand the concept of death."

"I wish he didn't have to."

"I do, too."

"That poor woman—lying there, unnoticed, all this time. It's unthinkable." Anne shuddered. "Her parents will have to be told. I can't imagine how awful that will be."

"Ghastly."

"What do you suppose they thought? That she just—just stopped writing? Stopped caring?"

"It's part of the mystery, I guess. It's hard to know how some families work."

Mitch poked his head out through the door. His glasses were steamy from bending over the oven. "Come on, you two," he said. "A very nice lasagne is waiting to be devoured. And I found some bread for garlic toast. A feast!"

As they followed him inside, Beatrice's chest warmed with nostalgia. Mitch in the kitchen, the table set for dinner, the smell of flowers in the air and the hoot of the last ferry of the night—it was perfect.

It couldn't last, though. Mitch would leave, though he had promised to stay until Easter. Anne and Benjamin would make some sort of decision, and they would go, too.

She couldn't bear to think about how empty the cottage would feel.

The call came as they sat together around the dining table, their dinner half-finished. Beatrice answered it, then held the receiver out to Mitch. "It's the Oak Hill police."

Mitch left his chair to stand beside the bar as he put the receiver to his ear. He pushed his glasses up onto his forehead, a gesture Beatrice knew very well. It signaled his shift into professional mode. "Dr. Minotti speaking."

The dining room went quiet. Even Benjamin, working his way through a second helping of lasagne, was silent, listening. Beatrice could hear the voice on the other end of the line, but not the words.

Mitch said, "Yes. Yes," several times. There was a pause before he said, "Forgive me for asking, Officer, but if I send the letters, will they be secure? We understand there is some question about undue influence."

There was more talk, while Anne bent her head and put her hand on her cross. Beatrice watched Mitch, impressed as always at how quietly and surely he took control of a difficult situation. When he hung up, she said, "They want you to send the letters?"

"They do." He had written an address on the phone pad, and he laid the pencil down. "I can go to the big island, I think, and organize special delivery."

"Did the officer say the letters would be safe?"

"He said that." Mitch came back to the table. He sat down and picked up his fork again but didn't use it.

Anne said, "You're not sure, though."

Mitch put the fork down again. "Not really."

"I'm not, either," she said.

"Just send half of them," Beatrice said. "We'll keep the rest until we know what's happening there."

Mitch nodded. "Good idea. We can sort out ones that cover the date span from when she was supposed to have disappeared until the letters stopped coming."

"We can't know for sure that they stopped," Anne said. "I never saw one, but James was the one who picked up the mail. "

Classic control technique. James no doubt controlled everything Anne was allowed to see. Or to do. He had built his life on controlling people, and he had been remarkably successful at it.

But a ghost was a different matter. *That* he had been unable to control.

She looked at Anne's lovely face, and Benjamin's sweet, vulnerable one, and in her own nonreligious way, she sent private blessings to Glenda Iredale. Glenda had saved them. Watched over Benjamin. Intervened for Anne. Beatrice wondered what that had cost her in energy, in anger, in heartbreak. She hoped she was now enjoying a well-deserved rest.

* * * * * ★ ★ ★ * * * *

Anne, The Island, 1977

The little chapel was full for Easter Mass. The sun shone over the island, and the worshippers had dressed for the occasion in island style. There were hats, a few dresses, cotton jackets instead of rain-coats, shoes instead of boots. It made Anne smile.

She had done her best with the few clothes she had with her. Benjamin had only one change of clothes, so his shirt and pants were looking a bit tired, but they were clean. Mother Maggie met them at the door and made a great fuss about escorting them to a pew at the very front.

Anne thought Beatrice looked uncomfortable, but Mitch had been raised Catholic. She could leave the guidance to him.

For herself, it was marvelous to settle onto her knees to offer prayers of gratitude before the service, and a joy to hear Benjamin's sweet, high voice joining in the hymns. They could be happy here, on this isolated island, more or less forever. She had no idea what the future would bring, whether she would receive her share of community property, whether any provision had been made for Benjamin's future. It was possible that James's legal defense would eat up any money there was. She didn't care. She had discovered how strong she could be, even how courageous. She would figure it all out.

She joined the Communion line, with Benjamin beside her to receive a blessing, and she felt more at home than she had in years.

48

Benjamin, The Island, 1977

BENJAMIN LIKED SINGING the hymns, because he never stuttered when he was singing. When Gramma Phyllis had taken him to church, the hymns were the part he liked best. Papa didn't go to church anymore, and that helped.

Dr. Mitch was a good singer. He held the hymnal low enough so Benjamin could read the words, and they sang together. Benjamin smiled up at him when one of the songs ended, and Dr. Mitch winked at him. Mama, on Benjamin's other side, seemed to glow, as if a light had been turned on inside her.

And past Mama, barely visible in the sunshine slanting through the colored glass windows, was the lady, right in the pew next to Dr. Bea. The lady looked like the people in the colored windows, because the sunshine came right through her, gleaming through her hair, glinting through her blue eyes. She didn't look sad anymore. She was smiling, but not at Benjamin. She was smiling at Mama.

The lady was dead. Benjamin knew that, because Dr. Bea had explained it to him. Dr. Bea said someone hurt her, and she died because of that. Benjamin was sad she was dead, but he was glad she didn't look sad anymore.

When he and Dr. Mitch were walking on the beach the day before, Benjamin asked him who had hurt the lady.

"You know, buddy," Dr. Mitch said. They had crouched on the sand looking for sea glass as they talked. "To be honest, we don't know for sure. We're going to have to wait to find out things. That's the way the law works, lots of waiting."

Benjamin thought hard about that, but it was such a great afternoon at the beach, and his little collection of sea glass was growing nicely. He didn't want to spoil the day by asking Dr. Mitch too many questions.

He was pretty sure Dr. Mitch didn't want to tell him everything he knew, but he was used to that. It was the way people were with kids, keeping secrets from them. They thought they were protecting them, and he knew Dr. Mitch and Dr. Bea wanted to do that. They thought the truth would scare him.

On the way back from receiving his blessing, Benjamin looked carefully at their pew, where Dr. Bea waited. He thought the lady might like a blessing, too, but she was gone.

49

Beatrice, San Francisco, 1977

BEATRICE SPENT HER first full day back in the city laboring in La Signora's tiny garden. Anne had given her specific instructions for salvaging the tangle of roses. She had written them down. She pulled on jeans and a denim shirt, pulled a cap over her hair, which had begun to grow back, and with the list of instructions in her pocket, set herself to tackle the chore.

She had dug a pair of hefty clippers out of the basement closet, and she began pruning. It was a little late in the year, according to Anne, but she felt it would work in California. Beatrice gritted her teeth, and though it seemed extreme, she cut every cane to about twelve inches, leaving the new buds where she could. She sheared off the suckers Anne had told her needed to go. By the end of the day she was dirty and sweating, but she had a pile of thorny canes in one corner of the garden and an alarmingly denuded rose garden in the center. She wished she could send Anne a picture to see if she had done it right.

Anne would be planting her own rose garden right now. Before Beatrice left the island, Anne had shown her the spot she had in mind, just to the south of the cottage, where the sun would be the warmest. With the support money awarded to Anne by the court in

Oak Hill, she had bought plants and compost and fertilizer and a couple of tools she couldn't find in the barn storeroom.

Benjamin had chosen a garden spot of his own, where he was already growing marigolds and pansies. Anne and Beatrice had decided, after much discussion, to let Benjamin wait until the fall to go back to school. He would start kindergarten over. His stuttering had decreased steadily once the drama had died down, and it seemed a good idea to give him more time to recover.

Beatrice had consulted a colleague in California who worked with small children, and his advice was a great help with Benjamin. She and Benjamin had taken long walks on the beach and through the evergreens, talking about everything that had happened, returning each time windblown and hungry.

It had been hard talking about his father and the abuse he had suffered at his hands. Sometimes Benjamin's stuttering returned in full force when the subject arose. Beatrice had spent hours sitting in the sand while Benjamin dug up bits of shell and sea glass, and they had fragmented but important conversations about it. Beatrice didn't force anything. She told Anne she thought it would be some time, years perhaps, before Benjamin could process his father's cruelty.

"He'll have to know eventually what his father did," Anne had said.

"You'll know when he's old enough to hear it, I think. Every child's tolerance is different, and Benjamin has already suffered so much."

Anne, on the other hand, flourished like one of the plants she was so good at growing. When the news came that James was in prison to await his trial, and that bail had been refused, it was as if five years dropped from her face. Her appetite grew, and her eyes and skin shone as they must have before she met James Iredale.

In the end, deciding the future for the two of them had been the easiest thing in the world. Anne was eager to stay on the island. With a nudge from Mother Maggie, the school had offered her a position as a teacher's aide, which she was delighted to accept. Her hours would match Benjamin's when the new school year began.

Beatrice had decided, having tried out several trips to the big island on the ferry, that she could manage the city again. There were still ghosts, but after everything that happened—and after meeting a real ghost, a true revenant—her perspective had changed. Now, home in her beloved San Francisco, she schooled herself to smile at people's faces rather than focus on the ghosts that followed them. In the Italian grocer's, or on the bus, she reminded herself that her ghosts represented people's history, their experiences, all the things that made them human. She didn't deliberately look away from their ghosts, but she didn't focus on them, either. If her throat began to ache with someone else's sorrow or fear, she did her best to breathe away the pain, and she was gratified at how much that helped. She was proud of how much her resistance had strengthened.

In a clinical situation, she believed her ghosts would be helpful. They could be clues to a patient's problems, even guides as to how to address them. It was hardly a miraculous transformation, but being home again, reunited with Mitch, was worth whatever the effort cost her.

And if Anne Iredale could face her demons with courage and grace, Beatrice thought she damned well could, too.

With the roses finished, and the pile of canes scraped into one corner, Beatrice pulled off her hat to let the lowering sun shine on her cheeks. She closed her eyes, listening to the familiar sounds: the clang of the trolley, the music floating from open windows, the twittering of city birds.

She opened her eyes, surveyed her work, and turned to go inside for a shower. She was going to cook dinner for Mitch: pasta with fresh shrimp from the bay, the way Anne made it. Tomorrow she would return to the community clinic, and as time went on, she would let the word spread that she had reopened her practice. She would reclaim her life.

Well done, busy Bea. You make me proud.

I don't know, Dad. Better late than never, I suppose.

Nonsense. I've always been proud.

She knew that was true, and she was grateful, whether it was deserved or not. She smiled to herself, acknowledging how humbling the past year had been, and imagined she heard a faint, fond chuckle.

Anne, The Island, 1977

Anne had splurged on six rose canes, already in bud, and a roll of wire fencing to keep the deer away from them. It had taken three days, but the rose garden was planted, composted, fertilized, protected. She poured a glass of cabernet and stood on the porch, surveying her work, considering where to put the vegetable patch. Mr. Thurman was going to drive his tractor up to dig out a spot, and she would do the rest with a spade and a hoe.

Benjamin sat cross-legged at her feet, organizing his collection of sea glass in rows along the inside of the porch railing. She glanced down, smiling. "That looks pretty, Benjamin."

"I have three colors," he said. "Green and b-blue and b-brown. I like b-blue the best."

"I do, too." Beatrice had said that Benjamin's stutter would probably ease, and Anne could already see signs of that. She had assured her son his father was not coming back, that he was safe, and so was she. That had been a big help.

Some of their conversations had been hard. She didn't want him to feel less secure, but she didn't want to lie to him, either.

The worst moment had been a long, circuitous talk, led mostly by Benjamin, about his lady being dead. Benjamin had chewed on the idea for a while before he lifted a solemn face and asked, without any stuttering at all, "Is Papa dead, too?"

Beatrice had advised Anne to be direct, but brief, in the discussions about death. "Answer his questions," she had said. "But there's no need to elaborate unless he asks to know more."

Anne had told Benjamin, "No, Papa's not dead. But he's not free to come see you."

"Oh," he said. "Because he did something bad?"

"I'm afraid so."

He had nodded, apparently satisfied. She was tempted to say more, to try to explain, but she let it pass. There had been no more questions about his father, nor about the lady. He seemed content on both counts.

Her mother had flown out to visit, bringing a suitcase stuffed with Benjamin's coin collection, his books, and all of his clothes. Phyllis said almost nothing about James, but she praised Anne's gardening efforts and her upcoming job, and promised to send anything she wanted from the house in Oak Hill. Anne understood it was her mother's way of apologizing. In truth, it was more than she had expected.

Her father didn't come. She wasn't sure she cared to see him, in any case. He had declared, on a telephone call, that he didn't believe it was possible James Iredale—the judge, as he still called him—had murdered his first wife. "He'll be found innocent, mark my words, Annie. Then you can come back, and the two of you can start over."

Anne had hung up the phone with unnecessary force, and she didn't feel at all sorry for the decisive clatter of it that probably made her father's ears ring.

Now here she was, managing Beatrice's cottage, planning a

vegetable garden, taking care of Dorothy and Alice while she and Beatrice tried to decide whether to breed them again or let them go dry permanently. Mother Maggie was all in favor of keeping the little dairy going, but Beatrice worried it was too much work for Anne.

Anne was inclined to do it. She liked the routine and discipline of milking, and she thought Dorothy and Alice did, too. She liked the idea of supplying milk and cream for the islanders. Once in a while she caught sight of herself in what she thought of as her milking clothes—jeans, rubber boots, a Pendleton jacket Beatrice had left for her that was a little short, but soft with wear—and she laughed at her image in the mirror. What would James's lawyer friends think of her now? She was the trophy wife no longer.

But then, what did they think of James? Would they, like her father, assume he would be exonerated? It didn't seem likely, after the discovery of Glenda's bones under the burn pile. It seemed to be merely a question of what his punishment was to be. That, she was glad to know, was out of her hands.

There were still problems, but most of them would be resolved by lawyers. The Oak Hill house would have to be sold, but that wouldn't happen until after the trial. She wanted to be divorced, but there was no need to rush into that, either. She would need to learn how to manage money, but she looked forward to the challenge, and she appreciated the freedom the money would bring. She hadn't yet told Beatrice, but she thought of buying the cottage from her. There would be, of course, a standing invitation to Beatrice and Mitch to come any time they liked for a holiday.

She drew a long, peaceful breath of sweet air, with its scents of salt and pine and fish. At her feet, Benjamin hummed to himself as he arranged and rearranged his sea glass collection. Alice lowed from the woods and appeared a moment later, leading Dorothy toward the barn.

Benjamin looked up. "Time to milk Alice and D-Dorothy, Mama."

"You're right. Do you want to help?"

He did, and moments later the two of them, in their rubber boots and woolen jackets, walked side by side to the little barn to do their chores.

50

Benjamin, The Island, 1977

AFTER DR. BEA and Dr. Mitch left, Mama moved into the bigger bedroom to give Benjamin and his collections space in the smaller one. Benjamin had a night light in the shape of a black-and-white orca whale that he and Mama had bought at the little store. It plugged into the wall, so it was always on. Mama left both their bedroom doors open, too, so he was never afraid. He was happy to see Gramma Phyllis when she came with his books and his coin collection, but he was glad when she left, and he knew for sure he didn't have to go with her. He didn't want to go back to his old house in Oak Hill.

He and Mama read books every night, separately and together. They bought food at the store, and Benjamin got to pet Petey. One day they borrowed the sisters' station wagon so they could drive out to the school, where Mama would help the teachers and he would go to kindergarten. They visited the island library, which had a lot of books for such a small building. They went to the church, where they saw Mother Maggie and sometimes they saw Petey again. They walked a lot, on the beach and in the woods, and they took care of Alice and Dorothy. Alice didn't like being petted much, and she bossed Dorothy around an awful lot. Dorothy was nicer, even though she had such a strange voice. She let Benjamin stroke her shoulder whenever he was close enough.

Benjamin was careful not to make Mama talk too much about Papa, because he knew it upset her, though she tried to pretend it didn't matter. He understood more than she thought he did about Papa. She said Papa couldn't come back because he wasn't free, but Benjamin knew what she really meant: His father was in jail. He had seen jails on television, and he understood that there were bars and lots of locked doors, and everyone had to wear the same clothes.

He still worried sometimes about Papa coming to the island and being really mad about the letters. No one said it was his fault Papa was in jail, but Benjamin knew it was. He had made it happen by pulling the letters out of the burn pile. He didn't do it on purpose, but it was still on account of him that Papa was in jail.

Sometimes he thought about what might have happened if he hadn't taken the letters. Papa could have made Mama go back to that rest place, or he might have hurt her really badly. He would have made Benjamin go back to Oak Hill, and he might never have seen his mother again. That would have been terrible.

It was all confusing. He wished he could talk to Dr. Mitch about it. Dr. Mitch knew a lot. It was Dr. Mitch's friend who made the police in Oak Hill dig up the burn pile, and that was where the remains were. Dr. Mitch would know whether Papa would get out of jail or not.

When he worried about those things, his stuttering got worse, so he tried not to do it. Mama said he could talk to her about anything, but he thought he would wait a while. See what happened. He could maybe call Dr. Bea, too, because she had left her telephone number, and Mama said he could call her any time. He knew how to call long distance, and he thought he would do it one day, just to talk about things. Maybe when Mama was out in the garden, or in the barn.

Then he could tell Dr. Bea he knew it was his fault Papa was in jail. He didn't think that counted as keeping secrets.

He did have one secret, though, and it was a pretty big one. He wasn't going to tell it to anyone, because they wouldn't understand. They would think it was bad. It wasn't. It was good.

The lady still came to see him at night, when Mama was asleep.

He knew Mama thought she was gone, now that Papa was in jail. Mama and Dr. Bea had been worried about Benjamin finding out she was dead, but he had figured that out before they told him. The lady could go wherever she wanted without a car or a boat or an airplane, and he guessed she had to be dead for that to happen. She had to be a ghost.

He wondered if she minded being dead. He wished he could ask her, but he didn't try, because she never said anything. She just stood at the foot of his bed, looking down at him. She usually came when he had been worrying a lot. Sometimes he waved at her, so she would know he was glad to see her. She never waved back, but she smiled at him, and stayed there until he fell asleep again.

He had another secret, too. He would never tell this one, either, because it would upset Mama, and maybe even Dr. Bea and Dr. Mitch, if they knew he understood. They forgot sometimes that he was extra smart for five years old.

He knew Papa had killed the lady. That was why the lady was a ghost, and that was why Papa had to be in jail. The police found out because of the remains. It was a very bad thing for Papa to have done, the worst thing Benjamin could think of. He wanted to tell the lady he was sorry, but he was sure she already knew that. He could feel it, the way Dr. Bea felt things. He *knew* it.

He was pretty tired of thinking about bad things, so instead, he spent a long time arranging his sea glass collection on a shelf in his room. He organized all the pieces by color, and then he counted them, twice, to make sure he knew how many there were. Seventy-six. He needed more blue pieces, though, so the collection would look just right. It looked pretty good already. It just needed one more thing.

He took the airplane pin out of his pants pocket and set it right in the middle of the collection. It looked good there, as shiny as the sea glass bits. He remembered the lady in the uniform on the airplane, looking at Papa in an angry way. He hadn't had a chance to say thank you for the gift. He wished he could tell her he still had the pin.

He stood back for a moment, admiring his collection. His coin collection was on a shelf underneath, and his stamp collection was on a little stand beside his bed. His room wasn't as big as the one in Oak Hill, but he liked it even better. The clothes closet didn't have a lock on the door, and that was good.

It wasn't dinnertime yet, so he left the bedroom to go in search of Mama to ask her to go down to the beach with him to find more sea glass. She was especially good at finding the blue bits. Then he could start on the shells.

Acknowledgments

I'm grateful to my late husband, Jake Marley, for escorting me on a field trip to the island to view the school and the library and the little store. It was great fun to do together. I will always miss him.

I'm also deeply grateful to Cheryl B. Levine, PsyD, the generous clinical psychologist who kindly read passages of this book to correct my errors and guide the development of Dr. Beatrice Bird. Any surviving mistakes are mine alone.

Warmest thanks and admiration go to Dean Crosgrove, PAC, who knew just how a ghost should attack a person. He would have gone even further! But I think he'll forgive me.

Dick and Mare Tietjen, who not only provided me with a space to work but have been the staunchest of friends through a challenging time. Thank you. I love you both.

I also want to thank my sweet friend, who prefers to remain nameless, who inspired this story. She worked as a psychic but had to stop when she couldn't keep spirits from intruding at all hours of the day and night. The idea of that intrigued me, and this book is the result.

Most importantly, my best love and eternal gratitude to Zack Marley, gifted beta reader, critiquer, and amazing writer in his own right. His insights and instincts are invaluable.

Author's Note

A fascinating book about controlling relationships is *In Control: Dangerous Relationships and How They End in Murder,* by Jane Monckton-Smith, a criminologist and former police officer. Very much worth a read.

Meet the Author

LOUISA MORGAN is a pseudonym for award-winning author Louise Marley. Louise lives in the mountainous Northwest, where she and her familiar, Oscar the border terrier, ramble the paths and breathe the clear air of scenic Idaho.

if you enjoyed

THE GHOSTS OF BEATRICE BIRD

look out for

THE SECRET HISTORY OF WITCHES

by

Louisa Morgan

A sweeping historical saga that traces five generations of fiercely powerful mothers and daughters—witches whose magical inheritance is both a dangerous threat and an extraordinary gift.

Brittany, 1821: *When Grand-mère Ursule gives her life to save her family, their magic seems to die with her. Even so, the Orchiéres fight to keep the old ways alive, practicing half-remembered spells and arcane rites in hopes of a revival. And when their youngest daughter comes of age, magic flows anew. The lineage continues, though new generations struggle not only to master their power but also to keep it hidden.*

But when World War II looms on the horizon, magic is needed more urgently than ever—not for simple potions or visions, but to change the entire course of history.

1821

THE LAYERED CLOUDS, gray as cold charcoal, shifted this way and that, mirroring the waves below. They obscured both stars and moon, and darkened the beach and the lane running alongside. Beyond the lane, in the field of standing stones, a handful of caravans circled a small fire. Firelight glimmered on the uneasy faces of the people gathered there, and reflected in the eyes of their restive horses. The invisible sea splashed and hissed, the only sound except for the crackle of burning wood. The flames cast their wavering light over the menhirs, making the stones appear to move out of their centuries-old alignment, to sway and tremble like ghosts in the night. The child Nanette whimpered and buried her face in her sister Louisette's rough skirts. The older Orchiéres glanced nervously over their shoulders, and at one another.

Two of the stones, collapsed on their sides in some unremembered era, formed a pit for the fire where a brace of rabbits had roasted, sizzling and spitting into the embers. The rabbits were gone now, their meat eaten, their bones buried in the ashes. One of the women stoked the fire, then stood back to make way for her grandmother.

Grand-mère Ursule, carrying a stone jar of salted water, walked a circle around the pit. She muttered to herself as she sprinkled the ground. When that was done, she brandished her oaken walking stick at the sky and whispered a rush of words. The clan watched in tense silence as she laid down her stick and reached into a canvas bag for her scrying stone. She carried it with both hands into the blessed circle, and lifted it into the firelight.

The stone was a chunk of crystal that had been dug out of a riverbank by the *grand-mère* of the *grand-mère* of Grand-mère. Its top had been rubbed and polished until it was nearly spherical. Its base was uncut granite, in the same rugged shape as when it emerged from the mud.

The scrying stone glowed red, flaring with light as if it burned within. It was a light reminiscent of the hellfire the Christians feared, and it reflected off Grand-mère Ursule's seamed face and glittered in her black eyes. Nanette lifted her head from her sister's skirts for a peek, then hid her eyes again, sure the blazing stone would burn her grandmother's hands.

Ursule crooned as she turned the stone, seeking the best view into the crystal. Her eerie voice made gooseflesh prickle on the necks of the watchers. She was the greatest of the witches, inheritor of the full power of the Orchiére line, and watching her work struck awe into the hearts of even those closest to her.

The men shifted in their places and worriedly eyed the lane leading from the village of Carnac. The women clicked their tongues and drew their children close in the darkness.

All the clan were fearful this night. Word of another burning had come to the ears of the men when they went into Carnac-Ville to buy beans and lentils. Nanette had heard them tell the tale, though she didn't fully understand it until she was older.

It had taken place in the nearby city of Vannes. It was said that one Bernard, a young and ambitious priest, had tracked down the witch. He took it upon himself to examine her for the signs before he denounced her in the public square. The archbishop, eager to be known as a burner of witches, had set the torch to the pyre with his own hand.

There was great excitement over the news of this burning in Carnac-Ville. The Carnacois applauded when Father Bernard, a man with sparse red hair and eyes too small for his face, appeared in the marketplace. Nanette wanted to cover her ears when Claude, having returned in haste from the town, told the story, but Louisette pulled her hands away. "You need to hear," she said. "You need to know."

"They say he hates witches because of his mother," Claude said.

"Why?" Louisette asked.

"She had a growth in her breast, and died in pain. Bernard accused the neighbor—a crone who could barely see or hear—of putting a curse on her."

Grimly, Louisette said, "There was no one to protect her."

"No one. They held one of their trials, and convicted her in an hour."

"Did they burn the poor thing?" Anne-Marie asked in a low voice.

Claude gave a bitter laugh. "Meant to. Bernard had the pyre laid. Stake ready. The old woman died in her cell the night before."

"She probably wasn't a witch at all." Louisette pulled little Nanette closer, absently patting her shoulder. "But he feels cheated."

"Been hunting witches ever since."

A grim silence settled around the circled caravans. The day was already far gone. The salt-scented dusk hid the ruts and holes of the lane, making it unsafe to travel before morning.

It wasn't safe to stay, either. They were only three men and five women, with a handful of children and one grandmother. There would be little they could do against a bloodthirsty mob.

The Romani had always been targets, and were always wary. When the blood fever came upon the people, when they were overcome by lust for the smell of burning flesh and the dying screams of accused witches, there was neither law nor reason in the land.

"We should leave," Paul, Anne-Marie's husband, said. "Move south."

"Too dark," Claude growled.

Louisette nodded. "Not safe for the horses."

They all understood. There was nothing left for them but to rely on Grand-mère.

⁓✦⁓

The old woman swayed in the firelight. Her cloud of gray hair fluttered about her head. Her wrinkled eyelids narrowed as she gazed into the scrying stone. She resembled a menhir herself, craggy, timeless, inscrutable. Her thin lips worked, and her voice rose and fell as she recited her spell. The gathered clan shivered in fear.

After a time Grand-mère's chant died away. She stopped swaying and lowered the crystal with arms that shook. In a voice like a violin string about to break, she said, "There is a house."

"A house?" Nanette lifted her head to see who was speaking. It was Isabelle, the most easily frightened of the six sisters.

Louisette put up her hand to shush her. "Where, Grand-mère?"

"Beyond the sea," Ursule said. "Above a cliff. Long and low, with a thatched roof and broken shutters. A fence that needs mending. A hill behind it, and a rising moor." Her eyelids fluttered closed, then opened again to look around at the faces in the firelight. Her voice grew thinner. "You must go there. All of you."

"But Grand-mère," Florence said. "How will we find it?"

"There is an island, with a castle on it. It looks like Mont St. Michel, but it isn't. You will pass the island. You must go in a boat."

The clan sighed, accepting. When Ursule scried, there was no arguing. Even four-year-old Nanette knew that.

The old woman sagged back on her heels, then to her knees. Her head dropped toward her breast. Nanette stirred anxiously against Louisette's side, and her eldest sister shushed her. They waited in the chill darkness, listening to the murmur of the ocean and the occasional stamping of one of the horses hobbled among the stones.

Sometime near midnight the clouds above the beach drifted apart, admitting a narrow beam of moonlight that fell directly onto the circled caravans. It gleamed on painted canvas and hanging pots and tools, and shone on the clan's tired faces. Grand-mère shot upright with a noisy intake of breath, and glared at the break in the cloud cover.

She commanded, "Put out the fire!"

One of the men hurried to obey, dousing the flames with a bucket of seawater kept handy for the purpose. When a child's voice rose to ask why, Grand-mère said, "Be still, Louis. Everyone. Silence." She reached for her canvas bag and covered the scrying stone with it. She got stiffly to her feet and bent to pick up her stick. She held it with both hands, pointing at the slit that had opened in the clouds. She murmured something, a single emphatic phrase that sounded to Nanette like "Hide us!"

Everyone, child and adult, gazed upward. For a long moment there was no response to Grand-mère's command, but then, lazily, the clouds began to shift. They folded together, layer over layer, healing the break as if it were a wound to be closed. No one moved, or spoke, as the light faded from the painted canvas of the wagons. The fire was nothing but a mound of ash smoking faintly in the darkness.

As the Orchiéres' eyes adjusted, their ears sharpened. The sea grew quiet as the tide receded from the beach. The wind died away. Not even the horses seemed to breathe. Gradually their straining ears caught the muffled tramp of feet on the packed dirt of the lane, and the voices of people approaching.

"Grand-mère," one of the sisters murmured. Nanette thought it was Anne-Marie, but she sometimes got them confused. She was by far the youngest of the six sisters, and the only one who had never known their mother, who had died giving birth to her. "Shouldn't we—"

"Quiet!"

Grand-mère Ursule was tiny and bent, like a doll made of leather and wood, but everyone knew her fierceness. She gripped her stick in her gnarled hands and whispered something under her breath, words so soft only those closest to her could hear. One last spell.

Mother Goddess, hear my plea:
Hide us so that none can see.
Let my belovèd people be.

Louisette clamped a hand over Nanette's mouth so she would not cry out as a deep shadow, more dense than any natural darkness, enfolded the campground. The footfalls of the approaching people grew louder. Some cursed when they stumbled. Some prayed in monotonous voices. One or two laughed. They reached the curve in the lane that curled past the field of menhirs, and the Orchiéres froze. The older children huddled close to the ground. The men braced themselves for violence.

The townspeople in the lane trudged along in an untidy crowd. They drew even with the campsite, with the dark sea to their left and the standing stones to their right, and walked on. Their steps didn't falter, nor their voices lower. They marched forward, a mindless, hungry mob in search of a victim, all unaware of the caravans resting among the menhirs, and the people crouching around a cold fire pit. It took five full minutes for the Carnacois to pass beyond the hearing of the clan.

Not till they were well and truly gone did the Orchiéres breathe freely again. In careful silence they signaled to one another and retreated to their caravans to rest while they could. The men murmured in one another's ears, arranging a watch. The women tucked their children into their beds and lay down themselves, exhausted.

But Grand-mère Ursule remained where she was, her stick in her hands, her eyes turned upward to the sky. She stood guard until the moon set behind the clouds. She held steady while the slow dawn broke over the rows of standing stones.

No one heard the sigh of her last breath when she crumpled to the ground. The man whose turn it was to watch was focused on the lane. The women, her granddaughters, slept on beside their children, and didn't know she had left them until they rose in the chilly morning.

It was Nanette who found Ursule's old bones curled near the fire pit, her hair tumbled over her face. The little girl shook her *grandmère*'s shoulder, but there was no response. Nanette put out her small hand and brushed aside the mist-dampened mass of gray curls.

Ursule's eyes were closed, her mouth slightly open. Nanette touched her cheek with a tentative palm. It felt cold as old wax. Nanette sucked in a breath to cry out, but Louisette appeared beside her, catching her hand and pressing it.

"*Chut, chut*, Nanette. We have to be quiet."

"But Grand-mère!" Nanette wailed, in a small voice that died against the surrounding stones. "We have to wake her!"

Louisette bent over the still figure, then straightened with a heart-deep sigh. "No, *ma petite*. We can't wake her. Grand-mère is gone."

"Where did she go?"

"I can't say that, Nanette. None of us can."

"I want to go with her!"

"No, no, *ma petite*. You can't do that. You have to go with us."

Louisette signaled to her husband, and he came to stand beside her, looking down at Ursule's frail body. Her stick lay beside her in the damp grass. The scrying stone was cupped against her with one arm, as if she had died holding it.

"We'll have to bury her here," Louisette said.

"Hurry," her husband said. "We need to go."

"*Oui. D'accord.*"

Nanette watched them wrap Ursule in a quilt from her caravan. Her *grand-mère* never complained, or tried to push them away, even when they covered her face. The other two men brought shovels and began to dig in a space between two of the menhirs. Louisette called Florence to take Nanette away to her caravan to pack her things. When they emerged again into the brightening day, Ursule and her quilt had disappeared. A mound of gray dirt marked the place between the stones.

Nanette turned to Louisette to ask what had happened, but her eldest sister's face was forbiddingly grim. The question died on her lips. She clutched her bundle of clothes, blinking away tears of confusion and loss.

The clan unhobbled the horses and smacked their hindquarters to send them running. They abandoned the caravans where they were, leaving them in their colorful circle in the field of standing stones. With their most precious possessions packed into bags and stuffed into baskets, they started away on foot. Louisette had charge of the crystal, and had packed Ursule's grimoire along with her own things. Nanette would learn later that her grandmother's staff had been buried with her, because no one else had the power to use it.

The Orchiéres left their grandmother, the great witch Ursule, resting alone with none but the deathless menhirs to guard her shabby grave.